Carlton Duncan hails from Kingston, Jamaica, the land of his birth and early education. As a child, Carlton became consumed with the idea of becoming a schoolteacher. The fervor, influence, and style of Carlton's own headteacher, Mr. Austin Constantine Pyne in the 1950s constantly spurred him on. Circumstances led Carlton to immigrate to the United Kingdom early in the 1960s in search of his teaching qualifications. Following a four-year University of Wales education, Carlton was at last a practitioner in the classroom. Despite the numerous obstacles and struggles, his determination and ambition ensured that Carlton reached the pinnacle of his profession, not once but twice, when he became Britain's first black headmaster of a secondary school in Yorkshire 1982 and repeated the feat in Birmingham in 1986.

I dedicate this title to my son, Kyme, whose degree studies were frequently interrupted to assist my underdeveloped computer skills whenever my desktop decided to show off its technical vagaries. Without such long-distance guidance and tuition, and there were many, I might not have completed this book.

The much-needed nourishment and sustenance that kept me going throughout the umpteen days and many late nights to complete this book was always readily and unstintingly provided by Miss Venecia Johnson whose concerns for my health and care knew no bounds. This book is in honor and recognition of this great lady.

Carlton Duncan

BRITAIN'S FIRST BLACK HEADMASTER OF A SECONDARY SCHOOL IN ACTION

Doubling as a Roving Sleuth

AUSTIN MACAULEY PUBLISHERS™

LONDON * CAMBRIDGE * NEW YORK * SHARJAH

Copyright © Carlton Duncan 2024

All rights reserved. No part of this publication may be reproduced, distributed, or transmitted in any form or by any means, including photocopying, recording, or other electronic or mechanical methods, without the prior written permission of the publisher, except in the case of brief quotations embodied in critical reviews and certain other non-commercial uses permitted by copyright law. For permission requests, write to the publisher.

Any person who commits any unauthorized act in relation to this publication may be liable to criminal prosecution and civil claims for damages.

This is a work of fiction. Names, characters, businesses, places, events, locales, and incidents are either the products of the author's imagination or used in a fictitious manner. Any resemblance to actual persons, living or dead, or actual events is purely coincidental.

Ordering Information
Quantity sales: Special discounts are available on quantity purchases by corporations, associations, and others. For details, contact the publisher at the address below.

Publisher's Cataloging-in-Publication data
Duncan, Carlton
Britain's First Black Headmaster of a Secondary School in Action

ISBN 9798891554924 (Paperback)
ISBN 9798891554931 (ePub e-book)

Library of Congress Control Number: 2024901163

www.austinmacauley.com/us

First Published 2024
Austin Macauley Publishers LLC
40 Wall Street, 33rd Floor, Suite 3302
New York, NY 10005
USA

mail-usa@austinmacauley.com
+1 (646) 5125767

Throughout my deliberations and writings, I never lost sight of the fact that I am influenced and motivated by my friends at DEEP and intellectual giants such as my long standing good friends brother Cecil Gutzmore and Professor Gus John. Their shoulders were important.

Chapter 1
Tony Brown's Disappearance

You must be a truly committed teaching practitioner to navigate the unfamiliar journeys on which just this one aspect (among many as will be seen) of British education is about to take me. Tedious, cumbrous and at times, downright dangerous are fitting adjectives.

Since the early 1960s, the black community has been expressing deep concerns regarding the performance and achievement of their children **(Bernard Coard had raised a timely alarm about this situation in his book *How the West Indian Child Is Made Educationally Subnormal in the British school system pub. 1971)*** and the frequency with which these children, especially the boys, are *excluded from British schools.* The view that British schools were institutionally racist and needed to change fast had rightly begun to take firm roots.

"Exclusion rates for black Caribbean students in English schools are up to six times higher than those of their white peers in some local authorities, highlighting what experts have called an "incredible injustice" for schoolchildren from minority ethnic backgrounds." Guardian analysis. Niamh McIntyre, Nazia Parveen and Tobi Thomas, Wednesday, 24 March 2021 17.00 GMT

https://www.theguardian.com/education/2021/mar/24/exclusion-rates-black-caribbean-pupils-england.

Wednesday, 24 March 2021 17.00 GMT.

No doubt, there will be some like Sewell **(Commission on Race and Ethnic Disparities: Sewell, et al)** and others like him who will continue to bury their heads in the political sands and deny what these figures and others like them (for example, those of the real-life experiences of everyday folks previously outlined in the Department of Education and Science (DES) Rampton and Swann Reports of 1981 and 1985 respectively) have clearly shown.

This problem, like nearly all the others affecting the black communities, is directly related to some unfounded and colonial stereotypes often associated with black people. The uninitiated teachers often make the incorrect assumptions that black children will be a source of problem in the classroom. These children are stereotyped into big bullies, constant troublemakers, and drugs pushers. A clear sign that we do not fully realize that we tend to behave in accordance with our expectations. In this way, let us not forget that teacher expectation, too, often influences the outcome.

"You see, really and truly, apart from the things anyone can pick up (the dressing and the proper way of speaking, and so on), the difference between a lady and a flower girl is not how she behaves, but how she is treated. I shall always be a flower girl to Professor Higgins, because he always treats me as a flower girl, and always will; but I know I can be a lady to you, because you always treat me as a lady, and always will." **(Pygmalion, G. B. Shaw).**

The independent by-stander in, or observer of, any classroom would, without bias, record that these assumptions are no truer for black youngsters than for the rest of the class. But if you begin from a racially jaundiced premise you arrive at decisions similarly tainted. Children will have conflicts between or among themselves. By their very nature, this is a truism. Part of the teacher's responsibility, in the pursuit of order in the classroom, is to be just and equitable in the umpiring of such conflicts. This is part of the hidden curriculum messages that teachers pass on each day spent in the classroom.

Yet, for the simple reason that our teaching fraternity may have been the product of past misguided schooling which supports white supremacy while being negative to non-whites, teachers sometimes find it difficult to be just where the conflict is between white and black. The negatively inculcated biases against non-white clientele can automatically affect teacher attitudes and expectations thus producing a skewed judgmental outcome which is rarely, if ever, in the black child's favor. Assumptions and stereotypes thus founded can have serious deleterious consequences for the black child. We saw this terrible outcome in the recent case (March 2022) of 'strip-search' at a London school producing headlines like this one:

Black girl strip-searched at London school to sue Met police.

Child Q to launch civil proceedings against Met and school to ensure this never happens again to any other child.

Dame Rachel de Souza, realizing that the child Q strip-search incident conducted by police was not an isolated case, requested the Met police data on their strip-search activities. This is what she found:

Of the 650 strip-searches of children from 2018 to 2020, almost a quarter took place without an appropriate adult present, the figures show. More than half of those searched were black boys.

Surely, the police, their controllers and conniving schools that can subject a 15-year-old girl to such inhumane and disgraceful ignominy must be held accountable one way or another. Child Q was a 15-year-old black girl, who, while on her menstrual cycle, was forced against her will to endure the uncaring exposure of her intimate body parts, all because her so-called 'caring school' wrongly suspected her of possessing marijuana. Clearly, this practice is signaling the prevalence of a pernicious stench of heartless racism: the type which begets the actions of white supremacy.

A beneficial case for having police officers in schools can be established. But before this can be done without the horrendous consequences feared and often experienced by non-white children, participating officers should be properly trained. The other big question emanating from this is: trained by whom? What is not needed is for untrained officers in schools turning out to be really immigration officers in disguise or drugs sniffers in a place of learning with a view to criminalizing whole sections of the schools in which they are placed.

Black children's school report cards, in these circumstances, constantly disproportionately reflect them as aggressive, troublemakers. In secondary schools, children could be taught by as many as eleven or more different teachers across the curriculum spectrum in any one week. If, as is very likely, most of these teachers are thus influenced by their own prior faulty education, this could have the effects of encouraging and generating staffroom racist gossips about black children. If repeated often enough, these gossips soon assume the status of facts.

Now, consider the collective views of these teachers when it is time to write their reports to parents about their children. The weight of these reports which are destined to follow these pupils for important periods of their livers is a strong determinant when headteachers and their governing bodies come to determine whether a child should be excluded from a school temporarily or permanently or not at all. This problem is made worse when we build in the impact of the 1990s academies and their controlling academy trusts. Driven by the "zero tolerance" motive, academies are seen to be responsible for a significant amount of school exclusions presently. Academies (grammar schools by any other name), as did Grant Maintained schools, receive funding directly from the government and are run and governed by academy trusts.

They have more control over how they do things than community or local authorities' schools. **The Department for Education (DfE) has data which shows that the national fixed-term exclusions rate has increased every year since 2014-15 and that some academy chains have been found to exclude children at very high rates, often using them to enforce "zero tolerance" uniform policies.** Throwing children out of schools for minor issues shows little regard.

For their entitlement under Article 5 of the Universal Declaration of Human Rights:

*"Article 5: No one shall be subjected to torture, or to cruel, inhuman or degrading treatment or punishment," a*nd this is what throwing children out of schools for frivolous reasons is.

Or their educational rights and entitlement under the **1944 Education Act,** The **Education Act of 2011** through to the **Skills and Post-16 Education Act 2022** and subsequent education Statutes that are relevant at the present time.

In recent days, Tyre Nichols, a young black American man, was brutally beaten to death by at least five Memphis police officers in the United States of America ostensibly for "dangerous" driving. At his funeral on February 1st, 2023, the eulogy was given by a black icon: Reverend Al Sharpton. A most poignant statement uttered by the eulogist was that Tyre Nichols was beaten and his life taken by the very people whose sworn pledge was to protect and save lives. Al Sharpton asked, was Tyre not entitled to the protection of the law too? The author sees a clear parallel here with the rate of exclusions for black children from their schools. Are they not entitled, like their white peers do, to the benefits and entitlements provided by the British Education Acts and Article 5 of the Universal Declaration of Human Rights?

Excluding a child can make them vulnerable to exploitation and can diminish their life chances. Over the years, black educationalists, me among them, have vociferously argued that not only is school exclusion in direct conflict with the aims and objects of the United Nations' Convention on Children's Rights, but it is also profoundly discriminatory, destructive, and uneconomic with scarce and limited resources. Schools and their authorities are most often reluctant to explore other measures in their behavioral management schemes on the grounds that they do not have the time or other resources.

Consequently, they employ the same old measures even if they are not suitable for all the children. No account is taken of those children who do not fit into normative patterns because their difficulties spring from psychological illnesses. These are the most vulnerable groups who are destined to be regularly excluded or suspended from schools thus driving the nails in their proverbial achievement coffins. The resulting damage is not confined to the excluded children, in most cases it also has deleterious and prejudicial effects on their families in economic and social terms. Teachers are also inclined to transfer their low prejudicial expectations to younger siblings who come to the excluding schools later.

Many schools do excellent work supporting children, but a significant minority are responsible for the bulk of known exclusions and suspensions, thought to be more than a thousand and one hundred and fifty thousand respectively each year.

A spokesperson for the department of education once stated: "Being excluded from school should not mean exclusion from high-quality education, but we will always back headteachers to use exclusions when required as part of creating calm and disciplined classrooms that bring out the best in every pupil."

These are the kinds of underlying factors which go to explain the disproportionately large numbers of black youngsters thrown out of their British classrooms daily either temporarily or permanently. Where these children end up will depend on the kind of provision that the schools, local authorities and academies put in place. Some make no provision at all; and the excluded children, and their parents, are left to suffer the consequences of exclusion all by themselves. The one thing that is certain, is that at such time, the excluding schools and the other relevant authorities are no longer discharging their legal and moral duties to provide proper education for such children in accordance with the relevant and prevailing Education Acts.

In this way, the time and education so lost, become a major drag on the life chances of these children. They simply never catch up and there is strong evidence that there are important correlations between exclusion statistics and the drifts to institutions of incarceration eventually. Unfortunately for parents and their children so affected, they have no leverage with which to fight back against a teaching force which is heavily unionized. Pre the advent of academies, parents had a right of appeal to school governors and subsequently to the relevant local authority against their children' exclusion from schools.

Although it was rear for governors or the local authority to over-turn a school's decision to exclude, the appeals system was, nevertheless, an avenue through which parents could seek justice for their excluded children. Today, the appeal system is non-existent or what is left of it is no more than a sham. Excluded children will most likely end up in some local authority provided "Sin bin" which is often euphemistically termed a sanctuary and offers no effective education for its occupants. Years of this kind of injustice have been suffered by our schools' black population: although not without notice, it is feared that, without more, many more years will similarly pass with the problem remaining unresolved. The time worn Parent Teachers' Association (PTA) tends to be episodic and hitched to a particular school.

As such, it has no national reach and is therefore ineffective as an institution for initiating sustained and positive change. Attempts at establishing national PTAs have failed mainly because of their operational impracticalities. The answer must be found in the institution of equality and justice measures for all our children whose life chances are at stake. Whatever that answer will be, it must incorporate parental and pupil industrial power that carry similar weight to that of the teachers' organizations for there to be a fighting chance of mutual respect in our educational kingdom. Black parents, their children, and other wide-ranging sympathizers, including teachers, urgently need to organize us into a 'force to be reckoned with' along the lines of the teacher unions. Failing this, their voices will not be heard in places where it matters.

The same Guardian analysis referred to above was concerned that this state of affair:

"Comes as campaigners and thinktanks warn of school exclusions contributing to the criminalization of children, while disproportionately affecting those from poorer backgrounds."

Magistrates, probation officers and judges are, in the same way as teachers and other important influential members of society, affected by the colonialist biases which affected their earlier education. Hence, the outcomes of their deliberations can be predicted as if predefined. Unless we use a vastly decolonized approach to our schools' curriculum, planned, hidden, or excluded, to put in place the seeds of the society we wish to see in the long run, we will forever experience the unjust society we have today.

I hereby vow to lead the charge to eradicate all these areas of injustices to make room for an education system which is equitable and just for every child.

Yet, it must be admitted that there are times when the school is backed into a corner and has no other satisfactory option but to exclude. It was one of those times that would get me very involved in my detective role. The case involving 14-year-old Tony Brown, an Afro-Caribbean young lad, is just such a case. Tony is known to be short sighted: a physical disability which could hinder his learning chances if not managed by the school. To accommodate his learning chances, all his teachers were advised to seat him near the front of the class where he would be able to read, with some ease, what is written on the black, sometimes whiteboards.

His teachers readily cooperate with this practice. Tony, as a student, is no more, no less difficult in classes than any other student at other times. He is keen to do well and responds positively to praises and earned good marks. He is typical for his age and, in many ways, the ideal student.

For some reason, Tony appeared to have some mental aberrations' one weekend and came back to school the following Monday morning with the expression "FUCK OFF" boldly barbered into the back of his head. Tony's physical disability fixed his normal seating position at the front of the class with most of his classmates always seated behind him. The resulting chaotic melee of laughter and giggles provided the kind of challenges that would have defeated even the most competent teacher seeking to maintain good classroom control in those trying circumstances.

Tony was rightly removed from the scene to enable the orderly resumption of the lesson. He was brought to my office because, at the time, I was the deputy headteacher and Director of Personal Development overseeing the pastoral system in the school. My first reaction was to reach out to Tony's parents but that failed because both of his parents were at work and were not immediately available. I could not allow any other class to be disrupted in the fashion of the earlier case. Tony was, therefore, destined to spend the remainder of the day in my office with as much set work as I could gather from his teachers for him. The school had a duty of care to discharge to all pupils and to ensure that they receive their lawful education. In Tony's situation, this was the best I could do until the base problem was removed.

Telephone calls to both parents and a letter taken home by Tony requesting parental representation at my office the next day were arranged by the school's administrative officer.

The next morning, with the rain falling slightly, only Tony's mother turned up—there was no Mr. Brown—with Tony in tow. Mrs. Brown, a tall well-dressed woman was not interested in polite conversations or hearing the school's viewpoint on the reason for her presence in school that morning. She burst into my office without knocking. She was raging mad as she demanded that her son be returned to his classes immediately. My attempts to calm Mrs. Brown were futile and, at least to Mrs. Brown, seemed provocative. I found this out when I found myself ratcheted into a far corner of my office, my tie being pulled in a choking action while an umbrella hovered above my head in readiness to strike. Mrs. Brown had used the element of surprise to get the better of me with remarkable speed and rampant accuracy.

I was just as quickly rescued by the school's caretaker who had, by coincidence, witnessed Mrs. Brown's unusual entry to the school and followed her closely up the stairs leading to my office. He saw when she irregularly burst into my office, not bothering to close the door behind her and went straight for me. It was my lucky day, the bulky and comparatively towering caretaker easily disarmed and pulled Mrs. Brown off my trembling frame. Till this day, I remain eternally grateful to Mr. Jackson.

Mrs. Brown, now disarmed, noisily departed my office shouting instructions to her son, Tony, to go to his lessons and that she would deal with any repercussions at the end of the day as she was now late for work. She stated that "we were all a bunch of racists who were not able to deal with a black boy who was expressing his individuality." And she was gone. I thanked the affable Mr. Jackson and headed in the direction of the headteacher's office, taking Tony along with me, in search of a conference on the matter at hand.

The headteacher and I, in the circumstances, agreed that since there was no one at the Browns' home to receive and be responsible for Tony, he should be kept in school, making ad hoc arrangements for his lessons, for the remainder of the day while we determined the way forward. My office and that of the headteacher's would share in providing the holding base for the day. We further agreed that, given the drawbacks of exclusion as outlined above, we needed to get Tony back to all his lessons as quickly as possible. To this end, Tony took home a letter that day to his parents which suggested the following options.

1. The school will allow Tony's return to all lessons immediately on condition that the offensive hair pattern is also immediately and completely removed from the boy's head.
2. Failing that, the school would recommend to the governors of the school that Tony be excluded for a period sufficient in length, to allow for the re-growth of his hair.

Here, then, was a school that was contemplating the educational welfare of all its pupils including Tony Brown's.

The next day the headteacher's secretary received a telephone call from Mrs. Brown emphatically rejecting option one because this would be an outright denial of her son's individuality and, therefore, the school can do whatever it wants. She confirmed to the secretary that that was also the position of her husband, Mr. Brown.

Apart from the comment that 'the school can do whatever pleases it', Mrs. Brown was silent on option two, which was, therefore, immediately formalized and dispatched to the Browns to be reviewed in ten school days: the school will leave prepared work at the reception counter for the Browns to collect for their son Tony while he is officially excluded. The necessary formalities, by way of the local authority and the school's governors, were actioned and the matter placed on the follow-up agenda.

On the second day of Tony Brown's official exclusion, I received a call from the BBC Television Studio in Pebble Mill, Birmingham. I was politely informed that the following Friday evening there would be a live broadcast involving a variety of school issues including school uniforms, dress ethos and children's individualism. Because one of my school's parents and her son would be featured, I was invited to give the school's point of view. I sought and obtained clearance from my headteacher and the Chairman of our governors to participate as requested.

To this day, I cannot understand why I was so alone. The live audience was made up of extremely vocal parents and students from diverse backgrounds. They might have been specially selected. That night, school uniform requirements took a bashing, but, at least, there were some supporters to give hope and encouragement to the school representatives who, like me, came to defend their schools. Tony Brown was asked to tell the viewers why he was not in school and to demonstrate his offending hair style. He received the loudest cheers of the evening with whistles and demanding calls to have him reinstated at his school. My attempts to raise the difficulties that meant for the school and other pupils were constantly drowned out with heckles and disapproving whistles. When the night was done, and I hurriedly left the car park, all I could ponder was, why were there no supporters? My profession can be a lonely one at times. That night was one of those times.

The worst was yet to come. Within hours of the BBC's presentation, it was reported that the 'star' of the show, Tony Brown, was missing from home. Two full days had passed and, still, no one had any idea of his whereabouts. The school was asked to give its corporation to the police who wanted to interview his friends and peers from the school.

We at the school found it difficult to separate this development from the fact of the boy's exclusion from the school. My personal involvement began to mobilize a strong element of compunction in me. That, together with that duty of care which every true teacher must have, hounded me night and day. This young man is somebody's child. He was a very promising student and would be a major loss all round. I became personally obligated to do whatever I could to find Tony and return him to his home, family, and school. The detective streak in me was yearning for immediate action.

The first thing I must do is obtain permission from his parents to visit the crime scene: Tony's home where he was last seen.

I arrived at the Browns' home at six o'clock in the evening by appointment. Visibility was already fading but there was still enough daylight to enable me to view the outside layout of the house even before managing a chat for details with the other members of the Brown's family. For the past month, the weather has been uncertain, mostly wet and damp; so much so that the ground around the house and garden was soft and, in some places, muddy and slippery. Signs of pedestrian skid marks were much in evidence.

The reports are that Tony Brown was last seen by his parents who left him in the home alone when they set off for their places of livelihood on the day of his disappearance. Tony's infant sister was left, as usual, with the child-minding neighbor three doors away and there she would remain until her parents, either one, fetches her at the end of the working day.

Three sets of footprints were still lingering in the muddy pathway by the side of the house leading to an unbolted side gate. The owners of these prints did not leave by the front door of the house which has a non-slip tiled pathway.

Two things struck me as being strange and unusual. Firstly, the three sets of footprints were not complete. Two prints revealed that the wearers wore sneakers with different sole patterns; but the third person wore only one shoe with yet a different pattern together with his naked footprint on the other foot.

Secondly, the footprints exited the property but showed no prints entering, at least, not the way they exited. Were they let in through the front door?

The Browns occupy a post Victorian semi-detached three-bedroom house situated in the Hill Fields area of the City of Coventry: the same area as Sydney Stringer School and Community College that has the responsibility to care for and educate Tony Brown. The house has a side gate to the property on the detached side of the house.

I had seen enough of the outside parameters of the Browns' home and needed to have an informative discourse with the family. Mrs. Brown was, surprisingly, not so hostile with me, in fact, not hostile at all, as she was on our last meeting at the school prior to her son's formal exclusion. As a matter of fact, both parents were visibly very anxious and distressed. They seemed overly ready to clutch at every proverbial straw in the hope that it would lead to the quick return of their precious son.

Inside the home, everything was neat and meticulously tidy except for one corner of the dining room that has a backdoor leading to the outside garden areas. Strewn all over that area were electronic games, gadgets (that, for Tony, would be considered age-appropriate), discarded mobile toys, his Aston Villa jersey all crumpled and abandoned. Mr. Brown assured me that Tony would not abandon his villa jersey if he could help it.

Little Angela Brown, just four years old, kept asking everyone about the whereabouts of her brother, Tony. She loved him and he loved her: there was an unbreakable bond between them. Tony would never voluntarily stay away from her for any significant amount of time, said Mrs. Brown.

A visit to Tony's bedroom revealed that his, otherwise neatly kept bedroom quarters, had recently been ransacked. His desk drawers, the drawers of his bedside furniture were drawn, riffled, and opened. Tony's mum speculated that Tony's Passport and birth certificate might have been taken because they were always kept in one of those opened and riffled drawers. All cupboard doors were disturbed and opened too. This looked like a hurried search had recently been conducted. Whoever conducted that search was not after money because Tony's last paper round earnings was still intact and was lying undisturbed on the table next to his bed.

All his favorite clothing was still in the dress cupboard; Tony seemed to have taken nothing with him except for the clothes he was wearing when last seen by his immediate family: a loosely fitting pajama top and an ill-fitting blue jean hurriedly pulled on for the purpose of joining his parents and sister for breakfast. He must, also, have been wearing just one foot of his favorite Nike sneakers; the other foot was left lying next to the fridge door in the kitchen. And he left his money behind.

The Browns confirmed that Tony returned home with them on the night of the BBC broadcast from Pebble Mill and that he had breakfast with them before they left him on his own while they went off to work the following morning. Tony's parents were dumbfounded that he had disappeared like this. He had been left on his own on many previous occasions, but he never left home and if he did, he was always back home before they returned from work. They found it so incredible that two days have passed, and Tony has not found a way to ring their house phone or tried to contact them in any other ways.

All their efforts to contact near relatives and known friends of Tony have drawn a blank. They were not saying it; but you could feel them thinking it, that had it not been for the exclusion from school, they might not be suffering the pains they are experiencing at the present time. Indeed, this impression that

I had appealed to my sleuthing instinct: we need to find Tony Brown before he is harmed.

The school was alerted to Tony's disappearance at the same time as the police. The school got to the Browns' home fast and first and I, as the school's representative, was extremely careful not to disturb anything which might be evidential in any criminal investigation that might arise from this unfortunate and suspicious development. It was time to bid the Browns goodbye while saying whatever I could to keep their spirits up and boost their seemingly fading hopes. This night, I would have much to keep me awake through a slumber less night while I itch with the desire to find answers: to find Tony Brown, alive.

"Two things struck me as being strange and unusual," I added a few others, and these, together, were the issues which held my thoughts throughout the long and baffling night. The night was far too long and drawn-out. I needed the morning to come so I could brief my superiors and let my headteacher know that I was now very emotionally involved in the search for our student, Tony Brown.

Chapter 2
Some Positive Developments Careers-Wise

On the professional side of my life, great things were happening. My work was recognized. The Department of Education and Science as it then was, organized a major Educational Conference at the University of York 16/17 December 1977. The theme of the conference was 'Comprehensive Education.' The Honorable Shirley Williams was then the Secretary of State for Education at the Department for Education and Science. Not only did she invite me to participate in that conference, but I was one of several educationists who was asked to prepare a paper to be published as part of the outcome of the conference. I remember feeling rather flattered to be invited personally by the Secretary of State; but daunted by the request to prepare a paper for such a high-level publication.

The only thing I had ever published before was a poem on my favorite headteacher, Mr. Austin C. Pyne while I was still attending an all-ages school in Frankfield, Clarendon, Jamaica. Mr. Pyne was away in England for several weeks and was due to return to the island in October 1960. This man was my idol and so to mark his return, I tried my hand at poetry, entitled: Mr. A.C. Pyne, and sent it off to the Jamaican Gleaner. Very impressively, it appeared in the Gleaner's 'Children's Own' that same October, to coincide with Mr. Pyne's return to the island. Seventeen years later, here is my chance to be in print again.

At the conference, I had the opportunity to meet the Secretary of State and other key officials in education across the country. I always hated staying in the background as I firmly believe that you can and are often overlooked in this way. I remember the time; Muhammad Ali came to Birmingham. When I arrived at the hall where he was, there were already thousands there to see the great man. Just to be part of that crowd was going to mean nothing to me. Systematically and gradually, I worked my way to the very front. Now, it would mean something to me because I was able to shake the hand of the world's greatest sports figure, Muhammad Ali who, very sadly, passed away on 4 June 2016.

In the same way, I grasped every opportunity I could get to make my educational points at the conference, and it felt good to hear more seasoned educationists applauding as I made my contributions. My paper for the conference was entitled: "The Development of the Individual Pupil, Personal and Academic." It was published, along with other contributions in an HMSO publication 'Comprehensive Education' December 1977.

Two years later, Gerald Haigh, renowned for his many publications in education and headteacher at a middle school, approached me to request a contribution from me for a book, which he was editing for the publishers Maurice Temple Smith. My name was getting to be known and that was never a bad thing for one's career advancement. My contribution, "Discipline and the Multicultural School," was subsequently published in a title called, 'On Our Side', 1979. A string of my publications would follow leading to some 46 in number up to the present time.

Roughly around the same time, I was approached by the Coventry Evening Telegraph, part of Coventry Newspapers limited, and a short time thereafter by Carrick Publishing. The former was preparing for publication a reference book, *Coventry Evening Telegraph Yearbook* and *Who's Who 1982* for Coventry and Warwickshire (including Warwick, Leamington Spa, Kenilworth, Rugby, Nuneaton, Bedworth, and Stratford-on-Avon). The latter was planning a similar reference volume, '*The Schools' Who's Who*', the first edition to be published in 1987. Each desired to include an entry about me in the document each was preparing for regular publication.

The publicity surrounding my appointment to Sydney Stringer School certainly drew a lot of attention to me. That coupled with my work at the school created platforms from which I was leaping almost daily to positive ends. Now my entries in these Who's Who documents would create wider openings for me.

But the big scoop was, in 1979, to be invited by the Secretary of State, Shirley Williams; right on the heels of the York Conference where I had made my big splash both in writing and in speeches, to serve on the 'Rampton

Committee of Inquiry' under the Chairmanship of Anthony Rampton. A Select Committee of the British House of Commons on Race Relations and Immigration had reported in 1977 (The West Indian Community) on, "The widespread concern about the poor performance of West Indian children in schools."

One of its recommendations was that a high-level and independent inquiry should be instituted as a matter of urgency by the government to enquire into the underachievement of West Indian children in maintained schools and make recommendations as to the remedies. The then Labor government responded by establishing a Committee of Inquiry to be concerned with the needs of all ethnic minority children but that the committee should give priority to West Indian children for its interim report: West Indian children in Our Schools. Her Majesty's Stationery Office (HMSO) 1981. Command: 8273. The commission consisted of 22 members. Only four were Afro-Caribbean, three others (Yvonne Collymore, Trevor Carter and Dorrette McAuslan), besides me.

Yvonne Collymore Trevor Carter Dorette McAuslan

For political reasons, Tony Rampton was removed from the chairmanship of the committee, indeed from the committee, soon after the publication of the interim report in June 1981. He was swiftly replaced by Lord Swann who would now lead the work of the committee for a further three years. The final report 'Education for All' (The Swann Report) was published in March 1985. Her Majesty's Stationery Office (HMSO) 1981. Command: 9453.

Following the publication of these reports, my work was cut out for me. Between 1981 and 1999, when I finally retired from education, I would be required to give over a thousand lectures on the work of the committee, its findings, recommendations, and educational issues generally to associations, schools, churches and universities, Oxford, and Cambridge among them, all over the United Kingdom and parts of Europe.

In 1980, I was appointed one of Her Majesty's Justice of the Peace— Coventry's Bench first Afro-Caribbean Justice of the Peace.

Coventry's Bench of Magistrates 1980

The train of successes was running away and gradually, I was becoming a national household name, at least among educationalists and associated officials at local and national levels. Clearly, the amount of work involved in serving on the Committee of Inquiry plus that from my service on the Bench was going to place a strain on my work in the school. The Director of Education for Coventry, at the time, was Mr. Atkin. He recognized that and gave my school extra staffing to compensate when he came under pressure from jealous individuals to revoke his permission for me to serve on the Committee of Inquiry. He took the view that it was good for Coventry to have one of its senior employees serving at such a high level nationally.

I completed three years as a deputy headteacher. This fact coupled with rising national recognition signaled to me that the time was right to take on the top job in my profession—the headship of my own school. In England, I had worked and learned under the leadership of five different headteachers, and I had successfully held every post from a probationer to deputy head all of which, I felt, had prepared me masterfully for the top post.

Hence, despite the parallel domestic struggles I had been experiencing, from deception, marital failure, cultural rejection, false arrest and imprisonment, hospitalization, and a hoard of gynecological issues to in vitro preparation, I felt that I needed to be more determined and vigorous in my aspirational drive for the top job. After all, the promise was that I would soon have an additional two mouths to feed. What I naively thought would be a somewhat easy road, turned out to be some of my most painful struggles.

At home, it was not so easy because it often meant being away from home overnight, sometimes for a whole week at a time as members of the Committee of Inquiry toured the country in evidence gathering exercises. Melvinder was often alone at these times. At the worst of these long absences from home, I would sometimes arrange for her to join me in different parts of the country just to break out of the monotony for her. On one occasion when Peter Sutcliffe, the Yorkshire Ripper, was operating at his peak, Melvinder had to join me in Leeds—the Ripper's country. I suggested in jest that it would be a good thing if I was the person who apprehended the Ripper who had been outsmarting the police for several years having already claimed thirteen victims.

The plan, I told her that in the dead of night, I would use her as bait as she walked the streets alone. Then when the Ripper pounced, I would be there to disarm and arrest him and hand him over to the police. Melvinder had a great sense of humor, but regarding this one, she thought I was the craziest man on earth. She was not amused. Little did either of us know that we would, one day, be living in the Ripper's country ourselves? And that one of my senior staff, Mr. Samuels, would be living directly opposite the Ripper's home. He told us the true story, when that time came, that the front garden of the house opposite his own was often unkempt and over-grown with grass and bushes.

This was not flattering to his own home so on several occasions when he was cutting his own front lawn; he would offer to cut that of the house opposite as well. The occupant of the house opposite was Mrs. Sonia Sutcliffe. She seemed very nice and kept to herself most of the time. She was always very grateful for the offer as her husband, Peter, was often away. Mr. Samuels also shared with us the story of how another of his neighbor's 15-year-old daughter was late from a disco one night. When she arrived home after 01:00 that night, her parents upbraided her about staying out late when she was fully aware of the Ripper's activities in and around the area.

The young girl reassured her parents by saying: "It's alright, mother, that nice man, Mr. Sutcliffe, from across the road, walked me home." Of course, no one knew the significance of any of these stories until long after the Ripper had murdered 13 women and injured several others and was finally caught on the 2nd of January 1981. A string of murders, which had begun on the 29th of

October 1975 and lasted almost six years, had ended. The young girl in the true story apparently fainted once the name of the Ripper was finally revealed.

120 Applications for Headship Positions

I had calculated that after three years in the position of deputy headteacher, it would be the right time to start testing the market for a headship. Thus, since the latter part of 1979, I had been doing just that without getting any response whatsoever. I was being called upon in the right places and by the right people. My work as an educationist was getting national recognition and I was making an acknowledged positive contribution to a very successful and nationally recognized school. At national level, too, I was having a strong impact, especially as Chairman of the Special Needs sub-committee of the Rampton, later Swann Committee of Inquiry; and yet my numerous applications were being ignored.

Now I was left to be wondering all sorts of things. Many of the authorities to which I sent my applications and from which I was getting no response, were, in practice, using me on their organized in-service educational courses for their school advisors and teachers. On occasions, I could not resist the temptation to ask education officials, who I recognized to be employed by the Education Authorities to which I had applied, what was going on and why wasn't anybody considering me as a potential head of one of their schools.

Replies ranged from, 'I really don't know,' to 'I promise to check it out for you,' but no one ever came back to me about that matter. I became so frustrated and disappointed about the silent rejections surrounding my numerous applications that I even actively considered, on one occasion, moving into Advisory Education and abandoning my search for a headship.

The Manchester City Council had advertised in all the mainstream papers for candidates to apply for the post of multicultural education advisor to the city's education department. As a head of department, later head of faculty, I was the first person in the UK to write a syllabus in multicultural education. The syllabus was accepted and examined by the then Middlesex Regional Examining Board. Children in Brent, at Certificate of Secondary Education (CSE) level, had the option of counting this subject as one of their CSE subjects.

I have also published a few things in the field of multicultural education. Added to these, I was also well known on the in-service training circuit throughout England, Wales, and Scotland. My contributions to their numerous Education Authorities and schools training days for advisors and teachers were always related to multicultural and anti-racist education. The multicultural education field was a relatively new development, and I was one of its earliest pioneers. Armed with these credentials, I felt able to make the switch since nothing was happening on the headship front. My application was duly sent to and received by Manchester City Council.

Miraculously, I was called for an interview on my first shot at this kind of post. On the day of the interviews, I discovered for the first time that my Afro-Caribbean colleague from my neighboring authority, Mr. Steve Stephenson, who held the identical post in Birmingham, had also applied for the Manchester post. He too was called for the interviews. The interviews were to be held over two days. Candidates who were successful at the first round of interviews would be contacted and invited back for the final interviews a week later. There were six candidates, one of whom was internal to the Manchester authority. He was a white candidate.

A week later, an official is alleged to have gone to the candidates' waiting room and openly summoned Mr. Carlton Duncan and Mr. Steve Stephenson. Of course, neither of us was present because we were never informed that we had been successful at the first round of interviews. By default, the post went to the internal white candidate. This information came back to me from an insider who followed the entire procedure. This incident served to re-focus my mind on the business of getting headship. But I still had the difficulties of silent rejections of my headship applications to resolve.

My suspicion was that a wall of silence was slowly building around me and my growing concerns about my applications. Were things going wrong from my end? If the Education Authorities were interested in my applications they would seek 'authority references' from Mr. Atkin, the Director of Education for Coventry Education Authority. Mr. Atkin would not normally write that reference. The usual thing was to delegate that task to an Education Advisor; usually the Advisor who has the candidate's school as part of his pastoral duties. That person, in my case, was a man called MF.

MF was a Caucasian Education Advisor who carried the Coventry Education Authority's multicultural education brief. In addition to the authority's reference, one from the headteacher would be requested as a matter of formality. I knew of no reason why MF or my headteacher, Arfon Jones, would be blocking my chances. After all, Arfon had been an outstanding friend, colleague, and boss right from the start. He often praised my work in my presence. There was a little friction between us on one or two occasions over my appointment to the Rampton/Swann Committee and my selection as a magistrate to the Coventry Bench.

There were those who felt that it was jealousy on Arfon's part, but I felt, at the time, that Arfon was overly concerned that these activities would place a strain on his workload if one of his deputies was publicly committed as I was going to be. The authority was pleased about my involvement and said so via its Director of Education who tried to accommodate my involvement by giving extra staffing resources to the school. I did not believe that Arfon would have been the problem here. After all, in times of his own difficulties, I was there for him. When forty members of his female staffs had reported him to the government Quango (The Commission for Sexual Equality for dealing with sexual discrimination), they were required to give him notice of their complaint.

It was on the last day of term, before the beginning of the summer holidays, that the notice was placed on Arfon's desk while he was out of his office. I was determined that his holiday should not be spoiled and quietly removed both the notice and the summons to appear before the commission later that year. In fact, Arfon never became aware of this development until he had enjoyed a great summer and returned to school the following September. I happen to know that Arfon was extremely grateful to me for protecting his summer break. He would not be rewarding me in this way.

MF, on the other hand, was the school's advisor and therefore knew of my skills and the headteacher's often openly expressed positive views about my work, he also had the opportunity to observe it first-hand. Additionally, he also served on the Rampton/Swann Committee and, indeed, on the sub-committee, which I chaired. At no time did he ever give me the impression that the authority was anything other than satisfied with my work and performance. Knowing all this, I continued to make my applications to numerous authorities across the country, to some of them repeatedly.

The Swann Committee was gathering evidence in the Birmingham area over several days in the early part of 1981. Many of Birmingham's maintained schools would be visited by appointment. One of these was Golden Hillock in the southeastern corner of the city. I knew the headteacher, Mary Stewart, from my Aylestone days in Brent. She was the deputy headteacher who left when the new head, Mr. F came to replace Mr. P.

It was good to be seeing her in action once more. The local education authority had courteously dispatched two of its education advisors to meet with the commissioners at the school. As it turned out these two advisors, one Asian and the other Afro-Caribbean were recently appointed to the authority and part of their brief was multicultural education across the city. It was therefore felt that they were the appropriate advisors to meet with us given the substance of our inquiry.

As we were introduced, it became clear that these advisors already knew who I was. They knew of me because their authority had received a good many applications from me for several headships, which became vacant in the city, but I wasn't considered because I was getting a "bad" reference from Coventry. It was hard to believe that, but it was true that I wasn't being considered. When I probed, it turned out that someone was taking it upon himself or herself to tell the nation that I was not ready for headship because I had hardly been in school since my appointment. This was a clear dig at my work on the government committee and on the Coventry bench of magistrates.

I would have to raise this matter with my school advisor, without giving away my source to see if he could throw any light on it. I would find a way. I was so determined. After the evidence gathering sessions were completed in Birmingham, I was back in school the following week. I did not have to see MF because he had made an appointment to see me when I was back.

At our meeting in my office that Monday morning, MF told me that I was causing the Coventry Education Authority a great deal of embarrassment because of the frequency with which they were receiving requests for references concerning my applications for headships. He went on to explain that it was an embarrassment because I had only done three years at Sidney School and Community College. I was, therefore, not yet ready for a headship, which is the top job.

"After all, I could not do it in three years," he said referring to himself. I cannot repeat the expletives which I used when I asked him to vacate my office forthwith and never to return.

I had always known that white bigots thought themselves to be superior to black people: a fault line in their education. But despite frequent rumors in the community about 'MF', I had still never expected this of him. I was quite prepared to debate the issue of my readiness with him with a view to convincing him that he was mistaken about my ability and my achievements thus far. And if he was willing to listen to reason, maybe he would remove those damaging paragraphs from future references pertaining to me. But once he took on that air of the superior 'white man,' he lost the reasonable me.

Before I even chatted with my headteacher, I got on the telephone and rang the Education Director's office. Unusually, the Director answered the phone himself. I was still very angry, and Mr. Atkin detected this. "Someone has upset you," he remarked. I then asked him if I could have an early appointment with him. "Why not come and have lunch with me, at 13:00 today?"

"Was my luck changing?" I asked myself, rhetorically. Usually, when you telephone the Director, you get his secretary who vets the purpose for your wanting to either speak with him or make an appointment to see him. When she was satisfied that your cause was worthy, you would gain an entry in the Director's diary sometimes as far away as two weeks hence or more. This time it wasn't so, and I was very grateful for the turn of events. His secretary was, in fact, off work that day on account of illness.

Lunch was at a known to-be expensive Coventry restaurant not far from the Director's office. I must have looked a bit taken back because he quickly remarked that lunch was on him. Once we discarded the menu and ordered our meals, we both had fillet steak, his well done, mine medium rear, served with fresh vegetables and a glass of red wine I told him that I had come to request that MF be taken off my reference. I then told him why.

The Director said, "Let's enjoy our lunch, and I will call you before the end of tomorrow." The Director did not say it, but it was clear from his demeanor that I wasn't the first person to raise questions about MF's attitude. Such matters were greater than MF and could impact the authority well beyond him. The Director had as part of his brief the wider welfare of the City of Coventry and he wasn't about to neglect his responsibility.

True to his word, that call, from the Director, came before the end of the following day, though not directly from him. Mr. Spiller, the senior Advisor with the authority's Science brief, called me at the behest of the Director. He was on his way over to the school to see me and was just checking that I was going to be there. I waited anxiously in my office to receive Mr. Spiller. I did not have to wait for long. He was gentlemanly and made no mention of his colleague MF.

He explained that the Director wished him to handle all my references from then on and he would appreciate it if I would keep him informed of what I had in the pipeline and any future ones. I agreed and advised him that I had recently made three applications, which could not have been processed yet. They were the three B's—Bedford, Bradford, and Brent. We thanked each other and he left for his office. I would be having one further conversation with Mr. Spiller, and it wouldn't be to tell him of any more applications, which I had made: it will be to thank him for "dispensing justice," as he had seen it.

Bedford, Bradford, Brent

The postman came early one December morning in 1981. I was just getting ready to leave for school when I heard the thud sound on the door mat. There were four letters there. I gave Mrs. Duncan hers and the other three were addressed to me. My heart was beating fiercely because I could see that they individually had stamp marks bearing the names of places to which I had sent applications for headships. The last time I had counted, I had already made 120 applications, and nothing had happened before: possibly thanks to MF; who knows? Many colleagues, white and black, male, and female, that I knew had often said to me that they would have given up after making ten or even fewer applications without positive responses.

Indeed, I knew this to be true because, at the time, I could point to several of my friends who tried to get teaching posts or promotions within teaching unsuccessfully and then gave up after a short while to work on the buses or the underground railways in London. Characteristically, however, I could not do that and would have kept on making applications however many it would have taken me. Once I had given up, I would have failed to achieve my deep-seated ambition, which I held since the age of seven. As a child growing up, I had always found that adversity fired my motivation to a greater extent than did triumphs. Who wants to be a loser?

Although I didn't want to be caught up in the morning traffic going across Coventry, I could not wait to get to school before opening my mail. I frantically tore the envelopes open one after the other and read enough of each to see that I was shortlisted for interviews at Bedford, at Bradford and at Brent. One day only separated the Bradford and Brent interviews. The Bedford interviews were first and by many days.

MF did not write the authority's references for any of these applications. Mr. Spiller did. I could hardly wait to thank him and tell him of the results. Even if I failed at landing one of these three, he had done enough to give me a fair chance, which reflected the measure of decency in the man: probably why he was the Senior Advisor and not MF. I shouted for Melvinder and broke the good news. She was delirious with joy and hope. That meant a great deal to me. That my wife was so happy for me boosted my confidence significantly. Now I had to get to school. My headteacher and certain key others needed to share in this.

Arfon and my fellow deputy heads said that they were pleased for me and wished me success at the coming interviews. I already possessed enough knowledge about Brent and the school, Slade Brook. After all, I had come directly from Brent to Coventry after working for the authority for five years. I was not only a teacher in the Borough but had involved myself more widely. For example, I was a teacher and governor of my own school. I was one of the founding members of the Brent Teachers' Center, served as a governor of the center, and helped in the self-help construction project of the Teachers' Center bar. I was also part of the staffing Rota for the bar. These activities meant that I got to know a great deal about the Borough and its schools.

But I knew nothing about Bedford and Bradford. I would now have to do some serious research and visit the areas so that at the appropriate time, I would not be handicapped. All three authorities had offered the candidates the opportunity to telephone the schools to make plans to look around and talk to key staff and external officials before the dates of the interviews, and I made good use of that opportunity.

During the period before the upcoming interviews, I picked up some gossip relating to an interesting development in the West Midland area. Immediately I wondered whether there could be a connection with Tony Brown's disappearance.

It would later be revealed that on the night of his BBC presentation at Pebble Mill, Tony not only attracted numerous fans, but he was also flushed with new friends some of whom were grossly unwholesome. At one of Coventry's regular Deputy Headteachers' meetings there was much rumor that a spate of human-trafficking was haunting the West Midlands and was creating significant pastoral problems for several schools throughout the area. The most frustrating thing for me was that there was no colleague who had anything more than hearsay about this phenomenal development in the area. One of my colleagues at the meeting let it slip that the issue was common talk among footballers.

It was then that I remembered Tony's love for football and his close ties to all things Aston Villa. This could be the breakthrough that I needed. I need to find Tony Brown and get him back into the school where he rightfully belongs. The football calendar revealed that Aston Villa was meeting Manchester United in a fortnight in Birmingham. Great news, I didn't have to go far, just next door to the City of Coventry. Tickets were still available. I got two of the cheapest. These would get me and my partner right where it matters: where the young people will be dressed in football splendor and competing regalia with their cans of beer often laced with spirit. It is in this atmosphere that gossip, truth and falsehood will thrive. My best hope was of hearing something that would lead me to Tony Brown.

The two weeks went by quickly, maybe because I was so preoccupied with all those other burning issues related to my career development. My partner and I had a fascinating experience down in the pits, sometimes it was too close to being dangerous but fun all the same. We did not learn anything which was directly related to Tony Brown but at least we came away knowing some of the tricks of the trade.

It seems, once a victim is identified, he or she is researched and located geographically. High profile victims like Tony Brown are located more readily with the aid of the media. At an appropriate time, the victim is pounced upon, usually aided by the victim himself/herself. The victim is drugged and hustled away in some waiting vehicle. His or her essential documents such as passport, national insurance and birth certificate are hugely important for a successful trafficking bust.

The next move is to have the victim initiated. This succinctly is to get the victim knowingly involved in criminal wrong doings such as burglary, theft, rape, and similar offenses. The victim is now locked into the ownership of his or her captives. There is no incentive to escape when you are fund less, being sought for by law officials and you have no identifying documents. At this point, you become priceless to your captives who eventually auction you off to the highest foreign bidder into slavery. Invitees to the auctions are usually wealthy foreigners. A little quiet village in Hampshire seems to be the hub for this very lucrative foreign trade with its easy access to Dover and open Europe: approximately **2 hours 20 minutes** (138.5 mi) via M20, M25 and M3.

If this was the fate of Tony Brown, no one really knows. And if it was, knowing what point in the processing chain he was at would be a matter of guess work. In any case, I have no reason to believe that Tony Brown has suffered this fate. This realization left me helpless: just where I did not want to be. Just then it occurred to me that the only thing left to me is to take blind chances in the hope of hooking a fish. Why don't I advertise in in some foreign newspapers that I am in the market for domestic and handy man workers and see what that turns up? My first three adverts produced nothing.

Just as I was beginning to think this was a waste of time and money, I decided to place one more advert in a local French gazette using the post box of a long-term friend, Nicole who lives in Paris. A week later, Nicole rang me to say that a catalog of some sort had arrived in her box for me. And that she had put it in the mail for me.

Eventually, that catalog arrived. In the section called domestic and farm hand workers, sure enough, there was a picture of Tony Brown over the name Gerry Hogan, Gerry Hogan, my back foot, I would know Tony Brown from a mile off. (Handles farm vehicles well). Will be in parade at a London venue on a date that was fixed for two weeks hence. I must be at this auction. It is good that he is still on British grounds and must not be allowed to leave our shores. I shall have to put on my thinking cap tonight. At the auction, I would be Mr. Phillipe Pascalle, and I will have to pay some attention to my French accent. After all, I am the French man who is seeking a handy farm hand.

The rules of auction say the product goes to the highest bidder who collects the product once the check is cleared on or before the fifth day of purchase. The product was allowed to show off his farm driving skills to those desiring to behold them. Here, the rules were a bit lax because the purchaser would have no lawful documents to leave the shores. This was just made for me and my intention.

When I set out for the auction in the London suburbs of Camden that rainy morning, I had no idea of what a beautiful day weather-wise the day would turn out to be. That it turned out to be a beautiful day was a blessing in disguise because I was going to the auction with the clear intention to re-kidnap Tony Brown if the opportunity presented itself. I would have to bid for the ownership of the boy like so many others who might be there and interested in having him.

I arrived at the back streets of St. Pancreas Railway Station about two hours before the scheduled auction. The spare time was most useful. My Toyota Celica which I had serviced and tuned up the day before, made light work of 100 or so miles in under two hours. Although no stranger to London, I was not familiar with this part of North London. Hence, the extra time was magically useful for reconnaissance. The auction yard was an old disused riffle range with some rugged dirt roads used for showing off the skills of potential farm hands. During the reconnoitering, I noted that the Edgeware Road was about two miles north of St. Pancras. This was a more direct route to the M1 motorway in Northwest London. This was good news should I need a quick getaway route.

The venue itself was lightly and inconspicuously staffed. Potential bidders arriving had to wander about aimlessly until they found their way to the center of affair.

Tony Brown (alias Gerry Hogan) was the last to appear on the parading stage. He was the guy dressed in a white open-neck shirt, khaki trousers, blue shoes and matching blue cap. He and his three peers were visibly chained together at the ankles. How the hell could this be happening in any place in the world let alone in the heart of central London. This wasn't the time for moral disapprobation. I needed to do my business and get out as soon as possible. There were four slaves on display and twice as many bidders…seven men (including me) and a woman. The slaves were auctioned in the order they came on stage. The first three fetched very high prices and were now unchained to the contract room. There were now five of us showing interest in Gerry Hogan, my boy.

At the extravagant heights of US$20,000, I knew I stood no chance of leaving lawfully with Tony Brown leaving me only option B which was to re-kidnap the boy and make a run for it. My intention and determination emboldened me. I entered a bid at US$25,000. Just as the hammer was about to fall our only female client intervened with a US$30,000 bid. On her face it said this was my last bid. I needed to test the waters and so advanced the bidding to US$35,000 where it stayed until the hammer fell. Tony Brown was now mine: only, I had no funds with which to pay. Before he was re-chained and brought back into captivity, I conditioned my future payment upon being able to verify that the boy was able to handle farm vehicles as advertised.

This meant taking him out to the range and the parked-up farm vehicles. For the first time Tony and I were in proximity. He recognized me but read my eyes that told him to shut up and play along. Tony was allowed into the passenger seat of my Celica for the quick trip out to the range but instead of pointing the vehicle through the gate to the range, I pointed my car northwards and sped off into the evening rush hour traffic knowing that by the time they could put a chase together, I would be lost in a sea of northwards moving traffics. Because of their criminality, they dare not involve the police.

In about 40 minutes, I was at the Cricklewood end of the Edgeware Road which is where I would pick up the M1 motorway heading north and routes to the West Midlands. I knew enough about English Law to know that what I had just done was against the law in a big way, but I shall plead the defense of justification. I didn't know, but common sense suggests that the slave traders might well be covering Tony's home tonight. We won't be going there: not even to my own home just in case someone guessed who I am. Instead, I will go directly to Inspector B who has known me from the days of my impromptu marriage to Melvinder as was arranged by the Chief Magistrate of Coventry, Mrs. Edwards, at the time.

On the way back to the Midlands I had the whole mystery cleared up by the victim himself. On the morning of his disappearance, as soon as the other members of his family had left him at home, he heard a knock on his front door. He answered the door only to be pounced on by two unknown faces, one of whom stuffed a strong-smelling cotton substance under his nose, and it would be many hours that day before he came to his senses. All those footprints, shoes prints, and ransacked cupboards and drawers now fall into place.

We shall be guided by Inspector B. At least, we have some helpful information to pass on to the police. Tony's parents and family will be delighted to have him home again. His school eagerly awaits him, and Tony is left with the horrible inconveniences of having to replace his stolen documents and hopefully expunge his record clean. All this was accomplished and still left me adequate time to prepare for the Bedford, Bradford, and Brent interviews.

Chapter 3

The Bedford interviews came and went. And although I thought I gave a good performance and had a fair interview; I did not get that job. The post was filled by the sole internal candidate. It was never always an advantage to be an internal candidate, but clearly, in this case it was. For me, this, together with the feedback, which was voluntarily given after the interviews, would be marked as good experience, which should help me in the future.

Wyke Manor Upper School

The First Headship

Because Bradford was such a far distance from Coventry and, indeed, a very awkward cross-country journey, I had timed my school visit for the day before the interviews. A member of the Rampton/Swann Committee of Inquiry lived in Bradford and she and her husband had offered me overnight boarding. That offer was gratefully accepted. The school for which I had come to compete, Wyke Manor Upper School, was situated in a small community called Wyke on the very edge of southwestern Bradford. The Bradford Education Authority had long-listed eight candidates who numbered four following a series of short-listing interviewing exercises by small interview panels put together for this purpose. These four formed the field from which the headteacher of Wyke Manor Upper School would be chosen.

My final interview did not go smoothly. About halfway through the interview, one of the other candidates, 'M', apparently so nervous, it was later reported, kept pacing the waiting room from corner to corner and fiddling with everything in sight. In this way, he eventually set off the fire alarm unwittingly.

Every member of the full panel vacated the interview room and left me sitting there wondering what was going on around me. It was some several minutes later that they all reconvened to continue my interview after establishing that it was an accidental false alarm. The shock from seeing the nature of the school from the day before together with the fire-alarm chaos did not instill confidence. Neither was I unduly bothered. The practice throughout the teaching profession in England and Wales of interviewing all candidates on the same day and then letting them wait together in some waiting room for the considered results is a nail-biting exercise.

In industry and various other places, you are sent home to await a call, which could be either negative or positive. I believe that the industry's way is a less stressful way of doing things. In our system, each candidate dreads the ultimate knock on the door, yet eagerly awaits it. This is because the candidates know that at that point a name will be called; that will signal to the others that they were unsuccessful. So, it was for all four of us on that day. Eventually, that knock came, and the name was called 'Mr. Duncan.' I quickly shook hands with the other three contenders, one of whom I had previously competed with for the Bedford job, accepted their congratulations, and hurriedly followed the messenger back to the interviewing room.

The chairman of the panel, Mrs. Doris Birdsall, who just happened to be the Chairman of the Governors for the school, thanked me, "for attending and giving such a strong and pleasingly engaging interview. The panel would like to offer you the post, would you accept?"

I had no hesitation in accepting and then reveled in the expressions of congratulations and well-done comments. I was then advised that the Bradford Education Authority would write to me formally within a few days to confirm the appointment. I was further advised that it would be perfectly alright for me to resign in Coventry in anticipation of the formalities from Bradford City Council.

The long and tedious journey home would not be so bad after all. On the way, I got around to thinking about two of the other three candidates. Firstly, I thought about the chap who had previously competed with me in Bedford. He had just seen me fall off the headship hunting list; hopefully, he will fall off soon. Then I thought about 'M.' It must have been enormously embarrassing for him when he mistakenly triggered the fire alarm. What I did not know was that I would meet up with 'M' again when he would successfully compete for another school, Carlton Bolling, right there in Bradford. He would eventually assure me that on his second visit to Bradford, he did not raise an alarm.

My journey home was made longer because of the seemingly endless evening traffic heading in every direction. Motorways were like endless car parking facilities as motorists inched their vehicles along the fume-tainted motorways toward their several homes. There was lots of time to ponder numerous things. Had my luck really turned? Firstly, I now had an opportunity pending for adopting James. This will be in the coming February. Melvinder is carrying our twins. Then there was the occasion when I met those advisors at Golden Hillock School; that led indirectly to my luncheon date with my Director of Education, Mr. Atkin. Mr. Spiller came on the scene and removed the blockages and now, here I am, just hours ago achieving my long-held childhood ambition: to be headteacher at my own school. I had just aspired to the top job. I had just done it.

In 1981, I had not even heard of the mobile phone much less having one of my own. In the moving traffic, you could not get out to telephone home from a phone booth. My wife would have to wait for my arrival before she could learn of the day's wonderful news. While I was aware that I was now Britton's first black headmaster of a secondary school, I had no idea that it was going to be such a newsworthy event or of the media frenzy that would follow. The long drive up to Bradford, the two days of heavy concentration and careful performance; and the long drive back in such heavy traffic fatigue; and all that thinking left me awfully exhausted as I slowly parked up my car at our front door that chilly December night.

Propped up only by the spirit of the day's success story, I managed to get the key into the lock just before my wife opened it. She knew at once. She guessed it; probably aided by my tired but joyful countenance. She had a way of making you feel even better about your successes than you did at first. That night was no exception. She was now a headteacher's wife and proud of it. I would take up my new position as headteacher at Wyke Manor Upper School in April 1982. Right then, I was interested in some sleep. Tomorrow morning, bright and early, I must not forget to telephone Brent to let them know that I will no longer be attending the interviews for Slade Brook School and why. I had a final term to complete at Sidney Stringer School and Community College. I would be giving it my all.

The Christmas school break was nigh and promised to be a great one. There were so many developments that we had to look forward to in the New Year. James would become our family; we would need to go house hunting in Bradford; a new job to start and the 'twins' were on their way. With all these positives in the pipeline, it made everything else seem very pleasant, whatever the circumstance. This would be the last Christmas that we shall be organizing for just the two of us. There is a saying that 'Christmas is for children and children there shall be after this one'. The builder had started some extension work on our home in February 1981 and had assured us that it would all be finished by early November that year.

As we drew closer to Christmas it seemed clear that the house was going to be opened and nowhere near finished on Christmas day itself. The various promises which we had in the air made us overlook little things like that. We had our suspicion confirmed about the house when we received a golden-edged invitation from the builder and his family to have Christmas dinner with them.

It was a great meal, and we had a great time in the builder's company and that of his very large family. The next day, Boxing Day, we traveled down to London and spent the day with my mother and my youngest brother, Raymond. Mother had never really told me how she felt about my marriage to Melvinder and the circumstances surrounding it. She always welcomed us into her home and showered us with caring hospitality. She was much more open about her feelings when I married Bronwyn and left home. Then, she had a lot to say, mainly negative, but in the final analysis, she accepted Bronwyn as my lawful wife and her daughter-in-law.

The work on our house was not, in fact, completed until the last day of the year. That night my wife and I took in the movie, 'Funny Girl' with Barbra Streisand and Omar Sharif. We got back home in time to see in the New Year with a bottle of Champaign. The toasts were to the New Year; to us; to the coming of James; to the new job, and to the twins' arrival.

Everyone at Stringer was happy for me, including my headteacher, Arfon Jones. The term went by very quickly. To me, it was most important that I should tie up all loose ends. The headteacher advertised my replacement as soon as he knew I was leaving. If such a person was known before the end of this last term, I would be able to do a hand-over directly to her or him. The most difficult part of the process would be to find a replacement Law teacher.

It was I who had introduced Law into the school's curriculum (as I had done at Aylestone Comprehensive School in Brent) soon after completing my degree (LLB) (Hons.), which I had started in Brent while I was employed by that education authority. Therefore, I felt a great deal of responsibility and obligation to my pupils. There were not many Law teachers and those that existed taught in tertiary colleges or universities. I had first and second-year Advanced and Ordinary Levels Law students to consider.

My 'A'-Level Lawyers

My economics students at these levels were less threatened because there were other Economists on the staff. Indeed, they were plentiful everywhere. We had plenty of slack in the staff because the Director had allowed extra staffing because of my service on the Government Inquiry and the Coventry Bench of Magistrate. The school used the extra staffing as it saw fit, so there was some flexibility available to the Time-Tabling Deputy. I suffered pangs of sorrow until I was eventually satisfied that all my classes would be professionally covered.

At home, we were now three. At the Adoption Hearing in February, the Coventry Magistrates ruled our adoption attempt successful and lawful. Since that time James (Jamie) Karl Duncan was kinship and living at home. Either Melvinder or I had to cease working to take on the full-time role of caring for James. In our given circumstances, Melvinder drew the straw. She would now give up her job at the library for this august task. In very short order, she would also be a mother of twins. Just as we had hoped and thought, James had brought a lot of life into the home. He brought the occasional embarrassment too. Looking out from our back door at our Coventry home, we could see the backs of a row of houses whose gardens were separated from those on our side of the road by a long and narrow passageway.

It was a frequent occurrence to find a particular woman from one of these houses peering over her fence into ours. Melvinder would often comment to me that that 'Nosey-Parker' from across the way was at it again. One day, this very same woman had reason to come to our front door. She rang our bell and as I opened the door and James saw who it was standing there, he ran back inside loudly shouting, "Mummy, mummy, it's the Nosey-Parker from next door." The woman heard this most clearly and was not amused and showed it.

It was greatly satisfying to watch Jamie learning new skills, gradually perfecting his dexterity, and witness him adapting to us as his new parents. On the weekends, we had new past times. We now spend a significant proportion of our time playing with little James in the public parks. He enjoyed having his food and drinks and really looked forward to feeding times. On one of our house hunting trips to Bradford, we were strolling along a busy pavement in the city center.

As we went by a restaurant, James shouted out in his loudest lovely little voice, "Daddy, eat shop!" This love for his food was a source of immeasurable joy and unimaginable satisfaction for Melvinder and me. While I was at Sydney Stringer School in the final days, Melvinder would sometimes surprise us and bring little Jamie in, ostensibly to see his dad, but in truth, to show him off to the staff and pupils at the school.

On three different weekends, James' 'park outings' had to be transferred to Bradford as we were keenly addressing the not unimportant matter of finding a place for us to live when we moved there in April 1982. Eventually, we found 19 Oakfield Grove: a secluded four-bedroom bungalow in Manningham. It had a portable swimming pool which would be ideal for James and later for the twins. We left all conveyance matters in the hands of the lawyers. Until we had to make the move, we would spend the remainder of the time at home in Coventry and at Sidney Stringer.

"This is your Life…"

Unknown to me at the time, the task had fallen to two of my Sydney Stringer teaching colleagues, Gary Quigley, English teacher, and Helen

Clarke, Science teacher to organize a leaving do and a celebration of my new headship. On my last official night at Stringer, I had the most touching presentation one could imagine or ever hoped to have. Its form was like the Eamonn Andrews' style of 'THIS IS YOUR LIFE', which was a British television regular and popular feature at the time. My wife was secretly helping to prepare for the night, and I did not guess a single thing. Helen Clarke was the researcher and compiler. The 'Red Book' story began:

You thought you came here to dance, But...

CARLTON GEORGE DUNCAN

A child prodigy, Megastar, Rampton absconder, Justice of the Peace, Headmaster alias Shaft...

"THIS IS YOUR LIFE."

It continued and covered stories about my childhood, university life, my boxing and dancing experiences, some of my travels abroad, my time at Stringer, my Justice of the Peace activities as well as those on the Rampton and Swann Committee of Inquiry. The 'Red Book' ended:

CARLTON GEORGE DUNCAN, YOUR HONOR.
"THIS IS YOUR LIFE"

They had to be outstanding researchers to have acquired all that information, and so much of it. To round it off Gary had written to Her Majesty, the Queen seeking 'a special message of congratulations.' I quote here from the response sent to Gary by the Queen's Private Secretary, Mr. Robert Fellows:

Dear Mr. Quigley,
  Thank you for your letter of 15th March. Her Majesty was interested to read of the appointment of Mr. Duncan as headmaster of Wyke Manor Upper School. The Queen hopes that your special session of "This Is Your Life" is a great success...

'Operation Bootstrap'

That weekend we had another reception in my honor to attend at the Coventry Community Relations Council's premises. Since my appointment at Sidney Stringer School and Community College, I had managed to use the school's premises on Saturdays to establish and run a voluntary supplementary school called 'Operation Bootstrap.' At the start, we had just three teachers, Christine Hall, my mathematics colleague from Stringer, and later Len Dore, another mathematics teacher from another school and authority plus me. Resources-wise, the supplementary school was mainly financed by the Coventry Community Relations Council under the leadership of Mr. Vernon Clements, its Community Relations Officer, in conjunction with the Coventry West Indian Association.

Operation Bootstrap became extremely popular with parents for their children, especially those of black origins. Since the publication of Bernard Coard's *How the West Indian Child is made educationally subnormal in the British school system* (New Beacon Books, London 1971), black people everywhere had become conscious of their children's underachievement in the ordinary schools right across Britain. Many black educationalists, including myself, felt that the least we could do is to give voluntary service in supplementary schools that had begun to mushroom around the country in church halls, people's living rooms, and similar places.

Some children from Operation Bootstrap came to tea

We, at Operation Bootstrap, set out right from the beginning not just to enable children, black, brown, or white, for such was the nature of our school, to develop skills in the three R's, but additionally, to build their confidence in themselves and in reaching for the stars. We wanted to surround our children with positive role models, which would encourage and support greater consciousness and higher aspiration. With these aims in view, we became very successful.

As I was now leaving Coventry and the Operation Bootstrap project, the parents wanted to show their appreciation for the roles I played at the school; hence the reception to mark my contribution and my departure. As did the staff of Sidney Stringer reception, the parents clubbed together to provide me with presents. These would always serve as visible reminders of my time with them. Christine and Len would lead the school into the future.

Moving home was always a difficult and stressful time. When I first moved to Coventry, I had found it necessary at different times to live in two different unsuitable temporary accommodations until such a time as I was able to acquire a suitable permanent home. Financially, it was often very difficult because, although the new authority usually assisted with relocation expenses, it was never enough, and it would take a long time for the salary increase associated with the new job to compensate. It was going to be extra difficult for us when we moved to Bradford.

This was because we were still paying mortgages on the Lady Margaret property in London and on the Coventry home in Aldbury Rise. It was a deliberate action on our part not to sell any of these properties. Instead, we attempted to find suitable tenants for them. We found tenants alright but never suitable ones. This meant that we had to make a hefty borrowing to be able to acquire the Bradford Bungalow. But who cared, we had Jamie and the twins on their way.

James had met new friends at the nursery. Melvinder and some of the other mothers had planned to take the children to the fun park very soon. The process of fitting into the community had begun. Our bungalow had no immediate neighboring houses. It stood alone on the land, which was once a tennis court before it fell into disrepair and was transformed into building land for the purposes of the bungalow. It was going to mean walking a little way to be friendly with our closest neighbors. However, Melvinder was of a friendly and talkative disposition so it would not take her long to break the ice.

Past to Present and Future

With all those trials in the past, here we are facing the present and anticipating the future.

At home, the focus was on James and the expected arrival of the twins. We had already found out that they were healthy and that it was going to be one of each: a girl and a boy. We know that made it so much easier to plan for their arrival. Everything was like magic; blissfully anticipating the greater joys to come.

Since the fracas and fray involving Melvinder's family on our wedding day, and, indeed, Inspector B's warning, we had had no further contact with the Sian's family. Melvinder had made one or two attempts to contact them by telephone at special times, for example, at Christmases, on Guru Nanak's and family birthdays, with no result. Now that we were no longer in Coventry, it would be even more difficult for the family to find us even if they were so inclined.

The last set of information they had concerning our whereabouts would have been Aldbury Rise and Sidney Stringer School. These addresses were no longer valid. My wife would now have to reconcile herself to the fact that any hope of her family re-contacting her, now that the grandchildren are near, is gone. Such a re-linking move would have to come from our side once the grandchildren are here. Still, life must go on for all of us. Of course, the publicity surrounding my appointment and what will surely follow the birth of the world's first black test-tube twins will bring us back into the lime-light and would make tracing us relatively easy. This fact was not lost to us.

Chapter 4

I had come a long and discouraging way to this point. Apart from Mr. P, who had predicted that I would, one day, become Brent's first black headteacher, the route was mainly a negative one. Maybe it was because my love for the teaching profession was already deeply rooted in Jamaica that I stayed the course with increasing enthusiasm. My love, respect and admiration for the profession was based upon the esteem and respect that teachers earned from the wider community. It is also very important to note that the teachers that brought me up were almost all black role models and that helped me to stay on course. It wasn't easy medicine to swallow when faced with a system that had set and marked the examination papers that were sat overseas and now, that same system, tells a young twenty-year-old who had successfully passed those examinations that his qualifications were not recognized in the so-called 'mother country' of origin.

It was pure raw determination, together with a character that makes my adrenaline flow faster in the direction of my chosen interest at that point that propelled me forward into repeating my general education in conformity. This intrinsically racist attitude, which was embodied in the British education system's rejection of people like me who were generally educated in the Caribbean, was fundamentally a relic of colonial mentality. It was also a visionary statement that would be poignantly echoed by the ex-so-called President Trump of the United States of America during his 2016 to 2020 tenure when he described countries like Jamaica as "shithole" countries.

That rejection only served to delay the gaining of the necessary training qualification. During the time I spent doubling up on my general education, I was able to advance my ambition. Instead of pursuing my goal via the Teacher Training College route, I was able to accomplish the extra qualifications necessary to go the university route which turned out to be both opportunistic and visionary. But this was not the end of the obstacles. Swansea University was nearly 200 miles from my parents' home in London. This meant seeking independent accommodation for the first time since my arrival in England that cold and wintry night in January 1961. Although I had variously seen signs in shop windows and on billboards indicating that there were "Rooms to let, sorry, no Irish, no colored and no dogs,"

I had never personally experienced their impact. Though the university gave non-white students first preference to halls of residence, I was asked to apply to digs from a list the university sent me. Clearly, because my name did not flag me as an overseas student. The taxi driver took me to Mrs. Yates's address, the address of the landlady I had chosen from the list. And here follows my next obstacle.

As we approached the address, the taxi driver, who obviously knew her, said to me, in a most splendid Welch accent, "There she is, coming down the road now."

A middle-aged woman with reddish hair, about five feet tall and stoutly built was hastening toward her address from the opposite direction as though she was expecting someone or a delivery. She arrived at her door at the same time as the driver pulled up the taxi.

"Mrs. Yates, I have another one for you," proclaimed the taxi driver to Mrs. Yates, as he put his head through the window of his taxicab.

Mrs. Yates peered sheepishly into the passenger compartment of the taxi and saw me. She immediately remarked, "I am full. I just have one place left and that is for a Mr. Duncan coming from London."

I instantly assured Mrs. Yates that I was Mr. Duncan whom she was expecting from London. Mrs. Yates became strangely whiter and agitated. All the blood swiftly drained away from her countenance as she uttered, "I told Mrs. Gilbert (the university accommodation officer) that I didn't want any overseas students."

In her moment of panic and obvious confusion, she had totally forgotten that Mrs. Gilbert had had nothing to do with the arrangement. This was all done by telephone between her and me. She continued, "I suppose you can stay the night and then leave tomorrow; you see, it is not me, it is the other students who don't want to share with any overseas students."

"Overseas student" or any other euphemism, did nothing to conceal Mrs. Yate's bigotry and did not hide the reality of what was happening to me. I had no room at the university halls of residence and my digs land lady rejected me in circumstances where I am a stranger some 200 miles away from home in total desperation as a young black man. The taxi driver, his skin tightly drawn around his glistening eyes as he listened, had realized that there was a problem and patiently lingered while I was still sitting in the back of his taxi. If there is one thing about me, it is that I am decisive.

I told Mrs. Yates I would not stay the night and turned to the taxi driver and asked him to take me to the university instead even though I did not know how things would turn out. On the journey to the university, as I pondered whether the outcome would have been the same had I been a white Australian, Canadian or American student, the taxi driver said he was sorry about what had happened and wished me well in finding alternative accommodation. Sometimes, negative things happen for a beneficial purpose. This time, it got me a place in the university's most prestigious hall of residence (Neuadd Gilbertson): a Victorian castle situated at Black Pill, only a five-minute bus ride from the university campus.

The tale of what had happened to me quickly spread around the university campus and made front-page reporting in Creft, the university Student Union daily newspaper. Despite what had just happened to me, my spirit was not broken, and I was even able to be magnanimous when an inquiry required my cooperation to remove Mrs. Yates' address from the university's recognized list of digs. I did not give it.

The next three years would see me reading for and acquiring a joint honors degree in economics and sociology without any major racial intolerance interfering. There were only comparative minor skirmishes, insightful though they were, such as when I had a first date with a white first-year student who, over dinner, wanted to know if it was true that my people "lived in trees." That was a very offensive point in an otherwise intelligent and jolly conversation on a delightful autumn evening. This young lady was not from a run-of-the-mill clique. After all, she had gained a place at the top-ranking University of Wales.

The ignorance reflected in the question she asked was the consequence of the faulty Eurocentric colonialist education that she received over time. She was able to absorb what was taught to her and used it to advance herself. She would have similarly aspired to the heights she had reached had she been taught differently. Clearly, the school curriculum, colonial attitudes, and values have much to answer, which must be part of my mission.

Three other minor racist skirmishes, but nonetheless significant, are worth mentioning before I move on to a more substantial obstacle that I had to circumvent to acquire my teacher status.

Maybe not so much today, but in my time during the 1960s, hitchhiking was a popular means of travel for students traveling between university locations and their distant homes. It was also a popular pastime to hitchhike to and from while on cheap foreign holiday destinations. Students' university scarves were always on flaunting display as their identifying feature to the passing motorists. I recall that it was a thing of joy when one of these motorists stopped in response to the student's lift-seeking gesticulations especially when the student has long distances to cover such as between Swansea in south Wales and the city of London in England as it was in my case.

Conversations between students and motorists covered many varied subjects: some dull and some very exciting. The black student, as I was, frequently encountered motorists who were quick to open conversation reassuringly with the statement: "I am not a racist." But this reassurance would be instantly canceled with the following: "But, I wouldn't let my daughter marry one of them."

When asked to explain this dichotomy, the rationale becomes: "It is in the interest of the children; society is likely to reject these bi-racial children." Is he saying that he was able to accept me, a black man, in his car but would not accept my children if they were multi-racial? Surely, he is part of that society behind whose tail, he was now hiding. The student is then forced into a hypocritical stance for the rest of the journey for fear of losing his precious ride.

On those occasions when I would travel on public transport, especially at times when seats are highly sought after, such as during rush hours, I would go long distances in comfort and style because no white person wanted to sit next to a black man. They would walk the full length of the train carriage and back looking for an empty seat while they carefully avoided the one next to me. I would silently pray that they would find one elsewhere thus preserving my comfort as the train makes light of the distance from New Street in Birmingham to Euston in the London Borough of Camden. This situation is equally true on the buses or even at the theater. The conclusion is that, but for the embedded racism in all of these, being black can be a gain.

My third minor skirmish also illustrates how racism can be a win for people of color. A chilly wind was coming off the Mumbles' shore as I stood shivering at a bust stop at Black Pill in Swansea. Standing there, too, was a white student from England wearing his green and white Swansea University scarf as I was. We were on a hitchhiking mission: he went to Cheltenham and me beyond there to London. It wasn't long before a red Rover 2000 pulled up almost on our feet in response to our thumbing gestures. The driver, a white man, rolled his window down. He was alone and in a distinctive Welsh accent, pointedly enquired of me where I was heading to. I eagerly told him that my destination was London and that my friend was also heading part way in the same direction all on the A40 highway.

The driver said it was my lucky day because he was, in fact, on his way to London. Then he said quite loudly for the English student to hear: "I will take you, but I won't take him."

In my own mind, I expected this situation to be the other way around. I was astounded, shocked even, by the open statement of the driver. Still puzzled, I quickly accepted the offer of a straight and direct ride (usually, a journey like mine would involve multiple lifts) to London, leaving the English student earnestly seeking a different ride.

It was not until we were some ways into the journey, that the Welshman mumbled: "Bloody English, I hate them." For the remainder of the near 200 miles to London, I was treated to a detailed historical account of the simmering resentment that exists between the Welsh and the English. A resentment which was born out of the conquest and the subjection and exploitation of Wales's natural resources not to mention sports and religious rivalry. No doubt, there is an English counteracting point of view. On this day, however, a black student was preferred over and above a fellow white student.

During the long journey, I tried desperately to find some parallel in the state of affair between the Welsh and the English which would help me to understand the personal and institutional racism to which every black person is a constant victim in white society whether we the blacks will admit it or not. I did not find that help. The Welsh resent being exploited and the other wrongs done to them and their land. It is easy to see how the Welsh might resent those who did them harm. But the black man did not harm or wrong the white man. On the contrary, the reverse is true. Black people were enslaved by the white man for hundreds of years until the grudgingly given emancipation became a reality in the 1860s, at least for some slaves, in the USA (thirty-two years earlier in Britain) and, yet slavery lingered on for a further two years for those slaves whose habitats, unfortunately, were in southern America.

And yet there is no resentment on the part of the black man; like Nelson Mandela, who was imprisoned by the white man for twenty-seven of his best years on Robben Island, he showed no resentment, no bitterness only forgiveness. It is wholly the other way around when it comes to the white man. Today, people of color continue to suffer discrimination in all the areas of life that matter: education, health, employment, housing and criminal justice. It makes no sense at all. And for this and other reasons, my resolve to be in the classroom where I can contribute to molding and reshaping minds in the direction of equality and justice was further heightened. Each day and night bring greater certainty that the school curriculum, aided, of course, by more transitory means such as legislation, training, policies, and even affirmative actions, must be the vehicle to permanent success, albeit a long and challenging route.

Desmond Tutu, the South African Bishop who fought all his working life against apartheid in South Africa has left these words ringing loudly for all classroom teachers to see, read, understand, and act upon "Children were not born racist, we taught them to be" using the colonialist white supremacist curriculum. We can and must undo the resulting evil of racism in all its forms—personal and structural—via a decolonized curricular replacement message.

And yet, I was almost denied the opportunity to make my contribution via the classroom. After a period of three years of what I then rated as the best years of my life up to then, I emerged with a fully-fledged Bachelor of Science—BSc (Econ) (Hons); but I was still not qualified to teach. To be able to fulfill my childhood ambition, it was necessary to spend another year studying for a Post Graduate Certificate of Education (PGCE).

Mr. Sharp was my tutor for the P.G.C.E. Course. He took me aside and put it to me bluntly that I should consider not proceeding with the course. His reasoning was that I would encounter many difficulties of a racial nature in the classroom and that I could spare myself the hurt and disappointment by going to do something else. My thoughts were that Mr. Sharp meant well, but his reasoning was somewhat faulty.

Was he saying that 'doing something else' meant that I would encounter no racism? If that was not the case, then why does it matter where I encountered that evil? I was already admitted onto the course as a graduate of the university, and I was determined to follow through with my childhood ambition to become a qualified teacher. I told Mr. Sharp that I would take my chances. It turned out that I was the only black on the course, and I found out that Mr. Sharp was deeply worried about his ability to find me placements in Welsh Schools to do my teacher training practice as was obligatory for the course.

I had flash backs of Mrs. Yates' refusal to accommodate 'overseas' students. But during the three years at the university, I had come across situations which did not always support the kind of attitude which she exhibited. The outcome of racial issues very often depended on the responses of the suffering individuals. 'It takes all sorts to make a world.'

In the end, Mr. Sharp found no difficulty in placing me either in the primary or secondary schools. Especially in the primary sector, my welcome was assured. At the end of the two weeks of training all the children in the class made me special farewell cards, examples of which are seen here.

Swansea Junior and Infants: Winter 1968

My secondary training, for a similar two weeks, was conducted in a boys' secondary school in Moriston, which is just outside of Swansea itself. Here the school's personnel found out that I had boxed for the university and invited me to join in some extracurricular activities when I was not in training. I undertook that task gladly. What Mr. Sharp feared, at least in training, was never realized. By June 1969, armed with my Post Graduate Teachers' Qualification, I was ready for the reality of the working world. I took it in my stride knowing full well that the outcome was largely dependent upon me.

In my climb up the practicing and promotional ladder to this pinnacle, Mr. Sharp has been proven right repeatedly. But for me not to have endured the pains, insults, and racial abuses about which he warned, it would have meant quitting on my ambition and quitting was never an option for me at any point along the 30 years journey to retirement. Once I had begun the journey, the pinnacle of the profession was my ultimate destination. Entering through the gates of Wyke Manor Upper School this day will be the confirmation that my goal, notwithstanding the rugged and difficult roads with more to come, was achievable.

Chapter 5

The village of Wyke is a ward within the city of Bradford Metropolitan District Council with a population of nearly 15,000. Most often Halifax City Center which is about the same distance from Wyke as Bradford City Center is the preferred shopping center. The only way to explain this preference is to note that Halifax was essentially white in complexion when compared with the immigrants pronounced Bradford City. Inner cities with large immigrant populations tended to be avoided or shunned by the less informed white population. The stories emanating from other large inner cities did little to encourage a rush to immigrant-populated cities by the white population for whatever reasons.

Though the 1824 Vagrancy Act (The SUS Law which gave almost unlimited powers to the police to stop and search people 'suspected of about to commit an arrestable offense') was repealed and replaced by the Criminal Attempts Act of 1981, for the black communities all over Britain, particularly for those in the Midlands and London areas in the south, the SUS law remained oppressively active.

Once the oppression became unbearable, some of these inner cities experienced black rebellion which, in nearly all cases actively supported by sympathetic white community members, was variously described as disturbances, uprisings, or riots. These communities then become unfortunate victims of a double whammy. Firstly, they are negatively and racially stereotyped by the police who use this to oppress them with the overuse of the SUS (suspicion) laws.

When this eventually causes the oppressed to explode, the explosions gave more reasons to perpetuate the stigmatization: a fact that is evidenced by the steady but certain drift away from immigrant cities and villages by the white people who once inhabited them. At the heart of the SUS law and its application is that wretched bogyman 'racism' but SUS is just one manifestation of this evil. It largely falls to us as teachers, at all levels, to eradicate it. This is the essence of my lifelong mission.

At the time of my appointment, Wyke Manor Upper School was a white school in terms of pupil composition and school management, clearly reflecting the ethos of the localities from which it drew its catchment. This fact made such a doubtful first impression on me that when I visited the school prior to the interviews I first thought someone was playing a prank on me by interviewing a black man for this lily-white school. Fortunately, courage and determination got the better of me, so I firmed up my resolve to go forward. From my childhood days, it was always a weakness in me (others thought it was a strength) when faced with daunting challenges not to be discouraged but become adrenalized instead. And so, I came to be telling this story at the present time.

As the first day of my first headship grew near, I began to look away from my obvious achievement and, instead, to check on my own understanding and the quantum of information I have about the new environment into which I will now take my family and myself to set up home.

I was almost a total stranger to any part of Yorkshire, north, south, east, or west. I had never set foot in that part of the country before. In fact, all the twenty-one years of residence that I had accumulated in Britain, before this point in time, were divided across periods in the English Capital, London, Swansea in South Wales, and Coventry in the West Midlands. Yorkshire was an uncharted sea for me. Any information I had about Yorkshire County was a mixture of hearsay, gossip, stereotypes, and some verifiable facts.

Earlier, my interest in literature had put me in touch with some of the written works of the Yorkshire-born Bronte sisters, Anne, Charlotte and Emily whose writings have found permanent places in the archives of great literature— 'The Tenant of Wildfell Hall, 'Jane Eyre' and 'Wuthering Heights' severally just to give a few representative samples of nineteen-century literature that could be said to have given me my earliest taste of Yorkshire. My love for the written words was well developed as a schoolboy in the Caribbean where I had the good fortune to have been taught by the almost legendary headmaster, Austin Pyne, fondly called Sugar Pyne or Teacher Pyne. He had taught me to love and appreciate the works of such stalwarts as Shakespeare, Byron and Goldsmith thus leaving in me a great lust and craving for the literary world.

Yorkshire seemed the place where that craving could be satisfied. Coupled with this, three years after my arrival in Britain in January 1961, the first General Election I witnessed and participated in first-hand, saw a Yorkshire man from Huddersfield become Prime Minister of Britain in October 1964. This was the Right Honorable Lord Wilson of Rievaulx KG OBE PC FRS FSS. He would go on to be the only Labor leader to have formed Labor administrations following four general elections and over two periods as Prime Minister of Britain—October 1964 to June 1970 and again from March 1974 to April 1976.

As a student in London in the early 1960s, I eked out my small parental allowance while I studied at the then Kilburn Polytechnic by working at J Lyons & Company—they ran a string of tea shops throughout the city of London. The company had an annual celebration for its workers at the Strand Palace Hotel located in Strand. At the first of these celebrations which I attended, the Toast Master, Ivor Spencer, spotted me dancing and invited me to attend an audition at the Tavistock Rooms in Charring Cross Road a few nights later.

For me, this was the kick-off for ten years of part-time professional dancing as 'Duncan Duncan' the Twist Champion from Jamaica and later as the International Dance Star. Ivor Spencer turned out to be a Royal Toast Master who was frequently called upon to manage the entertainment for numerous prestigious functions. That was how I came to be providing part of the cabaret arrangements for a function at the Dorchester Hotel in London Park Lane in the 1960s. Among the guests were Prime Minister Harold Wilson and his wife Mary, both of whom it was my fortune to meet.

Of course, Yorkshire was also the home of other political greats such as William Wilberforce who was born in Hull, eastern Yorkshire. This Yorkshire man was a British politician and philanthropist who in the late eighteen century was prominent in the struggle to abolish the slave trade and then to abolish slavery itself in British overseas possessions. On the other side of the Atlantic Ocean, almost thirty years after Wilberforce's death, Abraham Lincoln, the 16th American President, would issue on January 1, 1863, the Emancipation Proclamation that declared forever free those slaves within the Confederacy.

Sadly, two years later, in 1865, he was brutally assassinated by those who would stifle progress and let racism and inhumanity reign. In my drive to eradicate racism from its very roots, these two men will be the source of important and related material. It will all be of some poignant significance to do so from Yorkshire soil.

In my thoughts, there was also another well-known politician, Roy Hattersley. He too was a Yorkshire man born in Sheffield, West Riding of Yorkshire and was also considered a man of literature. In 1964 he gained his first Parliamentary seat in multi-racial Birmingham, the very place of my second headship and where I would end my teaching career on retirement. Life and things might have been so different for these Yorkshire men if another and much earlier Yorkshire man, Guy Fawkes who was born and educated in York did not fail in his attempt to blow up the British House of Lords—the failed Gunpowder Plot of 1605.

As my thoughts drifted in search of reasons why I should be confident and happy about making a new life in West Yorkshire, I drifted to another of my great loves. The world of cricket is the kind of activity that would do exceptionally well to absorb my leisure time. Would the people of Yorkshire be interested in this so-called English game? I was quickly put at my ease when I remembered such Yorkshire giants with the bat as Sir Leonard Hutton, Geoffrey Boycott, Brian Close and, of course, the great Freddie Truman with the ball and all-rounder Ray Illingworth—all of whom, much to their chagrin, had done competitive matches against my native team, the super West Indies team of my era.

Among these great Tykes, the record books were amplified by some 133,000 magnificent runs, 286 glorious centuries and 429 tumbling wickets in test cricket during their tenures. With such a rich history in one of my favorite sports, my confidence heightened in anticipation. I am not a football enthusiast, but it did not escape my notice that Sheffield Football Club is very prominent across the nation and brags of support of FIFA in this regard. Yorkshire, here I come.

During my 21 years journey in Britain, especially during the four years stretch at the University of Wales and during my working life since I had heard many stereotypes about people and places including the Yorkshire people. Many of these stereotypes masqueraded as innocent humor, some seeming to be genuinely funny, some embodied apparent truthfulness and others, still, were exceedingly racist and derogatory. For some examples of this last, I repeat two popular ones.

There is the view that the Yorkshire man is quite stingy and mean and we see expression of this locked up in "A Yorkshire man is a Scotsman with all the generosity squeezed out of him." And "In Yorkshire, hear all, see all and see nothing; eat all, drink all but pay nothing; and if ever you do something for nothing, always do it for yourself." To date, I had spent all my time in Britain fighting racism wherever it raised its ugly head. Attitudes and views such as these, however, held by our fellow men are exceedingly dangerous and must be confronted and must not be deferred. This job for education is an urgent one.

In those days, however, none of these attitudes, views and stereotypes registered with me to be of particular importance beyond the small-talk circumstance at the times of their utterances. Now, though, those pertaining to Yorkshire are vying for my further consideration. It was often said that the Yorkshire people are exceptionally friendly. They are always ready to go out of their way, go the extra mile, so to speak, to make strangers feel very welcome. Those mentions of the friendly conversations that were often initiated by, for example, shopkeepers with their customers, familiar customers or otherwise strangers, are now reverberating in my ears. But, along with this, there was always the caution that the Yorkshire people will always close ranks against outsiders.

This caution, if true, would be of a major concern to me being so visible a stranger or outsider. I had also picked up that no outsider could ever hope to play test cricket for Yorkshire. This was of little matter to me since my love for the game did not extend to such heights. I would, however, be taking with me my family consisting of my beautiful Sikh wife, Melvinder, who was in a state of advanced pregnancy (carrying at the time, the world's first test-tube twins), and my adopted son, James who was just three and a half years old. Of course, I could not speak for my family as far as their cricketing aspirations are concerned. I could only hope that times and practices would adjust in the right directions to accommodate them should they turn out to be so inclined and prove to be worthy of consideration from a residential point of view.

Time would tell. This worry wasn't proving to be seriously daunting at the present time.

I was more interested in learning more about Nigel Farndale's (himself a Yorkshire man) view of Yorkshire being "God's own country," and in using some of the spare time my family and I will have, beyond the challenges of running and managing a large school in pastures unknown, to sample some of the share beauty for which the County is known. Even in England and Wales, I had sampled the famous Yorkshire cuisine of roast beef and Yorkshire pudding followed with a dessert of rhubarb hopefully sourced from the Yorkshire towns of Wakefield, Morley and Rothwell which are known for their excellence in the production of this delight. The question is would these be more authentic when obtained in Yorkshire itself? I was sure that my wife would gladly join me in pursuing the skills behind preparing this 'national' dish. This was yet another reason to be looking forward to setting up a home in West Yorkshire.

Industry-wise, Yorkshire is widely known for its coal mines and that renowned trade unionist champion of miners, Arthur Scargill from Worsbrough, near Barnsley in South Yorkshire. There are still mental images of those "flat cap and whipped" Yorkshire men maintaining the woolen industry as a strong feature of the Yorkshire rural countryside and reminding us that "where there is muck there is brass," while Marks and Spencer (founded in Leeds from Jewish links) still rein strongly on the retail front throughout Yorkshire and elsewhere within the United Kingdom.

Some of the best hand-made chocolates which keep my family's taste buds craving for more are made in various places throughout Yorkshire. Steel, iron, and cloth remain the big manufacturing concerns with the digital industry becoming deeply rooted throughout Yorkshire. These truths formed major positives and encouragement for the venture my household was about to take.

My wife, however, had a major worry about going to live in West Yorkshire. Without wanting to trivialize her concern, I rehearsed with her the fact that the issue which was tagging her banefully had been settled and was now passed. During a five-year period (1975-1980) the women of West Yorkshire and to some extent those of Manchester in the north of England had every reason to be scared out of their minds. A dangerous serial killer was at large. He had proven to be an enigma to the police.

During the period, women were often murdered, and their bodies gruesomely mutilated revealing a hallmark of what was dubbed the Yorkshire Ripper. Two dead and mutilated bodies were discovered in Manchester and another eleven bearing the same hallmark of the Yorkshire Ripper over the period were discovered at various locations throughout West Yorkshire. In addition to these thirteen murdered women—most of whom were ladies of the night—seven other attempts left some of these luckier victims badly injured. During his spell of slaughter, the Yorkshire Ripper would taunt and mock the police and law enforcement generally. In doing so he mirrored some of the antics employed by 'Jack the Ripper' who had once haunted prostitutes in the Whitechapel area of the East End of London between August and November 1888. This serial killer who was never caught claimed the lives of at least 5 prostitutes.

The Yorkshire Ripper, however, though extremely evasive over a long period and murdered many more women than did Jack, was not so lucky. He was eventually caught in January 1981, a little over a year before my family was due to move to the area. At the time he was spotted with a woman sitting suspiciously in a car with false number plates in a well-known red-light area of Sheffield. The woman turned out to be a 24-year-old prostitute. She was lucky that a sharp-eyed policeman spotted the car and carried out instantaneous electronic checks that revealed the number plate deception. The Yorkshire Ripper was revealed to be one Peter Sutcliffe of Bingley, Bradford, West Yorkshire.

I am not sure whether I did a good job in removing her fear, but my wife showed no further resistance. Perhaps, the thought of being the wife of Britain's first black headmaster of a secondary school domesticated her fear.

Chapter 6
The Wyke Story and Student's Disappearance Case

Here I am arriving at the front gates of Wyke Manor Upper School on a sunny but chilly April Monday morning (the 5th of April 1982). Before setting off on the thirty-minute journey from home, I satisfied myself that my wife and son were safely ensconced in a wonderful four-bedroomed bungalow in Oakfield Drive, Manningham, Bradford, in the County of West Yorkshire. We, my family, and I had spent the entire Easter holidays settling in our new home. I had learned the route between Bradford and Coventry in the West Midlands extremely well because of the home-hunting process. Many weekends have been devoted to negotiating the one hundred and thirty miles on the M6 and M62 motorways for this purpose.

Because of this, I was this morning able to leave my family in our own detached space of choice. I nervously turned my Toyota Crown motor car through the school gates around 7.30 a.m. There is a driveway of a little over a hundred meters from the front gates to the reception building which also housed the office space that I will occupy. The driveway was decidedly very drab and uninviting. Yet I had read somewhere in the school's blurb which the Bradford Education Authority had sent me when I made my application for this headship that the school had an active handy man for a caretaker. This first approach to the school is what will give first impressions to parents, their children, and other visitors. Perhaps, when I meet with the caretaker the state of the driveway will make an appropriate ice-breaking conversation.

No Reception

The school was like a ghost town. No teachers, no pupils, no ancillary staffing, and certainly no welcoming officials for the new headteacher. I found it very strange that no one from the education office came to welcome me on my arrival: and, as I would soon discover, at no point throughout the day or even the first week. Richard Knight was the Director of Education. He was nationally recognized as an outstanding Director. His high profile inevitably placed a great deal of pressure on his limited time considering that he had a directorate to manage.

I, therefore, didn't expect that such a busy and important official would be here to welcome me in person. But surely there were education advisors, education officers and the like? There was not even a single member of the school's governing body. The omen was not good. Something was not right. It could not have been a memory failure. The local and national media was making a song and dance about my appointment and arrival at the school.

A parking space was marked out, for previous headteachers, just under the window of the headteacher's secretary's office window, I would later discover. I eased the Toyota Crown slowly into space and sat silently for a few minutes to see if I could attract some life. That did not work so I got out of the car and strolled to the double-sided wooden front door. The door was not bolted so it seems that the caretaking team had opened the school for what would soon be a hive of human activities—staff and students. I entered the building and as I approached the reception counter, I spotted George and Phyllis waiting in expectation. I recognized them as the two deputies to the headteacher when I first visited the school prior to my interviews.

George was visibly younger than Phyllis. He was quite short with striking red hair and a matching neatly low-cut beard. His appointment at the school was relatively recent. You shouldn't judge a book by its cover, but this young man struck me as the kind who would hide in the long grasses when the going gets tough. You know the type who prefers to stay silent in situations of open conflict. He would not openly take sides. This gave his kind the option to ingratiate himself to all sides when the others are not present. I had seen his type before. I hoped my first impression was wrong about this young man. His youthful energy and, I hope, ambition, would otherwise be ideal for the direction into which I want to take the school.

Phyllis, on the other hand, was in the school's service for a very long time. She too was on the short side with a slim frame, short black hair, and a lean face. Unlike George, she was talkative and obviously wanted to project herself as knowledgeable and experienced. I got the impression she was weary of George and wished to keep him in the shadows. Realizing that I was of Jamaican origin, she was quick to tell me about the holiday she once enjoyed in Jamaica even if she could not remember where in Jamaica. She was quick to invite my family and me to dinner when she would serve up a famous Jamaican dish—rice and peas. A similar invitation from George for my family and I to join his family for dinner would come at a much later date and would be the product of a Yorkshire kitchen I am pleased to report.

I would soon discover that Phyllis was a fraud when it comes to this Jamaican thing. Oh, that dinner: boiled white rice served with boiled green peas told us all we needed to know about her knowledge of Jamaican cuisine. Suffice it to say my family and I were truly embarrassed on that dinner date.

Both deputies and I exchanged very warm greetings, and I jokingly asked them; where is everyone, had they fled the school because I was coming? The deputies quickly pointed out that I had arrived far too early and that the school would come alive very soon. They, the deputies, are usually early because they live great distances away from the school and must beat the traffic in order not to be late. Just then, Madge, the lady who will act as my secretary and double as the head of the administrative team, entered the reception area on her way to her office.

She respectfully greeted me, and the deputies too and almost immediately took charge and launched me into what appeared to be a well-prepared, tried and tested customary induction program with the deputies hovering about watchfully and interjecting useful information here and there. The next whole school assembly was scheduled for Thursday morning, three days away. Madge and the deputies were hinting very strongly that I should use my first three days at the school to settle in quietly and face the whole school at Thursday's assembly which was scheduled to be led by Mr. Samuels. I was not happy with this fixedness and at once suggested some flexibility that would bring Thursday's assembly forward to Tuesday, my second day at the school. This was too golden an opportunity to miss on account of an unnecessary delay. An early and immediate impact was what I needed to make my mark.

My impromptu induction with Madge and the deputies immediately ended and was over-ruled. Their planned program of gradual introduction to the pupils and staff had to be adjusted in some important ways and I would see to this.

Sure enough, as the deputies had assured me, the school began to come alive. By the time Mr. Samuels, the next senior teacher below the rank of deputy headteacher, had sounded the bell for the beginning of the school day. The entire school, all eleven hundred 13-19-year-old and forty-two teaching and non-teaching staff, bar a noticeable line of late student stragglers and a tiny number of the teaching staff similarly late, had passed through the hall heading to their various classrooms as is customary.

Madge was Caucasian, a very respectable mature Yorkshire lady who ran a tight and efficient administrative office while acting as the headteacher's reliable Personal Assistance (PA). She carries a stout frame and always displays an exemplary professional seriousness of purpose on her quite charming face. She is meticulous about timing as she always is about her dress, coiffeur, and appearance. She was never late and always ensured that she got off on time at the end of the school day and held her staff to similar principles and standards. She had served the school in these capacities for many years and had seen many headteachers go and come. The entire school, pupils and staff hold her in high esteem.

The staff knows that they must have their registers and other admin documents kept strictly to regulations or suffer the wrought of the administration boss. Madge has a team of two other highly efficient ladies besides herself. In the early 1980s, her team was not overly conversant with word processing and so they relied heavily on Mr. Samuels who was the expert on technology and held a brief for dispensing his skills as widely as possible across the school as part of his job description.

Madge must have considered it extremely strange that, on my first day, I clearly ignored her induction advice by disrupting the scheduled assembly arrangements.

As rearranged, the next day at school I had all 1,100 pupils for my special morning assembly all gathered in the main hall. As I took to the platform, I realized this was a first for me. I had taken many assemblies over the years in my various capacities as head of department, head of faculty and as deputy headteacher and never did I stand before an entire school of solely white faces.

It struck me as being exceedingly weird not to have black or brown faces represented.

There was a discernible amount of friendly and enquiring curiosity in the sea of faces, of pupils and staff, before me. The overriding hum from the gathering had dramatically ceased to dead hush, as I took to the podium alone. George, one of the deputies, had suggested that he would introduce me, but I thought it would be psychologically more effective if I introduced myself. All the school's teaching and non-teaching staff were interspersed here and there strategically among the pupils. Beyond the strangeness of standing before a totally white audience, bar one Asian gentleman among the teaching staff, I quickly thought that some schools of thought might consider that multicultural and anti-racist education might not be relevant in an all-white school. My mental conclusion is that there could be no better starting place.

I began by saying, "Good morning, Wyke Manor Upper School," in tones, which told everyone that I was in charge. Next, I told them who I was as if they did not already know and needed to be told. Since my appointment, there were sensational headlines in the newspaper, radio, and television media, appearing everywhere in the country. Locally, there were newspaper headlines like these:

Telegraph & Argus

Twist king Carlton dances in

Former dancer is North's first black headmaster

THE TIMES TUESDAY APRIL 20 1982

TELEGRAPH & ARGUS 6/2/82

New head is black

Success out of limbo...

Carlton hot-foots it to top teaching post

My message continued to say that I wanted a meeting this next Monday (12th April 1982) at 19:00 with all their parents in this very hall and that they were now charged with taking that invitation home. I would arrange for their own form teachers to have 'prepared notes of invitation' to their parents. They will be required to take them home to their parents. Once this preliminary was out of the way, I explained that beyond the purpose of introducing myself to them I wanted to talk about 'standards.' The meeting was a dead hush as I explained my values and attitude toward attendance and punctuality, my expectations in relation to both class and homework; examination performance, respect for the individual, their teachers, their parents, strangers and themselves, and pride and care for the school and its property.

They should expect, here, to see greater emphasis in the contents of their lessons (in all curriculum areas) on equality and justice among all peoples of the world. More and greater revelations about the achievements and contributions of people from all over the globe. There will be the appreciation, respect and value of different cultures and people.

At the end of that meeting, I purposely and pointedly dismissed each class individually and invited the associated classroom teacher to accompany them to their classrooms. I deliberately allowed a sufficient time gap between dismissed classes, thus ensuring the kind of order I will expect in the future. What I did not tell the pupils and staff was that I was determined to be at the school gate to check on punctuality the next morning and thereafter.

During the day, I instructed my secretary, Madge, that, in addition to the note of invitation to parents, she was to get a note out to each member of both the teaching and non-teaching staff. The note invited them to a voluntary and impromptu staff meeting the following day, Wednesday, ten minutes after the end of the school day. No surprise, I had a hundred percent attendance at the meeting. Somehow, I had expected it to be that way because curiosity is in the air.

I thanked everyone for coming and explained that I would not keep them very long as I am aware that they have their domestic duties awaiting them. Over the course of the three days that had passed by the time of this staff meeting, I had taken the opportunity to meet each member of the school staff individually for the simple purpose of introducing myself while putting a face at their names.

So, because I had already introduced myself to each member on an individual basis, there was no need for further introduction at the staff meeting. I, thus, used the opportunity to give some insight into my educational background and philosophy. I explained the nature of the changes in the school's curriculum which they could expect (especially the introduction of the anti-racist or multicultural curriculum in all curriculum areas—what many educationalists are now referring to as the decolonized curriculum). At the mention of multiculturalism and anti-racism, I quickly scanned the faces gathered in front of me. I got the impression that I was using a language that was somewhat strange to them. I could tell what the main rhetorical question was. It was 'how does that apply to my subject?'

I took the opportunistic seconds of ominous silence to explain that this is about greater and wider research of our subjects to be better prepared in the preparation and delivery of our subjects in the classrooms. I explained that the key issue in all of this is to make every pupil that we teach feel very important by seeing himself and herself included in the lesson. We do this by proper research and inclusion. The result is that our pupils become positively motivated, and motivation means better performance and greater achievements not only by-passing examinations but, very importantly, by the way our pupils interact with their peers, school personnel and persons beyond the school environment.

I promised everyone present that my plans for the school on this front included training sessions with individual subject specialists to set the pace gently but firmly for everyone. I could see some lingering doubts, especially on the faces of those teachers responsible for delivering the mathematics and the science curriculum areas. I was, however, determined to deliver on my promise and my fervent mission. To this effect, I indicated, to all present, that we will all begin this journey in a fortnight. I had previously noted that the next scheduled In-Service Training Day (INSET) was just two weeks away. On that day, I would be leading generally on what a multicultural and anti-racist curriculum should be. This will prepare the way for the follow-up specialists' input in each of the curricula areas.

Additionally, I explained the organizational structures on which I shall shortly be consulting them. Also, I felt it important to spell out the attitude and performance factors, which are most likely to influence me when making decisions about promotion in salary and status. I expected the staff to assist me in promoting high standards among the pupils. This point I illustrated by pointing out that my presence at the school gate that very morning was to arrest the reported bad practice of pupils reporting late for school. I didn't expect teachers, who should be setting the example, to be caught in that web too, as was the case with three unnamed teachers that morning.

I ended the session by pointing out that the organizational structures mentioned earlier were mainly to give everyone the opportunity to be involved in the school's decision-making process and involvement in all aspects of the school generally. It was important that they found out quickly that I knew my stuff; that I was tough but fair and above all, that I expected us to work and pull together. I pointed out that the next morning; I would be meeting with their Trade Union Representatives in my office, to agree on the best ways to ensure the maximum chances for pupils, the staff working welfare and conditions, and the best way of promoting the school to the wider society.

As it turned out, this was a very useful exercise with the Union Representatives as it gave me the opportunity to figure out who was who, their strengths and weaknesses, but most importantly, the opportunity to put in place a mechanism for putting out industrial fires before they became uncontrollable flames.

The rest of the week went quickly and without anything, unusual happening except that the single Asian face on the staff, whom I had first met while I was introducing myself individually to everyone, came to see me. He wanted me to know that in all the years he had been teaching at the school, "This was the first time that he felt like a human being." I was soon to discover what he meant.

It seemed that I had created a stir in the school community. The main buzz circulating in all corners of the school was coming mainly from pupils who were caught in my morning late traps and found that they were punished in different ways. The measures were proving to be most effective because part of the buzz was that others should avoid this at all costs. Bits of advice on how to get to school on time became abundant and gratuitously given. Even among the staff, there were comments that the school needed that kind of tonic a long time ago. This was a sentiment, which would be echoed over and over at the meeting with parents the following Monday, commencing at 19:00 at the school. Within two weeks, the lateness among pupils had dried up to a minor trickle and the staff was having a good time too.

They Came to See Me

At the end of school, the following Monday, Phyllis, George, and the senior teacher, Mr. Samuels, stayed behind to help me plan for the meeting with the parents. Because all of us lived some considerable distances from the school, we decided that we would alert our individual homes to the fact that we would stay at school until the parents' meeting was over. There were several other teachers who said that they would be in attendance, but because they lived close to the school, they went home and would return at 19:00. I felt much supported. Those of us who did not find it convenient to go home and return for the meeting with the parents had all made individual arrangements for a snack and refreshment in the meantime and, therefore, did our own thing, while we waited for the parents to arrive.

I had picked up from some colleagues that the school was not accustomed to having a large turnout of parents and therefore I should not be too disappointed if only a handful turned up. These people knew the school from working there for years and their judgments ought to be respected. Somehow, however, my own inclination was to believe otherwise. With the media headlines and coverage, we, as a school, were having about this black headteacher, I think my colleagues were in for a surprise. An earlier lunchtime encounter with a potential parent of our school had helped me to be of this optimistic opinion. During the lunch hour, I had had cause to pop out to the nearest newspaper agent. That morning I was too rushed to collect the local and my favorite national newspaper—The Guardian—as was my wont. I knew that I would need to spend some time waiting for the parents' meeting and the newspapers would be a good way to do this.

Besides, I was most eager to catch up on what the papers were saying about the "dancing black headteacher in town." About a mile away from the school, I spotted a corner shop complex that sold newspapers and a variety of stationery, postcards, and souvenirs. The sole visible occupant of the shop came immediately to enquire about my needs. She spoke with a true Yorkshire accent which caused me to struggle a bit to understand her, she was tall and had reddish shoulder-length hair with piercing and engaging eyes. She seemed to be in her late twenties to early thirties in age. This was my first experience with that commonplace cliché about the friendliness of Yorkshire people.

"They are always ready to go out of their way, go the extra mile, so to speak, to make strangers feel very welcome." With little effort on my part the lady and I became very engaged in a wide-ranging discussion. She was particularly interested in my educational philosophy and practice. She said that, from the moment I set foot into her shop, she knew who I was. She had recognized me from the various newspaper articles and television reports and read about my presence in Yorkshire. She stated that she was picking up grapevine news about the positive impact I was already having on a school which had gathered a very bad name in recent years. I was able to answer as many of the lady's questions as the limited time I had would allow.

But before I could make an excuse to return to the school, she said quite enthusiastically that her daughter who would be leaving her middle school in the summer would need a place in an Upper School so that she could pursue her advanced levels ('A' Levels) and she was already convincing her daughter to apply for a place at Wyke Manor for the coming September. She chose Wyke because I seemed a rather nice headteacher with sound ideas for the school. I said thank you and goodbye, as I departed on the return trip for school.

It was only as I was nearing the school gate that it dawned upon me that I didn't have either the mother's or her daughter's name. Still, at least, I know where they are located and I know what the mother looks like even if I didn't see the daughter who, quite clearly, must have been at her school at the time I encountered her mother. There was no sign of a dad. I was now back at school feeling very hopeful about tonight's parent meeting.

When those parents started to arrive, my colleagues were gobs smacked. In minutes, it was like an avalanche of parents. For many, it would be a standing room only because the caretaker was not warned that there would be so many parents and he organized it according to his past experiences. George and Phyllis had cherry-red faces, and so did the senior teacher. I whispered to them that they were not necessarily wrong in their judgment. These parents had come to see me.

And see me they would. Here was an opportunity which had to be exploited. I knew and understood what my colleagues were saying to me. Other schools at which I had taught had similar experiences. We usually had those parents whose children were doing well socially and academically. The parents whom we truly needed to see, and to form working team alliances with, in the interest of their children, never bothered to come. Consequently, the school's philosophy and messages were only partially published to our parents. That kind of reality was bad for any school. Schools needed informed defenders as well as informed critics.

I would, now, use this marvelous opportunity presented to us, to get the school's values across; seek the parents' commitment to a better school and plan to involve them in the school generally. This would be the occasion to tell the parents about my community school philosophy and how it would benefit them and their children directly and indirectly. This was the opportunity to spell out in simple terms what was involved in the anti-racist or multicultural curriculum (phrasal synonym for the decolonized curriculum) and how it would benefit all children and contribute to a fairer and just society. I would spell out the routes which we would be taking to ensure that every child had a fair chance to maximize his or her talents and eventually leave Wyke Manor Upper School with quality qualifications and sound social skills and values.

I needed to say this myself directly to my parents. Hearsay was often associated with misinformation, sometimes deliberately perpetrated and perpetuated. As I went through all these issues, the parents listened intently and patiently. I knew I was winning because at key times there were intermittent bursts of ovation. As if underpinning what I was saying about direct information as opposed to the second-hand route, in the question-and-answer session one parent stated that she was feeling much better having heard what I had to say directly.

Another parent said she was feeling relieved because she had heard that the new head at Wyke (in only his first week at the school) had taken down the picture of the Queen and would be replacing it with 'colored people.' I could only deny my personal involvement in any such removal: I had been at the school only one week. The difficulty for me was that I did not know if anyone before me had made such a removal so I could not make a carte-blanche denial. As luck would have it, a well-established teacher on the staff came to my rescue. That twisted rumor of the removal of a picture of the Queen was reliably contradicted.

The senior teacher who had been teaching at the school for fifteen years, fortunately, spoke up to point out that in his fifteen years at the school, he had never seen a picture of the Queen hanging anywhere in the school. I closed the evening with a promise to my parents that I will personally seek to find a picture of Her Majesty and it will be hung prominently in the reception area. That promise was fulfilled the very next day.

That night I made my mark with the parents because many were taking pains to point out that they could see improvements in the school already. Their children were taking school much more seriously and did not want to be late in the mornings. And in the 'hell' that was soon to follow, parents and their children were all that I had.

Chapter 7

Tonight, I arrived home much later than usual. My wife sensed that something was wrong because I wasn't my usual joyful and optimistic self. Yet, I kept denying all her enquiries about what was wrong. James was asleep: he just couldn't wait up for me as he usually did. I had my sumptuously prepared dinner. It was a T-bone steak medium rear to my liking, while my wife sat patiently with me at the dining table; clearly dissatisfied with the loudness of my silence. I certainly didn't want to burden her with my work issues. After all, she was hugely pregnant with the world's first test-tube twins slated to make their entry into this world sometimes on the eighteenth of this month, April 1982. Dinner over, I expressed my appreciation to my wife for a deliciously prepared meal and politely asked to be excused. As I got up from the table, I pleaded exhaustion and made my way to prepare for bed. I wanted to be alone with my thoughts—two very serious issues had revealed themselves in just one week and a day at the school. I am not very good at finding workable solutions to problems unless I sleep on them first. This was such an occasion.

Firstly, the only non-white face on the staff, until me, was able to say to me in confidence that until my presence he "never felt like a human being." This sounded like the unwholesome effects of that horrible disease called racism is or has been very much at large in Wyke Manor Upper School. This did not auger well for me. I could take some comfort in the fact that I am the headteacher and would have much more power than Mr. Rashid, to protect myself against bigots and bigotry but that would be far too selfish and totally wrong. Where one person in the school community is needlessly unhappy, the entire school is by far the poorer for it. Racism is a cankerous cancer which must be irradicated wherever it raises its ugly head. The need to ensure that Mr. Rashid is treated equally as all other teachers in our school was clearly signposting itself, and the necessary action would have to come from me.

I tried to put myself into Mr. Rashid's shoes and wondered what it must feel like to work in a place for over twelve years and all the time feeling like a sub-human being. Once this was drawn to my attention, I asked Madge to let me see Mr. Rashid's file. Mr. Rashid joined the school twelve and a half years ago on the lowest pay scale. It is twelve years later, and he was on the same scale of pay. Yet, the records showed that during that time, 20 teachers with fewer years of service to the school had been given promotions—it goes without saying, all of them were white. I needed to know more from the horse's mouth and invited Mr. Rashid to see me in my office. It turned out that the sub-human feeling to which Mr. Rashid referred had largely to do with abusive and disrespectful colleagues and racist remarks and name-calling from some pupils.

Being called a "Paki" had become a way of life for him in the school. The worst part for him was not having a clearly defined route to redress and justice. The remuneration for his service was the least of his problems even though he barely got by on what he earned.

This situation with Mr. Rashid cared me right back to my first day at the first school to which I was appointed in 1969. My first term was due to commence at Ebury Secondary Technical School for boys in September 1969. The headteacher of the school thought it would make some sense if I turned up early in the capacity of a supply teacher for the last two weeks of the summer term. My duties would be all invigilation tasks as it was the public examination period. The head thought, rightly, that this way I would get a feel for the school before my official start date the following September. This could only be helpful, we both thought. Just coming straight from university, I could make good use of the extra two weeks' pay anyway.

Ebury Secondary Technical School was located on Ebury Bridge Road which ran to the rear of Victoria Station in London. It was a single-sex school for those 300 boys who never made it to any of the two grammar schools in nearby proximity. The school came under the control of the now-extinct Inner London Education Authority (ILEA). This school essentially catered for working-class white children drawn from areas not known, at the time, for diversity in their population. Nevertheless, some of these boys, at least one, had connections with black communities beyond their boundaries as I was to find out on my first assignment.

I reported to the school on the penultimate Monday morning before the school holidays. In the afternoon, the school management assigned me to room two where I would invigilate the Technical Drawing Certificate of Secondary Education (CSE) examination for the next two and a half hours. I gave out the pertinent instructions and relevant paperwork and accessories. At the stroke of 13.00, I gave the commencement instructions. The atmosphere in the room was a dead hush as it should be in most examination rooms. All the boys, bar one, began to work as instructed. This one exception decided that he would disrupt the examination by hurling filthy and insulting words at me. He was clearly showing off his knowledge of 'West Indian' swears words, the kind of foul language which characterized mainly the dregs of West Indian society.

These words were accompanied by his constant beating on the desk, thus guaranteeing that everyone's concentration would be broken. I called out to the young lad and instructed him to be quiet and to get on with his examination. The boy, whom I would later find out, answered with the name Fullwood. He saw that I was black and made the correct assumption that, if no one else recognized and knew the meaning of the words he was hurling, I would. The other pupils' examination chances were clearly at risk. I moved over to Fullwood and told him he had to shut up and cease interrupting the examination. He stared me in the eye menacingly and that was his first and last mistake.

Just out of university where I was still the University Athletic Union Welterweight champion boxer, in a flash second, I read his intention as his eyes caught mine and instantly stepped aside evading the vicious punch, he threw at me. He would not get another chance because I folded him up on the classroom floor like a freshly pressed handkerchief with one left hook to his solar plexus.

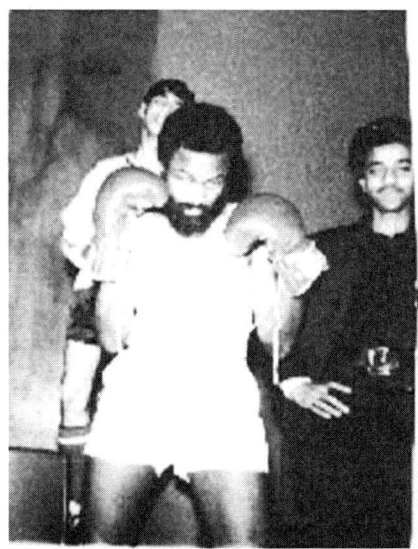

The other students looked on in awe, dismay, and total silence. I became frightened that Fullwood might have been badly hurt. However, in two very long minutes, Fullwood was back on his feet and went straight to his desk where he resumed his examination. Not a further word was said and simply no more antics. I would later learn that Fullwood was the school's bully much feared by everyone, staff, and pupils alike. He had acquired the black belt status in martial arts (Judo) and had previously injured the geography master using that skill because the master dared to challenge Fullwood's anti-social behavior.

When I eventually began at the school in the following September, news of the encounter I had with Fullwood had gone through the school like a village grapevine. For the next year that both Fullwood and I would be in the same school, he would find himself spending huge chunks of his time sitting and doing set work at the back of my classroom.

It was commonly felt that my classroom was the only one that extracted orderly behavior from this young man. When, at the end of the 1969/1970 school year, the ILEA executed its plan to amalgamate Ebury Secondary Technical School together with three other schools to create the new Pimlico Comprehensive, Fullwood and I went our separate ways. Most of the Ebury teachers, including me, were absorbed on to the staff of Pimlico and Fullwood went off into the working world.

In no way I am, here, arguing that Mr. Rashid's response to racism should have mirrored my example. Mine was a very risky response which might have landed me in all kinds of trouble. But my dignity as well as the other pupils' examination chances demanded defensive action.

At Pimlico Comprehensive, too I would encounter similar racial abuse from a white student and found absolutely no support from school management. The school had a policy of keeping classrooms locked until they were needed for teaching purposes. Someone felt it was funny to stuff chewed-up gum in the keyhole of the door lock to a classroom which I was due to use the second lesson one morning. So, when I turned up with my class of 31 pupils behind me, I experienced great difficulties trying to get my key into the lock to open the classroom door. I bent over to see what was hindering my key and that was when a fifteen-year-old white girl decided to kick me forcefully up my rear end in front of the other members of the class all of whom burst out in exhilarating laughter at my shameful humiliation.

My immediate response was to slap the hell out of the perpetrator. She began crying and went directly to the deputy headmistress' office to file a complaint against me. Minutes later, I was summoned to the headmaster's office. There, waiting for me, were the headteacher, the deputy headmistress and the offending 15-year-old. The charge against me was laid by the head. It was that I had physically handled a pupil in my charge. I was then asked to justify my action, and, so, I recounted my story. Even the offending girl admitted that my account was truthful in all matters. Yet, the headteacher instructed me in the presence of the girl and his deputy never to lay my hand on another pupil in this school. He then issued a warning, also in the presence of the stated audience, that if I disobeyed his instruction, he would report me to ILEA for disciplinary action which could lead to the loss of my job.

I got it: it was three whites against one black. I stood no chance. A white girl physically kicking the ass of a black man in public was seemingly acceptable to the school management team, at least the most senior duo. Here, too, I say again that my response, which was to strike the girl for what was clearly a racist and humiliating prank, is not a recommendation for Mr. Rashid and or other similar sufferers to follow. Many years on, it is now my view that if these things should happen to me today, I would want to react differently. But there would have to be a definite reaction. As a matter of fact, I did follow up my earlier response with a more appropriate one which turned out to be an important launching pad for furthering my career.

That Pimlico incident together with the totally unsatisfactory response drove me, at such an early stage in my career, to successfully seek promotion to a head of department role in another London authority—Aylestone Comprehensive School in Brent. These were some of the thoughts and recalls that kept me awake that night after my first parents' meeting at Wyke Manor much to the chagrin of my wife who knew something was wrong despite my denials.

The second matter which kept me awake that night was that untruthful comment that one of the parents made at the parents' meeting. You will recall that a parent wanted to know if I had removed a picture of the Queen and had plans to replace it with "colored people" images. I had been at the school just eight days and was certain that I was not guilty of that charge. Fortunately, Mr. Samuels who was, at the time, a fifteen-year veteran of the school came quickly to my defense. In all his years at the school, he explained, he had never seen a picture of the Queen on display. My contribution to this development was to make a solemn promise to the parents in question that I would source a picture of the Queen and put it on display as soon as possible.

What really troubled me about this matter was this. I had been at the school just eight days if the intervening weekend was counted. No parent visited the school during those eight days. The parent was very sincere in stating what she had heard. I had not mentioned my multicultural and anti-racist plans when I met with the pupils at the previous Tuesday's assembly. The first and only time I mentioned these issues was at my meeting with the staff at our impromptu, one hundred per cent attendance, staff meeting on the Wednesday of the previous week. How then, better still, who then informed the parents erroneously about my action pertaining to the Queen's picture? Images that reflected a diverse culture were in fact discussed at that staff meeting.

There was a grain of truth somewhere in the parents' concern. However, that grain of truth was deliberately twisted and given in such a way as to sew some seeds of troublesome unrest. In my own mind, there was a mole among the staff, and I didn't know who that might be. The one thing that is certain is that this person needs to be identified and watched with caution if sabotaging mischiefs is to be kept in check. I need to make this one of my missions. Knowing early that we have a mischievous mole on board was a useful piece of information in the context of my plans for the development of the school. I must lead and teach. I must investigate too. I must put my detective instincts to good supporting use.

The night went by slowly and I grew more restless while mentally yearning for the morning to come. I checked and saw that my wife had finally fallen into a deep slumber. I knew that she had been fiercely resisting going to sleep out of sympathetic concern for my strange mood at homecoming and throughout the time we had together that evening. The next day came, and, at the appropriate time, I set out for Wyke Manor feeling somewhat listless for want of sleep. Nevertheless, the day turned out to be quite normal and productive with many set tasks fully accomplished. In many ways, it could be said, this day would set the pattern for the work atmosphere of the school for many more days ahead. The INSET day came and went well with me leading on the multicultural/anti-racist curriculum as promised.

I delivered this paper.

THE MULTICULTURAL/ANTI-RACIST CURRICULUMCULUM (DECOLONIZING THE BRITISH SCHOOL CURRICULUM)

CURRICULUM COMPONENTS. As far as British secondary schools are concerned, the curriculum is that composition of recognized bodies of knowledge in a variety of fields (Mathematics, Sciences, English, History, Music etcetera) which we, as secondary school teachers, dispense to eleven to nineteen-year-olds on working days throughout the course of any school year. The pre-and post-secondary curriculum might well be of the same hue with their own idiosyncratic variations and, no doubt, will be filled in by colleagues with the relevant primary expertise and experiences.

The curriculum thus defined has, at least, three component parts (i). the planned or overt curriculum, (ii). the hidden curriculum, and (iii). The excluded curriculum.

Together, these component parts act in unison (the curriculum) to affect the life chances of the young people who consume it. This curriculum ultimately is a significant determinant for the kind of adults they become. These adults, so influenced, become political and industrial leaders; managers, teachers; lawyers, medical personnel, and law enforcers; workers and workmates; mothers and fathers who then are coerced by law to submit their own children to take the same routes to adulthood and hence the road to perpetuity becomes a predestined groove.

SELF-REPLICATING SYSTEM. If this system could, in any way be considered an invention, the colonialists would have to be given credit for cleverly creating a near-perfect system as far as serving their intended or unintended purposes are concerned. Whether wittingly or unwittingly they have put and left in place a self-replicating means for promoting the evils of white supremacy and non-white people's inferiority.

CURRICULUM COMPONENTS. To assess their effects on our lives, it would be helpful to consider the three component parts of the curriculum referred to above.

PLANNED OR OVERT

GOVERNMENT, QUANGOS, EXAMINATION BOARDS, AND THE PLANNED CURRICULUM. In most civilized societies, their governments, industrialized bodies, universities, quangos, and other quasi-governmental bodies often come together for essential purposes. In Britain, for example, in this way designated examination boards are agreed upon, created, and formed and are universally recognized for measuring the academic worth of individuals. Examination Boards are mainly concerned with the planned/overt curriculum. They regularly measure the performance of school students in the various curricular areas in accordance with previously outlined and sanctioned syllabi. Employers and other educational establishments are extremely interested in these measurements.

This component of the school curriculum, together with its measurement, commands strong and compelling societal interest. As teachers, we, and most of the rest of society, place particular emphasis on this informational purpose of the curriculum for the reason of enabling pupils to pass tests and examinations. There is no denying that this aspect or purpose of the curriculum is of great significance and importance because of the way the world beyond the classroom is structured and the world's expectations. Nevertheless, it should be noted that prescribed syllabi have the unfortunate effect of dictating what is taught by teachers as they prepare their students in limited time for examinations.

Still, given the perceived and actual importance of this aspect of the curriculum, it is clearly essential that all beneficiaries of it should have equal access to consumption. Yet this is not the case for non-white pupils generally.

The Hidden Curriculum

CONTENT ACCURACY, MOTIVATIONAL IMAGES, AND VALUE TRANSFER.

But while we are organizing and focusing on this examinational aspect of the curriculum, some of us pay scant regard to the content accuracy, motivational effects, and values transmission effects of the curriculum diet upon which we feed (indoctrinate, even) our pupils. The content accuracy, motivational effects, and value transmission, together, form the hidden curriculum which is vastly more powerful than the overt curriculum.

The Excluded Curriculum

WHAT IS SELECTIVELY OMITTED FROM THE CURRICULUM?

Just as significant is that aspect of the curriculum that is either wittingly or unwittingly omitted. What is not taught has the devastating effect of leaving all our pupils ignorant. Given that the curriculum must be regarded as **the measurable knowledge, skills, motivational values, and attitudes presented to the learners** to enhance their behaviors and aspirations to become effective functional, and successful human beings, this might be seen as short-changing for our young people of all races and cultures.

What is Wrong with the Curriculum So Prescribed

EURO-CENTRICITY, WHITE SUPREMACY, SEXISM, AND NON-WHITE INFERIORITY. The resulting British curriculum is essentially Euro-centric: that is, pregnant with white racism and sexism (the opinion, however, exists that we have made some advancement in ameliorating some of the worst effects of sexism in our schools in recent times) values used to promote the ideas of white supremacy and non-white inferiority. Although there is historical evidence to show that non-white people have had a presence in Britain and other parts of Europe for as long as anyone can recall, the school curriculum, in its creation and application, never contemplated these people. Were we to pull back the deceptive blanket of academia, we would reveal the most destructive remnants of colonization now coated with a hefty dose of imperialism.

The absence of non-white people on these august bodies that are responsible for the planned curriculum creation through to the measurement of its absorption ensures the dominance of white values and views. It is true that in the present-day situation, we can sometimes see non-white faces in key areas such as curriculum boards, examination boards, and school rooms. But even with the greatest powers of persuasion, these tokens are easily and often outvoted. Such non-white representation can no longer be justified given the multicultural, multi-linguistic nature of today's British society.

ABSENCE OF NON-WHITE PRESENCE, IMAGES, AND INPUT. Similarly, the hidden curriculum suffers from these same difficulties as far as non-white students are concerned. Classroom teachers, the inspectorate, and other interest groups which are mainly white in their composition need to be aware that it is in these three areas **(fact contents, motivational worth, and value transmission)** in particular, that colonization has done the most debilitating harm and racial injustice to **ALL** our pupils. The **ALL** here is very important to note. For example, what is the motivational value of teaching about Nightingale to white pupils? Could we have similar effects on black pupils by teaching about Mary Seacole's history and contributions similarly?

When the Home Economics Departments of schools focus only on roast beef and Yorkshire pudding or other European cuisines and ignore the foods from the Caribbean Islands, Africa, and the Asian Continent are they, by omission, demotivating their non-white pupils while transmitting a hidden message to all their pupils? I often told the story of my real-life experience in British schools as a teacher. Without exception, in every school in which I have practiced (six in total), I, being a black man, am chosen first for the cricket team. They realize their error when the first ball is bowled at me. Such is the misleading nature of stereotypes.

Just as pernicious, are the deliberate or otherwise omissions from the school curriculum. As already mentioned, this leaves all our youngsters ignorant and, I might add, dangerously misinformed. Where it is wittingly omitted, the ignorance it creates is intentionally and vastly more harmful for all pupils. Consider, for example, the racist use of laws and gubernatorial edicts being employed by Ron DeSantis of Florida and imitating fellow Republican governors to rule out black history as a source of knowledge in parts of the United States of America.

The damage that will result from such reckless and racist actions will be horrendous and unlimited in its reach. The question must be asked: whose values determine the omissions and to what end? We see these kinds of omissions mainly in the areas of black achievements in almost every subject area. The opportunities to motivate non-white youngsters and build their esteem both in their eyes and the eyes of their white colleagues are totally lost. The opportunities to dim the ideas of white supremacy and non-white inferiority are thus lost.

The Act of Decolonization

OBSCURANTISM, INADEQUATE RESOURCES, AND LIMITED RELEVANT TRAINING. Part of the obstacle to change in education is that there is a tendency to hide our intention in obscure language. One day, teachers are comfortably dispensing the prescribed curriculum in their classrooms and the next day there is an edict from above or elsewhere that they must be multicultural and or anti-racist in their practice. Their response is usually with a string of questions such as: "What does this mean?" "How does this apply to my subject area?"

In secondary schools, this could mean, how should I practice multiculturalism and anti-racism in "art, music, physical education, religious education, social studies, geography, history, information technology, food science, economics, law, and the big three—English, Mathematics and the Sciences" and maybe more, subject to the secondary school in consideration.

Another part is that there is a tendency to expect the same untrained soldiers to implement the desired changes. If existing practicing teachers were already familiar with terminologies like multicultural curriculum, anti-racist curriculum, and now, the decolonization of the curriculum, it would be a reasonable assumption that they would have already been practicing these policies under their own auspices. Relevant training by people with skills and know-how in the pertinent fields coupled with adequate resources will go a long way to avoid a result where our good intentions themselves become obscure, and then lack of understanding and know-how breed resistance and consequently discourages investment in any necessary resources.

Too many educational initiatives have fallen by the wayside because of the lack of clarity, resources, and know-how training. It might be useful if we just talked about a curriculum for Equality and Justice for ALL; in short, good practice in education. And then, ensure that all that is necessary for moving forward successfully will be in place.

This kind of essential preparation is vital for the decolonizing tasks ahead. We cannot afford to turn off teachers and other educational administrators before they embark upon the difficult and time-consuming tasks of decolonizing the school curriculum.

At the present time (the 1980s), both the Rampton and Swann government reports (your current headteacher served on both Inquiries) identified that, among other things, the school curriculum was a problem for non-white pupils. They clearly saw that a curriculum that was euro-centric could not deliver equality in a multicultural society. It cannot because it is essentially the product of colonialization which is, itself, about white superiority and dominance.

A "good" education should enable a child to understand his own society and to know enough about other societies to enhance that understanding.

A "good" education cannot be based on one culture only, and in Britain where ethnic minorities form a permanent and integral part of the population, we do not believe that education should seek to iron out the differences between cultures, nor attempt to draw everyone into the dominant culture. On the contrary, it will draw upon the experiences of the many cultures that make up society and thus broaden the cultural horizons of every child. That is what we mean by "multicultural" education.
RAMPTON: p26.

The essence of this statement is borne out when we realize that both non-white and white pupils through just those three examples mentioned earlier of Mary Seacole, the preparation of cuisines other than roast beef and Yorkshire pudding, and the non-use of odious stereotypical assumptions such as those involved in casting your headteacher in the role of a top-class cricketer could have learned that there are great achievers in every race in every field. We would be, in these ways, microscopically altering the value systems in our children, affecting positively their attitude and expectation of one another so that when these children become tomorrow's employers, administrators, politicians, and people in positions of power, influence, and responsibility, it will no longer matter what color is their colleagues.

They were not taught to hate and discriminate based on distorted curricular material. In this connection, it is worth remembering and heeding the wisdom of Desmond Tutu's (now the late Desmond Tutu's) observation: "Children are not born racist: we make them."

If there is any validity in Tutu's observation, then it stands to reason that if we can make innocent children become racist, then we can make them non-racist by the same process. I say we should use the same measures to unmake them—the task is made immeasurably more difficult and prolonged because of barriers of vested interests and those which are politically orientated. Difficulties, however, are never a sufficient excuse for not attempting that which is fair and just.

BENEFITS OF DECOLONIZATION. Instead, let all our children learn how to appreciate the good in themselves and others because we find the time and make the necessary efforts to alter the colonial messages embedded in the school curriculum waiting to distort their minds. We need a holistic approach to the development of young minds whose task will be to perpetuate what is truthful, just, and valued universally.

The colonialists, the British, have spread their wings far and wide—whether it was India, the Caribbean, and Africa or where have you—the stories of exploitation, spoils grabbing, plunders and enslavements are now freely available, not only from the point of view of the colonialists but also from those of the sufferers with greater authenticity.

TEACHER EDUCATION AND TRAINING. Given that the stakes are so high, we need all our teachers, lecturers, inspectors, and education administrators to metaphorically roll up their sleeves and embark upon ongoing nationally sponsored training along the lines recommended by Rampton and Swann. (See chapter 3, p. 60 of the Rampton and chapter 9, p. 541 of the Swann Reports for a detailed treatment of teacher education).

Considerable focus is given not only to content but also to **teacher attitude and expectation** to bring about the desired change we need for a fairer and more just society. Coupled with all of this, the reports gave considerable attention to supporting resources—human and non-human (see page 35 of Rampton) and the need to employ ethnic minority teachers as good practice (see chapter 9, page 541 of Swann).

The heavy emphasis that the two reports placed upon teacher education and the curriculum is a clear recognition that teachers and the school curriculum occupy the minds of impressionable young people for approximately 180 days in any year while the rest of the year is spent with the church, other religious bodies, and peer groups. Teachers are powerful agents of change. Let us use this agency for the better.

The British school system was largely designed to transmit the white man's values and view of the world. And there was glorification in everything he did or achieved even if it was enslaving his fellow men and plundering the wealth and products of other countries to take back to Cardiff, Bristol, and Liverpool, to mention just a few glaring examples. Underneath or resulting from such glorification is racial injustice which we see manifesting itself for non-white people in educational underachievement, poor housing, unemployment, police improprieties, exclusions from schools, the unjust criminal justice system including the wild and reckless use of the old SUS laws, and the kinds of poor health issues which bedevil these peoples all over the globe.

All of the issues raised and discussed above are essentially the kind of issues with which both Rampton and Swann grappled over a five-year duration.

A PLUG-IN PLATFORM FOR ALL SUBJECT AREAS. What, hopefully, I have created above is a plug-in curriculum platform with sockets ready for all subject specialists (not just history teachers) to plug in their subject areas having regard for the issues raised.

Let the action commence. **Rampton and Swann** have pointed the way. It is just, right, equitable and responsible to follow.

End of Lecture
Duncan/Headteacher

In the weeks and months that followed, everything was normal as good schools should. All visitors to the school are now greeted with a floral welcome.

Chapter 8

"Welcome to Wyke Manor Upper School" was seen as they walked or drove down the drive from the main gate. It was one of the first tasks on which I had set the caretaking team when I first joined the school. I wanted that entrance to display a warm, colorful and bright welcome in the name of the school and the caretaking team wasted no time in achieving a splendid outcome.

On the home front, things were moving in the right direction. We had found a suitable nursery for James and had made regular transport arrangements to get him to and from the nursery daily. On weekends, he would spend his time with mummy and daddy. A back gate from our secluded bungalow led directly to a well-maintained, well-equipped children-friendly public park which turned out to be heaven-sent for James.

James would soon have company at home. Melvinder is nearing her delivery date for the world's first 'test-tube' twins. August 16th would be the date. As my reflections will reveal, we had come a long way leading up to this expectation.

Reflections

It all began one rather dull day in the autumn of 1976 when the receptionist at my school put through a personal call to me. At the other end was an ex-student from my last school. Everyone at this huge multi-racial mixed-sex comprehensive school (Aylestone) in Brondesbury Park, London, knew her affectionately, as 'Mel.' That strange call came at a sour and sweet period of my life. I had just extricated myself from a broken first marriage to a young Australian teacher. I met Bronwyn Ellerman on the first day of my first teaching appointment after leaving the University of Wales (Swansea) in 1979.

The pangs and other consequences of this break-up were still lingering, especially the loneliness at home. Yet, even in such downtime, I was advancing my career. Here I was, just promoted to a senior position, just one step from the pinnacle of my profession. I was now the deputy headteacher of one of the country's most prestigious and forward-looking schools: Sydney Stringer School and Community College located in the City of Coventry, West Midlands. This was an astonishing achievement, for a black man in an essentially racist British society, in just seven years into my profession.

I should have been so excited and happy but that was not the case. My marriage to Bronwyn in July 1971 clearly meant more to me than I had realized when I decided that I wanted out of that marriage.

This was my reality when out of the blue; I received that call from Melvinder. I remembered her to be a not-very-bright student whom I had thrown out of my Ordinary ('O') Level law classes on numerous occasions for failing to produce set homework assignments. There were problems with her missing other lessons, too, in preference for smoking behind the school's canteen. In all, this was a very troublesome young lady who had just one good thing going for her. She was a very beautiful Sikh girl. Although she came from a very strict Sikh home, Melvinder was clearly rebellious and, it seems now, that that is what pointed her to my new school. My appointment with

Sydney Stringer was splashed all over the local and national media so it was not difficult to trace my whereabouts.

During the telephone conversation with Melvinder, she confirmed that she, too, had left Aylestone at the same time I did. She was now a first-year student of dental technology elsewhere. Melvinder then got to the point of her call. She wanted me to marry her. This was so out of the ordinary that I became both stunned and tongue-tied at one and the same time. I had to say something. I advised her to continue with her studies and, perhaps, at the end of it we could consider her suggestion. She left me her telephone number and her address, and we ended the call. My response in telling her to concentrate on her dental technology course was, I am sure, the right response in the given circumstances. But that response was by no means considered. It came automatically out of my repository of common sense. Yet, when I was alone that night, I took a completely different view of what had happened earlier that day.

I decided that I would call Melvinder the following day and tell her that I had changed my mind about her waiting and that I accepted her proposal that we should get married and that I wanted to do so right away. How crazy can one get in such awkward circumstances, when I knew so little about the young lady and what I knew, wasn't all that positive? As I decided, the next day I called Melvinder on the number which she had given me. It turned out that that number was not Melvinder's number. It was a number at the home of one of her best friends.

So, I decided to write, instead, to the young lady using the address she had given me, not realizing that the address also belonged to the same best friend. In the letter, I suggested that we could meet up in London during my half-term break from school. At that time, we would choose the rings and have a date penciled in at the registrar's office in Hampstead in North London.

It took some time to receive a response to my letter. Did my change of mind shock her into changing hers? The silence of her started to bother me considerably. Was this what being jilted felt like? I had to telephone that number again; maybe she is there with her friend now. I was, frankly, becoming frantic as each day passed without hearing from her. She should have received that letter ages ago. Maybe the letter was lost in the post. But if that was the case, why hasn't she made contact? She knows where to find me.

Nothing made any sense at all. It was nearing half term and I had suggested a meeting at that time in my letter, what shall I do?

When I rang the phone, Evette, her best friend, answered. It was then that I discovered that Melvinder had given me Evette's home address too. Evette told me that she hadn't seen Melvinder for a little while, but maybe she would the next day when she planned to call at her home to give her a letter, which came to her home for her. Now I knew for sure. Melvinder was hiding from her parents. Something was grossly wrong. We needed to find out more and straighten it out for the good of all.

Sure enough, the next day Melvinder received that letter. I know because she called me immediately after she read it. She was ecstatic with joy and readily agreed to the suggested meeting that was due in three days' time, for my half term would have begun. The meeting was arranged to take place at Queen's Park Underground Station, which is in Northwest London at 14:00, the following Monday.

It was at that meeting that we were able to clarify several things. She explained why she was using her friend's contact details and not her own. Her parents would not be supportive of any relationship, which she might have outside of their planning. She, herself, was totally against having her marriage arranged by her parents who were Sikhs from India. She completely rejects this aspect of her cultural upbringing. She was far too British in her way of thinking to have her life arranged in this fashion. To her, the most frustrating aspect of that way of life is that, oftentimes, daughters have no knowledge that their weddings are being planned. They know only days before the wedding and meet their marriage partners only on the wedding day.

There is no room for changing your mind if you do not like the person chosen for you. This made her shiver with anxiety with each passing day since she attained the age of puberty. It could happen at any time. She had no power or control over any of this. She wanted to escape from all of it to a man of her choice. Her choice was me. She was nineteen years of age and did not need parental consent to enter a marital relationship of her choice under British law.

I offered to meet with her parents to explain what we were planning. She would not hear of it. She thought that would be disastrous and that they would probably violently hurt me (she wasn't joking) in the process and, at the same time, they would, probably, have her banished off to India. Her suggestion was that she would leave home, marry me, and we would face the music thereafter. And she was right: there would be some 'music' to face.

We got into my car and then drove across to Cricklewood where there were long-established jewelers. We chose a diamond cluster to be her engagement ring and she slipped it on right there and then. The wedding bands for both of us, I would collect from the same store later. Our next stop was the Hampstead Registry Office, also in North London, where we went through the process of having the 7th of January 1977 penciled in for our marriage.

Melvinder needed to get back home and became restless. I offered to drive her home, but she said that she would make her own way if I took her back to Cricklewood as bus No.266 from there goes almost to her door. Her wish was my command. At Cricklewood, we hugged and kissed goodbye. She headed for the close-by bus stop and I headed for the M1 motorway less than a mile away.

The journey back to Coventry was uneventful. My thoughts were preoccupied with the fact that I now had just half of a school term to get everything ready for our marriage and a new wife. This wasn't going to be easy-going, because the half term leading up to Christmas is usually a very busy one for all schools. What was more, this was my first term in this very demanding job and all eyes were on me. The media's obsession surrounding my appointment had not yet died down. At the time, I was still temporarily occupying a Council flat, which was arranged for me by the Coventry education officials to assist me in the relocation process.

At least, the process of buying my own home had begun. I had already identified a property but could not say for sure how long it would be before 'we' would be able to move into that space. When I got back, I would have a good night's sleep and, in the morning, I could set the ball rolling. At least, I still had the better part of the week's half-term break, to get something done.

The rest of the term went well, and I found it very enjoyable; probably because of the frequent calls from Melvinder and what I had to look forward to soon after the Christmas break. As expected, it was like in any other school: very busy, perhaps more so, given the nature of Sidney Stringer School. Preparation for the Christmas festivities took up a great deal of time. Reports writing and parents' meetings would make their own impact on time. Most importantly, I needed to make the time to continue the important business of getting to know the staff of the school, especially the pastoral team who answered directly to me.

I was determined not to repeat the faux pas, which I made in the second week that I was at the school. The headteacher, Arfon Jones, had thought that it would be a good opportunity to get to know both staff and pupils if I relieved him of his morning lateness duty. This way I would get to know those pupils and staff who were persistent latecomers and could do something about it. What he did not tell me was that the Head of the Music Department, Mrs. Pat Jones, was his estranged wife and the mother of his three young children.

At the end of my first week on late duty Rota, Pat Jones was late four out of five mornings. I thought that I would better talk to her about this as it was not a good example for the pupils and the rest of the staff. When I knocked on Pat's office door, she was warm and polite as she invited me to come in and sit.

But no sooner than I mentioned the subject of lateness, she exploded, "I think you should know that I have Arfon's three children to look after and get off to school each morning before coming here. I get no help from him." I was immediately knocked off balance and lost all sense of purpose. At the first opportunity which I had to mention this to Arfon, he simply smiled.

The school was a very large one, so it was going to take much more time to get to know all the pupils, but that had to be done at all costs. At the same time, I had, myself, programmed in for a half of time-table teaching Law and economics. The more contact I had with pupils, the more effective I would be in my job. I was convinced of that, hence the heavy time-table load. By the time we had closed for the Christmas break, I was exhausted, but excited about the marriage plans. I would use my time now to carry on with preparations and head for London on the 30th of December. I still had a flat, for which I had no immediate plans, at 591, Lady Margaret Road. When I arrived in London on the 30th of December 1976, I decided to call on my best friend, Mark Waughray before getting to my flat.

Mark, I first met when we were students together at the then Kilburn Polytechnic, which was situated in Priory Park Road in Northwest London. He was the youngest of four brothers. He and two of his brothers lived in England and the other lived in Paris at the time. His brothers lived separately and independently while Mark shared his aging mother's accommodation in

Wembley Park, Middlesex, until he took unto himself a wife and set up home in Manchester, where his mother originated.

Mark's mother was an affable English Lady who no longer lived with her Indian husband who was at that time still living in India.

I knew that Mark and Janet, for that was his wife's name, would be down from their home in Manchester soon after schools were closed for the Christmas break. They were teachers too and Mark had already told me by telephone that he would be in London to spend some time with his mother as soon as their schools broke up for Christmas.

I was with Mark and his family when the doorbell rang. Mark answered it and it turned out to be a mutual friend who Mark had, in fact, introduced me to a long time ago. Graham was his name. Graham and his wife, Kay, lived in Perivale, Middlesex, which is roughly five miles or so away from Mrs. Waughray's. Graham spotted me in the background and barged straight past Mark and came over to me.

"Where have you been? I've been to your flat a dozen times trying to find you," Graham demanded.

"Why is this?" I inquired.

"A parcel has been delivered to my address for you," he replied. Graham was quite serious. How could this be possible? I began searching for my thoughts. I had never given Graham's address to any trader. Only mutual friends would know where he lived and none of them should be sending me parcels to his address. However, Graham wanted me to collect that 'parcel' there and then. I made my excuse and told Mark that I would see him before he went back to Manchester the following day.

Puzzling curiosity was still killing me when we pulled up at Graham's house. Kay let us in as Graham had forgotten to take his door key with him. I almost fainted. I could see over Kay's shoulder and there was Melvinder standing behind her, with a look of desperation on her face. Melvinder had left home taking nothing with her other than the clothes she was wearing. She went in search of Mark, but there was no reception at the Waughrays. They must have been out shopping. Instead, she made her way to Graham and Kay. Yes, I could remember then that I had told her who my closest friends were and where they were residing.

It had become imperative that she should leave home at the time she did. Melvinder had read my letter repeatedly. This last time, she felt it wise to destroy it. However, very unwisely she threw the torn scraps into her waste basket. When she got back from running an errand for her mother, she went to her bedroom and there, on her bedside table, she found the torn pieces of the letter taped back together, if somewhat disjointedly. Every bit of the letter's content, nevertheless, could be read very clearly. Fortunately, there was no address on that letter: just the date when it was written, and it was signed "your husband to be: no name."

Melvinder then snatched the mended letter and disappeared quickly before anyone could even realize that she was back from the errand for her mother. Now she was with me, it became all my responsibility. I did not shirk it. I thanked Graham and Kay for their kindness and Melvinder and I made our way to Lady Margaret Road. On the way home, I picked up a Chinese take-away and something to drink. There wouldn't have been anything at the flat given that I was away in Coventry for a full term.

The desperation had long gone off Melvinder's face. She was now hilariously happy to be with me, even though she realized a not very kind search party would be out looking for her and whomsoever she was with at the time. Melvinder's eldest sibling was called Terry. He was the only boy in the family. There were two other girls, Devinder, who was older than Melvinder, and Pinky, the youngest of all and was just about thirteen years of age at the time. Pinky was the member of the family that Melvinder trusted the most.

They were not only sisters, but unlike Devinder, Pinky was also her friend and confidante.

Although their mother and father were the nominal heads of the household, it was really Terry who ran things. The family was mobile peddlers of clothes and other bits and pieces in and around London and Terry oversaw setting up and manning the stalls and all that. As it turned out, at the relevant time, he was also responsible for things cultural at home, as far as the girls were concerned. He was the one to enforce the cultural strictness of their religion and culture in the name of the girl's welfare. Melvinder thought he was really a hypocrite in terms of what she knew of him. He would now be leading the search party for her.

The night was comfortable and relaxing despite the circumstances. We were both hungry so we 'licked the platters clean.' We drank all that we had bought on the way in, watched television for a while and then went to bed, both mindful that we were not yet man and wife and kept it that way in a tight hug.

The next day, we were in no mood for cooking, even if it was just breakfast. So, we decided to check out a local café in the Greenford area. I already knew that they had a splendid breakfast and it was not expensively. I had promised Mark the previous day that I would see him before he and Janet went back to their home in Manchester. The Waughrays had no working telephone at that time, so they were still in the dark about the mysterious parcel, which was addressed to me at Graham's and Kay's address. I needed to let them know all that was going on in relation to this parcel. After breakfast, we went back to the flat briefly. I was able to call Graham and Kay to thank them once more and to bring them up to date about events since leaving their home with my 'parcel' the previous day.

We decided to get to Waughray's early because Mark and Janet were dependent on public transport to get them back to Manchester. That meant that they may want to set out quite early as Manchester is some distance away. We were right about that because when we got there, they were ready to head out for Victoria bus station. When they heard our tale, they became most concerned for us. Mark had a good grounding in Indian culture, including Sikhism. He thought there was good reason to historically.

For the first time, I felt a tinge of fear, but quickly dismissed it as not something that should be taken seriously. Janet suggested that we come and spend a day or two with them in Manchester, while we worked through the situation. We agreed that we would do just that. So, we all stayed a little while longer with the elder Mrs. Waughray; and had some lunch before we said goodbye to her. All four of us got into my car and we drove the 200 or so miles non-stop to Mark's and Janet's home in the north of England.

On the journey north, Melvinder and Mark traded knowledge of Sikhism and the cultural dictates of the Eastern peoples. Janet and I were captured, but willing, pupils who sought clarification of statements made here and there by either of the scholars. Mark feared for our safety especially from the Sians. Melvinder and the other members of her immediate family are Sians. Apparently, the Sians were particularly powerful warriors.

It is amazing how quickly the miles go in such an atmosphere. Once we were indoors, depression began to set in on both of us. I could see that there was worry on Melvinder's face. She was missing her family; I could see that plainly. As for me, I was applying my rudimentary knowledge of the law pertaining to lost persons, to our case. Once Melvinder was missing for 48 hours or more, she could be treated as a lost person, even though she was an adult. This could mean the police would be looking for her.

It made me very anxious; and now her state of visible worry compounded my fear. Because everyone was so tired after the long journey from London, we made do with a light supper and had an early night. We didn't even wait to see the New Year in: Mark had nothing sparkling in the house, anyway. For me, the night was an exceedingly restless one and made for no sleep at all. I needed to speak with Melvinder's parents at all costs, otherwise I would not be happy with the situation as it was.

In the morning, I told Melvinder of my desire over breakfast. Janet had made us proud with a lovely breakfast. Melvinder thought I was crazy and begged me to forget it. Mark supported her and warned that I was playing with fire. Only Janet saw some sense in what I was saying but, nevertheless, cautioned that I should be careful.

This was the first day of January 1977 and I was going to take charge of the situation. I could not bear to see the worry on my wife's, to be, face. My own peace of mind was non-existent. I had to do something about that. I would call her parents and speak to them, no matter what she said. The phone rang for a long time without anyone answering. I was just about to hang up when someone picked up the phone at the other end. It was Melvinder's brother, Terry.

I said hello and introduced myself as the person with whom Melvinder was at the time. I told him that she was safe and that he and the rest of her family had no need to worry. He asked me to put Melvinder on the phone. I did. They talked for a minute or two and then she disintegrated into a pool of tears. I could not quite understand. I took the phone, but he was gone.

Melvinder then said that her father had had a heart attack and was hospitalized because of the shock, which she had brought on him by her fleeing from home. This was what Terry told her in that short telephone conversation. The young lady was now distraught, distressed and everything, which threatened to make her seriously ill. Even though I suspected that this was no more than some form of emotional blackmail, I rang Terry again and agreed to meet him the following day, 2nd of January at West Hampstead Tube Station in London. The meeting was scheduled to take place at 14:00.

On the morning of the 2nd of January, one day before my 36th birthday, Melvinder and I set off from Manchester quite early. It was around 08:30. Mark and Janet were still in bed when we knocked on their door to say goodbye. "Just let yourselves out and we will talk later," Mark said.

During the journey, Melvinder made it clear that she would not be going along with me to meet Terry. She didn't think the meeting was a wise thing. Had I not called her parents against her wishes, she would not be so down as she is now, she said. I had to accept that, but, on the other hand, other problems might have ensued. It was never my intention to take her to the meeting.

My own very close cousin Gloria (I called her Sister G.), who helped to bring me up in Jamaica when my parents headed for England, was living in Birmingham with her husband, George Clarke (I called him Georgie) and their two young daughters, Michelle, and Linda. My plan, all along, was to leave Melvinder with the Clarkes and then continue the journey to London in time to meet Terry. We arrived at the Clarkes' soon after 10:00.

George and Gloria Clarke
And their two lovely daughters below:

Michelle Linda Michelle Again

As usual, the Clarkes insisted on preparing a meal. We were very grateful for that. I didn't want to be late for this rather important appointment, so immediately made the introductions and gave as much of the background information as I knew it. As usual, Sister G. was silent nearly all the time. This was a most puzzling characteristic of my cousin. You never quite know where you stood with her or what she is thinking. As a boy back home in Jamaica, I was caught out numerous times misreading her silence. Just when I would think she was nonchalant in relation to my antics and then got careless, she would grab and soundly thrash me. Though the time when I could be trashed had long passed, her silence still bothered me. Georgie was much more forth coming. He asked Melvinder if she was tired and if she wanted to get some rest.

At exactly a quarter to twelve that morning, I left Clark's house to continue to London. I had precisely two and quarter hours to make my appointment there. At that time of day, most of the usual rush hour traffic on the M6 and M1 Motor Ways had already died down. Consequently, I made London a really good time. Some of the time saved was lost making my way from Staples Corner, along Edgware Road, through Cricklewood and Kilburn before turning left into Quex Road, which formed a 'T' Junction at its other end with West

End Lane. West Hampstead Tube Station was located on the right-hand side of West End Lane, about a half a mile to the left of the 'T' Junction with Quex Road.

When I reached West End Lane, I still had fifteen minutes to spare, and it would take me no more than a minute or two to reach the station. I did not want to be late; neither did I want to be early. I just want to be exactly on time. I turned left at the 'T' Junction and parked up about a hundred yards on the left even though it was unbroken yellow lines in a no parking zone. Two minutes before the appointed time, I set off and when I reached the station, I turned right into Broadhurst Gardens and parked about four cars down on the left. The station is situated at the corner of West End Lane with Broadhurst Gardens.

Now, all I had to do is make myself seem conspicuous and hope that Terry would approach my car to determine if I was Carlton Duncan. I did not know Terry and, therefore, could not tell whether he was already there. He recognized me. He had seen several television programmers and newspaper articles about me and some of them carried my photographs. I had not thought about that possibility.

Terry came from across the road and walked directly to my car. "Are you Terry?" I asked him.

"Yes," he replied and so I invited him into the vehicle so that we could sit and talk. Terry got into the front passenger seat of my car. He was unmistakably a Sikh young man without a turban. He was about five feet seven inches tall. He was slim and casually dressed. I introduced myself once more, this time face to face, and attempted to shake his hand as I did so but he was unfriendly. "How is your father? I understand that he is not very well."

"Thanks to you and my sister," he said. At this point, I decided to tell him in person about his sister's and my plans to be married in a short while. I told him everything. He wanted to know if he could see his sister.

"She did not want to see you right now," I told him. He kept on asking me to let him have a number for her so that he could speak with her by telephone. I said that I could not do that, but I would pass on a message and tell her of his desire to speak with her by phone. Maybe she would telephone him. Terry then asked if I wanted money.

"No," I replied, "I don't need your money." At several other junctures in our conversation, he would introduce this money thing, but each time I told him that I wasn't interested. That was very lucky for me because Terry was bugged with a listening device and there were plain clothes police officers close by listening to and watching everything. Finally, he said he was willing to be my best man, but please let him meet with his sister. I told him that his offer would be a good thing to say to his sister whenever they speak.

The Chase, Trap, and Arrest

We exhausted all that we had to say to each other. I reminded Terry that I would pass on his message to his sister and hoped that she would telephone him. He requested my contact address, and I gave him, in my own hand, both home and school addresses in Coventry. I said that I needed to go, and he let himself out of the car and I drove off with the return journey to Birmingham in mind. What I had no way of knowing was that I was being followed by three police officers in an unmarked car. Melvinder would eventually inform me of this. They followed me for a long way up the M1 Motor Way. They did not know where I was heading and did not prepare for a very long ride.

Unfortunately for them, luckily for me, their vehicle was low on petrol and so they stopped replenishing and, in that act, lost me completely from there. This was extremely lucky for me because had they been able to follow me, I would have unwittingly taken them to my cousins' address where they would have, no doubt, carried out a raid to find Melvinder. What an absolute embarrassment that would have been for my family in that quiet and respectful neighborhood! It did not happen, so post-mortem relief was in order.

At my cousins' place, I reported the meeting with Terry to Melvinder word for word and passed on Terry's message. With some encouragement from me, Melvinder used my cousins' telephone to call Terry. She was burdened with the same emotional blackmail, which was used on her when she was at Mark's and Janet's. It had the same effects, only worse. This made me terribly upset and had to do something about it. Besides, I wasn't too comfortable conducting this at my cousins'. I told Melvinder to get back on the phone and tell Terry that we would meet him in London that same night at about 19:00. We would meet him at my Lady Margaret Road address, nowhere else. She did and Terry agreed.

Tired as I was, we bade goodbye to my cousins and set off again for the long and tedious ride to London. During the journey, Melvinder was in tears for most of the way. I was pensive and anxious, but at least the matter would be cleared up one way or another. At least, that was what I thought. Little did I know what awaited us?

I pulled into the entrance to the Lady Margaret Road Flats and switched off the engine. Before we could exit the car, both front doors flew open. Several plain clothes police officers pulled me from the car and took my keys while several others pulled Melvinder from the other side of the car. From that moment, I saw or heard nothing of Melvinder until the 30th of March 1977.

In the meantime, what looked like fifty officers (turned out to be 15 in the end) surrounded me. They pushed me up against a nearby garage wall, searched for me from head to toe, handcuffed me and pushed me unceremoniously into one of their many unmarked cars. Soon, they dragged me out of the car again, this time I was handcuffed to one of the officers who led me to the front door of my ground floor flat. Everything was happening in the full glare of most of my neighbors. They demanded the key to the flat, but they had already possessed it when they took my car keys. It was on the same bunch of keys. I informed them of this. They let themselves in and started a grand search. They did not find what they were looking for or anything else.

I was then taken back to one of their cars in handcuffs and driven to Harlesden police station in Northwest London where I was stripped of my possessions and tossed into a grimy, cold, and damp cell. I was not even allowed to make the statutory one telephone call, despite my request. I would later discover from Melvinder that on the night of my arrest and her disappearance, there were several marksmen with loaded guns under cover as they waited our arrival at the Lady Margaret Road flat. They were very frustrated with having lost me on the motorway earlier that day.

Chief Inspector Harding of Harlesden Police

Chief Inspector Harding, a tall and imposing figure of authority, nervously handed me back the ring as his two colleagues watched in puzzled amazement. The usually commanding presence that would normally compliment the Inspector's stature was somehow absent. He, clearly, had been brought down a peg or two.

"She said that she didn't want it anymore." One of the other officers drew closer and brought my wallet with him. He showed the Chief Inspector a document, which was part of the contents of my wallet. The document informed the Inspector that I was to be married to Melvinder Kaur Sian at the Hampstead Registry in Northwest London in just four days.

The Chief Inspector then asked me in a quiet remorseful tone, "Why didn't you tell us about this?" He was clearly implying stupidity on my part, as he tried unsuccessfully to camouflage his most recent and obvious blunder. According to him, I had wasted the time of fifteen of his officers over a two-day period. The third officer came over sheepishly and gave to me the remainder of my belongings including my car and house keys. I signed for everything, and he mumbled, "Your car is in the car lot," as he left the room, in obvious disappointment.

I gradually became oblivious to my surroundings, all, and everything around me. Somehow, I found my way to the spot where they had parked my silver Toyota Corolla. As I entered the car, I remembered thinking, how was I going to negotiate my way out of this very tight spot and these badly parked police vehicles. That was the least of my worry. My head was spinning wildly with other more pressing commands. I fired the ignition and the next thing I knew; I was driving aimlessly and rather slowly as I pondered the complexity of the hell I had just gone through.

I was the recently appointed deputy headmaster of one of the United Kingdom's most prestigious and forward-looking mixed comprehensive schools at the time. I had just beaten all odds as a black man to aspire to the position of deputy headteacher and Director of Personal Development (DP) at Sidney Stringer School and Community College in Coventry, West Midlands.

This was still making the headline news locally and nationally. And, here I was, like a common criminal, locked up heartlessly behind steel bars in a dirty pungent police cell in Harlesden, Northwest London. The shackling handcuffs removed, men like I, only of a different hue, ushered me hastily in this dark and dismal place. It was not until 02:00 that morning, according to the clock on the wall in the interviewing room, that these same men came reluctantly to set me free. They had taken their time in checking their misinformation only to discover that they had either negligently, or deliberately, pent an innocent man based upon falsehood.

It was my release from this miserable cell that led me to be driving aimlessly in Harlesden on that early morning of the 3rd of January 1977, my 36th birthday, as I pondered Melvinder's fate. There was nothing that I could do. I had tried driving past her parents' home, which I had come to learn from her was in Fairlight Avenue in Harlesden, Northwest London, but Terry and others spotted me and came out to chase me in their vehicle and I had to drive speedily back to the same police station where I took refuge.

I eventually got back to my Lady Margaret Road flat in the wee hours of the morning when all the neighbors were still sleeping. When the day broke, some of the neighbors saw my car outside and realized that I was released from the ordeal, which they witnessed and came to my flat to enquire of my welfare and what it was all about. It was then that I learned that some of them had come to the station while they were still holding me to ask what was wrong and that the police told them nothing was wrong, denied them a chance to see me and sent them away.

They were all very relieved when they understood that I was charged with nothing, and they got to know what it was all about directly from me. I stayed in all morning until it was time to go and fulfill the Chief Inspector's request. Just before I left the station that night, he asked me to return on my own free will to see them at noon. But when I got there, the Inspector said he didn't want to see me after all, so I left the station for the last time.

Still not truly knowing what had happened, I contacted a lawyer in the Coventry area. He was able to ascertain that Melvinder's parents had lodged two complaints with the police. The first was that I had abducted their daughter. The second was that their daughter had stolen £600 before she left. This latter, till this day, has been the only possibly explanation for the search for my flat. Clearly, these were two inconsistent charges. Did she know that she was about to be abducted and thought that she would better steal some money, or did I just happen to abduct a young lady who had just stolen some money? None of the officers was bright enough, it seemed, to see through this inconsistency and continued to let Melvinder's parents blindly (or was there another more compelling motive like money?) lead them on their way to an obvious blunder.

Then they blamed the wrong person for wasting their precious time. I did not want to consider the possibility of corruption. After all, at our meeting, Terry was offering me money with the undercover police listening and taping our conversation hoping to trap me on the charge of abduction. Further, they had not charged Melvinder with anything. After questioning her, they simply allowed her to go home with Terry. The police clearly had the ingredients of a charge of wasting police time against Melvinder's family, but no charge was ever brought. This was quite telling!

As the days went by without any form of communication from Melvinder, I resolved to just get on with my job and my life, sadly bearing my disappointment, and let whatever will happen, happen by its own ordained accord, in its own predestined and timely groove. Most people who knew what had just happened to me were, at least, sympathetic, and genuinely sorry. There were four Sikh teachers employed at Stringer, and all, but one showed me no ill-feeling whatsoever. The one exception had nothing, but disapprobation and disgust for me and made it known. My headteacher was understanding and graciously helpful.

When the sole local authority official with an education brief started asking uncomfortable questions and implying that, maybe, the Authority had made an error in appointing me, Arfon Jones, my headteacher, rushed to my defense most robustly and permanently diverted any form of pressure that was in the political pipeline and heading my way. The pain never left me, but over the weeks that followed, I had started learning to live a life of hopelessness, which was so very clearly beyond my control.

Sydney Stringer School and Community College was like a soothing tonic for someone in my position. Managerial and pastoral matters coupled with a 50 per cent teaching load, helped significantly in the maintenance of my sanity. I dreaded being alone at night, not because of the absence of company, but because at those times my mind had far too much freedom to dwell on matters emotional, thus inducing the fierceness of self-pity with its ever-hurtful pangs.

To combat this tendency, I would often take home schoolwork, which would occupy me late into the night. In time, I had learned to develop other female interests, none of them serious, right there in Coventry, in Birmingham, Leicester, and Melton Mowbray and as far away as London. The traveling, time consumption, and the sexual gratification derived from these relationships were also instrumental to my continued survival and my ability to function effectively at work.

Escape from House Arrest

Just as I was beginning to feel comfortable in my despair and hopelessness, something happened. It was a warm and sunny day in March—30th March

1977. I was working at my desk when the telephone rang. I picked it up and said softly, "DP here."

The voice at the other end said, "It's me!" My instincts told me at once who it was. Three months, but for three days, had passed without a word from or about Melvinder; and now, just out of the blue, here she was speaking at the end of my telephone line.

"Where are you?" I asked. She told me that she had just escaped from the house arrest under which she had been placed since the night of the police operation. She was using a pay phone box at Queen's Park Underground Station to call me. She was very fearful that someone might track her down.

I told her to get back on the train and go to Trafalgar Square at the 24-hour post office there and call me again and I would need the number from which she will be calling me. The journey was going to take her about fifteen minutes. I paced the confines of my office about a hundred times before the phone rang again. It was her. She was now at the all-night post office in Trafalgar Square calling from one of its numerous public telephones. I took the number and told her that I would call her back immediately. This way, there was no risk of losing her because her money ran out before I could get someone to her.

She hung up as I suggested, and I called her back immediately. I then put her on hold and contacted my friend Graham in London. I told him where Melvinder was and how to find her. He agreed that he would send a taxi to fetch her and take her to me in Coventry, ninety or so miles away. Now, I reconnected with Melvinder and kept her chatting until I could hear the taxi driver asking her if she was Melvinder. She was now on her way to Coventry. Give her ninety minutes and she will be here. Only a week ago, I had moved into my own home, though completion had taken place a month ago. On this score, the timing was right.

Allan Edwards was my fellow deputy headteacher (curriculum brief). He was married to the Chairman of Coventry's Bench of Magistrates. I slipped across to his office, which was on the other side of the same corridor as mine. I told Allan what had just happened. Allan wasted no time by questioning me further. Instead, he got on the phone and called his wife. He told her what I had just told him. In about thirty minutes, Mrs. Edwards was in my office. By then, I had also alerted Arfon Jones. He was in my office when Mrs. Edwards arrived. Allan joined us too. Mrs. Edwards took control of everything. She was aware of the past and the problems with the police and was determined that any of that would happen in Coventry.

She called the Chief of Police for Coventry and put him into the picture. Mrs. Edwards then told me that she would receive Melvinder on her arrival, not me. She asked me if I was in love and wanted to marry this young lady. I assured her positively on both scores. The next thing I knew was that Mrs. Edwards was on the phone to the Registrar of Marriages, Birth and Death. When she got off the phone, she advised me that our marriage was arranged for 14:00 at the Registry Office the following day, 31st March 1977.

At that very moment, the taxi pulled up with Melvinder. She had no luggage, only blue jeans, a rust brown cardigan and a pair of matching brown shoes, which she was wearing. Mrs. Edwards greeted the taxi and transferred Melvinder to her car even before I could say hello to her. I paid the £40 cost of the journey, thanked the driver and he went on his long journey back to London. Mrs. Edwards 'instructed' me to wait for a call from her and then drove off to the Coventry police headquarters. About fifteen minutes later, the expected call came. Mrs. Edwards was on the line. She invited me to join her, Melvinder and the police for a meeting at their headquarters. It took me just ten minutes to reach their location and join the meeting.

As I entered the room, Melvinder ran across straight into my arms and burst into tears of joy as the magistrate and police officers looked on in awesome relief. After that, the meeting was quick and simple. The Chief Officer wanted to establish whether Melvinder came to Coventry freely. He questioned her on that point. Did she want to marry me the next day as had been arranged? She was positive about that. I, too, was still definitely positive on that point when the question was put to me.

The Chief Officer then assigned Inspector B as the officer to whom we should turn if we had any difficulties, which would require police assistance. The Inspector shook our hands and gave us his calling card. We thanked him as he smiled and left the room. Mrs. Edwards then advised us of the arrangements for the next day. Melvinder would be staying the night with her, and we would meet at the Registry Office at 13:00 the next day. My role now was to go away and find a best man and be prepared for the marriage.

Marriage, Reception, Hospital

The next day—31st March 1977—came in like any other day: no fanfare, no comets seen, just the sun rising magnificently in the east amidst the gentle murmuring morning breeze. Yes, that is precisely how I was feeling, ecstatically romantic and happy. All the gloom and depression of yesterdays had gone, and all was right with the world. I was feeling magnanimous. I will not now even bother to pursue the formal complaint, which I had lodged against the Harlesden police under the leadership of Chief Inspector Harding. Terry and Melvinder's parents were absolutely forgiven. They were just about to become my in-laws, though unwillingly and in absentia.

The corn flakes tasted extra special that morning, even the burned toast was favored. I pulled up my car in the school's car park at 08:00 precisely. I went immediately to the headteacher's office. Dilwyn Scott, the head of the mathematics department, was with him. These two Welsh men got on well together and I was an adopted son to the 'brotherhood' given that I am a graduate of a Welsh university. They were, in fact, talking about me in relation to the day, but the only detail that I picked up was that Dilwyn had volunteered to be my best man. Arfon would be taking care of all other relevant matters.

At 12:45, Arfon collected Dilwyn and myself from my office and took us to a wine bar, which was not far from the Registry Office. We all remarked how conspicuous the police officers were on almost every street corner that we passed on the way. It did not occur to us, at least to me, that they might have had anything to do with my day. The two Welsh men had a glass of red wine each. I had a pint of larger. The cheer was to the future of my marriage, which was about to take place just across the road in just minutes. Arfon paid the bar tender and we all walked across the road to the Registry Office. All three of us wore black suits and black bow ties. Dilwyn had arranged daffodils for our lapels.

Our shoes were polished jet black, with contrasting white shirts. At the door, we met Mrs. Edwards who escorted us to a nearby room. There standing and waiting with long and flowing black hair, was Melvinder Kaur Sian, soon to be Mrs. Melvinder Duncan. Mrs. Edwards had done a superb bridal transformation in such a short time. Later, she would present me with the monetary cost of everything and I would happily receive and repay the same.

Dilwyn had the wedding bands and the engagement ring, which Chief Inspector Harding had returned to me. He would produce them at the appropriate time. I had previously collected the wedding bands from the same jeweler where we had chosen the engagement ring in London. I had, at the time of ordering them, paid for them in full; therefore, despite the difficulties which ensued thereafter, the rings were already mine and had to be collected.

The wedding ceremony was traditional in its vows and statements. The signing of the Register was a brief and simple affair. The ceremony and signing were witnessed by about ten people, all staff at Sydney Stringer School. The wedding was over, Mrs. Duncan and I were driven back to the school where we would collect my car and head for our home. There they were again, only more of them. The police were out in force as though they were expecting some royal figure or something quite serious to happen. This visible presence of the law stretched all the way back to the school's gate. There were two burley officers even in the school's car park. It was then that it occurred to me, later confirmed, that the chief magistrate and the chief police officer of Coventry had left no stone unturned in enabling this marriage to take place without hindrance.

My wife and I thanked Arfon for taking us back and I thanked Dilwyn for his kindness, and we headed for the front entrance to the school's reception area. What a surprise greeted us! Pupils and staff with ribbons and confetti in awesome wonder paraded the reception area. Shouts of hooray, congratulations and good luck filled the air intermittently. Over in the far left-hand corner of the room, the food technology department had laid out an appetizing spread. In the center of it all was a magnificent cake that was bought and brought in especially for the occasion.

We were dumfounded with joy as both of us just simply embraced each other in a passionate but restrained first kiss as man and wife. The ceremonious cutting of the cake signaled the green light for all to have a feast and have a great time. In all the secret planning, careful as it clearly was, no one remembered a camera.

There were very few speeches. Even the best man forgot to give one. And once the celebrations were over, some of the pupils helped us gather up the impromptu presents, which we received at the reception and took them to our car. We then waved goodbye and headed home. My home was in Aldbury Rise, Allesley Park on the northwestern side of Coventry. Although Coventry had a large Asian population, not a single Asian lived in Allesley Park and certainly not on my road. My wife would be the first.

As we drove along, I was all the time hoping that Melvinder was going to like her new home. I thought it was lovely but needed a feminine touch. As I turned into Aldbury Rise from the eastern end, I noticed an Asian male going west the same as we were. Strange, I had never seen anyone other than white people around here. Still, we drove on until we arrived at no. 32, our very own home. Stranger still, there were two Asian males coming from the other direction walking toward the one, which we had driven past. Still, we ignored it and went into our home, anticipating all that newlyweds usually anticipate.

Melvinder went quickly up the stairs to look around. I lingered and peered through the front door glass panel. There were now five Asian males massing just across the road almost, but not quite, opposite our home. I became very suspicious then and there and decided to use the card that Inspector B had left us.

The telephone was placed right by the front door, so I was able to observe those outside as I made my call. The Inspector himself answered and I told him who I was and then described the gathering of Indians on our road as though we were witnessing the gradual gathering of Indians in some wild western movie. The Inspector didn't bother to ask any more questions. He knew Aldbury Rise quite well, he said, because he sometimes visited his station colleague who also lived in Aldbury Rise. "I am on my way," he said.

The moment I put the phone down and turned around, I saw Indians everywhere in our home. That morning when I was on cloud nine, I went to school and left the back door unbolted. There were those in the front, but there were also those at the rear. The next thing I knew was that I was being attacked by an Indian male around late 20's or early 30's. In the ensuing struggle, he stretched his hand and opened the front door and rushed those that were outside. I needed more space to call upon my boxing skills and so I collared my direct opponent and pushed him outside of the front door onto the street. I now had more room to let him pay for his folly. No sooner than I folded him up with a right to the head and a left hook to his mid-rift, two of his other colleagues pounced on me and brought me to the ground.

From the ground, I could see Melvinder being dragged down our stairs by her long hair, headfirst. They took her out to a waiting car and forced her inside. The rough and tumble and associated noise must have carried because a white male from two doors beyond mine to the right, came out and started to remonstrate with us about the noise. It turned out to be Inspector B's colleague who he had just told me about minutes ago. While I was held to the ground, and being kicked, the other members of the invading tribe began to load themselves into a second car close by the first in which my wife was being held.

Then there were flashing blue lights from either direction of the road. Inspector B and his men had arrived just in time to rescue my wife and me and he arrested all nine of the invaders, Terry, and Melvinder's father among them. It seemed Melvinder's father was no longer hospitalized with heart problems. The Inspector instructed one of his colleagues to transport my wife and me to the nearest hospital. He will need a medical report. Ironically, the first bed we found ourselves in after just being married, was a hospital one albeit separately. We did not have anything much wrong with us: just a few bruises from the rough and tumble. I had a sore side too. This was no great wonder, since there was where I was kicked a good many times.

The officer returned to collect us once the hospital had alerted him. His instruction was to take us now to the police station where all nine assailants were incarcerated in a dingy cell. At the station, and around the cell where all nine men were visibly held, Inspector B asked me if I would be pressing charges against these men. They, all of them, stared at me so sheepishly helplessly behind bars, to see and hear what my reply was going to be. My father-in-law was behind those bars and so was my brother-in-law. Also, behind those bars was one of my wife's cousins, he, himself, was a police officer from the London area. This would spell far too much trouble for them.

I remember thinking that it was some of these who had had me locked up in a similar police cell based upon their trumped-up complaints a few months ago. Should I let them stew a little in revenge? I relented and told Inspector B that I would not proceed with any charge. The Inspector opened the cell door and gathered all nine around him. He told them in no uncertain terms that they were extremely lucky with two scores. Firstly, that Mr. and Mrs. Duncan had suffered no great physical harm that the hospital could find. Secondly, Mr. Duncan was not inclined to press any charges. In view of their good luck, they should listen to him most carefully and follow his advice to the letter.

Leave Coventry at once, returning only for legal purposes, for, if Mr. or Mrs. Duncan complains of a 'stomachache' or the like, we will be looking at your door first. My wife and I thanked the Inspector profusely and left for a waiting police vehicle as we promised him, we would always remain keenly vigilant. Our police escort drove us to our house in Aldbury Rise, bade us good night, and left on his call. The night was a tender one in more than one sense of the word. We had bruises, remember! Tomorrow, life together would begin in earnest for both of us.

On the Week's Honeymoon

The first weekend after our marriage came quickly. We decided to spend some of it looking at our presents. They were not numerous but of considerable quality. There was a rather colorful envelope from Arfon Jones. Inside it was a note in Arfon's own hand. He was hoping that we would accept the gift of his country cottage in North Wales for a week to spend our honeymoon. The half-term break of a week from school was near and that was an ideal gift for our week's honeymoon. We gladly accepted, and what a wonderful week that was.

On the week's honeymoon, if we did nothing, we got to learn a great deal about each other's likes and dislikes. Melvinder was amazingly happy and chatty about everything. She enjoyed the collection of music, which I packed for the honeymoon vacation. She was particularly sold on two of the collections, namely, a 1974 Ace Cannon album entitled 'That Music City Feeling' and Nana Mouskouri's 'Passport' collection. These we played over and over and constantly; she loved them so much. I also discovered that Melvinder could not cook all those lovely Indian dishes to which I had become accustomed as a bachelor who frequented Indian restaurants.

That was disappointing because I enjoyed no other cuisine as much as I do those from the various corners of India. However, there was much more about Melvinder that would compensate. In any case, just as she was prepared to take steps to acquire the skills and 'know how' to prepare Jamaican cuisine, so too she was determined to practice cooking those delicious Indian dishes. Over time, my wife did acquire the skills to prepare several English, Jamaican, Italian, and even French dishes, but never succeeded with my favorite Indian ones. We just had to rely on the restaurants for those.

I discovered too, that unlike my first wife, Bronwyn, Melvinder was keen on having children and could not wait to have some. In this important respect, we blended rather nicely. I was very careful not to mention her parents and other siblings because it had become obvious that that could be painful for her and I enjoyed seeing her in her happy and vivacious mood. We left the cottage only to dine out and to take in some of the glorious northern Wales's sceneries.

We mostly stayed listening to music and doing everything else, which was fun for both of us. We had about two interruptions throughout the week. Both were at awkward times. Arfon when lending us the cottage for our honeymoon did not warn us that just weeks before he had put the cottage on the market for sale and therefore, we should expect potential buyers to call. The week went by quickly: far too quickly. We took our time in getting home as we drove leisurely back to England and the West Midlands. All the time, we were both praying that she was pregnant, so that we would soon be parents.

Earlier Procreation

One extremely cold night in early January 1961, I arrived in the United Kingdom, from the Caribbean on board an Italian vessel called the TS Ascania which docked in South Hampton: a journey part finished. From there I, and hundreds of others like me, boarded a train bound for its pre-determined destination at Victoria Station in London a few meters away from the back gardens of Buckingham Palace. Of course, I did not know and could not have imagined that some 21 years later, I would be an invited guest to a royal garden party in those very gardens. The 1960s were very eventful for me as a young immigrant coming to the shores of the 'mother country.'

It opened my first serious account in romance and the many concomitant heart breaks and attending woes to follow. During the 5,000 or so miles voyage, Marjorie Brown (known affectionately as 'Sweetie') was my constant companion. Once we separated at Victoria, both strangers in a foreign land, our relationship did not survive the numerous cultural shocks and racist struggles. It gradually faded to become a distant memory for both of us. My relative inexperience coupled with youthful lust was destined to land me in dangerous waters up ahead and very soon. Also new to the United Kingdom was a Blossom Campbell whom I had known from our island days in Jamaica but stayed platonic.

In England, though, this did not remain that way. Why delay the truth, our reunion quickly became sexual in circumstances when neither of us could afford a child or responsible enough to avoid one. And so it came to pass that my first child, Orville Duncan, was brought into this world when neither of us was ready. The story from this point is hard to tell. Suffice it to say that because

I was in no position to lavish on my son and his mother, Blossom decided that she would take me to the courts for child maintenance. The outcome of the trial, the circumstances of the parties considered, I was ordered to pay through the courts to Blossom for the child a weekly sum of £1 until Orville was eighteen years of age. Everything went downhill from this point onwards. The final reality is that I lost contact with Orville and his mother and so it remained with the two sides going their own ways without the involvement of the other. Every aspect of this matter faded almost completely with either side simply making no effort to contact the other side,

Once I had begun to establish a name for myself in the educational world, my whereabouts became well known with the aid of the media that was never too far from what I was doing. The next time I heard anything of Orville was that day in the mid-nineteen eighties when, out of the blue, my reception office alerted me that a Mr. Orville Duncan was on the line, and would I take the call which I did.

Orville and I had a long telephone conversation during which he disclosed that life had been unkind to him and remained very uncertain. There was more than a hint of mental and legal difficulties. We resolved that he would call me again so that a meeting could be arranged. That call never materialized and so the meeting never took place as was proposed. Time passed and I retired from Gorge Dixon an so he would have lost that avenue of contact.

Toward the end of 1961, September, in fact, I was enrolled at the then Kilburn Polytechnic in Northwest London for the important purpose of repeating my secondary education to counter the significant blow the 'mother country' had dealt me by rejecting my earlier Jamaican certificates. To eke out the financial cost of so doing, it became necessary to find and keep some form of paying employment. For this purpose, the string of teashops then known as J. Lyons and Company, came conveniently to the rescue. While working at Shop B11 in the Stand as a kitchen hand for the grand sum of £8.50p net of tax per week, I met many people, among them a young lady named Carmen Rochester who would become the mother of my next child, a daughter named Yvette.

Carmen was one of the most charming and well-meaning women that I have ever met. On many occasions, I have had cause to regret that things went the way they did for us. As it turned out, while I was at the University of Wales, and not in touch with her or my daughter, Carmen met and married another man, thus under pinning my loses. We remain solid friends even today.

Daughter Yvette Rochester-Duncan

In 1963, yes, I fathered my first daughter in circumstances which were very difficult and awkward. I was still a student at Kilburn Polytechnic and would be for a further two years after which I would be away at university for a further four years so my daughter, Yvette, and I would have had no opportunity to bond. My daughter was in London with her mother, who fortunately, remained linked to my own mother even if I didn't know about it, while I spent the next four years in south Wales at the University College of Swansea.

Mother was like that. She never shielded me when I needed that protection. I am sure she was convinced she was doing the right thing even if 'the right thing' left me in very awkward situations like the time when she told my girlfriend's father not to trust me because I was at the time in Sweden with another woman.

Even though I had no contact and therefore no relationship with my daughter, my mother's secret links to Yvette and her mother meant that it was not all lost and that at an appropriate time I could pick up those reins even if it was in circumstances of considerable shame and embarrassment as it turned out to be. I cannot recall the reason for visiting mother one evening after I had left university and had become an established teacher. But at mother's home there was this extremely attractive and well-turned-out young lady among others. The evening was jolly chatty if somewhat strange since there was no introduction, it was not until I was ready to leave that mother said rather loudly:

"Are you not going to take home your daughter?" that everything became clear. Mother had set me up by arranging the meeting to bring me face to face with the daughter I did not know. Mother was never able to handle delicate situations properly and this occasion was no exception. She just dropped me in it so that I sunk to the lowest depth with shame and embarrassment. The result turned out to be the best thing for me. It rekindled the friendship with Carmen, I found a loving and caring daughter and a grandson, my daughter's only child, in whose life I was able to play a role.

There would be other marriages that produced other children but the one that would show me most love and care even though we are separated geographically. Even as I write this it rings true that she crossed over 5,000 miles to be at my sick bedside.

In fact, daughter Yvette turned out to be the backbone of the family. At the behest of my mother, before she died in 2011, Yvette would become one of three Executors to her will. The other two Executors soon became dysfunctional leaving it all to my dear daughter to see through to the end a rather complicated and burdensome will. Along the way, it was my daughter who picked up the complete responsibility for my brother, Raymond, who was 56-year-old at the time of my mother's death. Since arriving in England from Jamaica when he was eight years old, Raymond was placed on the books of the London Borough of Camdem as a person with learning difficulties. For a significant period of years following mother's death, and under the auspices of the Power of Attorney bestowed upon her for the welfare of my brother, she provided accommodation, guidance, and care for Raymond.

Eventually, the accommodation aspect ceased when my mother's will was settled thus releasing funds to purchase a home for my brother. However, the administrative responsibilities of managing his home and daily life remain in the care and responsibility of my daughter. It is my daughter who, for example, organized his many trips (together with his lady friend of similar status) to visit me here in Jamaica.

It makes it more significant when it is realized that Yvette who has her own aging mother for whom to care, her own domestic household, a job to hold on to was, nevertheless, able to cross thousands of miles at the drop of a hat to be at my hospital bedsides.

I am in no doubt, whatsoever, that it is this showing on the part of my daughter that jointly with my home helper, Miss Venecia Johnson (the best there is) that brought me back to life from what was diagnosed as a very serious illness.

Yvette

Yvette grew up to be a beautiful and intelligent young lady who has independently established herself with great admiration. For much of the time, Yvette earned her living from show-business: in the theater, or in the classroom as a teacher and as an administrator in various fields. Ironically, Yvette would be the next person to connect with Orville in a telephone conversation to be followed up. The follow-up call never came, and the contact was once more lost.

Yvette gave me my first grandson, Jordan.

Jordan—my grandson

Jordan, in turn, gave me my first great grandchildren, Jessica and Joshua in that order.

Left to right are: my daughter's mother, Carmen; greatgrand daughter, Jessica; daughter Yvette; great grandson, Joshua and Yvette's partner, Theo—at dad, granddad and great granddad's home in Jamaica 2023.

Back in Coventry, life was real again. Melvinder had no friends simply because our circumstances and the shortness of time did not allow for friendship making. Melvinder thought of finding a job, but it was not much that she could do given her limited qualification. Eventually, she landed a job as a Library Assistant working in one of Coventry's libraries and then life was not all that boring after all. Additionally, a former boss, Mary Stewart, introduced us to a member of her staff. He taught Spanish at her new School in Birmingham but lived in Coventry. In time, Lois Cabrera, his wife Gabri and two children Carmen and Angelica became very close friends, especially Melvinder.

We did many things together including our first trip to Norway and at home back in Coventry, we spent time together seeing great musicals such as, 'My

Fair Lady,' 'Hello Dolly,' 'The Sound of Music,' 'Funny Lady,' and super films, such as 'Guess Who is Coming to Dinner,' 'In the Heat of the Night,' 'To Sir with Love,' and Alfred Hitchcock's 'The Birds.' Melvinder was now a great deal livelier and, in her own time and ways, began to expand her friendship circle all of which helped to take her mind off the circumstances of her parents and kinship.

More than a month had passed since our honeymoon in North Wales, more than three months since our marriage, but my wife was not pregnant. As time went by, I was beginning to wonder if anything was wrong with my sperm count. I was 36 years of age. We decided to give it another couple of months and if nothing happened, I would see my General Practitioner to arrange for a sperm count test. That day eventually came. The clinic said that there was nothing whatsoever wrong with my sperm. There was a lot of vigor there. Maybe it was just impatience and anxiety on our part. We should patiently wait and keep on trying.

The main reason my marriage to Bronwyn had ended was that Bronwyn hated children and ruled out having any of her own. She was up front about this on the very first day we met. Somehow, the fire of the new relationship, then, made me overlook her position on children and nevertheless conceitedly believed I could change her one day. There came a point when my persistence in pursuit of children was constantly met with excuses all about low funds and a string of debts. These debts were rapidly paid off given that both Bronwyn and I were full-time teachers, and I was a part-time professional dancer. We were no longer broke. Bronwyn then gave in to my persuasion and we began trying for a child.

Well, that was what I thought until I accidentally discovered that Bronwyn had taken to deceiving me. That day in Malagra, southern Spain, when I discovered that all along Bronwyn was secretly on the birth control pill, signaled the end of our marriage. Memory of this previous very painful episode in my life made me wonder to myself whether my current situation could be a Bronwyn's trick all over again. However, there was nothing whatsoever in our life at that time to justify that suspicion other than the 'once bitten' theory. The idea was rightly banished irretrievably from my mind.

Bourne Hall Clinic

Blocked Fallopian Tube to In-Vitro Fertilization

Not only was Melvinder not getting pregnant, but she was frequently having excruciating pains in the stomach area. Several trips to our General Practitioner revealed no cause. Yet, the pains continued and went off for several months. On one morning, it was so bad for her that I had to insist on a home visit from the doctor. The doctor took his time getting to our home and when he did get there, he told Melvinder it was just psychological, and she probably didn't want to have sexual intercourse.

When the doctor left, the pains became even more unbearable. I didn't think the doctor could be right, so I got my wife into our car and drove her to the emergency section of the Walsgrave hospital on the eastern edge of Coventry. It was the luckiest thing that we ever did. The doctor who attended to her, reported that one of Melvinder's fallopian tubes was so badly blocked it was only minutes away from bursting inside her and might have killed her. This tube had to be removed immediately and completely. The other tube had blockages too, but not nearly as bad. It was cleaned up and she would have to function with just one tube.

With just one tube, Melvinder very quickly experienced an ectopic pregnancy. She was rushed back into the same hospital where she had an operation to remove her second tube. Melvinder now had no fallopian tube. And both of us wanted children, so badly! Thanks to the Almighty, however, she had her life. Secondarily, however, it seemed that I was destined not to have children in wedlock. One marriage ended mainly because of my wife's adamant refusal to have children. She was so against the idea that she was driven to deceit. The break-up of that marriage had left its scars on me, and I will never know to what degree it has affected my outlook on life generally.

Certainly, Melvinder's appearance in my life, at the time she did, was a rich tonic for my mind, body, and soul. My hopes on the children's front had been rekindled. Even after all those problems, which we had gone through, and the entire trauma suffered on our way to the altar, Melvinder had injected new adrenaline into me. Melvinder's interest in children was as deep as mine, if not deeper. Nothing could possibly go wrong now, that was what I had thought. Thus, it was a soul shocking disappointment to face the truth that my wife could not now bear children the usual way. We would just have to allow the reality of this to sink in and record our joint reaction through time: find some way to be optimistic about life on a broader basis.

Chapter 9
Patrick Steptoe and Robert Edwards

All this happened soon after Patrick Steptoe, the world-famous gynecologist, who had joined forces with the Cambridge Scientist Robert Edwards in 1966, eventually produced the world's first so-called 'test-tube' baby girl. Louise Joy Brown was the scientists' first success at in vitro experimentation at their Cambridge private clinic. Just after the Louise Brown miracle on July 25th, 1978, the reported success rate for in vitro fertilization (IVF) was not high. In fact, it was more than disappointingly low. So, that we turned to Mr. Steptoe in our hour of desperation and gloom gave fresh meaning to 'the drowning man and the straw.'

We had no idea that it would have been so easy to meet with Mr. Steptoe. A telephone call to the well-publicized Bourn Hall Clinic, at Bourn in Cambridge, was all we needed, and we were well on our way to an arranged meeting with the great man. He made notes regarding our desires, medical histories, and my wife's gynecological condition. A further meeting was arranged for a non-invasive keyhole surgery (laparoscopy) to examine my wife's ovaries and for me to provide a sperm sample for sperm count purposes.

Once it was ascertained that my wife's ovaries were sound and that my sperm count was what it should be, we heard just what we wanted to hear from Mr. Steptoe. He advised us that, in the circumstances, and given that my wife was still very young, he saw no reason why an in vitro fertilization attempt might not succeed. This brought joy to our lives by way of hope once more although there was still a long way to go and there was no absolute guarantee of success.

Cambridge was a long way from Coventry. Largely because most of the journey was cross-country, it took approximately six hours to go there and back. Given our motivation that was a small matter. We had already done two of these journeys and were well prepared to take on any necessary others.

We didn't have a lot of money in the bank. In settling my earlier broken marriage, I had to put myself in extra debts to buy out Bronwyn's interest in the Lady Margaret Road property. Upon moving to Coventry, and with the Lady Margaret Road property not sold, it was necessary to incur further debts to obtain the mortgage on Aldbury Rise. Debts and high interest payments were accumulating. Now, Mr. Steptoe has stated that we would need to find £2,000 up front to cover all the cost of the IVF procedures. We assured Mr. Steptoe that we would have the money. He then advised my wife of the routines that she will need to carry out at home to identify the appropriate time to come into the clinic for the IVF procedures to begin.

Early in 1979, Mr. Steptoe took the first egg from my wife's ovary, fertilized it in a Petri dish using a sample of my sperm and at the appropriate stage of growth and development, implanted the fetus in my wife's uterus for nature to take its course. All we had to do now is to wait. We waited hopefully for several weeks before my wife's menses indicated the failure of our first attempt at in vitro fertilization. We were determined to try again, especially when we recalled what Mr. Steptoe had said to us about my wife's youthful chances. This would mean another £2,000, which was a lot of money in the seventies and eighties for people like us. There was no doubt that we were feeling the financial strain.

However, our desire to have a child domesticated those pressures. We would find the money. If the second attempt was to fail, we thought we would have to consider the possibility of adopting. We knew that adopting a child could be a long and drawn-out affair. For this reason, toward the latter part of 1979, we submitted ourselves to be vetted and considered as potential adopting parents. The Coventry Social Services department considered us willingly. They began the process almost immediately and after all the interviews and inspections, there followed a sufficiently long period of silence, we almost forgot our application. I certainly did.

Part way through 1980, we raised sufficient funds for our second attempt at IVF. Now there would be a repeat of home routines, traveling from Coventry to Cambridge several times and eventually the clinical procedures, which would place us back on waiting orders to see whether we succeed or fail. Let me not delay the truth: it failed for a second time. My wife and I were now beginning to think that we would never succeed in having a child of our own.

How strange can life be? Here we are, two people keenly desirous of having children, yet nature and fate are in blatant conspiracy against this ever happening. I started to wonder whether, if Bronwyn was as keen as Melvinder was, there would be these kinds of physical problems. Come to think of it, we closed the chapter on that relationship without me ever knowing why Bronwyn never wanted children. It simply was never a topic which we saw fit to discuss rationally. I never even knew if she could have children. I guess I will never know the answer to that question.

Adopting James

One day while sitting in the Coventry courts as a magistrate late in 1981, the clerk to our Bench passed up a note to me. It read, "Please telephone home as soon as possible." It sounded urgent so as soon as the case, which we were trying, was concluded, I used the telephone in the Magistrates' room to call my wife. She was excited about something.

"You will never guess what," she said. I did not have time for a guessing game since we had other cases to be tried. The Bench had only taken a pause to let me make that call.

"I have to get back in court," I stressed impatiently. It was then that she told me that the Coventry Social Services had rung earlier that day to inform us that they had a male child, about three years old, for whom they consider that we might make suitable parents. Melvinder's great excitement and bubbling enthusiasm infectiously transferred themselves to me over the telephone. I joined my other two colleagues on the Bench beaming with obvious joy all over my face. Part of the reason I was so carried away has to do with the naked fact that I had completely forgotten about our application to Social Services. Every time the whole thing seemed to die; new life seemed to be injected from somewhere. I wasn't grumbling.

I completed my day on the Bench and hurried home to share in the excitement and joy. It was good to see Melvinder in such a joyous mood. Since starting her job at the library, she had made more and more friends. She would sometimes go out with these friends, or they would sometimes come around to the house. Life was becoming more and more normal for her. She would laugh more frequently and hold long discourses on the telephone each passing day. I was most pleased to see that kind of development for her, especially knowing that her two or three attempts to reconnect with her parents and siblings had been spurned and that she was persona none gratis as far as they were concerned.

Even if it was not part of her reasoning for wanting children at first, I do know that since she realized that she was totally rejected by her family, there was this greater sense of urgency for having children of her own. She honestly felt that children would be the key to reopening those closed doors to her parents and siblings. She did not think that her parents would be able to turn their backs upon their grandchildren. For the past two years hope and hopelessness have been alternating for her, but she managed to stay focused on her burning ambition. Once more a bit of hope has emerged from nowhere and she is now happiness personified.

Social Services told us that the child would come to us in stages. The first stage would be in November 1981 for a period of three weeks and then they would take the child from us again. That didn't sound sensible to us in terms of the child's mental and physical stability; but then I was sure there must have been method in their madness. James came to us as planned, bright and early one chilly November morning.

James—at Start

We had had two weeks' notice of his intended arrival, so we had managed some preparation, including getting some warm clothing and some toys, to receive him. James was a beautiful child. He had the appearance of not been well cared for: probably because his life was not really settled. He was born on the 6th of July 1978 to his white English mother who cared for him all this time. His father, an Asian man, had been pulled from the scene by his own family to be married off in a culturally arranged marriage. Therefore, James had been brought up for the three years and four months thus far without daddy's input. James was placed with Social Services for adoption by his mother because she had met someone of her own race who wished to marry her but, for him, the child was an obstacle.

The next stage would come at an adoption hearing in the Coventry courts in February 1982. If the courts confirmed the adoption, we saw or knew of no reason why they wouldn't, James would come to live with us as our own lawfully adopted son. It was not for us to question Social Services as to how they determined 'suitability,' but it would take no great feat in imagination to figure out that the Asian factor to both this child and my marriage would have influenced their decision.

Expecting the World's First Test-Tube Twins

James was lovely, warm, cuddly, and adorable. As parents, we were going to have a great deal of fun bringing him up as family. We were now looking forward to February and the adoption hearing with great expectation. Yet, always lingering at the back of my mind was the regret that we were not able to have a child with our own genes. We had often heard stories of couples who were having difficulties producing children for no obvious reason and when once they successfully go through the process of adopting a child, the women in these circumstances suddenly conceive. Would this be the case with us, we wondered? And that was how we came to be, having one last try at Mr. Steptoe's clinic toward the end of November 1981.

We had emptied the last penny from savings so that we could put together this final £2,000 to enable the procedure for the third time. This time Mr. Steptoe took and fertilized more than one egg from my wife's ovaries. At the appropriate time he made multiple implants of two eggs inside her womb. We were, once again, left to wait while nature would take its course. We waited and waited until more than a month had passed. She did not begin her menstrual cycle. And bingo! Our GP confirmed my wife was pregnant. It turned out that both eggs succeeded so we were expecting the world's first black 'test-tube' twins.

It took so much pain, disappointments, humiliation, and sorrow just to get us to this point of promised joy at last. However, other developments were of a compensatory nature.

Chapter 10
History Repeated

Around the middle of June 1982, one Monday evening, my wife and I were entertaining some of my colleagues from school. Dinner was over and James had just gone to bed while we sat around chatting with our guests. There were three of them. Time passed quickly and it was just minutes away from midnight when our telephone rang. Melvinder took the call. It was her sister, Pinky on the other end. She was not calling from home because, that same day, she had run away with her Muslim boyfriend, Taj. She and Taj feared that Terry had an idea where Taj was living at that time and, therefore, could not risk be going to Taj's place. Terry would have, by then, had a posse of Sikh men out looking for them just as he once did to us. That was why they had fled, about 25 or so miles across London, from the danger areas to Croydon in Surrey, from where they were calling us to seek our help and assistance.

It was awfully quick thinking on Melvinder's part to take the number of the telephone box from which they were calling and asked them to hang around that kiosk and listen for the phone to ring. There was something strikingly familiar about that move. It might take a little while, she warned them. At that time of night and in that area, the chances were that not many people would be waiting to use the telephone box. To younger readers, it might be helpful to remind you that the mobile telephone wasn't commonly available until about five or six years later. People who did not have a telephone in their homes or who happened to be out when they needed to make a call had to rely on British Telecommunication roadside telephones or those in other public places to make their calls.

I must admit, that after Melvinder privately told me what the call was about, I became obviously anti-social; but even so, our guests did not read the signs and tarried well beyond midnight. The minute the last of the guests went,

Melvinder began calling that number, but the phone was engaged. Who could be using the phone at that time of night? Melvinder tried two or three minutes later but this time the phone rang out for about five minutes with no one answering.

Taj and Pinky had gone in search of another phone kiosk when the first one had been taken over by another user, for what seemed to them like years. At the times we were trying to get them, they were trying to get us desperately. At last, their call came through. We asked them to identify where they were, and we would come and get them. It was almost 01:00 and I had school that day. Croydon, I estimated, was nearly 300 miles away from Bradford. Melvinder was heavily pregnant, and no ordinary pregnancy either; James was fast asleep. But we had to help! We were once in similar circumstances and others helped us. Without further hesitation, I quickly backed our brand-new Toyota Crown out of the garage while Melvinder warmly wrapped the sleeping James and carried him to the waiting car.

We sped off into the night and hurriedly rowed back onto the motorways. The motorways and even the ordinary roads were almost empty of traffic. We could not say if we broke any speed limits, but no cops stopped us and by 04:00 that Tuesday we arrived at the pre-determined meeting spot in Croydon and there they were Taj and Pinky huddled together against the chilly night. On the return journey, we discovered that Pinky had never lost touch with us. She had followed our progress in the popular press and other media outlets.

One of the newspapers had mentioned the name of the road on which the new head and his wife were living in Bradford. Fortunately for her, there was only one Duncan living on that road in Bradford. Taj, on an earlier trip to Bradford to see friends, had checked out the telephone directory for our number. One day that might come in useful, they thought; and it did.

It occurred to me as we hastily made our way back that if Taj and Pinky could keep track of us the way they did, others could have done the same. In that case, I am now not so certain that it was such a good idea to have these two lovers come to us. We must not have a repeat of Coventry. Pinky's parents and family would have likely considered that our place would be a potential sanctuary for them, and they would be right. I decided that I shall have to put some precautionary measures in place. By the time we reached the outskirts of Bradford, the early morning traffic was beginning to get thick.

If I was to get to school on time, I would need to negotiate the back roads to home. I made it with just enough time to drop off my four passengers and turn around for the journey to school. I didn't want to be late, especially in view of my lateness policy for the school. I wasn't but had had nothing to eat and had driven about 600 miles without sleep.

I called S.F. a powerful and well-placed friend of mine. She knew the background and when she heard about the present situation, she was certain that I would need police protection. She was a friend of Bradford's Chief Executive Officer and said I was to leave it with her. That evening a police officer in plain clothes called at the house to see me and my wife. He later talked to Taj and Pinky. What we learned from the officer was that there would be some undercover police activities around us night and day and that we should not be unduly alarmed.

As it turned out, the couple stayed with us for exactly ten days. Taj made a couple of trips to London by train but was always back the same day. In the end, he lapsed into false security, became bored, and decided that they would then brave it back to London. It was beneath the Sikhs to have one of their own jumping their culture to become involved romantically with a Muslim. The only thing worse than that was to replace a Muslim with a 'black.'

We knew that, and Pinky knew that, and we all advised Taj. However, Taj, a young and stubborn Muslim man decided that they would go back to London. Bradford did not have the same vibrancy which London had. That move, admittedly, removed some stress and pressures from our household at a time when Melvinder really didn't need them. But we were rather sorry to learn that within days of returning to London, Pinky was recaptured by Terry and others while she was out shopping near the Taj's home. Taj, it was reported, was savagely beaten up at the same time. To the day Melvinder and I separated some nineteen years later, we had not heard anything from or from Pinky.

The Arrival of the Test-Tube Twins by Cesarean Birth

On the 16th of August 1982, my wife gave cesarean birth to the world's first black 'test-tube' twins at the Bradford Royal Infirmary.

The world's media were present at the Infirmary from the day before hoping to get a picture of the twins when they arrived. The birth was reported as far away as Canada, the United States of America, and Australia. I wanted, as the father, to witness the birth, but by the time I had penetrated the media frenzy and persistence, I had missed it all and had to make do with seeing them for the first time in their tiny cot and incubator. Natasha, at just over 4lbs, could be fed independently: she was in the tiny cot, but Nathan weighed in at only 2lbs and needed incubator care for several days, even after their mother and Natasha were discharged. It became part of my daily routine to go to the hospital twice daily to see, hold and feed Nathan until he, too, was discharged.

That day came, and soon all of us were at home: we just had to learn how best to live with the media frenzy as it gradually became less and less over the next three years, stories about the historical birth of the twins and of my historical headship appointment alternating and sometimes running simultaneously. The last reporter from the local BBC studio was with them for the last time on their third birthday. A nice thing about the media attention was that they never neglected Jamie. They always covered him from some appropriate angle, which fitted in with their stories. Both Melvinder and I resolved that it would be necessary to keep James' inevitable jealousy to its barest minimum; after all, two 'strangers' had just invaded his 'private' space.

The Royal Garden Party—Buckingham Palace

For a while, everything at home was peaceful and blissful. To top it, we had received an invitation from Her Majesty the Queen via The Lord Chamberlain to a regular garden party at Buckingham Palace. The garden party was on Wednesday, 27th July 1983 from 16:00 to 18:00.

It was a lovely and enjoyable afternoon, and we had the opportunity to talk to both HRH the Prince of Wales and Lady Diana. Lady Diana was graciously interested in knowing how far we had traveled to be there and what we would be doing after the garden party had ended. The prince (now the King) was surprised to learn that I was at the University of Wales at the same time as he even though at different colleges, he at Aberystwyth and I at Swansea. He thought that I must have been "a mature student!" He was right.

The Queen, Prince Phillip, and many other members of the royal family were present. After the party was over, we took the Princess's suggestion and had a lovely meal in one of London's finest restaurants before returning to Bradford.

Things at home and at school remained normal for a long while. We were having many distinguished visitors including Dr. Sally Tomlinson of the Oxford Education Department and Professor Lynch of Sunderland Polytechnic

(I was later to become a consultant in multicultural and anti-racist Education at the education department at Sunderland Polytechnic) to learn about our application and implementation of multicultural education at Wyke Manor. I had been called upon numerous times to assist other schools' teachers' in-service development programs around the topic of multicultural education. These were spread out right across the country and included six trips to various parts of Scotland. The real effect of this for me was that it all loaned credibility to what I was doing at Wyke Manor.

Chapter 11

Hell's Doors Open

RACISM

The happenstance of some strange occurrences and events indicated that there would be unwelcome changes at Wyke Manor Upper School. The omen was ominous.

A. On about three different occasions, I received anonymous letters through the school mail. They tended to be very unpleasant and mainly insulting about my race. They were usually saying things such as: "Nigger, get out of our country," or sentiments to that effect. I was never unduly worried about such things because I had heard of this happening to prominent black people all around the country and it was, therefore, unlikely that I would be an exception. Very interestingly, one of these anonymous mailings was a colorful postcard arriving during the summer break. At such a time, many of my colleagues would have been scattered all around some scenic countryside or on exotic foreign adventures enjoying their well-earned holiday breaks.

That card which arrived from a popular foreign holiday destination, France, was clearly meant to be a challenge to my authority. It pictorially depicted a natural layout and placement of granite rocks, of various sizes, which seemed to have withstood the ceaseless torrential beatings of waters falling on, beating against, and flowing through them creating an intricate network of meandering waterways. The sender's cursive inscription pointedly asked: "Who will go first, the water or the rock, my man?" The card was addressed to me.

B. However, things became exceptionally bad when one morning I arrived at school to discover that a brick had been thrown through the window to my office. There were glass splinters everywhere and my office looked like the scene of a motor car accident. The offending brick had landed on my desk. It had a message wrapped around it, which read: "Nigger, go home."

To this day, I remain almost certain that I recognized the 'n' and the 'h' in that note, and it wasn't from a pupil. During one of the school holidays, as already mentioned, someone sent me a postcard daring me to challenge my authority. The anonymous sender had written on the face of the card: *"Which will give way first, the rock or the water, my man?"*

The 'h' on the message around the brick was identical to those four used on the postcard and the 'n' was also identical to the only one used on that card. The police team from Bradford were called in and the previously received anonymously written postcard and other notes sent via the post were also handed to them, but according to Chief Inspector Larry Holms who led the police team, they had no way of telling who the culprits were. It seemed that they were powerless to do anything beyond taking notes presumably for forensic purposes.

A black man in distress, it seemed, did not merit pulling out the extra stops; did not justify going the extra mile to identify the offenders. I had expected the police would have wanted to know the holiday destinations of all the teachers that summer in 1982. Handwriting samples should have been gathered given the alphabetical commonality employed in some of the messages which were sent to me. But none of these happened and consequently, we never heard again from the police. We, in schools, must repair these shortcomings which clearly reflect the prior schooling that present-day police officers received. This is very much a job for the school curriculum aided by decent-minded members of the nation everywhere coupled with expertly given training.

The incident was reported instantly to the education office in Bradford. They in turn, from a distance, instructed the school's caretaker to replace the broken window immediately, which he did. The next morning on arrival at school, however, I discovered that the recently replaced window was shattered once more. This time a plank of rotten wood had been thrown through it as if to underpin the determination of the beastly culprit to obliterate my presence. There was no message on this second occasion. For reasons which were obvious, we did not bother to involve the police. They had previously declared powerlessness. Yet, again, the authority was informed. They responded this time, by sending a junior-ranked Education Officer to see for himself.

The officer simply advised the caretaker to have the window replaced once more and to have a shutter built over it, and as far as he was concerned, that was the end of the story. There was no desire to get to the bottom of these happenings around the authority's new and single black headteacher. The shutter should then be shut and bolted at night. Like a caged animal I was now the only headteacher in all of Bradford who had to operate from behind bars. The hellish and determined bigot was not to be defeated. The very next morning, the shutter was covered with racist graffiti and some of the foulest language you could imagine, all negatively aimed at my racial status.

C. Since the intake of pupils in September of 1982, it became clear that the school's population was undergoing a change in ethnicity. The induction assembly we had for the new intake that September was significantly different from that which I experienced on my second day at the school. This time, I was not standing in front of a sea of only white faces. Among the school's staff, Mr. Rashid and I were no longer the only non-white teachers. The school was changing its complexion character caused by an expansion in numbers and diversity among them. Dotted among the audience of 13- to 18-year-old students were several black and brown faces.

The messages at school assemblies are largely repetitive especially when there are new pupils to the school. It is important that all newcomers to our school should blend into the prevailing ethos of the school as quickly as possible. For those students who have heard the messages before, repetition spells consistency which is a safe way of inculcating the right behavioral attitudes and values even if it borders on the verge of indoctrination. Among all the new faces that September morning was one Alison Taylor. I was oblivious to that fact and certainly, I didn't know the name. However, later that day I would stumble upon these facts and, indeed more interesting facts.

My lunch was interrupted, rightly so, as I enjoyed a home-prepared meal for that lunch hour. This was not a regular thing as I prefer to dine with the pupils in their lunch canteen. Because she was at her middle school the day in April when I stumbled into her family business, I did not meet her. Her mother wanted me to know that she had kept her promise to send her daughter to Wyke. Her mother, Mrs. Marjorie Taylor, had told her to seek out the new head (who was caring and friendly, though, according to early hearsay, very strict) and let him know who you were. That was why this pupil was knocking on my door soon after enrolling at Wyke in September.

She was greeted with the same warmth and courtesy that all other visitors (pupils, parents, staff, and officials) to my office were entitled to receive. It was a sacrosanct part of school policy that pupils wanting to see the headteacher should be facilitated. Hence, Alison encountered no difficulty getting past Madge, my secretary. Readers will recall that several days ago in late August, I received that postcard with the foreign stamp on it. That card with the brazen challenge addressed to me: "THE WATER OR THE ROCK: which will give way first?"

I was rather suspicious about that card and believed a member of the school's staff might have sent it to me while on his/her summer jaunt. I was still curling inside about that accusation about the Queen's picture removal. The circumstantial evidence had pointed to a staff mole. I had no way of telling who sent me that postcard, but I would place the card conspicuously on the wall above the back of my chair. All the people entering my office would see that card above and behind my head as they face me in conversation. I would be watching out for facial expressions.

To my consternation, Alison remembered having once sold two cards like that at her family shop. She had sold them together with another depicting an Oaktree to a man with a short stumpy reddish beard and red hair at the beginning of her summer break. She was able to recognize the similarity because it was the last two like that and she was hoping to use one in a school project until the stranger bought them.

D. In fact, by the September intake of 1984, a fifth of the 1,140 pupils were non-white.

This demographic shift was not confined to pupil intake. Although Wyke Manor Upper School had an extremely stable staff, for example, over the years, one member of staff had sold and bought homes three different times in the village of Wyke so that she didn't have to leave Wyke Manor School. Another proudly bragged that he attended Wyke Manor School as a pupil, went to university in Bradford, did his teaching practice at Wyke Manor School while training to be a teacher, and got his first teaching post at Wyke Manor School where he was still in practice during my tenure: how parochial and insular could one get?

This insularity which characterized many of the school's staff was worrying in relation to the planned scheme of things to come. If the staff had no worthwhile exposure to what the wider world was about; no exposure to Changning values and more modern thinking, it is going to be exceptionally more difficult to move them willingly along with me. Occasionally, the opportunity came by for me to make my own staff appointment by way of replacement or because of increased pupil numbers. One such opportunity came in a very disturbing way. What was clearly a racist action aimed at me turned out to be very beneficial for the school. There was a knock on my office door one day. I shouted, "Please enter."

In walked our Head of Modern Languages. I stood up, as I always did, to receive visitors, no matter who it was.

"What can I do for you, Peter?" I asked.

"I have come to tell you that I cannot take orders from a black man," he said.

I fell back into my chair, not so much because of what he said but because of the directness and boldness with which he said it. His openly racist and honest admission stunned me momentarily. As I re-collected my composure, I said in reply, "But Peter, you have got problems."

Peter started fumbling inside the breast pocket of his jacket, "No, I have no problem," Peter said, as he handed me a brown envelope. He left before I could read its contents. I immediately opened the envelope, which Peter had just handed to me. It read:

"Dear Headmaster,

I hereby resign from my post as Head of Modern Languages at Wyke Manor Upper School to take effect immediately."

This was followed by his signature.

After recovering, I focused on two matters. Firstly, was Peter symptomatic of the rest of the staff? If that was the case, then I wished more of them would be like Peter. At least, he was right out in the open. I didn't have to watch my back with him. His kindness stabs you in the face, not in the back. His kind is easier to manage. The dangerous types were those who befriended you, smiled at you and pretended to be supportive of you and then, behind your back, stabbed you therein without remorse or mercy. This bothered me.

Secondly, there was now an opportunity to appoint someone whose attitude was more akin to what I was trying to do for school. Such a person was more likely to be non-racist in attitude and values. Incremental changes in staff numbers in this way meant that by December 1985, approximately six per cent of the school's 70 teaching and non-teaching staff were non-white. Including me there were now four non-white teachers at Wyke Manor. Life will not be easy for them as they were among some colleagues, some parents, and some students whose learning, upbringing and socialization is tainted with white supremacy while regarding non-whites at any strata of society as inferior.

At least, however, they will have shoulders on which to cry, unlike Mr. Rashid's experiences in years gone by. Far more worrying is the fate which belies the non-white pupils joining the school since my appointment. I bore some personal responsibility for their welfare. Deep down, I know they would not have come from so far away just to be at this school had it not been for the almost lasting streams of publicity surrounding my appointment and presence at the school. My early assessment was that these pupils were likely to have problems born out of bigotry thrown at them by some staff and some of their peers.

This was an important part of the reasoning behind my open-door policy, especially for my pupils. They would need my protection, encouragement, and support in the years ahead. This duty turned out to be nearly impossible at times. Firstly, the school had rules which must be followed for the good of all users. Secondly, I have a duty of care to all my students; and I must dispense equitable justice in all circumstances no matter what the complexion of the student. To illustrate this tight rope conundrum, I recount here the two most striking events for me in a single day. The day I was accused of being a racist by a white pupil and later that same day in an unrelated incident being accused by a black pupil of being a racist. It was a well-established rule laid down by previous management that, except in times of inclement weather, all pupils should vacate the school buildings and go outside for the duration of the break times.

A rota of teachers, including the headteacher, was identified to enforce this rule against pupil reluctance. A black fifteen-year-old girl (BG), for reasons best known to herself, at morning break that day, decided to remain in one of the many classrooms. It was on my duty route. I questioned her decision for wanting to remain inside on such a lovely day and required her to join the rest of the school outside. She insisted that she would not leave the classroom, and I was even more determined that she would honor the rules of the school. It was then that I was confronted with an outburst, which, to this day, is hard for me to decipher.

"Why must I go outside: is it because I am black?" The young lady enquired.

My only response was, pointing to my skin, "What color do you think this is?" She then quietly exited the building. I was then left to ponder how this could be real. Clearly, to this young girl, for whom racism is a real part of her daily life, racism is something which comes from those in authority, no matter their complexions. The task ahead is even greater than I had imagined.

That same day, when it was lunch hour, as I often do, convenience allowing, I went to the canteen to have lunch with my pupils. It was a great way to assist in maintaining social order and getting to know pupils on a one-to-one basis. Everything was going smoothly until a white boy (WB) suddenly burst through the canteen's double doors. He ignored several of his other white peers who were queuing for their lunches and went directly to the sole Asian girl about three spaces from being served. Without much ado, he forced himself in front of the Asian pupil with total disregard and utter disrespect for the pupils in front of whom he then stood.

This was not the kind of school I wanted to be a part of at any time. Without further hesitation, I left my partially finished lunch and approached the offending boy with instructions to apologize to the pupils behind him and to go directly to the rear of the queue immediately. This white boy then accused me of picking on him and siding with the Asian girl. He then removed himself from the canteen altogether and, seemingly, had no lunch that day.

That was a punishment he inflicted upon himself, as far as I was concerned, and therefore merited no further consideration. However, it was far more than disconcerting that, here I was, a black man with the ultimate authority in that school being accused of racism twice in one day first by a black girl and secondly by a white boy: the very cancer which I have pledged to irradicate. Racism can be a convenient fence behind which to hide, it must be noted. But such convenient usage must never get in the way of tackling this pernicious evil wherever it appears.

E. Mine and Melvinder's finances were somewhat shaky because of mortgage commitments in London, Coventry and now Bradford and we were still paying the hire purchase debt on our new Toyota Crown not forgetting that we have five mouths to feed. Therefore, when I saw an advert in a Sunday newspaper where an agency of Corn Hill *Insurance*, Chapel Ash, was recruiting representatives to build and manage a team of 'Managed Fund' salespersons in their own spare time. I jumped at the opportunity to eke out my earnings. I made good of this opportunity and that attracted a great deal of publicity in the financial media.

The progress I was making in my spare time even encouraged some head-hunting competition between Legal and General and Cornhill companies for my services. The word was out that I was an 'Insurance' salesman. I never appreciated the extent to which this was being viewed negatively by some until one Sunday morning when there was an unexpected knock on my front door. We had hardly gotten out of bed. It was my line manager, JA, the 13+ Assistant Director of Education. JA had never visited me before, not even at the school since my appointment was much less on a Sunday morning while I was still dressed in my pajamas. He was trying hard to be pleasant, but he wasn't doing a great job of it. He was the leopard still with its spots. He clearly did not like me. He and one member of the governing body of my school had always disapproved of my appointment for reasons best known to them. I discovered this because, behind the scenes, their actions did not match their face-to-face hypocritical attempts at pleasantries. This was more so in JA's case than in the case of the governor, who, in the end, made his attitude clear to my face and in a public governors' meeting.

I invited JA to come in and sat him in the living room while I quickly changed out of my pajamas and joined him. He went straight to the point. He had received word to the effect that I was working as an insurance salesman. I confirmed that I was involved in a 'Managed Fund' activity.

In that case, he said, "I am here to tell you that the authority views this as a matter of conflicting interest requiring a choice to be made." I told him that I would consider my decision and politely showed him the door. The audacity of the man: why did he think a black man's private home was his to invade at the most private of times? This could be explained only in terms of white supremacy bigotry. That same morning, I wrote to the Director of Education to confirm the meeting with JA and to advise him that with immediate effect, I have ceased my 'Managed Fund' activities. There really was no need for me to be pushed down this road, but I needed to avoid any form of scandal which would divert me from my purpose at Wyke Manor. Also, I was only too mindful of the contemporaneous scandal surrounding another Bradford school—Drummond Middle School—and its headteacher—Ray Honeyford. I did not wish Wyke Manor to be similarly distracted.

Richard Knight was one of the nation's top educationalists at the time, I had great respect for him, and it was important to me that my marginal activity did not bring any political pressures to his desk. I am glad I did because, as it later turned out, JA had sent a letter to a prominent local politician about me to the effect that I was reprimanded for selling insurance; just what I would have expected from someone like JA, and the same letter was mysteriously leaked (surprise! surprise!) to the press in a clear attempt, to discredit me as a black headteacher.

Then, there was the Ray Honeyford saga. Drummond Middle School in inner-city Bradford, in 1984, had 95 % of its pupils from ethnic minorities, mainly Muslims. The headteacher was Ray Honeyford, at the time. He was white. It was reported that he was against the concept of multiculturalism and said so in a low-circulation right-wing periodical called The Salisbury Review. There, he argued, Asian pupils, such as those in his school, should integrate into the British way of life. He criticized the Asian culture and way of life and ridiculed the Asian settlements as Asian ghettos.

All this was happening soon after Bradford had elected the country's first Asian Lord Mayor, Mr. Mohammed Ajeeb, who had pledged to use his office and all his efforts to bring about racial harmony in Bradford. The parents from his school and no doubt other interested agitators persistently demonstrated and picketed outside his school daily with placards calling for the removal of the headteacher and denouncing him as "Ray Cist." The Lord Mayor was sympathetic to the views of the parents and brought political pressures to bear on the situation at Drummond. Ray Honeyford was first suspended from his school and eventually sacked from his position as headteacher and never practiced again. None of this was good for me at Wyke Manor Upper School.

F. One Monday morning, as I arrived at the school gate, waiting for me there were six of our white parents. They did not want to be seen in the school, so they came very early so they could catch me going in that morning. Each of them handed me an envelope and remarked that all my parents (just the white ones, as it turned out) had received these or will be receiving them. All six were copies of the same letter, which they believed was drafted by someone in the school in conjunction with one of the school's governors and some local politicians (and I believed someone at the education office).

The letter asked parents what it was that the headteacher at Wyke Manor was doing with our children in the name of multicultural education. It insisted that parents should notice what 'they' were doing to one of 'ours' (a reference to Ray Honeyford) at Drummond School. 'You' (meaning the parents of Wyke Manor) should be doing the same to one of theirs (a reference to me). Motivated by racism and a not so obscured hint of revenge, enemies from within the school together with like-minded bigots from the political sector as well as the education department and from the governing body of the school were clearly in cahoots to destroy me.

So much so that they have conspiratorially gone to the trouble of seeking to incite the parents of Wyke Manor into action against me even in circumstances of no provocation on my part. I am pleased to report that the parents did nothing, at least, not in the way the instigators desired. The only reaction came from just those six parents who felt so strongly against what was obviously a case of injustice aimed at me, they felt it necessary to draw my attention to what was happening around me secretively. I believed that the parents failed to respond to the attempted incitement because they had all met me and understood my educational philosophies, of which they largely approved.

Personally, while I found it professionally necessary and proper to keep out of the affairs of other schools, especially political ones, I did sympathize with my primary colleague when he stressed the need for all children to learn English in a community and nation that measures achievements through the English language. I didn't, however, find that that pursuit meant abandoning the language, culture, and other inheritance from elsewhere across the globe to achieve it. Better still, whatever your convictions, you can hold steadfast to them without disparaging the culture and circumstances of others. Even so and although I stayed out of it, it nevertheless found me.

G. **THE CHRISTOPHER PERRY AFFAIR**:
Events were happening so fast that everything was now overlapping. The previous week, one of my teachers went off on long-term illness (more than three days). The Teaching Unions did not support the use of existing staff to cover more than three days of long-term illness. The headteacher was expected to use his Supply teachers' budget to buy in a Supply teacher from the Authority's pool for the duration of the illness identified.

In this case, I knew the illness was likely to last a month or more. The Authority's Supply Teachers' Pool sent me a Supply teacher, as requested. That Supply teacher was Mr. Christopher Perry. Mr. Perry was sophisticated and well-spoken. He had an Oxford accent and was not trendy. He gave the appearance of being a strict Union member (The National Union of Teachers—the NUT). He was white.

The other staff trusted him and in no time, he appeared to be part of Wyke Manor Upper School. After Mr. Perry was at the school for about three weeks, I returned from a headteachers' meeting to find a letter addressed to the headteacher on my desk. It was marked 'private and confidential'. Inside the envelope was a separate note-paper-clipped to another letter. That letter was addressed to the chief executive of the city of Bradford with copies to the director of education, Mr. Richard Knight, and the headmaster of Wyke Manor School, Mr. Carlton Duncan. The note explained that Mr. Perry had wished that he was able to speak to me in person first, but he did not know when I would return and as he was so incensed, he needed to act while the iron was still red hot.

How I wished that he had waited to see me. All hell broke loose uncontrollably from that point. Mr. Perry, in the letter to Bradford's Chief Executive, disclosed that in a recent Union meeting (the NUT) held at the school, he heard certain members of my staff, who he named in the letter, making racist remarks about the Headmaster of Wyke Manor Upper School while the headteacher was absent from the school.

One Department Head was alleged to have spoken rather disparagingly about my family, myself, and the 'test-tube' process involved in the birth of my children. Apparently, he had a test-tube vial demonstrating his imagined procedures. One other staff was alleged to have questioned the ability of a black man to lead the school. Mr. Perry had noted all this and left the meeting to do what he did. The staff obviously felt that he was one of them and that he shared their values. Mr. Perry went on to say in his letter that not one member of the meeting spoke up against such behavior. The remarkable thing is that, had I been in school that day, it might not have happened.

At least not that day; for the simple reason that I was also a NUT member and rarely missed Union meetings. The NUT membership accounted for more than half the total number of the staff. The other two Unions, the National Association of Schoolmasters and Union of Women Teachers (NASUWT) and the Association of Teachers and Lecturers (ATL) had split the remainder between them. If no one from over fifty percent of the staff and my own Union felt able to defend me in my absence, things looked bad.

To pour oil on troubled waters, unknown to anyone in the school (except the pupils involved), trouble was brewing among some of the pupils. The black and brown pupils together with some of their white supporting colleagues were planning a demonstration to take place outside the school gate against racist experiences, which they said that they were experiencing at the hands of white teachers at the school. Certain Organizations from beyond the school were assisting them with their preparation.

Clearly, what was happening reflected the fact that the staff had no experience in dealing with non-white children until my presence begun to attract them to the school. Staff comments, and sometimes attitudes, were found to be offensive and insensitive to some of the pupils. I felt it was a failure on my part that the pupils did not have the confidence in me as their headteacher to bring their concerns to me in the first place. It was only on the day of the demonstration outside our school gate that management at Wyke became aware of what was taking place.

It was at that late stage that I was able to go up to the school gate and address the pupils and the outsiders. I persuaded them in the end that it was doing the school no good to be attracting publicity in that manner. I managed to get them all into the school hall and there listened to their concerns; persuaded the outsiders to leave it all to me, at that point, to find answers. The teachers were now feeling that they were then under attack from Mr. Perry and now the pupils. There was nothing like having years of complacency and hearsay stereotypes unsettled by the real presence of other ethnicities around you to make you suddenly see yourselves as victims.

The NUT members called a meeting at which they passed a resolution asking that the headteacher should remove Mr. Perry from the school and that the headteacher should declare openly his confidence and belief in the staff of the school. I was asked to ignore the fact that I was under fire from some of the staff, to embrace them and declare my confidence in them. At the same time, I should shoot the messenger who stood up for me in those circumstances where no one else did. Did they really believe so much in their education that they remain convinced that black people were that stupid? That was never going to happen. But I had to recognize that it was conceivably possible that some staff might have been wrongly tarnished with the same bigotry brush.

I, therefore, published in the school's daily information sheet that I was sorry about the upheavals of recent days and that I recognized that the muddy waters were engulfing even the innocent for which I was even more sorry but that I had spoken with the Authority, and they agreed with me that an investigation was necessary to clear up the matter. A team of Advisors would come to the school to carry out that investigation as soon as possible. While everyone agreed that the Advisors' course was necessary, the NUT members were not satisfied with my response to their resolution.

They met and passed another resolution, which would go to the NUT headquarters in London asking that I be struck off the membership of the Union. Every NUT member had voted for this resolution. That fact caused me great pain. Mr. 'J' a white male teacher was a probationer teacher who could not find employment anywhere. He had been trying for nearly two years when he heard from an acquaintance that I might have a post going. He came to see me with his problem, and I listened and took pity on him and decided to give him a chance. He was on the staff for only two weeks when all this began. He was a NUT member too. He was at that meeting, which resolved unanimously that I be removed from membership of the Union.

The next day, I summoned him and asked him if he could recall his short history with me. That he could, and did, as he pointed out that I had been like a brother to him. "Then, my brother, why did you vote against me the way you did yesterday?" I asked him.

He said that he just had to follow the other members of the Union. That told me enough about my fellow men. The Yorkshire lads and lasses had closed ranks against Mr. Perry and me: both outsiders. Allan Evans and Shirley Darlington, the top officers of the National NUT Education Section from Hamilton House in London, decided to visit the school to speak with the membership and myself in response to the resolution. Nothing was ever sorted out. No matter how hard the Union Officials tried to make the Membership see their unreasonableness, they would not see it.

They wanted my guts for garters. But I remain in membership of the NUT to this very day. In the meantime, the member of staff for whom Mr. Perry was covering came back from illness. The authority had no further reason to be paying him and, I was made to understand much later, he was written to from the education office with the advice that for his own safety he should not return to the school. A special school event was scheduled for a few days later. I had raised enough funds to launch my community school project. **From the Cradle to the Grave.** All the bigwigs were invited, including the Chief Education Officer, Mr. Knight, the Chairman of Bradford Education Committee, Councilor Eric Pickles, the chairman of governors, Mrs. Doris Birdsall, and the press.

The Opening of the Community Initiative at Wyke Manor Upper School
From Left to Right: The Chairman of the Education Committee, Councilor Doris Birdsall, Chairman of the School's Governors, the Headteacher, Carlton Duncan and Mr. Richard Knight, Chief Education Officer

Mr. Knight was the official guest speaker. We were about half an hour from the start when Mr. Perry was seen approaching the school's gate. He had come to collect his bicycle and other belongings, which he had left behind. Mr.

Knight, himself, approached Mr. Perry and asked him to leave the school premises. Mr. Perry refused on the grounds that he was on public property. Mr. Knight asked the administrative officer to summon the police. The police officer also failed to persuade Mr. Perry to leave voluntarily. As a result, Mr. Perry was arrested by the police officer and charged with conduct likely to lead to a breach of the peace. He would never be able to teach in Bradford again. The launch was then able to take place in the presence of hundreds of people including the press.

> H. Two school days later, a team of six advisors arrived at the school to begin their three days inquiry. JA and the Chief Advisor (female) had put the team together and given them their briefing. Personally, I was rather disappointed in their work and told them as much. All that they did was to ask the named staff if they made these racist remarks against the headteacher. Of course, the staff sensibly denied the charge. It seemed the team was more interested in finding some muck to throw at me. It reminded me of the time when I was having some difficulty with a member of staff and rang JA to seek his support in dealing with this colleague. JA said he would send someone up. Well, someone did come up to the school but not to see the member of staff about whom I had complained. Instead, he was more interested in investigating me and my attitude toward the members of staff. That was his instruction, stated the investigator.

This, too, was rather reminiscent of the Asian people who, in East London, some months before, were experiencing racial attacks. They called for help from the police. When the police arrived, they did little by way of investigations into the attacks upon the Asian victims. Instead, they wanted to see the victims' papers to verify that they were not illegal immigrants, which they were not. The advisors completed their inquiry and sent it to JA who then published their findings. The findings were that the staff of Wyke Manor Upper was cleared of the racism charges. The press made a field day of this. Some papers were so eager to publish that their headlines were incongruous with the stories that they published under them.

Racism probe clears headmaster

Race charges are dismissed

The headlines were in fact damaging to me. Only when it became clear to the paper in question that I was about to sue them that they published a correction and made amends.

I. Could anything more go wrong? Two weeks later, I had to attend the regular headteachers' meeting. On my return to the school, the deputies explained that they were forced to close the school because asbestos was found to be part of the school's fabric in two areas. Because of this, the NUT, followed by the other two unions decided to down tools and their membership walked out. The deputies had no choice but to send the entire pupil population home with a note of explanation to their parents. The school remained closed for almost a week while the authority arranged to have the asbestos removed from the affected areas. The unions did not even offer me the courtesy of waiting until I was back in school before acting.

The truth is that there were forces on the governing body of the school who were working in conjunction with people at the education office, and at the local political level as well as with individual members of the school's staff to undermine and discredit the black headteacher. Only, I wasn't wearing out as readily as the granite rock was under the constant beating of the forest waters shown on that postcard, which, I considered, was sent to me by one of the school's staff, while on a foreign holiday break.

Those tactics failed and so something else had to be tried. That was the purpose behind the leaking of JA' letter which he had written to a prominent local councilor about me. That letter contained a falsehood claiming that I was the subject of a reprimand. No such reprimand was ever directed at me, and my ultimate professional superior did not know of one either. Fortunately, every sensible individual saw through the purpose of that letter and the leaking of it, including the highly respected Director of Education, Mr. Richard Knight, whose press release in response to the leaked letter is reproduced in full below.

City of Bradford Metropolitan Council
Press Information

Claims that Bradford Council was operating "double standards" in its treatment of two headteachers were firmly denied today.

General Secretary of the National Association of Headteachers, Mr. David Hart, said he suspected that the Council might be operating dual standards in its treatment of Mr. Carlton Duncan, headteacher of Wyke Manor Upper School, and Mr. Ray Honeyford, the headteacher suspended from Drummond Middle School.

Mr. Hart was speaking after the publication of a confidential letter sent to Councilor Norman Free about the support that a group of advisors had been giving to Wyle Manor Upper School. The letter was sent in reply to a request for information from Councilor Free.

But the Council's Director of Educational Services, Mr. Richard Knight, today dismissed the double standards claims as, "totally unfounded."

"The only thing the Wyke Manor and Drummond issues have in common is the sensationalized selective reporting of them in the media," said Mr. Knight. Let me set out the facts to correct the innuendo which is in danger of blowing up the issue relating to Mr. Duncan out of all proportion. Mr. Duncan was not 'reprimanded' as stated in press reports. He was asked by his Assistant Director to consider his position as an agent for a managed fund. On a purely voluntary basis, Mr. Duncan decided to finish his involvement with the fund. No reprimand was needed or given.

"The advisors who have been visiting the school recently did so with the agreement of both staff and the headteacher. This was part of a consultative and counseling exercise, which started as far back as November last year. The school has been affected by a series of disruptive events—a brief suspension of normal work after an asbestos scare, allegations of racism among staff, and a pupil demonstration—so it is hardly surprising that the advisors were asked to give the benefit of their considered opinions followed by suitable supporting measures.

"The cases of Mr. Honeyford and Mr. Duncan are totally unrelated. I can assure headteachers as well as their pupils and their parents that both cases are being dealt with sensitively, professionally, and appropriately according to the different circumstances.

"Any suggestion that we are favoring one compared to the other is totally unfounded. I am sure what will disturb many people is the irresponsible leaking of a confidential letter about Mr. Duncan to the media in what appears to be a blatant attempt to discredit a senior black headteacher.

"The raising of old issues concerning a black headteacher and criticism of his conduct in contrast with the current frenzy surrounding Mr. Honeyford lead me to the regrettable conclusion that Mr. Duncan has been targeted not for what he has done or not done but because he is black."

"For more information, please contact Mr. Knight on Bradford 752500."

All this was happening to me when the national context for race relations was worsening day by day. The lessons and effects of the 1981 Brixton riots had not gone away. In fact, we know that these riots, uprisings or national disturbances, call them what you will, were mushrooming in other places such as Birmingham, Bristol, Liverpool, and Manchester not to mention Broadwater farm in London. The racist 19 Century SUS Law (1824 Vagrancy Act) had given the power to the police to stop and search anyone they suspected of having criminal intent in cases of arrestable offenses. The power thus given was extraordinarily abused and overused against black people who were constantly racially profiled throughout the 70s and 80s.

On the advice of a 1979 Royal Commission on Criminal Procedure, the 1824 Vagrancy Act was repealed by the Criminal Attempts Act 1981 which received Royal Assent that year. Nevertheless, there was no letting up on racial profiling and the SUS law remained a bane in the life of black people all over the nation. It was this overuse which explained the Brixton 'uprisings' and, to a large extent, uprisings elsewhere across the nation. It would not take much to light similar flames around Bradford were the wrong flames to be fanned around the nation's only black secondary headteacher. Before things could be materialized into this, it was in everyone's interest to approach with wisdom and caution.

Teachers like me knew only too well that those riots were the direct and indirect function of a racist society. And this being so, points to the need for the nation's educators to begin and continue the long process of reforming the world in which we live. While there can be no escaping the truth that everyone and all institutions have a role in this difficult and long-term but achievable task, teachers and other educators must prepare themselves to take on the lion's share of this world-saving task. These others will tackle the issues from the leaves, branches, and limbs but these will grow back if more permanent eradication is not undertaken. Educators must, therefore, attack this pernicious problem from the roots for the benefit of both white and non-white consumers.

This is a recognition that has consumed me since the day I first set foot on English soil. It is a task that I attempted to provide a corrective contribution to at every level at which I found myself in my profession. And it is a task for which I felt I would be better equipped if I was operating from the top leadership position as head of Wyke Manor Upper School.

I tried with all the determination I could reasonably muster, not to bring any of this home with me. I had a very young family and did not want them burdened with these rather ugly and stressful things. My wife, at times, noted that I was pensive and questioned me about what was worrying me. Still, I did not let on about these awful incidents at school. But things were happening so fast around me that I would not be able to keep them hidden for much longer.

The Lives of My Children Threatened

The fact that I was still standing prompted the conspirators to try another tactic. They would now attack my family as well. I arrived home from school one day to find my wife in absolute distress. The postman had delivered a letter to our address addressed to Mr. and Mrs. Duncan. When my wife opened that envelope, she found a cutting from a newspaper. Someone had cut out a picture of the twins with Jamie. On the foreheads of all three, the word "death" was written in red ink. My wife was now scared out of her mind and rightly so in the circumstances. I now had to fill her in on all that had been happening over the last few weeks. I was getting scared too; not so much for myself but for my 'hard gained loving family.'

The evil conspirators were planning evil things and they clearly knew where to find us as their newspaper cutting and envelope showed. That summer break, I decided to take the entire family on their first trip to Jamaica. The sea, sun, and friendliness of the people, I thought, would soothe the mind and souls, and re-fortify us to return and face the future. The holiday was a great one. The children, though young, enjoyed it immensely. Playing at the edges of rivers, building sandcastles on beaches, and riding on donkeys did a great deal to make children their ages extremely happy. Nothing went wrong for anyone, except for James who, on one occasion, unwittingly stood in a nest of biting black ants much to his regret. But even that was temporary in its effects and soon James was enjoying the spirit of Jamaica once more.

On our return to England, we decided to spend a couple of days with my mother in West Hampstead in Northwest London. She would be delighted to see her grandchildren, and, in any case, we had taken back some Jamaican products for her. The children had a wonderful time with their granny and their Uncle Raymond, but it was time for us to make the long journey back to Bradford because I would need to prepare for the reopening of school. It was 15:00 one Friday afternoon when we arrived back in Bradford after the long summer break.

We found our back door boarded up with a blockboard and nails. We went across the road to our nearest neighbor to see if we could learn anything before, we entered that house with our young children. Our neighbor informed us that on the same day we left for Jamaica, that night our house was broken into, and the local police were informed by another neighbor when she discovered that our gate was left wide opened and checked to see how that had happened because, to her knowledge, we had bolted it when we left for our holiday.

We summoned the local police, using the neighbor's telephone to let them know that we had returned and that we were scared to take the young children inside without some support. The police were delighted to hear from us because they had a report to complete and only, we could tell them what was missing. The police came in the next fifteen minutes and helped us to enter our home. The house was ransacked from top to bottom. My wife's underwear garments were strewn all over the floor and passageways and so were the children's Smarties' (sweets). They were just emptied and sprinkled everywhere. Nothing, absolutely nothing, was taken from our bungalow.

The conspirators were showing us what could happen. We needed to take extra care while living at that address. My wife and I thought that it would be a good idea to get a dog. We needed to get it from the puppy stage so that it can grow up and be friendly with the children. The breed that we decided upon was a Doberman pinscher. That puppy (we named her 'Tina') was just about the noisiest puppy we had ever imagined. Just as well, we had no immediate neighbors, we thought. We had to suffer it alone.

Head Wins Dog Fight

Frankly, if there were complaints about the dog, we would have had to admit that problem because Tina (that was what we named her) barked incessantly even at a passing butterfly. We could contain some of the noise by keeping her inside when she was still small enough to do so. But the time came when the puppy was growing bigger and stronger, and she, therefore, needed more outside exposure and plenty of exercise. The Doberman pinscher, after all, is a large breed. When the dog was just over a year old, she had grown into a fierce watchdog, which was what we wanted in the first place given the kind of events which had surrounded us.

Cats, humans, and other dogs that chanced by our home would provoke a barking response from her. There was an awful amount of noise, though declining in frequency as she got older, generated by that dog. As she grew older, she was becoming more discriminating with her barks with the help of some professional training.

Low and behold, the postman brought me a letter in early April 1985. When I read the contents, I could not believe what I was reading. A neighbor from eight homes away from our bungalow had prosecuted me under the Noise Abatement Act current at that time. Because his home was so far away, he was not one of the neighbors whom I had met. I was to meet him for the first time in the Bradford Magistrates Court on Thursday, 23rd May 1985. Nothing that he told the Magistrates was true except that the dog was extremely noisy.

That fact I had to admit to the Bench and explained that things were improving as the dog grew older and received more training and the purpose for having the dog. My feeling was that the Magistrates would make an order against me in the circumstances, just when there was an outburst in rather poor English from Mr. Skorupka, he was my prosecutor, to the effect that I had been discriminating in reverse against him because he was white, and both my dog and I were black. I knew then that he had lost the case because I could see the change of countenance on the faces of the Magistrates who were completely taken back by that unwarranted outburst.

The Magistrates made no order and expressed the opinion that neighbors should expect to give and take. In any case, the situation was improving with the age of the dog plus training. They, therefore, dismissed the case. I went across to the section of the court where I had seen members of the press writing copiously as the case was proceeding. I said to the reporters, "You are not going to report that, are you?"

One of them said, "To tell you the truth, Mr. Duncan, had you been 'Mr. Smith', we wouldn't be reporting. But you are not Mr. Smith, are you?" They then left the courtroom briskly with me trailing closely behind them. The next day the following report appeared in the Bradford Telegraph & Argus.

When bigots fail, they become dangerously desperate. We would, wisely, remain conscious of that. My family and I were extraordinarily glad that we were allowed by the courts to keep our Tina because desperate people will do desperate things. Tina would be a source of alert and protection. We were truly sorry that we offended a neighbor and disturbed his peace in the way it happened. But there were evil forces beyond him, which made it necessary for us to have a dog in the neighborhood. It was about the preservation of life and limbs of those of our children.

They were innocent and, fortunately, far too young to appreciate any of what was happening. It was our responsibility to protect them. The dog would continue to be a vicious and noisy deterrent, but we had to remain alert and always expect the unexpected. We had no way of telling from what angle these sick-minded creatures will strike next. We just knew that they would.

The media was still following us on a variety of scores. Whether it was, my historical headship; my children's historical birth and development; a neighboring factory emitting fumes, which, it was alleged, was causing conjunctivitis in the eyes of my pupils and staff; pupil demonstration; racism allegations within Wyke Manor School; community education development at my school; multiculturalism and the school curriculum; improvement in the school's examination results; the impact of Drummond School and its headteacher, Ray Honeyford—there was plenty to keep the media interested in us. And they never let up at any time. There must have been grumbles about the media's frequent presence at the school, because, out of the blue, I received a letter from JA instructing me that I should seek clearance from him before I accommodate the media at the school.

Channel 4: Diverse Report: Schools Apart

Channel 4 was running a weekly series nationwide under the broad title 'Diverse Report.' This television company approached me to be the presenter of one of these called: 'Schools Apart.' All the prior filming for this was to be done in Birmingham and London over three weekends. To establish me at the beginning, the film crew needed to come to Bradford one day to get a shot of me leaving school at the end of the school day with pupils milling around. I agreed to be the presenter as suggested and to allow the opening shot for Channel 4.

The thirty-minute program was shown nationally on the 20th of May 1985. It began, as previously stated, with me leaving school and lots of pupils milling around. The voice-over said in words to this effect: "We have asked Carlton Duncan, headteacher of Wyke Manor Upper School to present tonight's Diverse Report…" No other mention was made of Wyke Manor Upper School, Wyke, Bradford, or even Yorkshire for the rest of the thirty minutes program.

One of the governors of my school had seen the broadcast and objected to the mention of Wyke Manor School in the opening shot. He was so aggrieved by that shot, so much so, that he summoned a special governors' meeting to consider what should become of the headteacher for such a heinous act. So important was this meeting that JA, who had never attended one of our governors' meetings before, was the first to arrive for the special meeting. After consultation with the headquarters of my Union (NUT), I was supported and represented by a regional officer of the Union, Ken Gravelin.

There was a 100% attendance of governors, some of whom were local politicians, clerks to the governors, and education officers at the meeting. This was going to be a lynching, and no one wanted to miss it. The initiating governor had made prior arrangements for a television and video machine to be set up for the meeting. He had a copy of the program, which was taped on the night of its showing. Once Doris Birdsall, Chairman of the Governors, had opened the meeting the initiating governor was invited to state his case.

He requested that the tape be played and once the first opening shot was played, he shouted to the technician, "Stop it there!" He explained that he wasn't concerned with the rest of the program only the shot, which mentioned that I was the headteacher of Wyke Manor Upper School. Ken Graveling, at my instigation, insisted that it was a statement of fact that I was the headteacher of Wyke Manor Upper School, and that fact alone could not bring disrepute to the school, which was the governor's claim, we, therefore, must see the entire half-hour program. Most governors agreed and the entire program was shown. Ken Gravelin had, in effect, demonstrated that this was 'much ado about nothing'.

Once JA saw that the drift of the discussion was going in my favor, he decided to plunge the knife in deeply by handing the chairman a copy of a letter, which he had previously sent me. He, clearly, came prepared with ill intentions to get me one way or another. That letter instructed me to seek his clearance before accommodating the media at the school. Because of JA's sneaky twist, the discussion now turned to the issue of what was meant by the accommodation of the media at the school. The camera crew never entered the school. In the end, the governor failed, and JA' letter failed to achieve its intended purpose.

Chapter 12
Staying One Step Ahead

On my way home that night, I thought to myself that they would get me some time. I needed to prevent that possibility. They only needed to be lucky once; I must be lucky every time. When I arrived home my wife had put the children to bed and was waiting for me. She was anticipating bad news. She probably thought that I was going to be sacked or at least suspended. But in my household that night, the joys existed. Those who had engineered my downfall had no joy in theirs. They will be even more desperate now and were either hatching or getting ready to mobilize on their next move. I didn't know what that might be, and I didn't want to hang around trying to find out. We needed to get away from this place, I told my wife and she agreed instantly: but to where and to what she enquired with an air of realism.

"Just leave it to me," I whispered and headed for our bedroom. I looked in on the children on the way. I was so exhausted that I didn't think I would be answering the children's calls that night. Since the birth of the twins, it had become my duty to answer their calls at night. Whether it was to change their nappies or to feed them; in the early days, their mother extracted her breastmilk so I could feed the twins when they came awake during the nights. Later, when they were no longer breastfed, there would be prepared bottles, I was there for them.

The next day, I earnestly began the search for a different job. It was a noticeable pattern in my life, so far, that I do everything twice, for example, I am in my second marriage, so why not look for another headship? Two days later, at about 19:00, my doorbell rang. At my door was a prominent, young, up-and-coming Tory Councilor (local politician) who was known to be aspiring for Westminster politics (central government). He wanted to check out a vicious rumor, which was circulating about me, and which was gaining strength in certain circles. He was undertaking measures to quash it but needed to check his facts.

This man, though white, sounded like a friend and so I invited him inside my home. Although his name was prominent in Bradford and was known nationally and I had also seen his pictures in the media, I had never seen him in person. This was the first time. It was a Labor Council in power in Bradford and this man's party was in opposition. Naturally, I was interested to find out what this "vicious rumor" was all about and how it would affect me.

Once we were seated, I said, "Well?"

The councilor was concerned that it appeared that 'they' (he never said who 'they' were, despite my asking) want to get you. And I want to prevent that. I remembered thinking; *"They want to get me"* was the biggest understatement of the time. I continued to listen intently. "The latest is that you falsely claimed on your headmaster application form that you have a degree in economics and a degree in law."

"I want to be able to quash it by saying that I have seen your certificates." I always kept my certificates in a readily accessible place and knew exactly where they were. I gave a sigh of relief, got up and went directly to the drawer containing my certificates and returned with them to the counselor. He looked closely at them and then apologized profusely for bothering me at such a time,

"But 'these idiots' must be stopped," he said, as he bade us (by this time my wife had joined us) good night. Ten minutes after he went, I realized that I had slipped up badly. I was completely taken in by the counselor's apparent concern for me and my family. In the process, I had lost a chance to make a significant amount of money by suing someone, or even more than one, for the worst kind of defamation—defaming a person in relation to his profession. I was under no obligation to provide evidence of my qualification to the councilor. I need only to say that I didn't know where to find the certificates and he might have taken that to mean the rumor was right. What a field day the media would have made of all that! I probably wouldn't have had to work again in my life. This was truly a lost opportunity.

The Search for a New Headship

The headship for George Dixon Comprehensive School in Birmingham, West Midlands was advertised for two consecutive weeks in the Times Educational Supplement. I did request the details from the first week that it appeared. At that time, I had also requested the details for one or two other advertised headships. Only the George Dixon one was appealing. The school had a distinguished history. George Dixon Grammar School for boys and George Dixon Grammar School for girls were two separate schools that had become amalgamated in 1976. At one time, it was 'The' Grammar School in Birmingham. Qualifying students came from far and wide to attend that school.

It was then entirely selective for around 600 students. It was caught up in the comprehensivization and amalgamation drives of the 1970s thereby losing its Grammar School status in 1983 and becoming one of Birmingham's largest mixed-sex 11-18 comprehensives with over 2,000 pupils. It was, in effect, an amalgam of three schools: the George Dixon Grammar School on City Road, the close-by Stanmore mixed-sex Secondary Modern on Stanmore Road and the not-so-far-away Portland mixed-sex Secondary Modern on Portland Road.

City Road was a main road with Portland Road crossing it runs north and south at a traffic light junction, which was just one property (a local church) away from the George Dixon building and car park entrances. The Portland School was situated some two hundred yards down (northwards) on the left-hand side of Portland Road after the crossing with City Road. Beyond the crossing with City Road, Portland Road (still southbound) forms a 'T' junction with Stanmore Road, which runs to the rear of the George Dixon Building. Stanmore School was separated from the George Dixon School only by a very extensive playing field, which was large enough to serve both schools when they were separate schools. Portland School had its own adjoining play fields at its location.

At the time of the advertisement, the school was still operating on all three sites and using all the buildings from all three schools, although the school was now experiencing falling rolls and consequently was in a period of contraction. The Birmingham Education Authority was advertising for a headteacher to lead the school's 115 teaching and non-teaching staff and 1,500 mixed-sexes 11-18-year-old pupils through that period of contraction and associated challenges. The salary was a group 13 salary (group 14 was the largest you could get anywhere in the country, and they were extremely rare). The salary scale at George Dixon was, in fact, two groups bigger than Wyke Manor's group 11 salary.

One very attractive feature of the school was its racial composition. This was a truly multi-racial school having groups of Whites, Asians and Afro-

Caribbeans, each forming roughly one-third of the school's population. Just over 6% of the school's teaching and non-teaching staffs were non-white. Only candidates with a proven track record and an innovative and imaginative flare need apply as per the advertisement in the Times Educational Supplement (TES).

Birmingham was next door to Coventry, where I had worked for some five-plus years and from where I was promoted to Bradford. I did know something about the City of Coventry. At the time I was there, I had known Birmingham to be a much more cosmopolitan and egalitarian city than Bradford was several years later. I could not imagine that the kind of bigoted idiots, who were baying for my head in Bradford, could be found anywhere else in the country and certainly not in Birmingham. How wrong could one be? They were everywhere as we shall see later.

I penned off my application with great speed and continued to peruse the Education Guardian on Tuesdays and the Times Educational Supplement on Fridays. There was little interest. It was the wrong time of the year. Advertisements, interviews, and appointments for the September term would either have been completed or be nearing completion. Most advertisements for positions to be filled in January usually appear early in the Christmas term. This meant that I would need to wait until September to have a strong field of advertised positions from which to choose.

The long summer break arrived and although we felt like it, we could not afford to go back to Jamaica or to go any other place abroad. Instead, we took the children on a touring holiday in parts of North and South Wales. First, we headed for Llandudno and the Colwyn Bay areas where we stayed in guest houses for three nights and took in the sites by the day. The children were only three and seven years old, but they had a great time when they visited the town of Anglesey to join thousands of visitors like us who were checking out the restored Railway Station in the little village of the same name: *'Llanfairpwllgwyngyllgogerychwyrndrobwllllantysiliogogoch.'* Apparently, in translation this means: *'The church of St. Mary in the hollow of white hazel trees near the rapid whirlpool by St. Tysilio's of the red cave.'*

I was eager to show off to my wife and children where I went to university and the surrounding attractions. Swansea will not only be nostalgic, but it will also create a form of escapism from that hell hole of a place called Bradford. In fairness to the people of Bradford such as the parents of my school, these evil plotters, conniving racialists, and ridiculous bigots are not representative of the area. They, in fact, drag down the place with them as they look up to see the gutters. Most of the people are good and decent people who are friendly to 'outsiders': that is, people who were born outside of Yorkshire.

I had some exemplary social relationships with members of the Bradford Blaize Rotary Club after I became its only black member soon after I arrived in Bradford. These were, all the members, fair-minded and decent people. But you see, these people held respectable positions in society and were people of worth. The evildoers had nothing and would never come to anything. Their greatest achievement would forever be in the way they spent their time pulling down others like crabs in a barrel. They made the loudest noises in criticizing and rejecting others whose barrels were overflowing while theirs were forever empty.

We arrived in the university town of Swansea late one summer night. With three young children, our only option was to go to bed. I had pre-booked bed and breakfast arrangements at a place I knew well from my university days, so they were still up awaiting our arrival. We were going to be at the bed and breakfast for five nights. It would be our base as we set out daily to explore the sheer beauty of the great Gower Peninsula. Although it was summer break, there was still a considerable amount of student life, mainly postgraduate researchers, on campus. I was thus able to show Melvinder and the children around my previous seat of learning for four long years.

Of greater interest to the children, however, were our trips out to Mumbles, Caswell, and Langland Bays because, although the seawater was very cold even at that time of the year, they had a good time playing on the idyllic beaches and collecting rocks at Mumbles as they watched the boats with sails go and come.

On the way to Mumbles, we diverted at Black Pill and went up to Clyne Castle (Neuadd Gilbertson), which is the hall of residence which accommodated me for a year when I was a student at the university. The castle had extraordinarily beautiful grounds and it remained a source of pride for me to know that that was once my abode.

Clyne Castle and my bedroom within it

The following day, we headed out to Rhossili, which is about seventeen miles out of Swansea on the coastline. Rhossili brought back sorrowful memories to me because I had lost a university colleague who, with another friend, tried to negotiate the rough waters in a single-seater canoe. The canoe capsized and nothing was ever heard of those two students again. However, Rhossili is one of the most beautiful places one can find for long and idyllic scenic walks. The air there is always fresh and invigorating. I knew my family would love it and they did.

Scenic Rhossili

What was most refreshing about this family trip was that during all the tours and visits to the pleasure spots, neither my wife nor I made a mention of what was going on in Bradford. It was as though Bradford and all that it entailed was all a sad dream from which we had awoken to pleasanter things. Now that the holiday was ending, I could feel a tinge of sadness re-emerging. My wife wasn't as bubbly and joyful either, but neither of us mentioned it.

On the return journey to Bradford, my mind was consumed with thoughts of the 1984 burglary. Because we were going away, we had to kennel Tina at great expense. Hence, the way was clear for a repeat of yesteryear. However, when we arrived home the house was intact. There was no sign of a break-in, or anything taken. The neighbors confirmed that all was normal during our absence. I had time to travel out to Shipley to retrieve our dog from the kennel, while Melvinder took care of the children.

When I got back with Tina, Melvinder had collected the many letters that were lying on the inside doormat. They were all addressed to me and so she placed them aside on the mantelpiece by the front door. I quickly shuffled through the pile looking at the postmark on each one in the process. There were some from Bradford, some from London, and one only from Birmingham. The others could wait, but I eagerly opened the one from Birmingham with trembling hands; no procrastination with this one. It was what I wanted; just what I wanted to see in print. The Birmingham Education Authority was calling me for interviews in mid-September 1985 in connection with my George Dixon School application. They had to act quite early if they wanted to fill the post in time for January.

The successful candidate will need to give three months' notice of intending resignation. My wife was in the kitchen preparing something for the children. I invaded her domain: handed her the letter and said, "Read this!"

She could hardly believe it. She was always dreading that I might have had to make another 120 applications before I would be called as was the case with the Bradford post. But this time it was my first application. The letter also invited me to join the other six candidates on a tour of the school on a fixed date. On that date, senior staff and education officials will be available to answer the candidates' questions and a week later, interviews will begin over a period of two whole days. The first day would be used to narrow down the long list from seven candidates to four or three final contestants.

When school reopened in September 1985, there was much to be joyful about too. The public examination results were published during the summer break and although the school was organized to receive the results and distribute them to the 'eagerly' and the 'anxiously' waiting pupils, the information would not become public knowledge to the entire school until the start of the new term. On our first day back, there were smiles on all our faces.

The pupils were happy, and the staff who taught them were happy because their hard work had paid off in good examination results. The 'A' level results were exceptionally good so there would be a good number of youngsters gaining places at the nation's universities. For me, there was also the fact that a book on multicultural education, which Ranjit Arora and I were editing, would be sent off to the publishers by the end of the week thus releasing more of my spare time to prepare for my pending interviews.

My wife had warned me not to say a single word to anyone, not anyone she stressed, about my oncoming interviews because I did not know who the enemy was. That was very wise counsel and I listened and carried it out to the letter. People around me must have suspected that something was right though because many genuine well-wishers had commented that I was no longer wearing a mask of depression. I simply put that down to the refreshing holiday, which my family and I had just had.

This month I would also be finalizing an in-service training program (INSET) for our staff. The list of speakers included HMI Eric Bolton, who would set the tone; Sue Watts on Science and multicultural education; Ray Hemmings on multicultural mathematics; Sylvia Collicott on multicultural approach to Humanities; Horace Lashley on multiculturalism and the Arts and I would be leading on pastoral care in a multicultural/anti-racist context. The staff had previously heard me address multiculturalism on the BBC Radio 4 Friday night and Saturday morning 'Any Question' program.

Rachael Evans, the then recognized expert in multicultural resources, was invited to come to the school and set up her stalls to support the day. Both deputies were roped in to make the INSET conference run smoothly and the day a complete success. It must have been a lucky omen for me because the Birmingham interviews had fallen on those two days (Wednesday and Thursday) after the INSET day, which would be on the preceding Monday. I could safely continue with my full and total involvement in the INSET day without giving anything away. One week before my interviews, however, I would have to join the other six competitors at George Dixon School for a normal briefing. That would not interfere too much with my involvement in the INSET day, fortunately. Whatever happened, Wyke Manor Upper School had to succeed.

Last term, lateness by both pupils and staff had become negligible and a big bonus of having a thriving community education program at the school was the greater discipline, which was broadly reported across the school. As it was at Sidney Stringer, pupils found it less free to prank or misbehave when their parents, grandparents, or other adults who are not relatives are present in their classes and milling about the school generally. The concept of community education had clearly caught on, for this term has signaled a significant increase in both pupil and adult intake.

I started to have similar pangs, about the expanding community education project, to those, which have always bothered me when I must move on and leave projects, which I started and not sure of whether my successor would be able or willing to continue them. If they were not continued, what started out as a big positive for the beneficiaries could end disastrously for them. I told myself that that was like counting chickens before they were hatched and tried to place that on my mind's back burner.

At home, there was no new development; well, not of the negative kind anyway. Melvinder was making all kinds of efforts to give the twins some experience at Jamie's nursery. It was important that we started them out on a socialization program before they would begin formal schooling. On the coming weekend, I thought that it would be a good thing to 'kill two birds with one stone and take the family out for a couple of nights' stay in the Birmingham area.

This would give me the essential opportunity of getting a feel for the community in which the school stood and its feeder areas. One of our neighbors agreed to put out some food and water for our dog. She would be left roaming the grounds of our home. All three gates to our premises would be securely fastened so that the dog could not escape and all that the neighbor had to do is push the food and water under the gate on Saturday and again on Sunday, the day when we would return. The dog would bark furiously at her but would not be able to harm her.

We left for Birmingham after school on Friday evening. I had previously arranged to stay for the weekend with my long-time former boss, Mrs. Mary

Sterling Stuart, the then current headteacher of Golden Hillock School in South Birmingham. It was her position of deputy head that was left vacant at Aylestone School when she aspired to her present headship. The journey down the various motorways was exceptionally tiring, especially after a full week's school. Melvinder was also feeling the strain of having to care for three children all week. We, therefore, headed directly to School Road in Hall Green, Birmingham, which was where Mary Stuart, her husband, Ron, and their last daughter, Lisa resided at the time.

Ron had left us some supper, which we had, and after chatting with the family for a while we took to the bedroom. The chat with Mary was most useful because after her ten years in Birmingham she had acquired useful information about the city, George Dixon School, and its communities. Mary passed on all that she knew and told me how to find out more that would be useful.

After breakfast the next morning, the children declared that they wanted to travel with me when I was looking around the area of the school. Hall Green was about 40 minutes away by car from Edgbaston where the school was situated. Melvinder got the children ready, and Ron decided to come for the ride too. Ron was an easy-going guy from Belize in the West Indies. He had met and married his Scottish wife, Mary a good many years ago. Although Mary had other children, Lisa was the only child of Ron's and Mary's marriage. I had always got on well with Ron when sometimes he would accompany his wife to events at Aylestone School or other events, which were often organized by the staff, and, of course, when he and Mary had staff colleagues over to their home in Southwest London.

 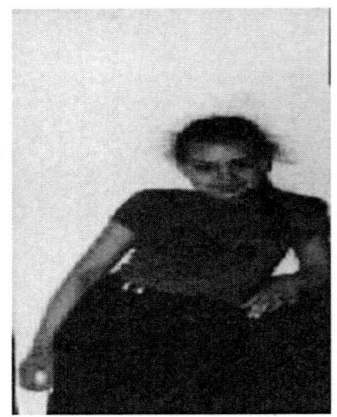

Ron Stuart Lisa Stuart

Mrs. Mary Stuart: Formerly Headteacher
Golden Hillock School
Birmingham

It was also at Aylestone School that I met little Lisa for the first time. She could not have been older than about seven years old when one morning, just after I had settled the sixth formers for their morning assembly; a little girl walked into the sixth form common room with the confidence and self-assurance of a headteacher and literally took over from me. I wasn't quite sure who was more surprised at this, me or the sixth formers who for the first time were dumbstruck. I later learned that it was the deputy head's daughter, Lisa. Lisa had no school that day and was spending the day with her mother when she wandered out of her mother's office and found her way to the sixth-form common room.

As it turned out, just as Mary had said, the school, despite its Edgbaston address, was not in 'proper' Edgbaston. The houses and facilities in the immediate surroundings of the school were more like those in the neighboring Winson Green area. The only thing that was notable about Winson Green was that a high-security prison of the same name stood imposingly on Winson Green Road. Some of Britain's most notorious criminals were held there. The children from Edgbaston proper would not be sent to state schools. Pre-comprehensivization (1970's) the school would have been considered a 'must' for Edgbaston children and the competition would have been fierce.

But this was not the case now, because of the amalgamation and subsequent loss of Grammar School status for George Dixon. I was able to see all three schools, which comprised the school because of the amalgamation. In getting to and from the Stanmore buildings (Martin Block) to the George Dixon buildings (Ritchie Block) there was no need to use the roads. It was simply a matter of crossing a playing field if the time was dry. However, getting to Portland buildings (Portland Block) from any of the other two blocks meant using the roads. I remembered thinking that that must have meant a time-tabling nightmare for the deputy whose job it was.

Most the school's population came from far and wide, for example, as far away as Erdington, Handsworth, and Harborne (the white children came mainly from Harborne) and anywhere on the No. 11 bus route. The No. 11 bus covered almost the entire Birmingham on a circular route around Birmingham, and it had a stop immediately outside the school gate. The area was well served by other buses besides the No. 11 and Birmingham town center was no more than three miles away.

On Sunday, we were able to make an early start back to West Yorkshire. Mary had given me a few contacts with whom she thought it would be useful to speak. I could do that from home, I thought. On the journey home, we had an interesting and sometimes challenging in car 'I spy with my own little eyes' competition. Daddy lost every time. Nevertheless, it made the miles slip by unnoticeably. The dog was waiting for us at the gate. She had clearly missed us. It must have rained while we were away because in her eagerness to greet us, she was all over us with muddy paws.

We went inside, telephoned our neighbor, and thanked her for looking out for our dog and keeping an eye on our home. The family then relaxed around a small fire and the television. Tomorrow will be a busy day at school and the children will be having another taster at the nursery followed by some entertainment activities in the nearby public park while I will be at school.

A few days later (mid-week), I headed back down the motorways to join the other six candidates and to meet key staff as well as the education officers who were chosen to spend the day with us. The day was quite normal. It was the usual kind of thing that candidates go through before the interview sessions. The candidates were gathered in the Ritchie Block staff room. When I entered, I received quite a shock. One of the candidates was Mr. Dave King. He was the Head of the English Department at Sidney Stringer School and

Community College when I was the Deputy Head and Director of Personal Development there.

Dave had gone on to be a deputy headteacher elsewhere and was now applying for headships. This was his second call for interviews. One other candidate was introduced to us as the existing Birmingham headteacher. He was interested in getting a bigger school. The other four candidates were all strangers to Birmingham but held deputy headships variously.

Our escort had planned that we would first meet the Deputy headteachers of the School. The school had four deputies because of its size and its scattered units. He took us first to see Mr. John Vickers, who was, in fact, the Acting headteacher. The school lost the headteacher at the end of the last Christmas term and Mr. Vickers has been acting ever since. My first impression of Mr. Vickers was how professional and knowledgeable he was. I couldn't help wondering why he wasn't a candidate for this post.

It turned out that Mr. Vickers had applied for the position, but it appeared that the authority at that time didn't readily appoint candidates who were internal to the school; hence he was not on the long list for this post. Most of the useful information I gathered throughout the day came from Mr. Vickers. He was so obviously of headship caliber, that I predicted that he would not be at the school for very much longer: and I was right. Not long after this, Mr. Vickers was appointed to his own school right there in Birmingham.

The next stop was at Mr. Phillip Naylor's office. He was the curriculum and timetable deputy headteacher. I needed to ask him how he managed the feat of time-tabling across three sites. It was from him that I learned that pupils moved from site to site on foot while teachers had two regular bus services going in opposite directions at morning breaks and at afternoon change of lessons. If teachers missed the bus service, then they must make their own way. Travel claims between sites for teachers using their own private vehicles were also honored. I asked and listened to all the curriculum and time-tabling questions and answers that Mr. Naylor could accommodate.

We next moved on to Mrs. Irene Gray. She was the longest-serving deputy headteacher at the school. She oversaw the pastoral brief. She had a bit of self-importance about her because her husband was the well-known Union official (NUT), Mr. Gerry Gray, and the existing headteacher of one of Birmingham's schools (Holt). I did not get the impression that it mattered to Mrs. Gray that she was practicing pastoral care in a multi-racial school. The significance of that might have been lost on her totally. Nevertheless, she was extremely affable and jocular. The sort of person who had the qualities to make anyone forget his or her sorrows in ten seconds.

Finally, we were taken to the deputy headteacher, who oversaw Administrative Affairs and associated staffing matters across the school. And here was where I had my second shock of the day. This was Mr. Robert Mason. I knew him as Bob Mason. He was the outgoing Head of the English Department at Sidney Stringer School and Community College at the same time as I was joining that school as its deputy headteacher. Mr. Dave King had, in fact, succeeded Bob as the head of the English Department. Bob, as it turned out, had left Stringer to go to his present post. Only I did not know to which school he had gone.

I got to know Bob very well because his wife, Jean Mason, remained at Stringer as the Chief Librarian and soon became an excellent and reliable friend. It was to their house that my crab-eating American friend Aaron Randal had gone and eaten them out of bread and cheese on his own initiative. During the time I was at Sidney Stringer, our families shared many dinner parties in each other's homes. Once I had left Coventry for Bradford, the relationship had gradually frizzled to just memories. What a coincidence, I thought! The two people whom I met again today have some past connection themselves. Not much reminiscence could go on after the niceties of enquiring about each other's partner and my children because there were six other candidates who were seeking information, only one of whom Bob also knew.

Once the sessions with the deputies were over, it was time for lunch. The arrangements were that the candidates would have lunch with the heads of departments in one of the school's lunch canteens (there were three, one at each site). This gave us the opportunity to gauge the performance of the school in the various subject areas and, most importantly, assess the kind of curriculum leadership one would have as support if one was appointed to the headship. It also gave us an excellent opportunity to gauge the discipline of the school.

Canteen order or disorder was very nearly always indicative of the order in the classroom and about the school generally. For the rest of the afternoon, the two education officers that were assigned to us for the day would wander freely about the school with us talking to the students and other staff that chanced by our ways. It was at that time, too, that we got the opportunity to pick the brains of the education officers about the Education Authority and the political scene. The session was optional. The candidates were free to depart whenever they felt like it.

Chapter 13
Day at Wyke

On the journey back to Bradford, my thoughts were interchanging between three subjects. Sometimes I wondered what was happening with the family at home. How is Melvinder going to react when I tell her about Bob Mason? Not too long now and I would be home. Sometimes it was about what the conspirators were planning for me next. And would I be able to outsmart them? And sometimes I wondered what the staff at George Dixon would be thinking of the candidates and what their reports would be. Candidates are always conscious that information-gathering days on occasions like today were as much about what the school thought of them as it was about what they thought of the school.

HMI Bolton set the scene and tone at our INSET day brilliantly. Mr. Bolton, at that time, was not only Her Majesty's Chief Inspector of schools, but a highly respected household name in education circles. There was the 'method in my madness' to invite him to open our INSET day. We had to plan the day in accordance with his diary, but there was no difficulty thereafter in getting him. It is true that I had met HMI Bolton on several occasions in connection with my work on the Rampton/Swann Committee and so that may have helped. The Inspector was known to be committed to equality of opportunity in education and that was a major factor, among others, in influencing my decision to invite him.

The rest of the day went just as I had wanted it, especially in the individual subject areas. Many staff had always argued that they did not know how multicultural principles could be applied to their subject areas, especially in mathematics and science. On INSET day, they had all the answers. The head, the deputies, the senior teachers, and department heads were then charged with seeing that the principles were applied in lesson plans and their executions.

After school on a Tuesday evening following the INSET, my wife packed me off to Birmingham so that I would be fresh the next day for the commencement of the two days of interviews, which began the next day. Ron and Mary had offered to put me up and I had gratefully accepted their kind offer of accommodation and hospitality. I had told my secretary that I would be away for two days and would be in regular contact with her as I always did when I was away from school. We didn't have mobile phones in those days.

I did not know what was happening on the reference front. At the headship level, some authority took up references only after the appointment was made, and then only at the Director of Education level. At this level, the writing of the reference is not delegated downwards. It wasn't all that long ago that I had spent a whole day at the House of Lords, together with my other colleagues on the Swann Inquiry, briefing the lords on the report, which was to be published the very next day, March 14th 1985. How would the blaze of publicity, several ITV, and BBC Television appearances, nationally and locally, which were associated with the publication of the Swann report affect me during these interviews?

All these things, and more, preoccupied my mind as I faced the long journey to Hall Green in Birmingham. Eventually, I was ringing the bell at School Road. Ron greeted me. He prided himself as a good chef and said he was going to prepare a steak his way for me. I must admit it was one of the best pieces of beef that I ever enjoyed. After a general chit-chat with the Stuarts, I was ready for bed.

Though tired, I could feel the determination and a definite flow of raw adrenaline flowing throughout my total being. I went out like a light and only responded to the triggered seven o'clock alarm bell the next morning. Interviews would begin at 10:00. All the interviews will be held at the education office in Margaret Street in the center of Birmingham. There would be three panels of interviewers and the candidates would be interviewed in turn by each panel. At the end of the first day, the hope was that four or three candidates would remain to go through to the big panel the next day for the final determination.

Ron and Mary served up ham and eggs for breakfast. Mary suggested that I leave my car behind, and she would drop me off at Margaret Street before making her way back to her school. In the evening, whatever happened, I would have to make my way back by a taxi service. That sounded like a good idea to me because parking in the center of Birmingham was not the easiest activity one could find and if you managed it, it was very costly. Ron and Lisa wished me good luck as we set off for the education office. Once there, Mary wished me good luck too and went on her way. I was grateful for everything, and they knew it.

The interviews were both exhaustive and exhausting. I felt sapped by the end of the long day, pausing only for lunch arrangements. All the candidates were now awaiting their fate as we sat in what was clearly someone's vacated office for the day. It took the deciders exactly one hour to let us know that three candidates would be going on to meet the final panel. They were the candidate from Derby, the Birmingham existing head and the headteacher from Bradford. We were told to report back at the same time and place the following day. On our way out, we shook hands with the other four candidates, including Dave King.

We also thanked them for their congratulations so far and wished them good luck in the future. It was general practice to debrief failing candidates immediately so that they could be on their way home quickly. This was, of course, an optional exercise but I expected the other candidates would accept it.

Although I felt most pleased with the outcome, there was still a tinge of doubt floating about. It concerned the existing Birmingham headteacher. Was this only a charade to hand this job to a person that was already in the house? There were two reasons why I did not conclude that this was a foregone conclusion. Firstly, simply appointing internally would mean another expensive advert and selection procedure soon to fill the vacating headship, and secondly, the Birmingham head was making it clear in almost everything he said that he was only after a bigger salary. This latter could never be a good reason to appoint a headteacher of a school if that was paramount in his thinking.

Mary and Ron were profuse with their congratulations. The arrangements for Thursday would be the same as they were the day before and so Mary would drop me off on her way to school. The other two candidates were looking at me with wondering eyes. I, too, was trying to weigh them up because we were called in alphabetical order; I was first in the hot seat. There were five people interviewing us today. Yesterday, there were three people on each panel. None of the five was on yesterday's panels. They were the chairman of governors for George Dixon School, Councilor Albert Bore; the Deputy Director of Education for the Birmingham Education Authority, Mr. David Hammond; the Education Advisor for the school and two other local politicians one of whom was black—Councilor Phillip Murphy.

After exactly 45 minutes, the interview ended. I came away thinking that it was a fair interview: I was given every chance to sell myself and had taken them. I felt shaky on just one matter. The panel was most interested in my community education ideas. It seemed I was beating about the bush on parts of it when the Deputy Director of Education just cut across and said: "Mr. Duncan, why don't you just admit that you are going to open up the school?"

Councilor Murphy was very interested in my ideas on multicultural education. He knew his stuff exceedingly well and had clearly researched my career to date.

The chairman of governors, who was also the chairman for the panel was more interested in what I saw as the most urgent physical needs for the school in a context of falling rolls and three sites. These were difficult questions, but I felt that I handled them well. The other politician questioned whether I had grit. It seemed that the school had known some troubled times on account of difficult staff. I summed up my attitude for her thus: "If I was going to suck eggs, I realized that I would have to crack a few."

The final part of the 45-minute interview was taken up with questions pertaining to wider curriculum issues, budget management, and team leadership. The Education Advisor and the Deputy Director of Education shared the lead on these. I was then directed to the same vacant office where we waited the day before. It seemed they intended to separate those candidates who were already interviewed from those who were not. A cup of tea and biscuits awaited me.

About an hour later, I was joined by the existing Birmingham headteacher. He did not think his interview went well, however; he was smiling as though it didn't really matter to him. He already had a headship! In an hour-long conversation, I learned a great deal about the man. He told it all to me. I did manage to gain some very useful information about Birmingham. Some of it I had already got from Mary Stuart, so his information was just verification. To the extent that I relied on any of it during the interviews yesterday and today, I now felt even more confident.

The tea lady brought in a fresh pot of tea and some more biscuits. Shortly after that we were joined by the candidate from Darby. He was looking rather pleased with himself. He oozed confidence all over. He must have had a very good interview. It was about thirty minutes later that the office door was opened. Candidates always dreaded that moment and yet they always waited for it so eagerly.

"Mr. Duncan," the visitor said. "Would you follow me, please?" The other two candidates were most gracious with their congratulations and I, in turn, wished them better luck for the next time. Councilor Albert Bore offered me the position of headteacher at George Dixon School to commence in January 1986. I gladly accepted. All members of the panel were happy for me and I in turn thanked them profusely. The normal course of action now would be for the Birmingham Education Authority to confirm officially in writing so that I can resign from my present position within the specified time, usually three months' notice must be given. If the Birmingham Authority acts straight away, I would be well in time.

I was the happiest man on the planet. I asked the officer if I could make two telephone calls to Bradford. I was allowed. First, I rang my secretary because it was nearing the end of school hours and I wanted to catch her before she left for home. She confirmed that all was well, but that I had lots of letters and other paperwork to see in the morning. All that will be fun now, I remembered thinking. 'Mum' was still the word on my plans. Next, I rang home to share the good news with my family. My wife was so ecstatic; I could feel it down the telephone line. I just took the time to say, please don't tell anyone yet, and rang off instantly.

Taxis were rather commonplace around the Margaret Street zone. I hailed one and headed for School Road in Hall Green where my car was waiting for me. Only Ron and Lisa were at home. Mary never leaves her school before five in the evenings. I decided that I would wait and share my joy with her. In any case, it will be advantageous to see off some of the evening traffic before hitting the road myself.

Ron popped open a bottle of bubbly, it wasn't champagne, but it would suffice. "Here is to work in Birmingham," he said, as he took a sip. We drank and chatted for a while. Mary was home by six-thirty.

Before I could break the news, she enquired, "How did it go?" I told her, and she gave me the biggest hug and the biggest kiss that I had known for a long while. Her congratulations were plentiful, and her vision focused on my working with her as a colleague when I came to Birmingham.

It was around 22:00 when I arrived home in Bradford. Unfortunately, the children could wait no longer. My wife saw it when I drove in and so was waiting at the door. She just held me tightly and said, "Well done, let's leave here before they kill us," or words to that effect. She had made Lasagna Verde al forno for dinner.

My Italian friend's, Gabriella, recipe had come in rather handy. It tasted extra special and went down very well with a glass of red wine served up at room temperature. We discussed the pending impact on the children; the business of home-hunting all over again. Whatever happens, we are going to be happier there, I said, as we went to bed. My secretary had warned me that there would be a lot of work in the morning.

The Final Rounds at Wyke Manor Upper School

I got to school as early as I could on Friday morning. My secretary wasn't joking. How did so much paperwork accumulate over just two days? I sifted them for those that could not wait until Monday. In the meantime, I called the Director of Education, Mr. Richard Knight. I told him that I needed to see him urgently. I had a good relationship with Mr. Knight. A few months back, he had selected me to travel with him to Oxford to meet several Oxford Dons. Those were very influential opinion formers. Many of them were part of the government 'Think-Tank.'

On that occasion, ironically, white society accepted me fully; my blackness didn't seem to matter in academic circle; only my contribution to the important matters of the day mattered. But once I was back on my own in unremarkable circumstances, I had rubbish—the used paper from which a fish and chips meal was just consumed—tossed mockingly into my face and called a "nigger bastard" by the scummy dregs of the same white society. I wasn't equipped for a violent outcome, so I suffered in silence and went home that night.

Mr. Knight said that I could come straight away. He would be leaving for London afterward.

When I got to Provincial House, which is where his office was located, his desk was cleared for the weekend, but he waited for me. I went straight to the point and told him about my success in Birmingham. Mr. Knight was delighted for me; and he said so in the sincerest way that could only have come from a man of high integrity and honesty. He also said that I made his weekend for him as he set off for the long journey to London. He would, no doubt, deal with any ramifications and administrative necessity once he was back in the office.

Alison Taylor

Birmingham wasted no time in formalizing my appointment. By Tuesday morning the letter was handed to me by the postman as I was setting off for school. There was nothing to hold me back from telling anyone now. Unfortunately, some of the shine had gone off this ball, to borrow a cricketing metaphor, on the local TV news last night Wyke Manor School was, sadly, in the news; and in this morning's local papers, next to a picture of her, it was stated that, Alison Taylor, a star pupil of Wyke Manor Upper School, was gone missing since Sunday afternoon and the police was conducting a house-to-house search for her as they conduct related investigations. Anyone with information concerning her whereabouts was asked to contact their nearest police station or ring 999.

As I got into school, I rang Councilor Doris Birdsall, the chairman of the school's governors, and informed her about Alison Taylor's disappearance. The chairman had already seen and heard the same news I had. On that subject we decided to keep in touch. I then broke my good news about Birmingham. The chairman piled on a heap of congratulations and wished my family and me very well for the future while expressing her sadness that Wyke will soon be without me. I thought to myself that some of that sounded genuine but at the same time I detected sighs of relief.

Doris was coming under considerable strain from all quarters to roll back my influence on the school. She knew that although Bradford was a professed equal opportunity employer, it was more words than practice. She sensed that the racist mobs were gaining grounds and she was between them and me. That I am now going, would take some of that pressure off her and the fabric of Yorkshireman loyalty. I decided that I would take my time informing others who needed to know. My secretary and the two deputies were the next to be informed simultaneously.

They too were congratulatory in less enthusiastic terms. Madge, I am sure, would be contemplating the possibility of retiring while the deputies would now sharpen their rivalry in contemplation of their chances of filling the resulting vacant headship post. They were all feeling sad and there was a sense of urgency about Alison as they hoped for more positive news about her.

Thereafter, the news about my leaving and Alison's disappearance had spread like wildfires rolling across the Californian prairies.

Now I would be a lame duck headteacher. But I was determined not to allow that fact to be abused by those who had no good intentions for me or the school. I needed, therefore, to put in place strategies to prevent the school from suffering during my final days. At the full staff meeting where I announced that I was going to Birmingham, I also explained that I was not neglecting the promotional aspirations of all my fellow colleagues. It was my intention to leave a reference for every colleague, teaching, and non-teaching, on his or her file because that would be useful for the new headteacher who will of necessity, take some time to get to know the staffs and do justice by them if there was a request for a reference at any time.

Additionally, I announced that I had agreed a program of visits by some of the governors to the various departments. The governors will be keen to see and note how each department was incorporating the new ideas, gleaned at the recent INSET day, into the curriculum. There would also be my final report to both the governors and the authority on the entire school, especially staff initiatives and departmental performances. Finally, the deputies, senior teachers and I would remain vigilant to the last day of that term. If anyone saw through that, I would never know because the business of the school flourished to the very end. I ended the meeting by asking the gathering to pray for the safe return of Alison Taylor. The staff response was mainly one of silent disbelief on both issues.

The chairman of governors had arranged a typical send-off for a leaving headteacher where I was able to thank those governors and the staffs at the school for their valiant and professional work in taking the school thus far. There were several notable absences, both of governors and education officials. In fact, these were the same ones that were absent from the final governors' meeting, when I delivered my final governor's report. I felt nothing of the warmth and goodwill that I could recall on leaving either Aylestone Comprehensive or Sydney Stringer School and Community College. But then, in those earlier times I was not living in the capacity of a headteacher.

By chance, I ran into JA while I was at the education office one day in my final week. He pretended that he knew nothing about Birmingham, so I told him. He asked only two questions: what was the size of the school? I told him that it was two sizes larger than Wyke Manor. He then asked who wrote my reference. I told him truthfully that I did not know and bade him goodbye. Now I shall have to use the Christmas holidays to property hunt in Birmingham, my family in tow. It looked as if, so far, that my family and I had escaped the creeping trap but, for me, a mountain of sorrows remained because the police had not made any progress on finding Alison.

Chapter 14
George Dixon Comprehensive Mixed School Commuting

My family and I had immediately placed Oakfield Grove on the market for sale. The signs were that selling was not going to be easy. The people from whom we had purchased the property on our move to Bradford had difficulties selling, then, too. They had the property on the market for years until we came along and bought it for their asking price. The estate agent who handled the sale had written to them expressing surprise that we had come along and paid the asking price. We discovered this because when the vendors moved out, they left that letter behind inadvertently and we found it. Meanwhile, before I closed school for the end of term, I took the opportunity to make a couple of quick trips to Birmingham on my own, one on a weekend and the other mid-week. I needed to feel the temperature in the housing market for buyers as we would soon become. The weekend was deemed best for that purpose. My conclusion was that we wouldn't have many difficulties finding somewhere to live in time, but would we sell in time?

I had used the mid-week trip to do some looking around too, but the main purpose of that trip was to visit George Dixon School before they broke up for the Christmas holidays. It would have been considered traditional and courteous for me as an incoming head to meet with my team 'to be' to introduce myself and meet with other staff and the Acting Headteacher before the official 'take over' day. Word of my appointment had clearly gotten around given that everywhere I went in the school I was constantly thronged by students, young and old, whose expressions were of 'wonder', 'disbelief' and 'hope' all rolled into one. Above the melee, I could hear a voice stating very clearly, "He is going to be the first black Prime Minister of England." I had never heard of Barack Obama in those days!

No one was expressing any interest in Oakfield Grove, Bradford. Yet, if we did not sell, we simply could not buy in Birmingham. It wasn't that our asking price was too high. It wasn't much more than what we had paid for the property almost four years ago. Bradford and the entire West Yorkshire generally, did not make for good housing markets if you are a seller. It soon became clear that I would have to commute between Bradford and Birmingham until we could dispose of our Bradford home. Nevertheless, we continued looking for a property in Birmingham to be our home eventually.

That was how we came across 185, Pineapple Road in Stirchley, Birmingham. January came and as expected, there was still no movement on the Bradford house, therefore, the family had to remain behind while I went to Birmingham to commence my new position as headteacher of George Dixon Comprehensive School. Bradford was about 200 miles away from Birmingham so daily commuting was totally out of the question. I would simply have to commute on the weekends, whether I liked it or not.

In the end, Mary, Ron, and Lisa came, once more, to my rescue. The arrangements were that I would stay with them Sunday to Thursday nights, and I would travel to Bradford on Fridays immediately after closing school. I would do the return journey on a Sunday afternoon. And so, it was until we were forced to sell the Bradford property for exactly what we had purchased it for four years before and were thus able to process the mortgage on the Pineapple Road property. Almost five full months had disappeared out of 1986 before we were able to conduct the move from Bradford and bring the family back together once more. During the commuting stage, my principal worry was that my family might be exposed to those who were hell bent on doing us harm.

Meanwhile, I had begun the process of settling in at the school. As usual, there was a sea of media publicity and interest to navigate.

Duncan leaving for Midlands

City's biggest school names its new head

New Head for City school

One of Birmingham's largest schools, George Dixon, in City Road, will have a new head teacher in January.

Staff Reduction

At once, I had to consider the thorny issue of staff reduction. This was never a pleasant task for any headteacher. To tell a colleague, probably one with whom you have been working for years, that he or she is being made redundant is a heart wrenching task. In the case of a new headteacher, on the one hand it might seem easier because of the absence of any historical relationships, but on the other hand it is not a good way of establishing oneself if you are going to earn the tag as a 'butcher' or 'the axe man.' The school had fifteen staff, too many.

Rolls were falling across the city, and it was now seriously uneconomical to employ so many teachers. The teacher-pupil ratio had changed drastically over the last few years making it a far too expensive proposition for the Birmingham Education Authority to staff their schools in this uneconomic fashion. The Birmingham Education Authority insisted excess staff had to be made redundant.

In effect, these staff would not be returning to the school after the summer holiday. The task of calculating the areas where the axe must fall and identifying the relevant staff fell to me and I had just one school term in which to do so because the staff so identified had to be given the proper period of notice. This would have been a very tall order for any incoming head. Fortunately, the deputy who was the acting head during the interval was still with me; and this made the task considerably easier. The knowledge that redundancy was in the air, encouraged some staff to behave obsequiously whenever I was in their vicinity.

But much of their ingratiation was of no avail because of the dire circumstances of rapidly falling rolls. Then was simply not the time for curry favoring. It was interesting to see how much of this curry favor turned into resentment and reluctant cooperation once any of these staff were identified for redundancy. Nevertheless, by the appropriate time, we had accomplished that mammoth task and the school was trimmed down to its economical size, ready for the start of the new academic year.

Curriculum Reform

As it was with most schools around the country in those days, the curriculum at George Dixon was mono-cultural and euro-centric in nature. This was the undesirable remnant of colonialism. Changing this to a multicultural and anti-racist curriculum was going to take some time and effort, not to mention opposing obstacles. But it had to be done. First, we would have to try changing the teacher's attitude and expectations because that was the most crucial component in this herculean exercise, which we were about to put into operation.

In my book, 'Pastoral Care: An Anti-racist/Multicultural Perspective,' (Basil Blackwell Ltd 1988) Chapter 7, I demonstrated how important it is that we, as teachers, should have the right attitude and expectation if we are to enhance and further all pupils learning process and opportunities. I repeat here two quotations used in my book in support of this view:

"From the further work we have done since the preparation of our interim report we find ourselves more convinced of the major role which the expectations and attitudes which many teachers have, not only of West Indian pupils but indeed of pupils from the whole range of ethnic minority groups, can and do play in the educational experience and perhaps the academic achievement of these pupils. We believe that if teachers allow themselves to be influenced by, and even to perpetuate, stereotypes of different ethnic minority groups, their ability to educate an individual pupil from such a group

according to his or her actual "age, aptitude and ability" may, however unwittingly, be undermined and it can become all too easy to ascribe the pupil's behavior or performance to the assumed stereotype rather than to exercise professional judgment." (Swann, et al 1985, pp. 25/26).

And,

"...You see, really and truly, apart from the things anyone can pick up (the dressing and the proper way of speaking, and so on), the difference between a lady and a flower girl is not how she behaves, but how she is treated. I shall always be a flower girl to Professor Higgins, because he always treats me as a flower girl, and always will; but I know I can be a lady to you, because you always treat me as a lady, and always will." (Pygmalion, G. B. Shaw).

**An INSET Day at George Dixon GM School
From Left to Right are Miss Jane Gurd, Miss Tamara Karim
And Mrs. Jaspal Dhanjal**

It is for this reason that I would discuss with the George Dixon Team the need to call upon the services of the same team of experts, and possibly others, which assisted me at Wyke Manor Upper School in moving forward. It will be necessary to get the strategy right if we are to minimize resistance. Staff need to own the program from the start and at no time feel that the headteacher, especially a black one, is compelling them down roads that they would never have voluntarily gone. Every aspect of the program of actions must be fully discussed and shaped by the entire staff at every level. The school, however, did not have the machinery of government and management in place to allow this to happen. I would have to put this in place. We needed a structure whereby things can happen from the bottom up as much as from the top down. Getting our management and decision-making structures right and operational took the better part of the first two terms.

A key component of this was the role teacher unions representatives would play in promoting the welfare and working conditions of their membership while simultaneously maximizing the learning opportunities for all children. This was of great importance to me because one of the indices of success in any school which is led by me will always be good industrial relations. I did not quite achieve that at Wyke Manor, but I was determined to applaud that at the end of my time at George Dixon. [When I did go in 1999, I had led the school for over thirteen years without a single Union dispute in all that time].

Our built-in industrial strategies of inclusion and joint operations worked. Whereas insularity strongly negatively affected the character of the teachers at Wyke, it was far less so at George Dixon whose staff shared greater cosmopolitan exposures. The teachers here have been around and have experienced a greater reality of the nature of multicultural Britain. To the extent that this was true, my team and I encountered less resistance simply because of my color. When I first arrived at George Dixon, the school was roughly evenly split three ways in terms of pupils' ethnicity: black, Asians and white.

One of the nicest things that happened to me soon after coming to George Dixon as its new headteacher was to have received an invitation from my old University Education Department in Swansea to come up to Swansea on May 12th, 1986, and address the Post Graduate Certificate of Education (PGCE) course about the Swann Report and multicultural education. This was particularly flattering because I was once a student on that very same course at the very same university department. Some of the lecturers and professors who knew me as a student there in 1965-1969 presented themselves at my lecture. It was gratifying to answer their searching questions at the end as I seemingly turned the table. My lecture on these subjects must have been successful because it became an annual event.

School Refurbishment

I was allowed some honeymoon as a new headteacher, even a black one; it was important that I used that period wisely and without undue delay. If I am going to ask the staff to review and alter their approach to teaching and give of their spare time voluntarily to be part of the school's decision-making machinery, I ought to be doing something which is clearly in their interest too. The school had no obvious entrance and no reception at Ritchie Block. Yet, of the three buildings, Ritchie was obviously the main one. It was the most central. For entrances, there were two arches, one showing 'Boys' indicating the entrance for the boys at the eastern end of the block and similarly the other showing 'Girls' indicating the entrance for the girls at the western end.

This reflected times past when the school was a mixed-sex institution. Apparently, the sexes were strictly kept apart; so much so that they could not use the same entrance for fear that they might meet each other. Sometime later, the schools would cease their separate existences and duly amalgamate. Yet, that block was considered the main block to the school, probably because of its prestigious past and its prominent and convenient location on the popular City Road, not to mention its architecture and its listed building status.

The entire corridor was dilapidated and badly in need of repairs. There were instances when the teachers were known to have their umbrellas up during teaching when it rained. Finally, the library and close-by staffroom could use some refurbishment. Facilities on the other two sites were better because they were more modern buildings. But they were not the main sites. To motivate my colleagues, and indeed to have my pupils function in a more positively stimulating environment, our team suggested we approach the Birmingham Education Authority about allocating some funds to undertake the necessary works at the school. I was a new head, and the chances are that we would succeed. Also, on our side, was the fact that the school's chairman of governors was Councilor Albert Bore (now Sir Albert Bore) one of the most powerful politicians in Birmingham at that time.

It paid off. My meetings with the education officials and several politicians including Councilor Bore, bore fruit (excuse the pun). The works to be done over the next three years included the complete refurbishment of the long corridor; the classrooms carpeted and refurnished; a new entrance and reception facility; roofing repairs to prevent leaks and a new headteacher's suite of rooms to include the head's office, shower and toilet facility, a kitchenette, headteacher's secretary's office and a parents, pupils and staff waiting area.

Unfortunately, some mischievous person leaked it to the media that the new head was having a jacuzzi built into his office at the Birmingham rate payers' expense. Just like the story about me having taken down a picture of the Queen at Wyke Manor Upper School, this one was a blatant untruth and clearly mischievous in intent. As did the Wyke story, this was the first sign that there were enemies about the place. This was a deliberate lie, which the architects did much to dispel after the media stubbornly clung to it for an extended period.

On the Home Front

On the home front, the family was together again. The purchasing arrangements on the Pineapple Road property were completed and the local doctor who had owned the house moved out on May 8th, 1986, and we moved in the following day. This was a four-bedroom detached family house.

The bedrooms were exceptionally spacious. It had a very spacious living room and a very large kitchen.

The Conservatory and Garden half of the Livingroom

The Front door and Bay Window Half of the Livingroom

The garden had the benefit of expert landscaping; it had many fruit trees and plenty of lawn areas for the children to prance around at will.

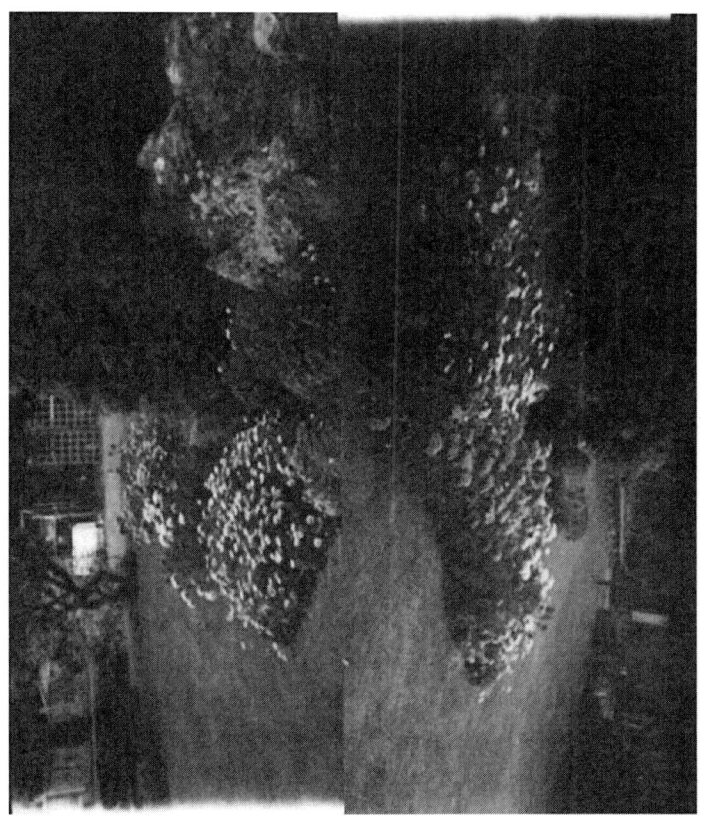

Some of the Gardens

More of the Gardens

In all, it was the ideal home for our family. Once more the immediate focus at home would be to find a suitable nursery school for the twins who were approaching their fourth birthday and a suitable junior school for James, who would soon be eight. Following a great deal of search, research, visiting and advice, we decided that the children would all be enrolled at the nearby Colmore Junior and Infants School. The twins would be enrolled in the infants' while James would be enrolled in the juniors. Their school was within easy reach of home and turned out to be a very good school conveniently located.

It was not a surprise to me but was a major blow when the current deputy head and former acting head announced that he was successfully considered for another headship in the east of Birmingham.

Appointment of a Deputy

I had always wondered why Mr. Vickers was not long-listed for the George Dixon headship. He was so obviously a head in waiting. Everything about him was strictly professional. In the short space of time, I was at the school, his guidance and support were immeasurable. His well-deserved promotion represented a significant loss to me as a new headteacher. The true professional that he was, he worked unstintingly to the last day of the summer term. He would take up his new appointment at the beginning of the coming September. This loss was not altogether without merit. I had inherited four deputies, none of which was my appointment. Here, already, I was given the opportunity to field a deputy of my own choosing.

The necessary steps were immediately taken to advertise the vacancy which John Vickers would be leaving behind. We were very fortunate we had a good response to the advert and were thus able to short-list a very good selection for the interviews. There were six strong candidates in total competing in an all-day set of interviews before a panel of four governors, including the Chairman of the Governors, plus myself. Mr. Tayeb Chekera finally emerged the victor and would join the team in September 1986 as one of the school's four deputy heads.

As if the loss of an outstanding deputy in the early days of my new headship was not enough, the headteacher's secretary, who had been at the school for very many years suddenly resigned. This was rather puzzling given that she currently had a new headteacher that needed to be settled in office. That is considered one of the foremost responsibilities of any secretary. To go in such circumstances, was not only bad for the school but was personally bad for me (rather reminiscent of the Head of Modern Languages at Wyke but done differently) and for her team of six other administrative team members only one of whom was black.

The deputy, Mr. Bob Mason, who oversaw administration, moved swiftly to find a replacement. None of the existing members of the administrative team applied to be considered. The haul was a poor one, but the urgency of the situation meant that we would take a risk with the best of the bunch. It was in this way that 'Mary C' came to be appointed. The appointment was a disastrous one and lasted just three weeks. In the meantime, I had taken some personal interest in the performance levels of the rest of the team and had concluded that Mrs. Julie G had the necessary potential and credentials to make a suitable headteacher's secretary.

I questioned why she did not apply for the position first time round? She did not apply because she did not think that she would be considered. This was simply a matter of confidence. On the second outing, Mrs. Julie G did apply and eventually became the personal secretary to the headteacher and the head of the Administrative Team of seven including her.

For the new headteacher, this was a very difficult and fiercely critical time. I had survived a hellish experience in Bradford and narrowly escaped their guillotine thus enabling me to assume the headship of one of Birmingham largest comprehensive schools. I did this in circumstances of falling rolls requiring me to make fifteen staff redundant almost immediately. The Christmas break of 1985 was the only separator between the management responsibilities for these two schools. There wasn't even sufficient time to settle my accommodation issues before picking up the reins in Birmingham.

My wife, and three young children had to endure a substantial period of separation and being left behind in a town which didn't welcome them and had, indeed, threatened the children's lives. It meant commuting the near 200 miles each way there and back on all weekends for the better part of five months while enduring the real fear and stressful worry for the safety of my family until I could bring them to a settled home of safety, as we have done now. To accomplish the results we have now, I had to make do with temporary accommodation. Along with all this, the new school was under well needed refurbishment.

Moreover, I had quickly suffered the loss of two key members of the George Dixon established team—an important and solidly effective deputy headteacher and the headteacher's secretary who had optimum knowledge of the school. This latter is a loss that would have caused any new headteacher to wince. Amidst all this, the main business of the school had to go on: providing the students with high-quality education which would enable them to function properly in Britain and in a multicultural world as well-rounded individuals. To this end, staff development and related training was paramount. My team and I wasted no time in mobilizing on these areas.

Chapter 15
Murder Announced

We were consumed with all this when the news broke that the almost forgotten Alison Taylor's disappearance was once more in the headlines of the national and local media. Most people I knew and with whom I was in contact thought the case had gone cold. It was not. Deep into the privacy and beauty of Ilkley Moor's ground nesting birds' upland habitat, a shallow grave was found at the end of May 1986. A keen bird watcher had stumbled upon the contours of the grave and immediately raised the alarm with police headquarters.

Ilkley Moor is arguably the most famous tourist attraction in Yorkshire especially for nature lovers. Its fame, at some point in time, will touch all mankind. Which university freshmen group did not have the great and popular Yorkshire National Anthem and Folk song "Ilkley Moor Baht 'at" as part of their sing song repertoire at all their jolly events throughout their university tenure? But Moors are not just known for their sheer beauty, they can also be infamous. Saddleworth Moor for example, also in the north of England (part of the West Riding of Yorkshire), has the distinction of being associated with what is still regarded as Britain's most gruesome and heinous crimes. This was the platform on which the Moors murderers Ian Brady and Myra Hindley tortured, raped, and murdered five children and teenagers.

They slaughtered their young prey and sadistically recorded the children's sufferings and cries for merciful help during the commission of those horrible crimes between 1963 and 1965. The victims murdered by these heartless brutes included John Kilbride, Lesley Ann Downey, and Keith Bennett. These brutal serial killers were eventually caught and imprisoned in 1966. Myra Hindley died in West Suffolk Hospital prison in 2002, aged 60 years. Ian Brady variously fought his incarceration: he went on hunger strike in 1999 and made several complaints about his treatment at Ashworth Hospital where he was held. The author has personal knowledge of this because he was a non-executive director and deputy chairman, on the Ashworth Board of Directors between 1999/2002. The section of the hospital that was covered by his brief was the very section that housed Ian Brady until his death in 2017 at age 79.

I am recalling all this misery suffered by the parents of those children in Brady and Hindley times and wondering what agony Mrs. Taylor and her family must now be enduring.

Since leaving Bradford, I would frequently telephone Mrs. Taylor to update my information on Alison's case. Mrs. Taylor was always optimistic about eventually having her daughter returning home safely even though she always admitted in the same conversations that neither she nor the police had any helpful lead. Now, all that optimism will have gone, leaving Mrs. Taylor in absolute and total despair.

According to the reports, Alison did put up a fight before she succumbed to her fate: tiny clumps of reddish hair under her nails were still discernable when the remains of her skeleton frame were exhumed. Her handbag found under the skeleton still contained new notes amounting to twenty-five pounds Sterling. Whoever killed Alison did not do so for her money.

Ringing in my mind's ears, were the words "tiny clumps of red hair" and the untouched money in Alison's handbag. These matters gave me a strong hunch and I wanted to go where they would take me for Alison was a superb student and a great asset to her school and her home. Going through my mind was a burning question: did Alison die because she knew too much? Did she unwittingly share information with me that led to her death?

It did not take too much to convince me that I must hurriedly return to West Yorkshire to investigate my hunch. Alison was one of my prize students and she is entitled to all that I can give even in death. I am determined that her killer or killers must be brought to justice.

Fortunately, my newly appointed Personal Assistant (PA) was familiar with the school's administrative systems. She was already in situ and was, therefore, able to assume her new responsibilities immediately. With the team of deputies and I remaining in constant touch, she should be able to hold the school in progress for the two or three days I expected to be gone.

After dinner on Sunday the 1st of June, I said goodbye to my family who by then, and to the extent they could understand, were fully in the know about the circumstances which were pulling me back to West Yorkshire. I turned the

Toyota Crown, a thing of luxury and beauty just this side of its fourth birthday, northwards heading for the M6 motorway. It was then that I noticed the flashing blue lights behind me signaling me to pull over and stop. This was becoming all too familiar. Since purchasing this car from new in 1982, I have been pulled over by the police in different parts of the country four times. This would be the fifth occasion. And if I include the first one, I experienced back in 1969, this current one will make a total of six times.

As the officers cautiously sauntered toward my stationary car, I could prophetically recite verbatim the procedure that they will follow.

"Good evening, Sir. Would you please switch off the ignition and step outside the car, Sir?" instructed the first officer.

"Yes, officer," I said, as I obeyed his instructions.

"Is this your car, Sir?" The first officer further asked.

"Yes officer, some of it. I am still paying for it," I sarcastically replied.

This was a signal to the second officer to intervene.

"Please open the booth, Sir, I want to look inside as part of our routine check," instructed the second officer.

I willingly obliged and flew the booth catch. The second officer turned the booth inside out and even carefully examined the spare tire looking for any compartmentalization. That done, he left all my stuff on the ground and moved to the inside of the car. He removed all the mats, checked the glove compartment and side pockets. It was only then that the first officer intervened once more.

"How are you able to afford this car, Sir? What is your occupation?" He asked.

"I am a schoolteacher, Sir," I replied.

To some amazement, he asked me to produce my papers. I gave the folder containing the car's first M.O.T. certificate, my insurance papers, and my driving license. After a detailed and meticulous examination of the documents, he returned them to me with a final question:

"Where are you heading to, Sir?"

I told him that they had just delayed my arrival for an important meeting in Bradford by some forty-five minutes or three abouts. They both said sorry and went their way leaving me to put my car back in order.

The message was very clear, if somewhat repetitive, it was all my fault. A black man had no right to be driving a Toyota Crown, especially given what they would have known: that it was only eleven of these cars in England at the time. Except for a brief hint at frivolous sarcasm, I was both docile and polite throughout the ordeal. I had learned from early on in my British experience, that it does not pay to be smart with police officers especially if you are a black person.

In 1969, soon after I was appointed to my first teaching post at Ebury Technical Boys School in London, I began purchasing my first car. It was a new Morris 1100. Just like I was experiencing now, I was pulled over by the cops on a routine stop on my way to school one morning. Apart from the staring ignominy from the drivers and passengers of passing morning traffic, the officers were carelessly delaying me and causing me to be late for school. Minute by minute my young and foolish head got the better of me until I was extremely angry at the antics of these cops. The effect of my visible indignation was to encourage those officers in the ruthlessness they employed in their search of my car.

Even the upholstered fabrics were ripped away from several areas of my new car. I got nowhere with the complaint my solicitor lodged on my behalf at what, for me at the time, was a heavy financial burden that I could ill afford. There were four other similar instances of this kind in the past. All have prompted complaints to the relevant police authorities. Other than the eventual letters containing rationalized apologies for the inconvenience I suffered, nothing known to me ever happened to these xenophobic zealots.

It is not realistic to expect the police to police the police. Now, despite the history of these police stops, I shall have to file a complaint to the West Midlands police authority for being so frequently targeted for these stops and searches: the traffic version of the old SUS law. It is a massive task that we teachers have ahead of us and for well into the future.

While reports to police headquarters may or may not remove some of the limbs of racism, they cannot do so permanently. Those limbs will spring again, even more vigorously, as we continue to manufacture more and more racially tainted policemen and women in our white supremacy school factories. We cannot carry on doing the same thing and expect different results. It is to the teachers of the world, armed with their decolonized curriculum, that will, eventually, eradicate this pernicious evil called racism from its roots.

It was a good thing that I had decided to travel on Sunday. Had it been a weekday there would have been very thick evening traffic compounded by this racially instigated stop and search?

In those circumstances, I would have been set back in making progress against the magnifying workload for the busy people I wished to see as the day progressed.

Despite the unwarranted stop, I would still get to Bradford in time to book myself in a local hotel and still get some sleep, in readiness for the meetings that I had mentally planned for tomorrow.

I did not tell Mrs. Taylor that I would be visiting. But she would be my first call on my detective venture. When I first contemplated teaching as a profession, I never envisaged that I would, by extension, be engaged in the business of a sleuth repeatedly.

I made a telephone call to my wife to assure her that I was safely ensconced in a four-star hotel in the city of Bradford. I found out that she and the children were missing me but were all ok. She wasn't impressed when I told her about the West Midlands Police stopping me and giving me the going over. She fully supported my intention to lodge yet another complaint to the police authority regarding these constant harassments.

I woke up the next morning at the Bradford Metro Hotel at 06.30 on the dot. This was good timing. I could freshen up and get a good breakfast inside me. There was no certainty that I would have time for lunch. At nine o'clock I telephoned my PA in Birmingham. All was well on that front. Everything was going like clockwork, she assured me.

I pulled up outside Mrs. Taylor's corner shop on the edge of the village of Wyke at precisely 09.30. I entered the shop, but Mrs. Taylor was nowhere to be seen. Instead, in her preferred corner of the shop was a tall and slender gentleman with brown hair and a heavy mustache. He was friendly and quick to assist me as Yorkshire people are often said to be. This was my first meeting with Mr. Andrew Taylor, husband to Mrs. Marjorie Taylor. These are Alison's parents.

I politely enquired about Mrs. Taylor's whereabouts. Mr. Taylor told me that she is inside the home but has not been on shop duties since they received very bad news about their daughter, Alison. He was tearful as he made the unsolicited disclosure that his daughter was murdered—a fact they discovered after Alison's long disappearance.

I told Mr. Taylor that I was Alison's former headteacher and that it was the news about Alison's death that had brought me back from Birmingham where I am now based. Mr. Taylor was suddenly jolted by belated recognition.

"Oh," he said, "I know I had recognized you. I will let Mrs. Taylor know that you are here. She never stopped singing your praises."

With that, he departed and quickly returned, Mrs. Taylor in tow. It seemed there was little left of her. She had lost some weight and her appearance seemed neglected, but she was, nevertheless, happy to be talking to me in person once more as both she and her husband listened to me with the hope of any miracle, I might be able to perform. They were both impressed that I had come all the way from Birmingham so quickly after the news broke about this matter which is so personal to them.

I asked questions such as whether there was anything unusual about Alison's modus operandi on the day she went missing. There was nothing unusual that they could recall except that a call came to the shop, and she answered it. During the telephone conversation, Alison agreed to meet someone at the bus station on Toller Lane at 16.00 that Sunday afternoon, but that was not strange. Alison had made meeting arrangements with friends before. Alison did not mention the name of the person she was going to meet, and her parents settled on the assumption that it was one of her many friends. I didn't think it was going to be needed but I asked the parents if they would let me have a list of Alison's best friends.

It didn't take them very long and soon I had a list consisting of seven names with addresses and telephone numbers. Only two of these seven were males one of whom I immediately recognized. He was an Asian boy from Wyke Manor. I secured this list in a special compartment in my briefcase just in case it is going to be needed. However, my hunch had become much stronger after learning of Alison's meeting point on that, seemingly fatal Sunday afternoon. What I had in mind was going to need the magic of some police authority. I expressed my sincere sympathy to the Taylors and told them that I would leave no stone unturned until the police is able to arrest and bring to justice the killer of their daughter.

Only when that happens, will their woes be assuaged somewhat; only then will there be closure for the Taylors. I bade the Taylors a very good day as I set off on my next visit. Around the corner, there was a telephone booth. No one was using it, lucky for me. I pulled up next to the booth and quickly made a call to Bob Mason, the administrative deputy at my new school. I felt more comfortable calling Bob because our friendship went back a long way to our present relationship. I did not know Phillip Naylor or Mrs. Irene Gray, the other deputies, all that well and therefore not sure of their trustworthiness. Tayeb Chekera, though appointed, would not join the team of deputies until later that year. As did Julie, my PA, Bob, assured me that the ship was sailing nicely.

I needed a meeting with Chief Inspector Larry Holms. He was the officer who had failed to do anything about the anonymous postcard, letters and the brick which was thrown through my office window when I was at Wyke. After ending my call to Birmingham, I went directly to the Chief Inspector's office in the city of Bradford and asked at the desk if I could see the Inspector. The young girl at the desk enquired who I was before informing me that for a month now, the Chief Inspector was transferred to the City of Leeds. He was no longer at the Bradford office.

Thirty minutes later I was pulling up to the station's car park on Main Street, Leeds City Center. The Inspector was not at his desk when the clerk rang through, and no one really knew where he was. Did I want to wait indefinitely or leave a message for the Inspector, the clerk asked. Before I could reply the Inspector was seen emerging from the luncheon canteen on the compound. Luck was on my side again. The minute he entered the reception area, he recognized me and greeted me by name. This was a good sign; it would make my mission much more manageable.

The Inspector beckoned me, and we walked to his office. Once we were seated, the Inspector said to me, "You are looking as if you could use a good cup of coffee" while reaching for the telephone perched precariously on the top right-hand corner of his desk. I nodded as he ordered two cups and a pot of coffee.

During the wait for the coffee to arrive, the still puzzled Inspector queried: "Mr. Duncan, the popular news was that you had left the area for the West Midlands, why are you in Leeds? And how did you know that you could find me here. The last time we had any dealings I was still based in Bradford?"

I confirmed to the Inspector that his opening premises were correct and that I am the current headteacher of a school in the West Midlands. However, I told him he knew that I had some unfinished business in West Yorkshire and recent developments seem to have some relevance in connection with that business.

"I am not sure that I understand what you are saying to me; you seem to imply that I should know something. You will have to refresh my mind as clearly as you can," the Inspector said in a puzzled tone.

At this point, a chap from the canteen arrived with the coffee and the Inspector beckoned him in. He seated the tray on a nearby side table and then quietly left the room. The Inspector poured us both a cup of steaming hot coffee and we then resumed the conversation.

"I am recalling my early days at Wyke, Inspector, when you led a team to investigate several shenanigans involving anonymous, racialist mailings and a brick crashing through the window of my office at Wyke Manor Upper School. Is any of all this finding a route down your memory lane, Inspector?"

"Yes, Mr. Duncan, it has all come back; and I remember that we, the police, were unable to proceed with those incidents because there were no leads. I presume that explains your reference to unfinished business which I should know about?" said the Inspector as he outlined his recall.

I confirmed that he was spot on. The coffee was awful, too bitter for my taste buds, but I didn't tell the Inspector that in so many words. I simply politely declined his offer of a refill.

Now, the Inspector began probing the connection between his recall and 'what recent developments?' He was not aware of any. Earlier this morning I had picked up a copy of the Yorkshire Post which still carried the Ilkley Moor shallow grave find as its front-page headlines. I reached inside my briefcase and produced a copy of the paper and handed it to the Inspector. He was aware of the story but still could not fathom the relevance to my past Wyke Manor story. I wasn't quite sure either, Inspector. It is just a very strong hunch I have, Sir, and I am hoping that the police will assist me this time round in following through my hunch because this time a white girl has lost her life leaving her white parents in excruciating mental pain. This last remark was deliberate.

I was hoping that the Inspector would have picked up my oblique reference to racism and that it would have stimulated some compunction in him. Maybe this would cause him to do better than he did almost four years ago. It worked. The Inspector wanted to know how he could help me with my hunch. I referred the Inspector, once more, to the article on the front page of the Yorkshire Post. He read audibly the section which said that 'almost new Sterling notes were found in the handbag that was found under the skeleton body and the reference to tiny clumps of red hair being still visible in the areas of the dead girl's nails.'

I immediately focused the Inspector's mind on the banknotes. That was where I needed his help. The red hair clumps had meaning to me too, but this was something I could handle on my own.

"Inspector, the report says that the notes found were new and of the same sequence as if they were just issued by a bank. What I would like to know, Inspector, is which bank issued those notes. Is this something the police could find out?"

Chief Inspector, Larry Holms, thought very deeply about this before breaking his silence to say: "Mr. Duncan, leave this with me for a couple of days. I will see what we can do. How can I contact you?" The Inspector asked.

I gave my school's telephone number and that for my home to the Inspector. Although the mobile telephone had made an appearance in Britain in the earliest part of 1985, one was not yet available to me or yet in common usage.

I would now be able to join my family tonight and be ready for school in the morning, much earlier than I had previously anticipated.

With no police interference, the Toyota Crown made light work of the miles and I was home before the children retired to bed. James, who was already seven years old, was playing big brother entertaining his twin siblings with his own made-up version of bed-time stories which I had told them in the not-so-distant past. The twins were now approaching their fourth birthday. The media was no longer showing any interest in them. In fact, their third birthday was the last time there was a media presence. Mummy and daddy listened in for a while before we had to discharge our parental responsibility and see them safely in their several beds. Having accomplished this with only little resistance, mummy and daddy were left with some quality time for ourselves.

The Bank Noters

The deputies and my PA were surprised to see me back so early. They were expecting me to be away for at least another couple of days. Nonetheless, I was properly briefed, and we set about conducting the business of the school.

The Chief Inspector was true to his speculation that it would take him a couple of days to find the answer to my query. On Wednesday, soon after the morning break, the phone on my desk rang. My PA advised that she had Chief Inspector Holms' office on the phone for me. Once connected to the Inspector, I realized that I had hit a jackpot. The Inspector had not only traced the bank notes to the bank of issue as I had asked, but he traced the branch, cash dispenser; the date, the time, and possible people who might have visited the cash dispenser on the date.

The notes were traced to a Toller Lane cash dispenser which I knew very well. I had personally used it on numerous occasions during my time in Bradford. It was the closest and the most convenient to my home in Manningham. Those notes were taken from a batch used to stack that dispenser. The notes were taken on the same day Alison went missing (Sunday) at 15.45.

The Inspector informed me that, on that day, there were 70 withdrawals from the said cash dispenser. According to the information gained from the 70 extracting cards, there was only one schoolteacher among them. He was Mr. Dale Stewart of a Bingley address, and he was a teacher at William Holt school. He became a customer of the bank and branch, at least, since September 1978 when he opened his bank account at the Toller Lane branch of Yorkshire Bank.

I knew that there was a Dale Stewart at Wyke, and I remembered he lived near me in Manningham. The discrepancies in address and school were not terribly significant. Afterall, teachers do move addresses and seek promotion to other schools. For this reason, I was able to express my gratitude to the Inspector and assured him that his efforts were extremely helpful. I did not share with him that Alison Taylor rendezvoused with someone, possibly her killer, at Toller Lane Bus station fifteen minutes after the funds were taken from the cash machine. The cash machine is only a short walk from the bus station. The Inspector bade me good luck and good day as he signed off saying that he will keenly listen out for any developments that I can share and that I should not hesitate to let him know if there is anything else with which he can assist me.

I put through a call to William Holt school as headteacher to headteacher, albeit from different authorities. The headteacher, Mrs. Brown, was helpful. She confirmed that Dale Stewart was no longer a member of her staff and that he moved to a new school in September 1979. The school was Wrigley Secondary in Sheffield. (He could have moved his home address too, I thought to myself). My calls to Wrigley School were resisted on grounds of privacy even though I was a serving headteacher. I decided that it was worth a trip to

Sheffield in South Yorkshire. Maybe my personal charm would work on Ms. Grandison who was the headteacher of Wrigley Secondary.

On Friday morning, I arrived at George Dixon bright and early. Spent just enough time to see the school settled and advise my PA that I would be leaving shortly. I told her that she should brief the deputies and I will be in touch before school breaks for the weekend. Sheffield is a lot closer to Birmingham than Bradford. By 13.00 I was at Wrigley School. I was so wrong. Ms. Grandison would not see me.

I overheard her muttering to her secretary that I was so rude turning up like that without a prior appointment. You could see unpleasantness written all over her countenance and enough to tell even the dumbest person that they would not get past her. I had no prior knowledge that someone in my profession could be so rude, or was it prejudice? All I wanted to know was if she still had a member of staff known as Mr. Dale Stewart.

It became very clear that I was going to need the assistance of Chief Inspector Larry Holms once more. I would leave this until after the weekend and make my way back to my family. As it turned out, I was able to do better than calling George Dixon, I was in the school a good half an hour before the school was dismissed at 16.00.

On Monday, I placed a call to the Chief Inspector at 10.00 on the dot. The Inspector told me that if I was one minute later, I would have missed him because he was just leaving for a two-day conference for Chief Inspectors in Sheffield, of all places.

"Wow!" I said, "Inspector, the help I need is in Sheffield and gave him a quick synopsis of Ms. Grandison's tale. All I wanted, Inspector, was to know if she still had a Mr. Dale Stewart on her team of staff."

"I know the school quite well. One of my close nephews goes there. While I am in Sheffield, I will see what I can uncover for you." The Inspector assured me.

I thanked him in anticipation, and he was gone. Before the week was out, the Chief Inspector rang me at home one night and shared with me his findings.

The chief discovered that Dale Stewart was no longer at the Sheffield, Wrigley School but has been at Wyke Manor Upper School since September 1981. He made a call to the Acting Head of Wyke Manor to confirm that Dale Stewart is still there, and he is. His current address is given as the one I knew in Manningham. Once more I expressed my gratitude to Chief Inspector Holms for the very useful information he shared.

I pointed out to the Chief Inspector that Dale Stewart, I knew, had red hair. The significance of that was lost on the Inspector.

I advised him that if he did me one more favor, I will hand him on a plate, the killer of Alison Taylor, with all the motives he will want.

The Inspector was quizzical. I want you to search for this guy's place in Manningham. You need samples of his writing that will connect this guy to the postcard and anonymous notes plus the objects thrown through my window when I was at Wyke.

The Inspector asked: "What the hell has all this got to do with Alison Taylor's murder, Mr. Duncan?"

"Inspector, Alison may have sold that mysterious postcard to Dale Stewart. And if she did, he may have killed her," I replied.

"OK, we will do that, but we will need a lawful pretext. This guy also smokes marijuana, so we can use that," the Inspector acknowledged.

A few days later, the search revealed a foul smelly dump that has never seen any tidiness or order. This dump indicated a total lack of organization. The kind of person living there was the kind that seeks out his cleanest 'dirty' shirt if he must go anyplace. Nevertheless, the Inspector was able to retrieve enough writing samples that were of major interest to me. Very significantly, the Inspector found two unused postcards. One was identical to the one which was sent to me and the other was of a huge oak tree with a small axe leaning on it.

This card, too, was unused. Finally, in a wastepaper basket which seemed to have been forgotten for several months, were three pieces of paper. On closer examination, the Inspector found that two of the three pieces were, in fact, related. They were the two pieces of a letter angrily torn into those pieces and tossed into the wastepaper basket. The content of that letter was revealing. The letter was dated the 14th of April 1982, which was two days after my first parents' meeting at Wyke Manor.

It read: "Dear Mr. Stewart, You made me look like an idiot at the parents' meeting last Monday evening. You got me to ask about the Queen's picture which no one knew anything about. How could the black headteacher move the picture which was never in the school according to the teachers who were all there before he came just one week earlier? Were you creating mischief? If so, please don't use me in this way again. I am going to tell your Uncle Ralph about this and ask him to warn you. Madge Ellis."

This letter was dynamite. This guy hated me from day one and began enlisting accomplices, though not always successfully. The third piece of paper was unrelated but hugely relevant. That piece of paper revealed that Dale Stewart's bank card was used to withdraw fifty pounds from the Toller Lane cash dispenser at 15.45, Sunday, 15th September 1985. Here is the evidence I needed.

A. The handwriting collection which revealed some matching consonants with some of those on the documents sent to me anonymously at Wyke Manor.
B. The unused identical postcard, together with that of the Oaktree.
C. The letter which explained the Queen's picture slander.
D. And the fact that this guy is one of the two red heads and stumpy reddish beard at my former school.
E. The telling cash machine receipt.

These were the missing jig-saw pieces I needed. I was, at last, able to rule out my deputy who also had red hair and who had figured in my suspicion. It seemed Alison had recognized Dale Stewart as the person she sold those cards to and the route to her shallow grave was mapped out therefrom. Now, I would like to make a special trip to Leeds. I have a promise to fulfill.

It was a Saturday afternoon in Leeds. The Inspector was expecting me for 13.00. I was punctual.

As I promised, Inspector, I said: your killer of Alison Taylor is Dale Stewart. Alison had seen my card which I had placed on purposeful display in my office when she first joined the school in September 1982. She remembered selling a redhead stranger with a stumpy red or ginger beard, the last two cards of the same type. She remembered because she was hoping to use one of those cards for a school project, but the stranger bought both plus a card showing a large oak tree.

The dilemma I had, Inspector, was that I had two members of the staff answering that description and had no way of eliminating one without giving away my internal thoughts. What was most strange to me was that both these red heads had visited my office on numerous occasions and would have noticed that postcard on prominent display and never was there the slightest facial giveaway.

Inspector, I will leave you to figure out whether there was a case of someone knowing too much here. Was Alison being paid to shut up? Was there a trace of blackmail? Was she lured to her death?

All the credit must go to the police, I told the Inspector. There must be no hint of my involvement. The last time I was involved in some other project which was extraneous to my main job, this city cried "conflict of interest." I should not want my current employers to make a similar charge.

I was now feeling far better than before about leaving West Yorkshire for the West Midlands.

Dale Stewart had just taken out a long-term lease in one of the HMS Prisons. Much of the evidence for establishing his right to occupancy was provided by himself. He was by no means the only character who wanted to destroy me as a black man, but he operated surreptitiously and had to be dug out.

There were named others who got flushed out by Christopher Perry in his letters to Bradford's Chief Executive, Chief Education Officer, and me. They had denied the charge leveled at them, as I would have done, when the advisors asked them if they were guilty. Additionally, they sought the protection of their Union, the NUT. But what was most telling, they never confronted the man who named them.

People from the education office, the advisory team, a named school governor, and conniving staff members, and political contributors were exposed by the parents who came to see me about the Ray Honeyford related plot.

The 13+ Assistant Director of Education had written to a prominent politician about me in adverse terms. Mysteriously, that letter was leaked to the press. It took the Chief Education Officer to stem the flow of damaging publicity emanating from that leakage. The same 13+ Assistant Director approached his aim from other angles too. He and one of the school's governors had failed miserably in their attempt to bring me down at that special governors' meeting. These guys could not hide. They were right out in the open.

I would have liked to know who was responsible for breaking into my home just to ransack it while my family and I were abroad, who was responsible for threatening the lives of my children, and, finally, who was it that instigated the pupil demonstration that took me by surprise on that day of action. This last I consider to be deserving of a prize for gallantry because it brough to light the racial injustices many of our students were silently suffering.

But you cannot win them all. Somethings require more long-term measures like relying on an anti-racist multicultural curriculum to produce future actors and actresses whose behavior would be the reverse of that coming from their present-day counterparts. This remains my drive on the platform now moved to Birmingham, West Midlands.

Chapter 16
The Sunday Times and
The Sunday Telegraph Defamations

The first half of 1986 at George Dixon had gone extremely well. Physical and structural improvements of the school's fabric had begun and was continuing; the staff development programs were taking root and both students and staff were happier, and they were showing it. Staff were now able to participate meaningfully in the management of the school because of the new management structure that was now functional. They could now rightly say that they owned the school's decisions especially regarding learning programs. This was so much the truth that I had begun to lose sight of the fact that I was a black man in charge on the 'bridge' of this ship: and that is a luxury no black man at the 'bridge' should ever allow to happen. You forget that fact at your peril.

Complacency in our situation is a very dangerous avenue. Too much complacency can hide the signs of trouble lurking. And lurking they were, but in some different shades from the ones encountered in Bradford. Nevertheless, it is just as troubling and, in some cases, more terrible, as we shall see.

Pressures on a Black Headteacher

There were the demands and pressures from the local black and Asian communities. The Asians represented in the school were predominantly Muslims and Sikhs. The communities from which these children came were very concerned that schools were not nurturing their religious and cultural values. At a time when inner-city schools were losing children to their suburban counterparts, it was difficult to ignore parental wishes. But to give in to some of the demands, which the Asian parents made, had very complicated repercussions.

To take just three examples: (i) some Muslim parents did not want their girl children bearing their bodies even in the company of other girls. This complicated school arrangements for physical education and shower facilities.

(ii) Many Asian parents considered that the daily Christian worship requirements in schools was in direct conflict with their own religions and made demands for separate worshipping arrangements. It was not easy to accommodate that because of the need to find a 'double coincidence' of sufficient staff that had the necessary knowledge and sympathetic understanding to arrange and supervise separate assemblies daily. Daily worship was a lawful requirement imposed upon all schools.

(iii) Thirdly, many Asian parents wanted the school to keep the sexes apart once their daughters attain the age of puberty. They felt that unless the school did that, there would be an active threat to their way of life as it appertained to the institution of arranged marriages. That was feasible in single-sex schools. But in the mixed-sex secondary schools, such as George Dixon was, it is almost impossible to ensure that kind of division. Because of this failure in schools, like George Dixon, there was a drain on the school of its female Asian pupils.

All the single-sex girls' schools in Birmingham and neighboring authorities were full and bursting at the seams even in those times of falling rolls. Apart from the loss of numbers, we were losing 'brains' too. No one in the business of education could have remained oblivious to the numerous media reports and research findings indicating that girls were outperforming boys everywhere in the country and internationally. This would seriously impact upon our ability to produce good examination results later in time.

The black community had its own demands and imposed its own challenges too, both on the school and on me, as a black headteacher. Almost every black community organization in and around Birmingham has begun issuing invitations for me to either address their memberships and/or become an active member of their organizations. It could not be done. I would have had no time left to manage the school and certainly no time for my family. I had to be selective and offer my best. It was in this way that I became an active member of the Afro-Caribbean Teachers' Association (ACTA). In due course, I became its chairman and gave accommodation facilities to the organization at George Dixon School premises.

Bernard Coard and others had revealed the weaknesses in the British educational system as far as it pertains to black children (West Indian children). ACTA was formed with the precise aim of remedying the identified weaknesses in state schools.

These weaknesses were negatively impacting pupil performance and achievement mainly in the areas of English, mathematics, and history. ACTA responded by organizing and running its own supplementary school on Saturdays (hence the popular terms "Saturday Schools" or Supplementary Schools at the time) where great emphasis was placed on preparing all pupils (white and non-white), who attended these schools, in these three subjects mainly. Inevitably, I was bound, out of a declared commitment to become one of the school's regular voluntary teachers on Saturdays. Even so, I was often criticized for non-involvement with my own fellow blacks.

Similarly, the Asian communities had concerns about the adequacy of the educational provision in British schools. As did the black communities, the Asian communities responded by creating their own community organization, Asian Teachers' Association (ACTA), which, in many areas of the country, established and ran supplementary schools. In these schools, in addition to mathematics and English, a strong focus was given to religion and cultural values of the countries of origin of the pupils. Under my leadership at George Dixon School, and as did ACTA, ATA was also accommodated at George Dixon School.

As did Bernard Coard's work (How the West Indian Child is Made Educationally Subnormal in the British school system 1971) in the 1970's, the Rampton and Swann Reports of the 80s had also left no one in any doubt that things were wrong educationally for black children. As a member of both Inquiries, which produced these reports, I was seen by my fellow blacks as the person with all the answers. One of the many problems, that black children encountered disproportionately everywhere as we have already seen, was exclusion from schools. This had the effect of driving parents in search of my school or even to my home with tales about the 'racist' exclusions that had befallen their children. What they most wanted at those times was for me to take their excluded children into my school. If I didn't, I would be viewed as not caring and a 'sellout'.

Yet, I did not see this 'Carlton Duncan was the savior' thing reflected in a rush to enroll their children in my school in the first place. Over the years, I would see dozens of black children passing my school either on foot or on the buses, to go to neighboring, white-run schools. Yet, in times of trouble, these very same children and their parents were at my doors seeking help. In such circumstances, I had to be just and judicious in how I handled such cases.

There was more than one side to every story. And I had to be as professional as any other headteacher if not more so given my racial status. I, also, did not want to unnecessarily load my staff and school with clear cases of disciplinary problems. In short, not all such parents left me feeling satisfied and to that extent, I was often condemned as 'one of them.' But I wasn't 'one of them' whatever that term meant. I wanted to be given an early chance to get things right for all my pupils. Too often black youngsters were finding my door only after they were messed up elsewhere.

There were also the benefits of being a senior black individual in the black community. Invitations to be present at important and informative events held by the black community were almost guaranteed.

When the Honorable Michael Manley, the then Prime Minister of Jamaica, visited the Afro-Caribbean Center in Dudley Road, Birmingham, in October 1986, an invite to meet with him was quickly off the mark. Similarly, when Nelson Mandela was released from prison and made Birmingham one of his first trips abroad, I was one of the senior blacks to meet with the great man at the International Convention Center (ICC).

And I can recall too, just how excited I was to have received the invitation from Mrs. Rose Thompson, then Chair of the West Midland Chapter of the Association of Black Lawyers, to meet with Johnnie Cochran, who was visiting Birmingham as guest of her association soon after he had got O. J. Simpson off the double murder hook in the United States of America. Hence, if you linked with the community and could withstand at least some of the pressures, there was occasional compensation.

Rendezvous at No. 10 Downing Street: Mrs. Thatcher

To close off the first year at George Dixon, the then Prime Minister, the Honorable Margaret Thatcher and her husband, Mr. Denis Thatcher, extended an invitation to my wife and me to join them at a Reception at No. 10, Downing Street, Whitehall, London on Monday, 1st December 1986.

After what I thought was a most scintillating and interesting conversation with the Prime Minister and her husband, we were left to wander among the other invited guests. Because of my interest in boxing, I was quick to recognize the then British Heavyweight Boxing Champion, Frank Bruno, among the other guests. For a man of such great physical power and achievements, he was exceedingly charming, humble an attentive even in a situation where everyone was seeking his attention.

We drifted, next, to a couple, who were clearly enjoying their tiger prawns and freshly poured wine. We said hello. They turned out to be Mr. and Mrs. Ian and Penny Skipper. Nothing about them told us who they were, except that, like us, they were gathered in the Prime Minister's reception room having a good time. During a conversation with Mr. Skipper, he enquired about my occupation.

Once he realized that I was in education and where, he simply asked his wife, "Penny, did we not make a financial contribution to Birmingham University once?" Mrs. Skipper acknowledged the truth of the question.

With tongue in cheek, I questioned, "What's wrong with us then?"

Mr. Skipper replied, "What would you like?"

I replied, "I would like some computers for my school."

He then asked how many, and I replied, "Twenty-five."

Mr. Skipper then replied, "You shall have them."

I remembered whispering to Melvinder that that was 'drinks talk' because the liquor was flowing on that occasion.

Nothing more was said until it was time to depart. Mr. Skipper asked us how we got to Downing Street that night. We explained that we had driven down from Birmingham and left our car at Kilburn underground station some four or five miles away and took a taxi to the reception. By this time, we had bid the Prime Minister and her husband farewell and were now standing on the steps of number 10, when Mr. Skipper waved and in seconds a gleaming black chauffeur-driven Rolls Royce drove up to collect the Skippers. Mr. Skipper took us aboard and instructed the chauffeur to drop them off at their hotel and then take us to wherever our car was parked. He was also told to get our contact details.

It was during the journey to Kilburn that we learned from the chauffeur that we were in encounter with one of the richest men in Britain. A few months later, Mr. Skipper was featured in the Sunday Times magazine "Britain's Rich," as the 40th richest man in Britain.

The very next day, after the Reception at Downing Street, I received a call from Mr. Skipper confirming that the computers were on their way. Within two days the computers were up and running in the school. They were the very first set of computers the school ever had. The school laid a "thank you" reception for Mr. Skipper and invited the Chief Education Officer of Birmingham, the school's chairman of governors, and other important officials in Birmingham to meet Mr. Skipper.

It was noticeable at the reception that Mr. Skipper spent most of his time talking to the students as they charted their way around the computers on open display. It was so obvious that Mr. Skipper loved children and was prepared to do a lot for them. The next school year and beyond, Mr. Skipper would become greatly involved in the life of the school, both as a governor and as a philanthropist.

Thoughts About Me

During the Christmas holidays, while the children were consumed with their toys and presents galore, I got to reflect on my life so far. My mental occupation enabled me to identify some stark facts about myself. I did not necessarily like some of the conclusions which I came to, but they were reality, and I would have to live with them. As a kid, I was not a very bright child at school. This will probably alarm many of my schoolmates and contemporaries who thought I was brilliant. To pass my examinations, I had to work exceptionally hard, and even then, sometimes needed to repeat examinations to get my certificates.

This fact followed me through to university in England where I failed my first term examinations and had to repeat several subjects to remain on the course. In the end, I left the university with just a third-class honors degree. The same was true with my LLB examinations. I also struggled with these and had to take over some subjects many times before I ended up with another third-class honors degree. Hard work and determination then were the key to my passing any academic examination. And, yet all the evidence showed that I was a very good teacher; one of the best when measured in terms of my pupils' examination results, their later achievements, and ways of affinity with pupils.

The Evidence:

KILBURN POLYTECHNIC

1. Hi Carlton; Going back to 1961 at KP you gave me £1 so that I could eat, and you refused repayment. I have wanted to thank you for that for many years and the memory of your birthday night party when you got Carmen to try to dance with me. **Barry Harden.**

Aylestone Comprehensive

2. Dear Mr. Duncan, I wonder if you remember me! Aylestone School Law 'O' level, The Buccaneer Pub in Harlesden, **Natalia Martins then now Manley (Portuguese!)** Very proud to see all your achievements but then you always were a very inspiring teacher and i nearly went on to study law because of it. It would be nice to hear from you but of course I understand if you don't remember! Thank you for being such a wonderful person and teacher. I will always be grateful and remember you and Aylestone for giving me a great education and friendship. Thank you, Mr. Duncan! I hope you are well and happy!

Thrasos Vassiliades
Great to meet up with Carlton Duncan my secondary school teacher at Aylestone High many decades ago (known as Mr Duncan then). Carlton inspired many pupils success. For me it was high grades in A level economics and law. One of the top 5 people to influence my career and life.
Thanks Carlton — with Carlton Duncan.

Wyke Manor Upper School

3. Wow...I cannot believe I have found my old headmaster from Wyke Manor...the amount of times I caused you problems...flooding the science room, setting of the fire alarms, stink bombs on the corridor...I thank you for your guidance...without your firm but fair policy I don't think I would have the career/wife/children I have today...hope you are well and your family are well too...funny how adulthood makes you see your childhood in a different light...thank you

1. **Jamila Butt**
Hello Sir. Thank you for accepting my request. You wouldn't remember me at all. I used to go to Wyke Manor Upper School when you were the headmaster. It was around 1983 which seems such a long

time ago. You were a great head and ran the school well. Thankful I never had to see you for any behavior issues as there were none.

2. **Shazia Ahmed**

Mr. Duncan—I was a pupil at Wyke Manor during your headship—remember you being a fantastic headteacher!

Oh Mr. Duncan, I really did not expect you to remember me or my name as such, but you will recall that the children from the ethnic minority were a minority at the school during those years. However, we felt safe while you were the head although we suffered terribly with racism from the teachers as well as our white peers. You had a certain presence, you commanded authority and my friends, and I had great respect for you, and we were so sorry to see you leave. I remember your wife and you were blessed with twins shortly before you left.

Well, I can't blame you for retiring to Jamaica—it's quite depressing here in the UK! Hoping that the COVID situation gets better eventually, and people can travel as before. Yes, I am a solicitor—I think not having much encouragement and support from the teachers at school just made me even more determined to pursue further education and realize my dreams. Wishing you all the best and for your son too—I'm sure he will become a fine lawyer someday.

3. **GREGGORIE MITCHELL**

"Carlton Duncan was the single most influential headteacher Wyke Manor Upper School ever had…pushed me through my boxing and as I was rare at that school he was someone I could turn to as most of the other teachers were ignorant to my issues."

4. **MARK COUP**

"Yes, Greg, I imagine he did. I always thought he was a real gent and a super influence for the school and students. Carlton Duncan, thank you."

George Dixon Comprehensive/Grant Maintained School

5. **AMBER JESSAL**—Hello from a former student from George Dixon! I hope you are in good health and that life has treated you well. You protected us so much from what's happening in the world today when growing up and I wanted the opportunity to thank you for that 🙏

6. From **Angela Tippa** sent via Facebook:
   Subject: Old Times
   "You may not remember me, but I left GD in 1986 and I remember when you first started and we were all messing around in Richie block hall, and then we heard your voice, and everyone started to run. You were a very good headmaster, and very fair. The school really needed you at the time. You may know my dad John Rawlins who played the steel pans? Anyway, hope you're fine and take care."

7. Dear Carlton, I have been truly touched after reading about all the challenges in your life you have tackled head on. I attended GD just after your retirement from Sept 1999 to July 2006. Just purchased your Autobiography and it is a real page turner! Members of staff (Mr. Coley, Mr. Vyse, Mr. Forrester, Mr. Mann, Mr. Hayes, and many others) at GD have always spoken very highly of you. I have always loved GD and even did 3 years as a Voluntary Teaching Assistant! I am now teaching Psychology in Stratford-upon-Avon and am always inspired by your belief in aiming high. Hope to hear from you soon. **Bhupinder Kuwar,** Birmingham UK.

Dear Sir, it is wonderful to hear from you. I have had a fortunate life in that I have had a very good career and been involved in some of the biggest cases in history. I have stood for Parliament and hope to be a judge next year. However, I have helped hundreds of people along the way. In so doing I want to follow in your footsteps. Thank you for giving me hope and opportunity. May God bless you and yours. Yours forever grateful, James.

1. How are you?

View Monica's profile

Good morning yes, I knew, you were in Birmingham. Good to know all is well with you and yours. We here always remember and remark about your headship management leadership of our children while at school. Stay well and enjoy. Monica Coke.

2. From **Natasha Thomas** via Facebook:

   Subject: Hello
   "Mr. Duncan, hope you remember me, I moved to G.D. from London in 1989 after a messy case of abuse. I was always being hauled into your office and no matter what I did you never ever gave up on me. Thank you for that, and I so wish there were still headteachers like you now that I have my own going to secondary school. Well, take care. **Natasha Thomas x**"

3. Pam Kaur: Hello Mr. Duncan, what an honor to be able to speak to you again. I am one of your ex-students from George Dixon School in the U.K. How are you and your family?
4. From **Steven** via Facebook:
   "Yes Mr. Duncan. First, thanks for adding me. I just wanted to say thank you for being an inspiration. Even though I only had you for one year (my final year at GD) the impact you made on my life was unforgettable. I left GD with all my 'O' levels bar English, which I eventually got. I was a forensic scientist and now I teach the beautiful subject of science…Love my job and love the kids. Oh yeah i love the holidays too. Once again Sir, thank you. **Cave.**"

Perhaps, it was because my pupils and I sync in terms of sympathetic understanding; especially those of my pupils who needed to struggle to learn. I knew just what and just how to enable them to circumvent or dismantle any learning barriers.

Another uncovered fact about me was that I had to push myself to the forefront of many issues to be noticed. Essentially, I was a very shy and withdrawn child. Many will find this hard to believe, but until this day that fact remains inescapable. I am shy now and will always be. I have always had to actively tell myself that I must not go to the back of the queue, or I will be overlooked or forgotten. The same at meetings and other gatherings; it is a conscious decision that I take to speak up, so that I am noticed.

None of that came naturally. My boyhood shyness was tamed just a little when, by accident, I got caught up in the world of show-business for some ten years. Having the gift of dancing and anticipating the applause that would follow when I put it on display helped considerably to bring me out of my shell. It certainly made it far easier for me to push myself forward.

At interviews and other evaluations of my worth, my performances were learned. I usually prepared myself extremely well and deliberately relied on the human inclination to follow leads. I acquired the skill of hanging pegs on which others would hang their hats. I hung out only those pegs about which my prepared knowledge was extensive and thorough. If you took the bait, you were bound to be impressed, which was what I wanted. Even when the interviewer came with their own prepared questions, I would find a way of pegging their routes.

For me, winning at interviews was never going to be based upon any innate brilliance for that was not the case with me. Preparedness and manipulation then, was the key to my climb up the professional ladder thus far. These techniques did work for me, and it will have been observed that in every situation I have done it at least twice over. To date, I had to run the general education gauntlet twice; I gained two first degrees; I was married trice and I was appointed to two headships of secondary schools.

Another thing about me was that I could be a realist; always willing to accept what I cannot change. In those circumstances, I searched for ways and means to make a negative situation into a positive one. Take my blackness in a white society, for example. What good was there in moping that I am viewed negatively by white society? There was greater joy in seeking the benefits of being black. I have told the story that as a student hitchhiking the 200 or so miles between Swansea and London at the end of terms, the bigots went out of their way to pick me up so that they could tell me they were not racist, but that they wouldn't want their daughters to marry one of my kind because the children of such a marriage would encounter discrimination.

But I was getting my ride. My seat on buses and on trains was always the most comfortable. The white passengers preferred to sit on top of each other rather than sit in the empty seat next to a black man. In professional competition, I am usually underestimated and ignored while I listened to the plans and strategies, learning all the time. Much of the media exposure which I received was very good for me personally, for my schools, and for my family. That was only possible because I was black and the first. Other headteachers did not get similar exposures because they were white and commonplace. I had learned how to manipulate my blackness to get what I wanted from the media.

Finally, it had become extremely clear from as far back as I came to know myself, that adversity and disappointments do not put me down. They are the spur to my adrenaline sources. Many people who I knew, told me out rightly that they would never have made as many as ten applications for a headship, much less the 120, which I made. Quitting was never a part of my DNA.

That was the problem for the Bradford conspirators. The more they plotted, the more determined I became. I was no crumbling rock against the relentless pressures of flowing adversity. But for my young family, I would have been there fighting them today. But my family's life and future were not mine with which to do as I liked: not mine with which to gamble. That very same determination was much in evidence as I struggled for academic success and in all else that seriously engaged me throughout life.

Chapter 17
Community Education and School Discipline

Back at George Dixon School, it was the beginning of the second term of the school year. This coincided with the first anniversary of my appointment at the school. Last term, I had noticed here and there that classroom and corridor discipline was not all it could be. I needed to sell the idea of a 'community school' to the staff as having a huge bonus in terms of school discipline. This was true, and true for discouraging bad habits and practices, such as lateness to lessons and failing to mark books correctly, among the staff. However, it would have been functionally sabotaging to advance this latter advantage as a reason for moving forward with the idea. That was one I had to keep to myself.

This was also the term when we would have the big kick-off on training for multicultural education and I needed to be mindful of that. Mr. Steve Walker, the school's Careers Officer, had agreed to lead a committee of Staff in discussing a draft of a whole school policy on equal opportunities (antiracism and anti-sexism), which would eventually be refined by the whole school and ratified as the school's policy and be the foundation for all individual departments.

While all that was happening, the task fell to me, as it always does to begin fund raising initiatives to mount a community education program based upon the concept of 'from the cradle to the grave.'

From 'cradle to the grave'

If I was successful in raising funds it would be good motivation for the staff. as I discovered with the Wyke Manor project. I had to find the ways and means of replicating everything at George Dixon. In every application, I would include a photograph of myself as the new headteacher at George Dixon School. Many made the connection with the media publicity, which had surrounded my appointment, but others saw the incongruity of a black man heading up a school in Edgbaston and came to visit mainly out of curiosity.

It was always a good omen when potential benefactors came to visit for whatever reason. This gave me the opportunity to explain the project in context. In this way, over the next year or two, I raised almost £200,000 to launch the project at the school. Because we had excess building capacity, all we had to do was to adapt some spaces and we had a functioning 25 places nursery, which met all the Social Services criteria; a senior citizens' project which provided daily luncheon for the beneficiaries together with a variety of light craft work and educational endeavors such as English for beginners in the case of older Asian citizens.

This part of the project was of great benefit to the senior citizens, as they made good savings on heating bills by not being at home throughout the days. In between, were the fit and able mums and dads who had both the time and desire to join their children, in some cases, grandchildren in their classes? The school did not ask why it was that parents and grandparents wanted to join the classes. But we understood that there were those who simply wanted to be able to help their children with their homework or were trying to improve their own job marketability as well as using their leisure time in some way.

Both the nursery and the senior citizens' projects needed staffing on a permanent basis, and we also required an overall coordinator for the entire project. The co-coordinator was primarily responsible for negotiating classroom places for those parents who wanted to join classes, and to team with me in fundraising exercises. In time, we began to have engaging hands from the school's normal staffing both in terms of ideas and hands on projects.

The New Community Team and Some of its Students and Workers

Community Education at George Dixon Grant Maintained School

Community Education at George Dixon Grant Maintained School

Community Education at George Dixon Grant Maintained School

All that was then necessary to enable the community project to function effectively was the formation of a Community Association as the over-arching governing body of the various projects. The association met on a regular basis to ensure accountability for raised funds, and to monitor the timetabled performance of the workers. By the end of the final term of the academic year, that body was in place and operating effectively.

George Dixon School: The Interest of the Colleges

Some of Birmingham's colleges were following the progress of George Dixon School in the media and showed some selfish interest in its development. Falling rolls meant that they, like secondary schools, must find creative ways to attract college age students to their fold. This need puts them in direct competition with schools with sixth forms like George Dixon. Three of the Birmingham colleges made direct contact with me in with ideas seemingly in the interest of my school but was a way of multiplying their intakes at our expense. Take, for example, the Birmingham College of Food. It seemed that the news that our Community Association's nursery was full had traveled out to them.

My secretary had made an entry into my diary for one Mrs. SY to meet with me on the 15th of February 1988 at 14:00. When she walked through the door to my office, it was impossible not to notice her stunningly good looks, shapely figure, and mouth, which was reminiscent of the Italian international sex symbol Sophia Loren.

I don't know what impression I was giving her, but she started to explain that I had met her previously. That, she said, was soon after I had arrived in Birmingham, I had met with her in my office, right where she was at that moment, she emphasized. She was even able to give me a date and time, which was later corroborated by one of my earlier diaries. She went on to explain her mission.

One of the Vice Principals of the Birmingham College of Food had asked her to sound me out on a project that was of some importance to their college. She explained that because of the location of the college, the college had no land upon which to build a nursery, which was badly needed to support the work of the college. Although I was still dazed just by looking at the heavenly structure and attendant attributes seated before me; my head still whirling with romantic projects, the drift of her mission immediately became clear to me. She needn't have said anything more.

The college, as with all other colleges in Birmingham, was trying to identify ways and means to encourage more students to come through their doors. Pregnant teenage girls and existing young mothers who want to continue their studies, despite motherhood or pending motherhood, would find a college, which offers nursery facilities as part of their attractions, to be infinitely more attractive than other colleges that do not have such a facility. I could see that, but I wanted the blanks filled in for me.

Mrs. SY continued to explain that the college was aware that the nursery, which was in operation at George Dixon, was full. However, the college had substantial funds, which they would be willing to use to expand the nursery to another 25 places in return for the right to advertise their courses as having the support of a nursery. If I was, at all, interested, she would go back and arrange a further meeting for me to come to lunch at the college and meet with all the key players.

I could not see a problem with any of this and so advised Mrs. SY, thus giving her the green light to go ahead and set up that luncheon. In any case, I would need some time to consult with my governors and the Community Association on the proposals. Before Mrs. SY left, I found the courage to ask her if we could meet socially. She was delighted that I had asked and was quite keen on meeting me socially as well. She winked at me as she handed me a card, which had her home and college contact details there on and then left my office.

I just could not wait for the next meeting with Mrs. SY and her colleagues. I was too hooked and curious about how far things could go. She was a 'Mrs.', so there could be a husband somewhere. Did she have children? What would she want of me? Would it be only sexual as it was with me? I needed to know all the answers and I could not wait. The same day she left my office, I called her that evening. She was available to meet me that very same evening and so we decided to go to the 'Old House at Home' public house, the midway point between her home and my school, to meet for a drink and a chat. By the time she had arranged the luncheon with her colleagues, Mrs. SY and I were very much involved.

Ostensibly, she had wanted only the same sexual companionship from the relationship as I wanted so it was going to be all fun at no one's expense, at least, not hers or mine. But only a few days into the relationship Mrs. SY was hinting, much to my chagrin, that I didn't have an escape clause built into our arrangements. What is more, she had become so confident and self-assured that she was telling me unsolicited stories of all the tricks she had played on men who dared to succumb to her wiles. It soon became only too clear, to me, that I was in a trap and that all those stories were meant as warnings and guard fences against me ever attempting an escape.

Chapter 18
Going Wrong at Home

Meanwhile, at home, my wife was beginning to sense that all was not right. Yet, I continued to deny all her suspicions most vehemently. I will say this, though; it is a foolish man who underrates a woman's intuition. My wife was right nearly all the time.

The luncheon was scheduled to be on the 10th of March 1988 at 11:00. The college had several commercial restaurants serving the public and doubling as training venues for their students. Our luncheon would take place in the 'West Indian' restaurant. We were joined by the then Principal, his Vice Principals, and several other important others. At the end of lunch, the college and I had struck this deal. The agreement was that the college would fund the cost of extending the capacity of the George Dixon Community Association Nursery to double its capacity.

The college would meet one half of all running costs, staffing and otherwise, resulting from the doubling of capacity. In return, the college was entitled to advertise all its courses as having nursery support. At all times, the school and the association should guarantee a maximum of 10 places to be used by students at the college. All extension work was to be commenced immediately. I rightly predicted that our association would be happy with that.

Once the extension work was completed, the terms of the agreement were rolled out operationally, and for some time, all seemed to be functioning extremely well. It was observed that up to ten children, babies or toddlers were registering daily under the college's name. This continued unperturbed until Mr. Fred Trowman, one of our very active school governors, came to see me. He showed me a letter, which he had received from one of several banks to which he had written to seek funds on behalf of the school. That letter stated quite clearly that the bank in question considered that it was already contributing to the school by buying several of the school's nursery places.

The governor was rightly alarmed because none of this was in the deal that I had brought to the school community. In effect, all along, the college had envisaged a trading opportunity with different banks. At the rate they were charging the banks per place, they would have long recovered their original investment and we would have known nothing of it. This could not stand, and I told the college so. They wanted nothing less and this situation signaled the parting of ways.

However, things became so bad at home that when we received a second invitation addressed to Mr. and Mrs. Duncan, to be guests at the Royal Garden Party on the 11th of July 1989 at Buckingham Palace, my wife refused to go with me. To this day, I have remained both regretful and embarrassed because I wasn't able to attend for want of a legitimate partner.

My very frequent appearances in the media were beginning to annoy Melvinder. They were no longer a source of pride and joy for her. They had become a bane instead and she said so frequently enough for me to believe her. This was somewhat odd because when it suited her, she would often remind me that the media was very interested in me and that she would not hesitate to refer our difficulties to them. Not only that, but it was beginning to appear that anything positive that was said or published about George Dixon's school made her both irascible and scornful of the school. She was known to laugh critically at its teachers and make disparaging remarks about the work and aspirations of the school.

No doubt, much of this was aimed at hurting me. It was punishment for what she deemed was my bad behavior. I found it difficult, though, to understand why she scorned the very source of her livelihood. Had it not for George Dixon School none of us would survive. Under those circumstances, I had expected her to wave the flag for the school; but no, the school and everything associated with it as well as teaching per se, were to be damned. Reasoning did not come into it at all. And as it turned out, I was quite foolish to expect that kind of rationality from her given the circumstances and her not unfounded suspicions. The atmosphere at home had become so poisoned; I dared not invite a colleague to come to the house.

Three things happened around the same period that kicked me into making some serious efforts at home to pull back my marriage from the brink of disaster. Firstly, an unexpected letter from my wife's solicitors fired a serious warning shot across my brow. That letter indicated that my wife was contemplating a divorce and a parting of ways. It required me to give an accurate valuation of our joint assets and advised that it would be in my interest to enlist the advice of a solicitor for myself. Secondly, for the first time in my life, I came to appreciate the importance of both the gender and the age gaps, which were important characteristics of our marriage.

I was 17 years older than my wife. She was a woman, and I was a man. Like it or not, these characteristics were making a difference. I was brought up not to 'hang out my dirty washing' in public. That was an important feature of my upbringing and has remained so till this day. I simply cannot make a shift from that. It will always be deeply embarrassing for me if others discover that I am having domestic problems.

The portrayal of 'sweetness and light' is what was inculcated as the only acceptable thing to do at such times even if inwardly I am suffering great pangs of distress. To discuss your troubled marriage, even with family members, was not the thing to do. You must 'keep a stiff upper lip' as the English would say. Consequently, even my closest relatives were ignorant about what was taking place in my immediate family. It became clear too, that women find it much easier, to discuss their troubled relationships, than men do. Because of this, I lost the public relations battle every time.

Honorary M.Eds.

Thirdly, I had just received notification from the principal, Mrs. Janet Trotter, of St. Paul's and St. Mary College Cheltenham (now Cheltenham and Gloucester College of Higher Education) that I was chosen to receive the college's first Honorary Master of Education (M.Ed.) on the 10th of November 1989. I was flattered to be chosen for this honor but was frightened at the thought of not having my family with me on such an august occasion. I just did not want to relive the experiences of the second Buckingham Palace garden party almost four months earlier. The college bestowed this honor for all the contributions I made to their education courses both in terms of my publications, some of which were used on their courses, and my personal input on a regular basis. I certainly would not want to receive this honor in absentia.

Maybe, I was being too much of the strong man at home when trying to convince my wife that she was all wrong about me and that it was all her unfounded imagination that I had broken our marriage vows. Maybe, I should have been rightly humbler and truthful. I was in a mess and needed help. What I was doing was letting pride and deceit domesticate humility and honesty. And maybe I was too weak in terms of how I was handling the relationship with Mrs. SY. Clearly, the emotional blackmail, that underpinned those dreadful stories, which Mrs. SY told me about her cunningly arranged downfalls of those other unfortunate men who traveled the same road as I was then traveling, was having the desired effects. It was time for the right actions both at home and abroad.

In the weeks ahead, I genuinely made efforts at home to ameliorate the situation for all the family. This effort was paying off. I was spending more time at home with the family; the children were not so openly taking sides with their mother anymore and above all, everyone was looking forward to my honorary graduation. My mother was also coming up from London to be at the graduation, which was going to mean spending a day or two with us and we didn't want her to feel upset about anything. The problem was the more normal the situation was at home, the more strained the relationship between me and Mrs. SY became. I had for some time concluded that the relationship must end.

In effect, it had ended, but cowardice had prevented me from saying so to her. Now, I told myself, was the time to force discipline out of resolve; it must be done. Mrs. SY was not going to assume that the relationship was non-existent because she was still pushing me into ending my marriage so that all would be well between her and me. And she certainly wasn't going to end it; therefore, I would have to take that dreaded risk of cutting the umbilical cord. Procrastination would cease immediately after my graduation in November, I told myself.

The event afforded us the opportunity for the entire family to spend a long weekend in London with my mother so that all of us could go shopping in Oxford and Regent Streets in the London West End for our outfits to be worn on graduation day. There seemed to be nothing like shopping in expensive stores in London for healing domestic wounds. Ipso facto, everything then seemed right again. Yet, I knew that there was more trouble to come because I had not yet faced up to the real challenge.

The graduation came in all its colors and splendor. The citation was given by Mrs. Janet Trotter and could not have been more elevating for me. But what was most satisfying was to see not only my mother but also my wife and children in the congregation taking it all on board.

Mrs. Janet Trotter
Principal of St. Paul's and St. Mary College Cheltenham And the Guild

The Christmas of 1988 was grand. I had worked hard and succeeded in putting in a little extra money to compensate, especially the children, for the grief which I had caused the family. Nothing was too good, or too much, that Christmas. I even offered to take them on a trip with me to Amsterdam early in the New Year. Professor Chris Mullard of Focus Consultancy and holder of the Royal Chair in Ethnic Studies and Education at the University of Amsterdam in the Netherlands had invited me to deliver the keynote Speech at an International gathering at the University of Amsterdam.

That offer was reasonably declined by my wife on the grounds that the children would have to miss out on their schooling as school was in session.

The Education Reform Act (1988)

That year before my honorary graduation, 1988, the British Parliament passed The Education Reform Act (1988). That Act was widely regarded as the most important piece of education legislation in England, Wales, and Northern Ireland since the passing of Butler's Education Act 1944. The passing of the 1988 Act by the then Tory Administration in Great Britain was timely.

Although George Dixon was doing so well as a school, it had no answer to the effects of falling rolls, which was affecting the economics of the city of Birmingham. The city was forced to consider the closure of several of its inner-city schools. The rumor ran wildly that three schools had to be taken out of the Central Area and that George Dixon would be one of them.

Admittedly, this was all rumors. None of them came from the Education Authority, as far as I knew. But the effects of such rumors were sometimes worse than what might have been the outspoken reality. Parents were not inclined to register their children at schools that were likely to be closed. This intensified the drift away from inner-city schools, George Dixon being one of them, to the sub-urban schools, which were not so threatened. We, at George Dixon, had done much to stem that drift to a trickle, but the job was not complete. The rumor of closure once more pulled the plug and we saw a real loss in terms of numbers.

Birmingham, at the time, funded and staffed its schools according to the number of pupils on their rolls. This meant a decline in our income and staffing annually. Declining income and staffing meant that we were not able to meet the needs of our pupils. The quality and ability levels of our pupils required more input of resources, human and otherwise, no less.

Senior management and I came to the regrettable conclusion that what was happening was a deliberate policy and political strategy on the part of the education department and the Education Authority, respectively. It was never a popular decision for any local authority to announce the closure of any of its schools. Political careers could disappear because of it. It was safer to let rumors do it for them.

My team and I had worked too hard to bring the school to where it had reached to just let it wither away without a fight. I was not prepared to let political maneuvering blight the future of a thriving school any more than was the undoubted case already.

The 1988 Act had many important provisions. For me, the two most important provisions were: (1) It allowed schools to ballot their parents on the question of whether they want their children's school to opt out of local authority control and be funded directly by Central Government. (2) It allowed schools to manage their own budgets. Schools which exercised these lawful rights were termed Grant Maintained schools.

For understandable reasons, the Labor Council in Birmingham did not want any of its Birmingham schools to opt out. That would significantly affect the Council's annual income and related budgets. To the extent that schools opted out of their control, they would lose all the monies that these schools would then receive directly from the Central Government. Their Central Government grants would be slashed by the total of those amounts. Given that local authorities did not spend 100% of their grants on schools, this would mean a loss of income to spend on other things.

Additionally, there was provision in the Act for opted out schools to take the lands, buildings, and other physical resources into their ownership. In funding such schools, the Central Government made an allowance for any neglect for which the local authority was responsible over the preceding years. By my calculations, George Dixon School stood to benefit by another £600,000 annually, if we opted out of Birmingham's control.

The problem was that Birmingham City Council actively opposed many attempts by its schools to opt out of its control. It used its financial might and other resources to leaflet the parents of any school attempting to exercise that right. This way, it often managed to crush such attempts by schools. What was also very clear, however, was that the city council did not go all out in its opposition in all cases. It was very selective in its choice for full scale opposition. It had the resources to translate all its canvassing papers into the languages of the various communities that might be affected. I was not satisfied that Birmingham was giving schools a fair chance under the Act to try for Grant Maintained Status especially its inner-city schools, which were impoverished compared with sub-urban schools.

Yet, when sub-urban schools and the King Edwards Grammar schools decided to opt out, they met with only tame opposition, if any, from the city council. To them that have, more shall be given. In such circumstances, it was no surprise that all these schools had successful ballots.

Yet, when it came to the inner-city schools, they faced the full discriminating might of the council. I am sure that there was a political explanation for that, but it was never disclosed. However, there is a view that inner-city schools attract larger amounts of central government's grants, hence, they take more with them when they opt out of local government control.

Two of the tactics that were used successfully to get the parents of inner-city schools to vote 'no' and against Grant Maintained Status were: (a) a specially prepared document, which took all the arguments in favor of Grant Maintained Status and turned them on their heads to show a disadvantage. At all times, this document was prepared in the same format. It was, in fact, a ready-made document just sitting there on someone's computer waiting for the name of the next inner-city school, that would dare an opt out proposal. (b) Next, there was a team of foot soldiers, mainly Asians, whose role it was to visit the homes of Asian children under the auspices of helping the parents with translating any information, which may have come from the Council, the school, or the Electoral Reform office.

There was some evidence that many of these foot soldiers were shams. They took away some of the parents' ballot papers, it was often reported, and voted on behalf of the parents. Invariably, these schools failed to obtain Grant Maintained Status (GMS).

Honorary Lecturer: University of Birmingham and Second Honorary M.Ed.

Late in 1989, Stewart Ransom of the Birmingham University Education Department invited me to be an honorary lecturer at the University Education Department. Previously, the department had relied on our school for placement for budding teachers year after year. What was more, as it was with St. Paul's and St. Mary, the department had been making considerable use of many of my publications. To solidify the relationship between the department and the school, the idea for me to serve as an honorary lecturer was conceived.

I was glad to be working with the university in this way because I had sixth formers who were seeking university places all over the country each year. Such a relationship could only help that process. But then, straight out of the blue, toward the end of 1990, I received news that the university's Senate would bestow an honorary M.Ed. on me on the 14th of December 1990. This was fabulous news because it offered a further opportunity to unify things at home and to get my mother up from London for the occasion once more.

That event came and served its purpose well. There was a terrific citation that even I found overwhelming. I could hardly have expected more. My family all accompanied me as before and the university made a great fuss about them, perhaps more than they made of me.

Now the joke was among friends, "Will I have a 'third degree?'"

By the middle of 1991, the pressures from the Mrs. SY affair were building and getting far out of control, especially with all the publicity, which was directed my way. I had vowed that following the degree ceremony of 1989, I was going to be brave enough and bring about a definite end to that relationship. I did not. Another year has passed, and another degree ceremony has taken place. I shall pretend that I did mean after the 1990 one as if I did know that there was going to be a 1990-degree ceremony. But even so, the 1990 ceremony has long passed. To hell with it I said and called Mrs. SY on the telephone. She agreed to my suggestion that we should meet at 19:00 in a local public house (pub) for a drink: still too craven about the outcome to state the true purpose of the meeting.

Showdown with Mrs. SY

I arrived at the public house (pub) somewhat early and secured a strategic parking space, which would enable a quick getaway. I had no intention of being out too late because that would exasperate an already diminishing peace at home. Once there was a dent in the relationship, no matter how hard you tried, there is always a remnant of suspicion, which like a volcano, could erupt at any time. Mrs. SY was as usual, punctual. This lady's timing was always perfect. Not a minute early and not a minute late. You could set your watch to her movement.

That night she was having gin and tonic water and I was having a rum and blackcurrant which was my favorite shorts. I got in the drinks and casually threw my bunch of keys on the table at which we were seated. That was a very serious error. My keys were an unusually heavy bunch of metals. It had car keys, house keys and school keys on it. The pub was very crowded for a Monday evening, and it was only just past 19.00. Many of the customers seemed to recognize who I was; you could tell from their frequent stares and finger pointing.

I then calmly said to Mrs. SY, as she took her first sip of the gin and tonic, "This is our last drink together, we need to call it a day." The moment I said that she must have read the seriousness of purpose in my eyes, she made a double shot at me: firstly, she threw the gin and tonic straight into my eyes and then grabbed hold of my bunch of keys and crashed it, with all the force she could muster, into my head. The crowded pub became a dead hush, and all eyes were then focused on our direction. All I could do was to retrieve my keys from where they had landed and left the room, my drink untouched, as I headed straight for my car. My clothing was all soaking with gin and tonic, and I smelled like a rum-bar.

I pointed the car in the direction of home as I pondered what next? If what I had tonight was the sum of it, then I would have got off very lightly. Twenty minutes later, I pulled up outside the driveway to my home. I didn't notice the car that was parked about 20 feet away on the same side of the road as my house. As I got out of my car and approached my front door, Mrs. SY alighted from that car and came toward my front door as well. "I am coming in," she said. I refused to open the front door and for the next ten minutes or so, she remained adamant that she would not go away until I let her into my home.

"Very well," I said, as I put the key into the door lock. "Come in and I will call the police." At the sound of that, she decided to discontinue her entry, which she had begun. She turned around, as I shouted for Melvinder, and got hold of the front door and slammed it so thunderously the entire house shook with a horrific tremor.

Melvinder emerged about ten minutes later. All the children were asleep, and she was in the shower when it all happened. She enquired about the loud bang, which she had clearly heard. I lied. I said that when I came through the front door both my hands were full, so I kicked the door shut. I had no appetite for the meal which my wife had prepared. Something told me that Mrs. SY was going to return. I was right. She had gone away to fetch her 19-year-old son, and both were now standing outside my front door ringing its bell, persistently.

Melvinder answered the door and when she saw who it was; that it was the woman she had suspected all along; she slammed the door shut in their faces without bothering to hear her gripe. They left without further incident. I explained to Melvinder that Mrs. SY was here because she was refusing to accept that I didn't want to have anything more to do with her. That was clearly true and might have worked in my favor at a different time.

She just said, "You will be hearing from the lawyer." She then went to bed in my daughter's room. For the next several weeks, I had to fend for myself on the domestic front. Even the children refused to speak to me. That was harsh punishment.

Chapter 19
George Dixon Grant Maintained School

John Patten: Birmingham Short-Changing its Children

I had deemed Grant Maintained Status (GMS) was the way to go to rescue George Dixon School. But it would be first necessary to convince the remaining staff. Many had already fled to safer pastures because they could see the redundancy sledgehammer hovering. Those who stayed thought, like me, that that was the way to go and that it would be worth taking the risks. As always, it was the better qualified and most experienced staff that are the most mobile.

I dreaded having to retrain new staff into our ways of practice. It can be time-consuming and costly. The ethos of the school alone cannot suffice. It was at risk, too. Deliberate action and coordinated activities purposefully designed are what a school needs to remain at the cutting edge of its performance capabilities. I decided that the best way to approach the staff would be to give them the naked facts and let them decide in which camp they wanted to be. The facts were simple and straight forward.

1. As John Patten, the then Education Secretary, was quoted in the Birmingham Post of 30/03/93 as saying: *"Children in this city are being short-changed by their local authority and that saddens me. I want to see that situation change."* That, in effect, meant that we, as a school, do not get all of that to which we are entitled annually. We were "short-changed" approximately £600, 000 annually.
2. With that money, I could improve the teacher-pupil ratio and not lose as many teachers. The impact of smaller classes upon performance over a few years would be quite telling.

3. Better performance, together with the absence of rumors about closure would help to stem the drift of pupils to the sub-urban areas; and attract more able pupils to our school.
4. Managing our own budget would mean more local and thus more relevant decisions with quicker outcomes. For example, we would not have to wait six months or more, as we do now, for a decision to go ahead and mend a leaking roof.
5. We could set up our own 'in-house' special needs services for pupils instead of having to wait for months before a pupil can be seen by the educational psychologist, for example. We could more readily identify those pupils who come to us from deprived circumstances for whatever reason. Thus informed, we would be able to put in place compensatory measures against class and race deprivation. This last point is very important especially in inner-city areas where we find large population of non-white children.

Their circumstances of parents with no jobs or low paid jobs, both parents having to do multiple jobs to make ends meet, poor housing, poor health conditions and resulting lack of home help and resources with education, often meant that these children are educationally and socially way behind their more fortunate peers when they come to us. It is part of the school's role to spot such deficiencies and make appropriate compensation for such candidates. Inner cities schools need more funding, not less.

Against these advantages, we would have to weigh the loss of most of the Services which we currently get from the local authority. For example, we currently get all our Advisory and Special Needs services, fuel, and heating services from the Birmingham Authority and would have to buy these from another authority if Birmingham refuses to sell to us, as I suspected they would.

As it turned out, other authorities, including Birmingham, were queuing up to sell us those services, albeit at exorbitant prices. Luckily, under GMS, we would be able to afford these services and the option to seek out the more economic. packages.

After a full deliberation among all the staffs on the merits and demerits of becoming Grant Maintained, I was able to say to the governors that I had the support of 98% of all the teaching and non-teaching staff.

Next, I would need to convince the governors that GMS was our only way out. Now that I could show that all the staff, except for two individuals, were behind me that would be manageable. There was just one problem: The chairman of governors was councilor Albert Bore and from the Labor-led city council. Politically, it would not be possible for him to be seen to support GMS. That ideology was strictly conservative. I spent many late nights talking to Councilor Albert Bore at his home about this. The best I got out of him was an agreement that it seemed the only way the school could survive.

Once we had all the staff and other governors wanting to go that way, the councilor knew that he was out on a limb all by himself, but, as he indicated, he would now await the outcome of the parental ballot. At that time, he would decide what would be his next step as far as being a governor at the school was concerned.

A team of governors, notable Miss Trail, Mr. Trowman, and the indefatigable Mrs. Ade-John together with staff input and my leadership took up the challenge. We have done all the research necessary. We knew why the other inner-city schools had failed in their battles. That gave us an advantage. We were determined that we would counter the tactics even before they were used against us. And that was what we did. Our case for GMS was briefly and simply outlined and explained in an expensively produced eye-catching document. The finance for this was a gift from a well-wisher and philanthropist.

Every child in the school took one of these brochures home to his or her parents. Next, we prepared a further document using the same format, which we already knew the authority would be using to confound parents about the evils of GMS. But the similarity ended when it came to contents. Point by point, we took each of the authority's outlined drawbacks and showed that, in fact, it was a distortion. When the authority released their document, as we knew they would, their falsehood was already countered.

To ensure that we got to our parents first, we, as a school, resisted the authority's demands and pressures to release to them a full list of all parents with their addresses for as long as we were able to do so in the light of all the threats of disciplinary actions, etcetera. First off, the mark for seeking that list was the education office's representative Mr. Peter Lee. When he failed, they sent in the big gun, Mr. David Hammond. We knew that we had to give them that list, but it would be at our own timing.

Peter Carter-Ruck and George Carman, QC

When the authority realized that we were ahead of the game, the full blast of all hell's fury was unleashed against me personally. One councilor, Phil Rose, then Vice Chairman of the Birmingham City Education Committee, took the lead with a document, which was very libelous of me as a professional and which he sent out to the parents of George Dixon Comprehensive school. In it he claimed that I had mismanaged the school and wasted its funds. The inference to be drawn was that I was no good at management and that I could not be trusted with the increased funding, which the school would receive under GMS.

As I saw it, this was no longer about denying the school GMS, it was now about my professional integrity. I wasn't going to have it. When my friend '**David**' chatted with me about the libelous matter, we both took the view that this was '**Goliath**' seeking to trample on whosoever was in his way. With the splintering of the Inner London Education Authority before now, Birmingham had become the largest and most powerful Education Authority in the United Kingdom. Its financial might was awesome. It could destroy little 'people' like me by just dragging them out and prolonging any legal battle that anyone dared to bring against it.

This knowledge that the tax and rate payers provided a great wall of defense in their favor made them somewhat careless, even reckless, in how they dealt with others who were not so fortunately protected. This was certainly the case with councilor Phil Rose (a Sandwell Labor councilor) as we shall see from his first reaction when my lawyers asked him to retract and apologize.

What they did not count on, however, was that I might have had a friend called 'David' and that, that friend might have had a 'slingshot', which was as powerful, if not more so, than their might. 'David' said that he would back me all the way throughout the legal battle that I would now wage against the councilor and the authority jointly in defense of my professional integrity. Europe's best and most successful libel lawyers were **Peter Carter-Ruck**. They were also the most expensive lawyers around. 'David' said I should instruct no lesser firm than they and so I engaged that one; the very best. Andrew Stephenson at Peter Carter-Ruck was satisfied that Rose and the Birmingham City Council jointly had a serious case to answer.

Rose had sent out a defamatory letter dated 18/01/93 to the parents of our school. The governor of the school got hold of a copy and brought it to me. By the 27/01/93 Rose had received a letter from my lawyers asking him to retract and apologize. Rose contemptuously disregarded the letter from Peter Carter-Ruck's firm despite several reminders dated the 2nd and 10th February 1993; yet he continued to aggravate the defamation in the press.

In fact, a reply was never received until both Rose and the city council had become joint defendants. Had he replied when he was supposed to do so, at that point, that case would have ended there? But the knowledge that tax and rate payers' funds were paying for insurance protection for him against this kind of reckless behavior, unleashed his overbearing and ridiculous arrogance, which was unbecoming of a public official. In a letter dated 19/02/93, the Municipal Mutual Insurance Company signaled their interest in the defendants' case to my lawyers.

In the meantime, the canvassing was over, and the parental balloting was on the way. Many of our pupils reported that they had callers and visitors telling them how to vote. Some callers even wanted to collect the ballot papers. How many of these bogus helpers succeeded in their mission, I will never know. What I can tell you is that 59% of the school's parents voted and that a resounding 79% of those votes said yes to GMS.

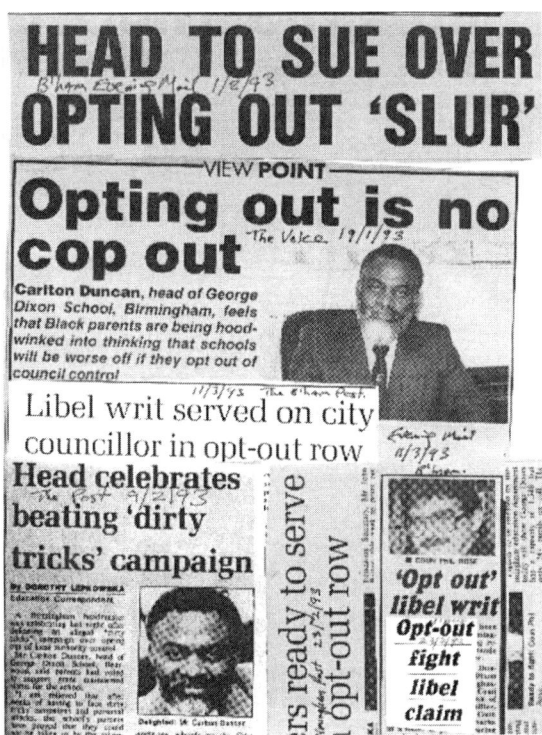

That result brought jubilation to everyone at the school and to those connected with it. For Councilor Albert Bore, this was a defeat for which he would never forgive me. Naturally, he promptly resigned from the Chairmanship and membership of the Board of governors. As the leader of the Birmingham City Council, at the time, he went on to become the Knighted Sir Albert Bore. On a subsequent occasion, when my name was advanced by others for a similar title, requiring the support of the Birmingham City Council, Sir Albert Bore revengefully denied that support.

Albert Bore was, just as promptly, succeeded by Mr. Gus Williams as chairman of the new George Dixon Grant Maintained School to be.

The parents spoke and spoke very loudly. As a school, we could then only await the decision of the Department of Education and Science (DES) on GMS. That decision came in the positive in September 1993. GMS would eventually take effect on the 1st of January 1994.

The Parents Say Yes to GMS

In the meantime, the defamation battle between Rose, the Council and me raged on relentlessly. The writ was served to them by post on 05/03/09 to be answered in the High Court of Justice, Queen's Bench Division case number: 533, within 14 days. The defendants resorted to awkward tactics of delay and complication.

My lawyers detected that their tactic was to complicate the issue. On the 16/08/93 we asked for 'Better and Further Particulars' of their defense within 14 days. Those Better and Further Particulars did not reach us until 01/10/93. They persisted with their tactic of complication. Andrew Stephenson, the solicitor dealing with my case at Peter Carter-Ruck, wisely arranged a consultation for me with the distinguished and world-widely renowned Libel Counsel, George Carman, QC in his chamber on 06/01/94 at 11 a.m. After that consultation with the great man, it was decided by our team that our answer was to ask the court to strike out all the unnecessary complexities, which meant most of their justification defense, and their entire plea of fair comment.

Nothing could be done about their defense of qualified privilege. This defense of qualified privilege would stand or fall according to whether there was the absence or presence of malice respectively. There was an overwhelming amount of malice on the part of the defendants and both sides were fully aware of that. In due course, we would make our application to the high court and after listening to arguments from defense counsel, the court ruled our application successful in its entirety. It was now time to have the case settled down for trial.

At that point, the defendants decided that their case was hopeless and threw in their metaphorical white towels. The result was that, in addition to their own legal costs, they had to meet mine and pay an undisclosed sum to me in damages. Suffice it to say, I was satisfied with the outcome, and they were not.

As of January 1994, I would be able to start the process of school improvement for the benefit of our so deserving pupils. My team and I will first consider the business of having smaller classes. In an area where there were so many selective grammar schools, over 10 of them, the five King Edwards plus those funded and run by the Birmingham Education Authority as well as private institutions, not many bright pupils came to George Dixon School.

Coupled with this was the fact that the school was relentlessly rumored to be under threat of closure on account of city-wide falling rolls. As we have already seen, this meant that the more mobile students headed for the sub-urban schools. The pupils who came to us could not be catered for effectively in classes of 31, which was the usual class size. We needed to do better for them and that we would.

Teacher Fellowship, St. Ann College, Oxford

In 1992, Oxford University, St. Anne's College had invited me to take up a Teacher Fellowship there. Unfortunately, for me, it was a bad time for me to accept that honor because of the prevailing pressures at school. This was the time when we were taking over our own budget (LMS) and the GMS campaign had begun. In all, prestigious though it was for the school, it was not the right time for the headteacher to be away for four weeks. The governors of the school to whom the invitation had been sent wrote back to the Principal of St. Anne's College, Mrs. Ruth Deech, to thank her for the invitation for their headteacher to be a Teacher Fellow at St Anne's College and to explain why it could not be accepted on that occasion.

Mrs. Ruth Deech had, in the past, addressed my staffs, governors and pupils at George Dixon School on the principles of equal opportunities as part of the earlier staff development program, which I had launched at the school. Her lead lecture, on that occasion, will long be remembered for its quality, seriousness of purpose, humor and to have been given by a person of such sharp intellect.

Mrs. Ruth Deech was determined to grant me that honor, which I could not accept on the first invitation. Early in 1993, the invitation was once more extended to the governors for me to take up a Teacher Fellowship at St. Anne's College, Oxford. This time the governors accepted the offer. The school was then awaiting an answer from the DES regarding the resounding 'Yes' vote, which our parents had given to GMS. In a sense, we were in limbo until we heard from the government regarding this matter.

The situation was not without some doubt, because it was all over the media that the Birmingham Education Authority was seeking or was going to be seeking an appeal to over-turn our ballot on grounds of misrepresentation because, in our campaign, I had used a document, which was like that which they normally used to oppose schools that were seeking to opt out of their control.

While we were waiting for the government's response to our ballot, it was a good opportunity to go to Oxford for the month. I would use the month to do some research for my next book and establish contacts, which would be useful for my school and, indeed, for my own children in future years. During my time away from the school—from 21/06/93 to 16/07/93—my deputies would act jointly and would inform me immediately if anything was heard from the DES.

The Fellowship covered my full board, lodgings, and research facilities for the month. While I was there, I was asked to give two lectures only. Both lectures were given at the education department: one to budding teachers and the other given to lecturers at the university on the multicultural curriculum in schools. The highlight of my stay was receiving an invitation to the robed degree ceremony at which the then Secretary for the United Nations, Mr. Perez de Cuellar, would receive an Honorary Doctorate. And afterwards, for a special reception at Prime Minister Margaret Thatcher's old college, Somerville.

**Perez de Cuellar, Secretary to the United Nations
At Somerville College, Oxford,
After Receiving His Honorary Doctorate
From the University 1993**

Before I would end my fellowship, I had taken the opportunity to invite the family down to spend a weekend with me. It was a special day at St. Anne's. It was their annual garden party and so, my family was able to get a feel of life at the college and enjoy the special reception and meet some key members of the staff. Melvinder came but remained aloof all the time so nothing much was gained by having them down except that they all had a nice weekend out of the home. In June, just before I went to Oxford, I had for the second time received a letter from my wife's solicitors stating that she was considering a divorce and that it was in my interest to consult a solicitor, as well.

I had heard that song before and so did not take it very seriously. Nevertheless, I had taken the precaution of consulting with a London solicitor who was recommended by Andrew Stephenson of Peter Carter-Ruck as a good specialist in family law. I was rather hoping that the trip to Oxford would have helped to lessen the heat in that kitchen, but it didn't. The coming September, the twins were due to transfer to grammar schools. I personally tutored and prepared them for the 11+ examinations, which they passed with flying colors. Natasha had gained a place at King Edward Grammar School for girls, Camp Hill, which was within walking distance of our home.

Nathan had gained entry for both King Edward Grammar School for Boys, Camp Hill, which shared the same campus as the girls' school, and at Handsworth Grammar School for Boys, which was a decent bus ride away from our home. I was very happy when he chose Camp Hill, not just because it was close to home, but most importantly, because the Camp Hill schools had consistently come top of the league table of all schools in Birmingham every year, without exception. James did not make the Grammar School because he failed at his 11+ largely because he had less preparation time when we moved to Birmingham in 1986. In 1989, he had transferred to Wheeler's Lane Boys' School, which was also within walking distance from our home. He was very settled there.

Chapter 20
Divorce No. 2 And the CSA

I had hoped and thought it more than reasonable that while I was away in Oxford, Melvinder would have, at least, begun the preparation for equipping the children ready for their new school experience in early September. She did nothing and left it all until I was home in mid-July. The storm that blew over this matter, I maintain till this day, was the proverbial straw. Melvinder had noted from an earlier time that leaving the bedroom and taking up abode with Natasha was a very effective way of hurting me. I never saw her in our bedroom ever again.

Melvinder's tactic was now three-fold. Firstly, she had gone to the Child Support Agency (CSA) and claimed that we were now living in two separate households. This meant that, although I continued to meet all household expenses as previously, I was now bound by the CSA's ruling to provide additional monthly income as determined by the CSA to Melvinder's household, which she claimed consisted of herself and two of the three children, Natasha, and James. She had difficulty trying to turn Nathan against me, so he was counted in my household. This extra income to her was backdated to the day she first moved out of the bedroom. So not only must I pay a regular amount, but I must also pay a backdated lump sum of £25,000, which I chose to pay in installments because I could not afford a lump sum of that amount.

Secondly, she actively and successfully brainwashed the children against me. The very fact that I needed to earn to support my family and a household gave her the opportunity to do such an unfair thing. The fact that my job took me away from home frequently meant that she had all the time and access to the children to carry out this appalling deed. Somehow, Nathan, who was the brightest of the three children saw through what was taking place and resisted it.

He was ostracized by his mother and his siblings because of it. That would have been awful for Nathan because I was often out of the home, and he was on his own while the others had their own company. Effectively, I had become a one parent household. Keeping Nathan fed and properly ready for school meant on many evenings coming home to take him with me to a variety of restaurants. It also meant getting back on time to do his washing and ironing for him so that he could hold his head high at school.

While I could understand how Natasha, who had been the closest of the three to me, could turn away from me, after all her mother slept nightly in her bed, I found it difficult to comprehend James' behavior. He was the eldest of the three and he knew that I had to fight many battles for him against his mother who was often less than kind to him. He knew that I often had to threaten to call Social Services to save him from what I considered to be child cruelty. How then could he side with her against me? Was it because he was so scared of her?

Thirdly, Melvinder was not satisfied that I should support the children, at least Natasha and James, according to my financial ability. She asked the CSA to intervene, and they determined that I should pay her £350 x 2 = £700 plus income and installment of £400, making a total of £1100 monthly from my monthly income after taxation of £2,200. With this amount I was left to support myself and Nathan while maintaining a sizable mortgage and all other household expenses on the house in which Melvinder had established that hers was a separate household. This arrangement would continue until the children reached the age of eighteen years of age.

Legal expenses were also building up at the London lawyers who I had retained against a possible divorce petition from Melvinder. In the circumstances, I decided that I would have to bell the cat because Melvinder was quite comfortable the way things were at great expense to me. I asked the lawyer to serve a writ for divorce upon my wife. The Decree Nisi was made final on 10/08/95, but living arrangement continued as it was before for almost a year afterwards until Melvinder was able to buy a house of her own using the £60,000, which the lawyers on both sides agreed would be a fair settlement. I did not have anything like that amount. I had to take on a crippling further loan on the house at Pineapple Road to raise that £60,000.

Melvinder and the two children eventually found a home for that money about a mile and a half from Pineapple Road. With some transport aid from me, they moved out and left Nathan and me at Pineapple Road. Once she had gone, the relationships began to improve. Natasha and James would often come around to visit. I had bought Natasha a Labrador puppy for her birthday, but I had to keep and look after it for her because her mother insisted that she could not take the puppy home. Natasha would often come on her way from school or on the weekends to see me, her pup and her brother Nathan who also had his own Beagle puppy for which to care. In the summer of 1996, Natasha was allowed to accompany Nathan and me on a holiday to Jamaica.

Everything was fine again from a distance even though I was struggling financially. During my defamatory battle with the Birmingham Council and Rose, Melvinder had got her lawyer to register an interest in any damages that I might win. Even that did not make me dislike her. Her greed would eventually catch up on her, I thought.

To date, apart from the blistering blemishes of Bradford and the legal skirmishes of Birmingham, I would conclude that I had had a very successful career. I wished, most sincerely, that I could have said the same about my domestic life. However, the tide was about to change, at least, on the career front. On the 2nd of May 1997, the Tory Government of Britain, under the leadership of Mr. John Major, was routed. It was expected that Tony Blair and 'New Labor' would win the election, but the immense scale of the defeat for the conservatives was not anticipated. In a massive land-slide victory for 'New Labor' the Tories, in fact, lost many of their notables and key candidates who were former members of their government?

This loss for the Tories was received by the Labor Administration in Birmingham with triumphant glee. I knew, at once, that this signaled the end of the GMS era and vindictive repercussions and consequences for schools, such as mine. Nevertheless, together with my team, we were determined to soldier on, whatever the future held for us.

Chapter 21
They Are Out To Get Me

Now that we had acquired GMS status, everyone in the school, or at least so I thought, was looking forward to a smoother road ahead for improving our children's academic and social future. I was at one time allowing myself to consider the luxury of not having to fight on the racism front while I was raging a legal battle with the Birmingham authority and some of their officials. It was a nice thought, which I had put down to the more racially cosmopolitan nature of the staff at George Dixon. But with me, luxuries can only be transitory indulgences. My secretary, Mrs. Julie Griffiths, rang through to my office on the 13th of May 1994 to inform me that she had a freelance news reporter on the line asking to speak with me and did I want to take the call? I agreed that she should put the call through. My deputy, Mr. Bob Mason, was with me at the time.

The freelance reporter wanted to confirm whether there was any truth in the rumor that I had beaten and physically injured two children at my school. Because there was no truth whatsoever in the question which the reporter was asking, I simply dismissed it as not true and after sharing the query with my deputy forgot about it completely.

Apart from the occasional racially motivated documents, which I had, from time to time, received through the post from cranks, I had experienced nothing at George Dixon School that came anywhere near the scale of those experiences at Wyke Manor Upper School in Bradford.

The call from the freelance reporter did nothing to disturb that growing confidence in my staffs as far as racism was concerned. After all, as a school we had gone to great lengths to be a place of anti-racist values. Many of the school's staff were frequently in the media advocating for the school and its values and outlining their roles in all of it. It was a frequent occurrence that staff from the school were involved in INSET delivery at other schools because of what we stood for openly and publicly. So, the last thing I was expecting was some cowardly racial attack of any kind from any of the staff at George Dixon. Six days after receiving that call from the freelance reporter, on the 19th of May 1994, I was advised by my secretary that an urgent call had come in from my Union, the National Union of Teachers (NUT) and that they wished me to return the call right away.

I did just that. They had picked up the same story as did the freelance reporter and understood that it was having 'legs' as they say in American journalism. I was in the same position knowledge-wise as I was at the time of the freelance reporter. I knew of no such incidents. Had I done such an awful thing, surely, I would know about it and would have heard from the parents of these children by now. After all, in the past six days I have heard this from two different outside sources. And according to the freelance reporter, these acts had happened before the date of his call.

All that I could say to my Union was that I had heard about that matter from the freelance reporter previously, but that I was ignorant about it and remained no further informed. What else could I do? Short of calling the entire school together and asking for the two children who I had beaten and injured to come forward, I wasn't going to be any wiser. That was what I thought. My Union assured me that they would keep a listening ear and keep me informed and I, again, left it at that.

Eight days later, on the 27th of May 1994, Julie Griffiths informed me that there were Inspector Bates and a PC Sangha waiting outside to see me. This still did not seem unusual. As a school, we had good relations with the police and shared many sporting activities with them. It certainly was not unusual for the police to call in and out of curtsey call to see the headteacher. I told Julie to invite the Offices into my office. She showed them in and then returned to her office. I greeted and seated the police officers.

Once seated, Inspector Bates informed me that they had come in response to a call, which they had received from an unnamed member of my staff who informed them that I had beaten and injured two boys, Khawar Ali Raza and Michael Reid. The police officers assured me that they had only come to let me know that such anonymous reports were emanating from my school and as they were bound by rules to follow up reports of this nature, they were also asking me if there was any truth in the matter. At this point, I summoned my deputy, Mrs. Irene Gray, to be with me.

I told the officers that, while I do know the boys to be difficult customers, I cannot recall having beaten and injuring them or any other pupil at any time. Mrs. Gray confirmed that to her knowledge, there were no such incidents. When I pointed out to the officers that from the time I had first heard of the incidents until their visit, 14 days had passed and, yet, I have had no complaint from the boys' parents, they thought it odd and bade us 'good afternoon' and left the school.

Now I have enough to make some enquiries. I thought it wise for Mrs. Gray to handle the enquiry and to report back her findings to me. She did. Apparently, about a month before all this broke out the two boys were causing some disturbance in their class, which was being held in one of our halls in Ritchie Block. It was reported to my deputy that I was passing through that hall conveniently and saw what the boys were doing. The teacher, Miss Bold, simultaneously asked me to intervene, which I did, and instructed both boys to stand in a corner of the hall with their hands on their heads facing the class so that they would feel ashamed of their behavior.

Apparently, so it was reported to Mrs. Gray, both boys became very fidgety and were reluctant to do as instructed. I then got both by their lapels and led them to the corner, shook both and re-issued my instruction, which the boys then obeyed. We had no more encounters and the next thing we know is the story, which had unfolded. Clearly, there was an enemy in the camp, as the police had said to me, but who, and why? This matter had become very serious because one of the parents of the two boys, I was made to understand, was to be visited by a Child Protection Officer about this matter on the 1st of June 1994.

The white Child Protection Officer was visiting only the Asian pupil, Khawar Raza, and not the Afro-Caribbean pupil, Michael Reid. I also wondered why that was. Something was odd and clearly wrong. I had some detective work to do with some urgency and purpose.

This matter was then of a proportion that the governors of the school had to be informed. Two of the governors are also teachers at the school. Neither of them had said anything to me about that matter, so I assumed that they, like me, were just being informed. During the governors' meeting they both behaved as though the whole thing was a surprise to them. I had informed the governors that two police officers had visited the school after receiving an anonymous telephone call from someone claiming to be a teacher at this school.

The caller informed them that the headteacher, Mr. Duncan, had beaten and injured two pupils of the school. Naturally, I had to tell the governors all that I knew to date including the fact that I had received no complaint from any of the two parents. It is fair to say that all the governors, bar the two teacher governors (one male: Mr. Tom Rickard and one female: Ms. Kay Lewis), were furious. The two Afro-Caribbean governors, Dr. Joyce Trail and Mrs. Camile Ade-John made known their total and absolute support for me and was rather scathing of the 'low-down' coward that had done that dastardly deed. They were certain that the motive was racism. The full board, again barring those two teachers, pledged their determination to find the culprit and to expose any underlying motive. It was in my interest to help them. I would.

Dr. Joyce Trail Mrs. Camile Ade-John

The next morning, I got to school a little earlier than usual because I needed to catch up on my paperwork before going on my usual morning patrol. Sitting in the waiting area just outside my office was Tom Rickard, one of the two teacher governors. He was waiting for my arrival. I was expecting that visit to take place, somehow, but not so soon after the governors' meeting. Without an invitation, Tom followed me into my office. His countenance transmitted enough to tell me that he was clearly troubled and worried. I would wager my last penny that he did not sleep last night. I would let him provide the evidence against himself: self-incrimination as they say. Voluntary confession is good for the soul.

Tom Rickard was the current head of my science department, the third person to hold that post since I joined the school in January 1986. Tom then confessed that following the governors' meeting the night before, he was feeling rather bad and thought that the best thing was to come and see me as quickly as possible. He then went on to admit that he was the person that was responsible for the matter, which I reported to the governors. He had come by it because another nameless colleague had referred it to him in his capacity as a teacher governor.

He was investigating the story with the two boys and things had leaked out of that way. However, he denied that he was the person putting it beyond the school. I wasn't going to take any chances. Although Tom was admitting this to me, he might later deny having any such conversation with me. I did not have a witness in the room. I thanked Tom for coming to see me and made an excuse that I had an appointment to keep so that Tom would leave my office. As any good detective would do, I decided to pin down the unsolicited self-confessed evidence that I had just gathered from Tom Rickard in a document created as contemporaneously as was humanly possible.

Once Tom was out of my office, I quickly dictated a note to my secretary. It was addressed to Tom Rickard and my secretary was to deliver it by hand personally to him once she had prepared it. In that note, I confirmed our meeting earlier that morning and accurately recounted the story, which he had told me in all its details except one. That 'one detail' was his denial that it was he who had published the matter beyond the school. I deliberately distorted the truth of what he had said to me regarding that matter. In fact, I stated that he had admitted that he was the one putting it beyond the school.

There was method in my madness. I correctly assumed that Tom would reply in writing to correct that aspect of my note. He did just that and so, I then had a written record of Tom's conversation with me that morning and confirmed by his own hand. He would not be able to deny that story and his involvement.

His problem was, though, he had admitted carrying out an investigation in his capacity as a governor. Fresh off the sleuth's trail in Bradford, I was still feeling the adrenaline and urge to expose those who would seek to harm me and in so doing sabotage the school's development plans. I would leave no stone unturned to flush out those who would entertain racially motivated actions that do not have our pupils' welfare at their core.

Tom had corroborated in written evidence that he was the investigator because it was referred to him by a member of the school's staff in his capacity as a staff governor representative. At the special governors' meeting I would focus the governor's attention on the fact that one of them should have a report to present to the rest of us. Among the governors' pre-prepared agender and documents for their meeting, there would be a copy of what took place between Tom and me with his own written response to what I had written.

The governors reconvened and insisted that Tom should report his findings to the full board and disclose the name of the colleague who referred the matter to him in the first place. Tom would do neither and that brought him into full conflict with the rest of his colleagues, barring Kay Lewis. The governors were never going to let it rest because he said that he was acting in their name. That made it an obligation to report his findings to the full board. Despite the pressures which he was then under, he remained uncooperative to the very end. Tom Rickard did not last much longer at school. He soon became ill and was off school for a while before we received his resignation.

In the meantime, the police had already told me that they were duty bound to follow up the report even though they received it anonymously. Some days later, I received a request from the police to come into the station at Rose Road to give a statement about the matter and that I would be cautioned, and the interview would be taped. My friend, David (you remember him, he was the one who helped me win that libel battle against Rose and the City Council earlier in the year) thought that I should, at his expense, be accompanied by a lawyer with whom I should have a consultation before going to give a statement on tape at the police station. This was very wise advice because the lawyer suggested that I should obtain statements from the boys and their parents in my defense. That I duly did.

Once the session at Rose Road police station was over, I then had an agonizing wait for the prosecution service to decide whether I should be prosecuted in a court of law. Even though I knew that I had not done the acts for which I was accused, and the two boys and their parents were ready to testify to that end, I could not stop worrying until I received that communication from the Prosecution Service. This agony was different from that at Wyke Manor Upper School in West Yorkshire, but just as painful if not more so. The response from the Prosecution Service was a long time coming but when it came it was a massive relief.

While all that was happening, I was being shot at from another angle. I had never found out who was behind this one. It defied my detection skills. I believed, however, that I had a reasonable hunch of who it was, but no evidence. I didn't believe that Tom Rickard was at it again. This was a different teacher: and if my hunch is right, it would surprise even me. The reader will recall my plans for the quadrangle. It was to be stocked with peafowls and other pheasants. Well, I had gone deep into the Derbyshire countryside to acquire a pair of adult peafowls and an extra hen. I took them back to the school and kept them confined for three months, as was advised by the breeder, before letting them loose in the quadrangle.

Probably because they had never seen so many children all at once, led by the peacock, they first flew onto the roof of Ritchie Block and thereafter, never to be seen again. This was a setback, but that only made me more determined to succeed next time. The breeder from whom I had purchased the birds had advised that if I was going to free the birds before the expiration of the three months, I should clip the tip of the wing feathers on one of their wings. I had not done that because the birds were confined for the full three months. As a boy growing up in the country in Jamaica, I had seen that technique used successfully to ground flying birds and had learned to use it myself on, for example, hens, ducks, and other domestic birds. I was no stranger to the technique.

I managed to get hold of some more peafowls and, instead of confining them for a lengthy period this time; I used the 'wing-clip' method and freed the birds in the quadrangle immediately. Although they all attempted to fly away, they were unsuccessful and soon learned to settle in their new home. It was just over a month since the Coventry freelance reporter had broken the news of my then current troubles, when on the 20th of June my secretary announced the presence of an R.S.P.C.A. officer waiting outside my office door to see me. Most people, including me, are familiar with those abbreviations, but somehow, on that occasion they did not ring a bell immediately. I told my secretary to invite the officer into my office. In walked a slim and frail looking middle-aged Caucasian character with an over-grown Dickensian mouth stash.

"Please be seated," I said. "How can I assist you?" I then asked.

He told me his name, which I have conveniently forgotten and repeated that he was from the R.S.P.C.A. Only, he spelled it out for me. "I am from The Society for the Prevention of Cruelty to Animals," he repeated. I still didn't get it. Isn't it odd how innocence has a way of making you unwise?

He then told me that his society had received an anonymous call from the school to tell them that I had personally 'cut off' the wings of an unspecified number of birds, which are being kept here at the school. My mind immediately flashed back to the ongoing police investigation: was this to be part of it? There was that 'anonymous' thing again? I was shocked. I had no idea that I was hated by anyone in the school so much so that they would go to this great length to do me harm. Furthermore, it seemed that I was leading a school that was full of cowards that constantly hide in the long grass from where they discharge their hateful shots at me. The worst part of all this is that no one knew anything; yet the school of anonymity was very much active.

I timorously explained to the officer what I had done with the birds and why. He agreed that, on my account, I had done nothing that was either wrong or illegal. Nevertheless, he rightly insisted on seeing the birds in question. Heartened by his earlier comment that I had done nothing wrong, I then took him to the quadrangle, whereby simply observing the birds he could tell that my account was right and that the call, which the R.S.P.C.A. had received, was either 'mischievous' or based upon 'total ignorance.'

Coincidentally, a full staff meeting was due in exactly fifteen minutes from the time the officer and I left the quadrangle for the return journey to my office. The officer very kindly accepted my invitation to stay for that meeting where and when he would, at my request, explain the situation with the birds. Mindful of the officer's time, I made this the first item on the meeting's agenda. This would allow him to get away as soon as he was ready. I introduced the 'visitor' in terms of his office, carefully watching faces to see if I could detect any unease. I couldn't detect any sign whatsoever. The officer explained to the staff why he was at the school.

In particular, he emphasized that he was answering an anonymous call from the school but had found no cause for concern and added that the "headmaster" clearly was experienced in the management of the birds. He then invited questions from the staff. The silence which then fell on that room was deafening. The officer bade us goodbye and made his way toward the exit. I had nothing more to add, so I moved the meeting on to its original agenda. The best sleuths sometime fail to solve some of their cases. This seemed to be just such a case.

OFSTED

The Office for Standards in Education (OFSTED) was in the process of examining all schools across the land. Early in 1994, we, at George Dixon School, received notice that we would be inspected soon. The usual fore runner in the form of a questionnaire was completed and returned at the end of February 1994. For reasons best known to OFSTED, they did not, in fact, carry out that inspection until the week 10th-14th February 1997.

Eleven official OFSTED inspectors came and, for the entire week, carried out the most vigorous inspection, which was possible. The experience was a humbling one for the entire school. No stone was left unturned. The official Inspection Report, which followed that inspection, was a fair and accurate assessment of where the school was at and where it was heading. Eleven highly trained OFSTED inspectors spending five complete school days at our school could hardly have failed in their task as we shall later be led to believe. Let me repeat, eleven inspectors acquiesced in the report, which was presented to the headteacher and his staff; the governors of the school and placed in the public domain.

One further point I must stress: none of the eleven inspectors was known to anyone connected to the school in any way. The inspectors unanimously concluded that there were areas which, as a school, we needed to address. In other words, we were not perfect. No school is or will ever be. There is always room for improvement. There were areas which were flattering to us as a school. All schools have good points too. We knew that and appreciated the fact that the eleven inspectors took the time and space to say it to us. The eleven inspectors' overall conclusion was that we were "an improving school."

Chapter 22
The Defeat of the Conservative Government in 1997

Following the defeat of the Conservative government in 1997, there were those in Birmingham local government and some of their educational officials who were surreptitiously and covertly telegraphing vindictive messages to me that they would now get their own back: "scores would be settled," it was said. Others with my interest genuinely in mind told me more directly that the knives were out for me; I should watch out.

Let me be clear, the fact that I had dared to vindicate my good name and professional reputation against their libelous actions back in '93/'94, had remained a matter for political revenge, as far as certain players were concerned. After the General Election and the loss of the conservatives in '97 it had become politically convenient and so the conspiratorial knives came out. If you are the largest local authority in the country and a Labor one at that, you have connections in Whitehall and in the nation's Civil Service and you use them. It happened all the time and it is not a practice, which is confined to just one party. We have all heard of the term cronyism whichever government is in office.

This was what would then be employed to get even with me. They began their vindictive measures by deploying another OFSTED Inspector of lesser ability than those previous eleven whom he would now follow into the school. His presence in the school, unlike his predecessors, was of no significance to the children. Instead, he provoked constant laughter among the children and, I am ashamed to admit, some staff because of the way he dressed. He was a tall man whose trousers' legs noticeably didn't quite make it to his ankles. He, single-handedly, over the course of one and a half days conducted a cursory inspection just one year after the full and complete inspection, which was skillfully and properly executed by those eleven properly trained and chosen OFSTED Inspectors.

Even though everyone knew and understood the puppetry purpose of his presence in the school, we all cooperated with him for the full day and a half he was there. I, for one, felt rather sorry for him because he had to play the game, which he was maneuvered into playing, possibly unwittingly. I told him that I was aware of his role and explained it to him in minute detail but, of course, he denied that it was politics. As if he could have acknowledged the truth even if he knew what that was? Nevertheless, he put his credibility on the line and declared that what his eleven other colleagues took five whole days to find was all wrong and that we should accept that what he single-handedly investigated in a day and a half should be preferred.

Unethical Predictions

In the meantime, and before we had heard from the lone Inspector, an agent of theirs had clumsily let it slip in talking directly to me, that if I remained in charge of the school, the Inspector would place the school under 'Special Measures.' She felt certain that if I were to announce that I was taking early retirement, the Inspector would report favorably. Of course, I disregarded her unethical predictions, much to her annoyance, not because I didn't think she was right, but because she was clearly a conspirator using her own initiative.

Once the news of this attempted bribery was leaked to the media, she was quickly thought by others, deep in the quagmire of conspiracy themselves, to have acted out of place and was permanently removed from the scene. She was allowed no further involvement with me, or the school. She was simply banished. The whole inspection charade was meant to be a cover-up and she made the rest of them look like visible fools. It was too far gone, and 'sweet revenge' rested upon it, so even despite the exposure, the Inspector was made to deliver the deed.

George Dixon School had gone from "an improving school" in one short year to one being put under special measures for political purposes. We were probably the only school on record anywhere in the country to be inspected twice in so short a space of time, especially after the first inspection had reported that we were, "an improving school."

I had defied plan number one. Plan number two was the special measures option. The new Labor government did not embrace GMS and was in the process of abolishing the funding agency, which, under the conservatives, had replaced the local authority regarding the funding of schools. What 'special measures' meant was that the local authority had 'good reasons' to send in their Inspectors to turn the school upside down; find as many faults as they could concoct and then blame it all on the headteacher. That would have been a disciplinary matter punishable by dismissal. The only trouble was I was ahead of that game.

One step ahead of the game

Now, I would dumfound them. Plan one or plan two, either way, they would get me; but they never thought of plan number three because they were not all that smart. I had always said to my fellow black heads and deputy heads in BHDNA, you must have a plan in readiness that deals with the inevitable. They will get you one day. When that time comes, you will need a plan that foils them. Following my own advice, I had a plan that would be mesmerizing. Had I gone before the Inspector reported, they would have gotten rid of me and have "an improving school."

If I stayed, they would have gone down the dismissal route using special measures as their reason. But what if I go now? They would be left with a self-inflicted special measure wound. That wound will take a lot of dressing and they couldn't touch me. I would have to act quickly though because the Funding Agency (FA) is on their way out. I didn't stand a cat in hell's chance of getting early retirement from the city council or their education department. The funding agency never had cause to be concerned about my performance as a headteacher, in the same way as Birmingham never did. On the contrary, there was always much about which to sing my praises.

The FA could not understand the sudden change and so offered me a handsome package by way of early retirement, almost by seven years.

My only other option was to stay and put up a fight. Fighting was what I had done my entire teaching career and I was good at it. I knew the ring well. I had seriously considered that road but was cautioned against it by my chairman of governors who thought that I couldn't just go on fighting all the time. In any case, he was leaving the chair and governorship because he would be taking up certain business opportunities in the Caribbean. He was a powerful ally; without him, I would be considerably weakened in any fight.

Taking the funding agency's offer was probably the most sensible decision I ever made in my entire life. It seemed that as part of the conspiracy, there was a calculation that the funding agency could not conduct early retirement arrangements once it was announced that they were to be closed. Had that been the case, I would have been left to the mercy of the Birmingham education department; and I know what kind of mercy I would have received? I was once their 'blue eyed' boy, but now they considered me a Judas for not only taking the school out of their control, but also for successfully challenging them legally on the libelous assertion. I had it on good authority that they resented my escape, but there was nothing that they could have done to prevent it.

A few of the staff at George Dixon Grant Maintained School

A few of the staff at George Dixon Grant Maintained School

Chapter 23
Early Retirement

However, there was still one outstanding bit of detective work to be done before I could truly enjoy my retirement arrangements.

The non-white communities, served by George Dixon Comprehensive, and subsequently, Grant Maintained School, placed many pressures on the school. The responses at school levels have not always been positive. Take, for example, the time worn legal requirement of delivering physical education as part of the school curriculum in our schools. In a mono-cultural all-white setting that would have been the backdrop and focus of the requirement, this requirement would present little or no difficulty at all. It would have been a timed and managed physical arrangement for all pupils followed by the hygienic practice of having a shower before any other activity. If we then add some cultural differences to the same situation, the reader would be alarmed to find out the resulting numerous complications that would follow.

The school, with its one set of facilities, must now accommodate numerous cultural dictates. The Asian communities have as much right as any other community to be educated in accordance with the laws of the country and this should not mean surrendering their cultural expectations in the process. In these circumstances, what must the school do at the end of a physical education session if culturally, morally, and religiously some children may not expose their bodies in the presence of others? Do you just let those who must not shower go without a shower?

Such a way out would be considered unjust by those not allowed to go without a shower and that decision would be questioned and challenged many times over. The ramifications here are many and should focus relevant minds on the genuineness of our stated goals.

In the same way, the school will face cultural turmoil when cross cultural romance enters the picture. And the author should know.

Jamaican born Lloyd Thomas of class 11/2 clearly had a romantic interest in his Muslim classmate, Jameel Akthar, and she in him by way of reciprocity. The school had picked this up since both were in class year 9/2. As a caring institution, we were not only interested in their academic development but ensured that both students had the benefit of counseling in relation to the relationship in which they were so obviously involved. The effects of counseling seemed to have deepened the relationship and were of no match for Cupid.

In the meantime, information about this developing relationship surfaced in the homes of both sets of parents. Both sets of parents wanted the school to nip the relationship in the bud before it became uncontrollable. The Akhtar's were the most anxious and concerned about this. In due course, that is exactly what happened. Despite the efforts of the school, the relationship became uncontrollable. So much was at stake for these pupils. It was the year of their first set of public examinations upon which their futures largely rest. Other considerations included the perception of cultural shame and dishonor as well as society's likely rejection of the offspring of such a relationship. From the point of view of the school, reasoned arguments did not prevail: the youngsters were far too locked in their romantic venture.

Then Akthar's family suddenly announced to the school and the local media that their daughter, Jameel, had disappeared and by innuendo, impugned Thomas' family, and the school. They reported that Jameel never returned from school on the day she disappeared. The police were brought in and they, in turn, launched a manhunt following a consultation with the school.

Instinctively, my detective skills became activated once I read what was being reported. This story resembled too many like it and about which I had read and heard. Some of the eventual outcomes were never good. Some bodies were found floating in rivers with limbs severed all in the name of 'honor killing.' The thought of any such thing happening to our Jameel got me moving once more in search of a precious pupil who was entrusted to my care.

Jameel and Lloyd were exceptionally bright and lovable students. It is hard to conceive of a scenario where they would not have built into their story the experiences of so many other couples in the same situation as themselves. Such stories with different shades were often rife.

As it turned out, they were prepared, and their preparation turned out to be the big break which I needed to bring back Jameel to the school and to pave the way for her alleged kidnappers to have a very smooth road to a secure penitentiary. I was not prepared to follow any of the red-herring trails that the parents of Jameel were flaunting and so I decided to get to know as many of her friends as possible. In this regard, Lloyd was useful for pointing me in important directions.

For me, there was a sense of great urgency since, alongside this disappearance story, I was deeply involved in the celebratory arrangements for my retirement from the school after thirteen years of service as its headteacher. As far as I was concerned, to depart the school leaving the disappearance matter unsolved would be a major blot on an otherwise unblemished career. This possibility provided the extra oomph needed to my sleuthing drive to wrap this matter up successfully.

In the meantime, the police were employing a considerable amount of resources investigation the alleged disappearance of Jameel without any leads which they considered useful.

I was determined to interview everyone who was flagged up as Jameel's friend, especially those referred to me by Lloyd: and just when I was about to throw the towel in on this case, Lloyd, unwittingly, pulled the rabbit out of the hat. He suddenly remembered that Jameel had another friend that he did not tell me about. That friend was Sally Tomlinson who was in class 9/2 with both Lloyd and Jameel. He had forgotten her because at the end of year 9, Sally Tomlinson and her parents had migrated to live in Copenhagen in Denmark.

My motto was, 'no giving up' until I had exhausted the list of Jameel's friends. Lloyd undertook to research Sally's current address. It took him exactly seven days to provide me with an address for Sally on the outer fringes of Copenhagen in the Scandinavian Peninsular. And that was how I came to be taking a long weekend in Denmark in search of an ex-pupil, Sally Tomlinson whose parents were very welcoming, accommodating and even remembered me from their last parent meeting for Sally.

"Do you remember Jameel Akhtar of year 9/2?" I asked Sally in the presence of her parents who had just served up some tea and Danish scones.

"Of course, I do. She was my best friend. Why, is anything wrong?" Sally asked, anxiously.

"Yes, she went missing and the whole world is searching for her and that is what brought me here," I told Sally.

"Well, she cannot go very far because I still hold her passport and birth certificate," said Sally, still clearly puzzled as to how I found her whereabouts.

She must have seen my eyes popping at the utterance of her possession of Jameel's documents.

"How did you come by those?" I enquired.

"Jameel was always suspicious about her parents' intentions as far as her marital future was concerned. She was also very worried about the many stories about Asian girls disappearing and then either found dead or back in India married off to men they had never met before. She sneaked out her documents one day and asked me to safekeep them. Without them it would be difficult for her family to take her out of the country to do anything against her will. She wanted me to release them if anything suspicious ever happened to her," explained Sally.

"Well, Sally, something suspicious has happened to Jameel and I am prosecuting enquiries on her behalf. I hope you will trust me to look after your "best friend's" interest and let me have those documents for which I will give you a receipt duly signed in my name."

There was no hesitation on the part of Sally, especially after she received a glance of approval from her parents standing close by.

On the KLM flight back to Birmingham, the predominant thought was that Jameel was being held against her will somewhere in the United Kingdom. I was of this belief because in my possession were her legal papers without which she cannot travel to foreign parts. We would need to intensify the search on British soil to find Jameel. I called the Inspector in charge of the search for Jameel and told him so. The one good thing is that no 'body' has turned up dead as with many in similar circumstances. There was hope, yet.

Eventually, after all the troubles and use of resources, it was let slip by an inebriated bragging uncle who may have had one too many scotch at a close-knit family gathering that his niece, Jameel, was married and settled in a village called Mawlynnong in India. This blunder did not stay confined to the family gathering. In days, it had surfaced by way of gossip with no foundation in the school playground and eventually drifted to my casual ear.

About this, I remained in considerable doubt because I was in possession of Jameel's travel documents. How could she have left the country? However,

I was interested in the village called 'Mawlynnong' because it sounded like one which I heard of before. That night (I always think better at night) it came back to me. This is the home of my good friend, Indra Du Mungur. Tomorrow, I will link with Mungur, he owes me a favor.

The next weekend, Mungur and I was on a flight to India all at my expense. Mungur was certain that he knew all the families of the said village and he knew of the Aktar family very well.

The nearly 12-hour journey got us to the village close to midnight, so we made ample use of Mungur's grandparents' hospitality for the night. The next day, Mungur would get to work on verifying if there was a new bride living in the village. To my amazement, he discovered that the parents of Jameel had deliberately arranged the shipment of the young girl to India using false names and false papers arranged in India. The girl was made to believe she was going on a holiday to her grandparents and extended family.

Quick thinking on Mungur's part a meeting between Jameel, who was not yet married but was soon to be, and me, was arranged. Jameel could not believe her eyes when she recognized me as her former headteacher and immediately asked us not to leave her there because she wants to be back in the land of her birth where she can be happy.

I assured her that we had no intention of leaving her behind: we just wanted her to cooperate with us. We had that assurance and Mungur, who knew the ropes and short-cuts, took care of the acquisition of another ticket on the overnight flight back to London Heathrow. At least, we didn't have to use false papers and made-up names to embark upon our travel back to the United Kingdom, Jameel's rightful home.

The Inspector in charge of Jameel's mysterious disappearance will now have much to aid his enquiries when I deliver her to him tomorrow morning very much alive. As to her parents and associated others, I am sure the law will take its rightful course. Kidnapping across borders, wasting police time could be just some of the issues raised at law enforcement level. I shall only ask that my role and involvement remain unpublicized for fear of conflict-of-interest kickbacks, as my true purpose was that of education. And now I can give myself with all conscience to the joys of retiring.

On Saturday, 20th March, in the evening, following the pupils' send-off, I was treated to a magnificent arrangement at one of Birmingham's prestigious hotels in the city. This was organized by Mr. Martin Blissett, the head of Mathematics at the school, together with his wife, Gail, who were very prominent members of the black community in Birmingham. I was truly stunned with pleasant surprises to see so many of my friends and relatives gathered in one place to mark the end of the line in the teaching profession for me. I could now retire with my new wife and son, Kyme, to that glorious island of paradise called Jamaica in the Caribbean. I thought it so appropriate when the curtains came down with a substitute artist's rendition of R Kelly's *I believe I can fly*.